ICEBERG

A NOVEL OF SUSPENSE
BY CLIVE CUSSLER,
AUTHOR OF *RAISE THE TITANIC!*

A megaton ice mass conceals the murderous lever of an incredible conspiracy to hijack South America.

And it's just the first surprise in a nonstop, chain-reaction caper that explodes with lethal action—as it rockets to a last-second climax beyond suspense, terror or shock . . .

ICEBERG

Clive Cussler

BANTAM BOOKS · TORONTO · NEW YORK · LONDON

This one is for Barbara,
whose enduring patience
somehow sees me through.

*This low-priced Bantam Book
has been completely reset in a type face
designed for easy reading, and was printed
from new plates. It contains the complete
text of the original hard-cover edition.*
NOT ONE WORD HAS BEEN OMITTED.

ICEBERG
A Bantam Book / published by arrangement with the author

PRINTING HISTORY
Dodd, Mead & Company edition published September 1975

Bantam edition / December 1977
2nd printing .. November 1977   5th printing ...... February 1978
3rd printing .... December 1977   6th printing .. September 1978
4th printing .... January 1978   7th printing .... December 1978
8th printing .... July 1979
9th printing
10th printing

ICEBERG

Prologue

The drug-induced sleep wore off into nothingness, and the girl began the agonizing struggle back to consciousness. A dim and hazy light greeted her slowly opening eyes while a disgusting, putrid stench invaded her nostrils. She was nude, her bare back pressed flat against a damp, yellow, slime-coated wall. It was unreal, an impossibility, she tried to tell herself upon awakening. It had to be some kind of horrifying nightmare. Then suddenly, before she had a chance to fight the panic mushrooming inside her, the yellow slime on the floor rose and began working up the thighs of her defenseless body. Terrified beyond all reason, she began screaming—screaming insanely as the abomination crawled ever upward over the naked sweating skin. Her eyes bulged from their sockets and she struggled desperately. It was useless—her wrists and ankles were chained tightly to the ooze-covered surface of the wall. Slowly, ever slowly, the ungodly slime crept across her breasts. And then, just as the unspeakable horror touched the girl's lips, a vibrating roar and a phantom, unseen voice echoed throughout the darkened chamber.

"Sorry to interrupt your study period, Lieutenant, but duty calls."

Lieutenant Sam Neth snapped the book in his hands shut. "Dammit, Rapp"—this to the sour-faced man seated beside him in the cockpit of the droning air-

1

craft—"every time I come to an interesting part, you butt in."

Ensign James Rapp nodded toward the book, its paperback cover illustrating a girl struggling in a pool of yellow slime—kept afloat, Rapp deduced, by a pair of immense buoyant breasts. "How can you read that crap?"

"Crap?" Neth grimaced painfully. "Not only do you invade my privacy, Ensign, you also fancy yourself my personal literary critic!" He threw his big hands up in mock despair. "Why do they always assign me a co-pilot whose primitive brain refuses to accept contemporary style and sophistication?" Neth reached over and placed the book in a crudely constructed rack hanging from the side panel by a coat hanger. Several dog-eared magazines, depicting the unclothed female body in numerous seductive positions, also rested in the rack, making it quite apparent that Neth's taste in literature didn't exactly take in the classics.

Neth sighed, then straightened up in his seat and peered through the windshield at the sea below.

The United States Coast Guard patrol plane was four hours, twenty minutes into a dull and routine eight-hour iceberg surveillance and charting mission. Visibility was diamond-clear under a cloudless sky, and the wind barely moved the rolling swells—a unique condition for the North Atlantic in the middle of March. In the cockpit, Neth, with four of the crew members, piloted and navigated the huge four-engined Boeing aircraft, while the other six crewmen took up office in the cargo section, eyeballing the radar scopes and other scientific instruments. Neth checked his watch and then turned the plane on a sweeping arc, settling the nose on a straight course toward the Newfoundland coast.

"So much for duty." Neth relaxed and reached for his horror book. "Please show a little initiative, Rapp. No more interruptions till we make St. John's."

"I'll try," Rapp responded dourly. "If that book's so absorbing, how about letting me borrow it when you're finished?"

Neth yawned. "Sorry. I make it a point never to

lend out my private library." Suddenly the headset crackled in his ear, and he picked up a microphone. "Okay, Hadley, what have you got?"

Back in the dimly lighted belly of the plane, Seaman First Class Buzz Hadley stared intently at the radar set, his face reflecting an unearthly green glow from the scope. "I have a weird reading, sir. Eighteen miles, bearing three-four-seven."

Neth flicked the mike switch. "Come, come, Hadley. What do you mean by *weird?* Are you reading an iceberg, or have you tuned your set into an old Dracula movie?"

"Maybe he's picking up your sexy terror novel," Rapp grunted.

Hadley came back on. "Judging from the configuration and size, it's a berg, but my signal is much too strong for ordinary ice."

"Very well." Neth sighed. "We'll have a look-see." He frowned at Rapp. "Be a good boy and bring us around to course three-four-seven."

Rapp nodded and turned the control column, executing the course change. The plane, accompanied by the steady roar of the four Pratt-Whitney piston engines and their endless vibrating beat, gently banked toward a new horizon.

Neth picked up a pair of binoculars and trained them on the unending expanse of blue water. He adjusted the focus knobs and held the glasses as steady as possible against the quivering movement of the aircraft. Then he glimpsed it—a white inanimate speck, sitting serenely on a glistening sapphire sea. Slowly, the iceberg grew larger inside the two circular walled tunnels of the binoculars as the cockpit's windshield closed the distance. Then Neth picked up the microphone.

"What do you make of it, Sloan?"

Lieutenant Jonis Sloan, the chief ice observer aboard the patrol plane, was already studing the berg through a half-open cargo door behind the control cabin.

"Run-of-the-mill, garden variety," Sloan's robot-like voice came over the earphones. "A tabular berg with a mesa top. I'd guess about two hundred feet high, probably about one million tons."

"Run-of-the-mill?" Neth sounded almost surprised. "Garden variety? Thank you, Sloan, for your highly enlightening description. I can hardly wait to visit there someday." He turned to Rapp. "What's our altitude?"

Rapp kept his eyes glued straight ahead. "One thousand feet. The same altitude we've been at all day . . . and yesterday . . . and the day before that—"

"Just checking, thank you," Neth interrupted pontifically. "You'll never know, Rapp, how increasingly secure my old age becomes with your able talents at the controls."

He fitted a battered pair of flying goggles to his eyes, braced himself for the blasting cold, and opened his side window for a closer look. "Here she is," motioning to Rapp. "Make a couple of passes, and we shall see what we shall see."

It took only a few seconds for Neth's face to feel like the embattled surface of a pin cusion; the icy air tore at his skin until it thankfully turned numb. He gritted his teeth and kept his eyes glued to the berg.

The huge ice mass looked like a ghostly clipper ship under full sail as it floated gracefully beneath the cockpit windows. Rapp eased the throttles back and twisted the controls slightly, sending the patrol plane into a wide, sweeping bank to port. He ignored the bank and turn indicator and judged his angle by peering over Neth's shoulder at the gleaming mound of ice. Three times he circled, waiting for a sign from Neth to level the plane out. Finally Neth pulled his head in and picked up the microphone.

"Hadley! That berg is as bare as a newborn baby's ass."

"There's something down there, Lieutenant," Hadley came back. "I've got a beautiful blip on my—"

"I think I've spotted a dark object, skipper," Sloan interrupted. "Down near the waterline on the west face."

Neth turned to Rapp. "Swing down to two hundred feet."

It took only minutes for Rapp to comply. More minutes passed and still he circled the berg, holding the aircraft's speed a bare twenty miles an hour above stalling.

"Closer," Neth murmured intently, "another hundred feet."

"Why don't we simply land on the damn thing," Rapp offered conversationally. If he was overly concerned, he didn't look it. His face wore the expression of one who was about to fall sleep. Only the tiny beads of sweat on his brow betrayed the total concentration upon the risky flying job at hand. The blue swells seemed so near, he felt as if he could reach past Neth's shoulder and touch them. And to add fuel to his growing tenseness, the walls of the iceberg now towered above the plane, the summit disappearing entirely above the frames of the cockpit windows. One twitch, he thought, one tricky air current, and the port wing tip could catch on a wave crest and instantly transform the giant aircraft into a self-destructing cartwheel.

Neth became aware of something now . . . something indistinct, something flying across the unseen threshold between imagination and reality. It slowly materialized into a tangible thing, a man-made form. Finally, after what seemed an eternity to Rapp, Neth pulled his head back into the cabin, again closed the side window, and pressed the mike switch.

"Sloan? Did you see it?" The words sounded stiff and muffled, as if Neth were talking through a pillow. At first, Rapp thought it was because Neth's jaw and lips were frozen with the cold, but then he sneaked a fast glance and was surprised to see Neth's face frozen, not with cold but with the blank look of genuine awe.

"I saw it." Sloan's voice came over the intercom like a mechanical echo. "But I didn't think it was possible."

"Neither did I," Neth said, "but it's down there—a ship, a goddamned ghost ship inbedded in the ice." He turned to Rapp, shaking his head as if he didn't believe his own words. "I couldn't make out any details. Just a blurred outline of the bow, or maybe the stern, it's impossible to tell for certain."

He slipped off the goggles and raised the thumb of his right hand in the air, motioning up. Gratefully Rapp sighed and leveled out the patrol plane, putting a comfortable margin of space between the aircraft's underbelly and the cold Atlantic.

"Excuse me, Lieutenant." Hadley came through over the headphones. He was hunched over his radar set, painstakingly studying a little white blip almost in the exact center of the scope. "For what it's worth, the overall length of that thing in the berg is in the neighborhood of one hundred and twenty-five feet."

"A derelict fishing trawler, most likely." Neth vigorously massaged his cheeks, wincing at the pain as the circulation began to return.

"Shall I contact District Headquarters in New York and request a rescue party?" Rapp asked matter-of-factly.

Neth shook his head. "No need to rush a rescue ship. It's obvious there are no survivors. We'll make a detailed report after we've landed in Newfoundland."

There was a pause. Then Sloan's voice came through.

"Make a pass over the berg, skipper. I'll drop a dye marker on it for quick identification."

"Right you are, Sloan. Make the drop at my signal." Neth turned again to Rapp. "Bring us over the high part of the berg at three hundred feet."

The Boeing, its four engines still turning at reduced power, swept over the stately iceberg like a monstrous Mesozoic bird in search of its primeval nest. Back at the cargo door, Sloan raised his arm, pausing. Then at Neth's spoken command, Sloan tossed a gallon pickle jar full of red dye out into space. The jar grew smaller and smaller, shrinking to a tiny speck before finally striking the smooth cliff face of the target. Peering back, Sloan could see a bright vermilion streak spreading slowly down the million-ton mound of ice.

"Right on the button." Neth almost sounded jovial. "The search party won't have any trouble spotting that one." Then suddenly grim-faced, he stared down toward the spot where the unknown ship lay entombed. "Poor devils. I wonder if we'll ever know what happened to them?"

Rapp's eyes took on a thoughtful look. "They couldn't have asked for a bigger tombstone."

"It's only temporary. Two weeks after that berg drifts into the Gulf Stream, there won't be enough left of it to chill a six-pack of beer.

The cabin became clouded by a silence, a silence that seemed intensified by the incessant drone of the plane's engines. Neither man spoke for several moments, each lost in his own thoughts. They could only look at the ominous pinnacle of white rising out of the sea and speculate on the enigma locked beneath its icy mantle.

At last Neth slouched backward nearly horizontal in his seat and became his old imperturbable self again. "I strongly suggest, Ensign, unless you have a hankering to ditch this lumbering bus in forty-degree water, you take us home before the fuel gauges die from thirst." He grinned menacingly. "And please, no interruptions."

Rapp threw Neth a withering look, then shrugged and turned the patrol plane once more on a course toward Newfoundland.

When the Coast Guard patrol plane had disappeared and the last steady beat of its engines had faded away in the cold salt air, the towering iceberg once again lay enshrouded in the deathly stillness it had endured since being broken from a glacier and forced into the sea off the west coast of Greenland nearly a year before.

Then suddenly there was a slight but perceptible movement on the ice just above the waterline of the berg. Two indistinct shapes slowly transformed into two men who rose to their feet and stared in the direction of the retreating aircraft. From more than twenty paces they would have been invisible to the unaided eye—both wore white snowsuits that blended in perfectly with the colorless background.

They stood there for a long time, patiently waiting and listening. When they were satisfied the patrol plane was not returning, one of the men knelt and brushed away the ice, revealing a small radio transmitter and receiver. Extending the ten-foot telescopic aerial, he set the frequency and began turning the crank handle. He didn't have to crank very hard or very long. Someone, somewhere, was keeping a tight watch on the same frequency, and the answer came almost immediately.

Chapter
1

Lieutenant Commander Lee Koski clamped his teeth a notch tighter on the stem of a corncob pipe, jammed his knotted fists two inches deeper in his fur-lined windbreaker and shivered in the intense cold. Two months past forty-one years, eighteen of them in the service of the United States Coast Guard, Koski was short, very short, and the heavy, multi-layered clothing made him look nearly as wide as he was high. His blue eyes beneath the shaggy wheat-colored hair gleamed with an intensity that never seemed to dim, regardless of his mood. He possessed the confident manner of a perfectionist, a quality that helped in no small measure in his section as commander of the Coast Guard's newest supercutter the *Catawaba*. He stood on the bridge like a gamecock, legs braced apart, and didn't bother to turn when he spoke to the tall mountain of a man standing beside him.

"Even with radar, they'll play hell finding us in this weather." The tone was as crisp and penetrating as the cold Atlantic air. "Visibility can't be more than a mile."

Slowly, deliberately, Lieutenant Amos Dover, the *Catawaba*'s Executive Officer, flipped a cigarette butt ten feet straight into the air and watched with analytical

9

interest as the smoking white tube was caught by the wind and carried over the ship's bridge, far out into the rolling sea.

"Wouldn't make any difference if they did," he mumbled through lips that were turning blue from the chilly breeze. "The way we're pitching, the pilot of that helicopter would have to be extremely dumb or dead drunk or both to even consider touching down back there." He nodded aft toward the *Catawaba*'s landing platform, already wet from the blowing spray.

"Some people don't give a damn how they die," Koski said severly.

"No one can say they weren't warned." Dover not only looked like a big bear, but his voice seemed to growl from somewhere deep within his stomach. "I signaled the copter right after it left St. John's, informing it of the building sea and strongly advising against a rendezvous. All I got from the pilot was a polite *thank you*."

It was beginning to drizzle now, and the twenty-five-knot breeze flung the rain over the ship in driving sheets that soon sent all the men who were on duty above deck scurrying for their oilskins. Fortunately for the *Catawaba* and her crew, the air temperature held at 40°F, still eight degrees away from the dread of freezing, a nasty situation that would have quickly covered the entire ship with a blanket of ice.

Koski and Dover had just slipped into their oilskins, when the loudspeaker on the bridge crackled mechanically. "Captain, we've just picked up the bird on radar and we're guiding it in."

Koski picked up the hand transmitter and acknowledged. Then he turned to Dover. "I fear," he said casually, "a plot is brewing."

"You're wondering why all the urgency to take on passengers?" Dover asked.

"Aren't you?"

"I am indeed. I'm also wondering why the orders to stand by station and receive a civilian helicopter came direct from the Commandant's Headquarters in Washington instead of our own district command."

"Damned inconsiderate of the Commandant," Koski growled, "not to tell us what these people want. One thing's certain, they're not going to find themselves on a pleasure cruise to Tahiti—"

Koski suddenly stiffened and cocked an ear in the direction of the unmistakably thumping beat of a helicopter's rotor blade. For half a minute it was invisible in the heavy overcast. Then both men spotted it at the same time. It was coming from the west, through the light rain, and heading in a direct line toward the ship. Koski recognized it immediately as a two-seater civilian version of the Ulysses Q-55, a craft capable of nearly two hundred and fifty miles an hour.

"He's nuts to try it," Dover said dryly.

Koski didn't comment. He grabbed the transmitter again and exploded into it. "Signal the pilot of that copter, and tell him not to attempt a touchdown while we're pushing through ten-foot-high swells. Tell him I won't be responsible for any insane actions on his part."

Koski waited for a few seconds, his eyes glued to the helicopter. "Well?"

The speaker crackled in reply. "The pilot says he's most grateful for your concern, Captain, and he respectfully requests that you have some men on hand to secure the landing gear the instant he touches the pad."

"He's a courteous bastard," Dover grunted. "I'll say that for him."

Jutting his chin out an extra half inch, Koski took another viselike grip on the pipe stem. "Courteous, hell! There's every possibility that idiot will wreck a good-sized piece of my ship." Then he shrugged in resignation and picked up a bull horn, shouting into the mouthpiece. "Chief Thorp! Have your men ready to secure that bird the second it lands. But for God's sake, keep them under cover until it's firmly on the pad—and have a crash crew standing by."

"Right about now," Dover said softly, "I wouldn't trade places with those guys up there for all the sex goddesses in Hollywood."

The *Catawaba* could not head squarely into the wind, Koski calculated, because the turbulence dealt by the superstructure would hurl the aircraft to sure destruction. On the other hand, if the ship ran abeam of the sea, the roll would be far too excessive for the helicopter to land firmly on the pad. All the years of skill and judgment, coupled with the knowledge of the *Catawaba*'s handling characteristics, made his decision almost routine.

"We'll take them in with the wind and sea broad on the bow. Reduce speed and make the necessary course change."

Dover nodded and disappeared into the wheelhouse. He returned a few moments later. "Broad on the bow as ordered and as steady as the sea allows."

Caught in the cold grip of apprehension, Koski and Dover stared at the bright yellow helicopter as it swept through the mist, headed into the wind and approached the *Catawaba*'s stern on a thirty-degree angle above the ship's spreading wake. Though the wind was buffeting the Ulysses badly, the pilot somehow managed to keep it in a level position. About a hundred yards back, it began slackening speed until it finally stopped in midair, hovering like a hummingbird over the rising and falling landing pad. For what seemed an eternity to Koski, the helicopter maintained its height while the pilot gauged the high point of the cutter's fantail each time it lifted on the crest of a passing swell. Then abruptly, when the landing pad hit its apogee, the copter's pilot cut back his throttles, and the Ulysses dropped neatly onto the *Catawaba,* a bare instant before the stern lurched downward in the trough of the next wave.

The skids had hardly kissed the pad when five of the cutter's crewmen dashed across the tilting deck and began struggling under the strong gusts to secure the helicopter before it was blown over the side into the water. The engine exhaust soon died away, the rotor blades idled to a stop, and a door opened on the side of the cockpit. Then two men, their heads bowed against the driving mist, leaped to the platform.

"That son of a bitch," Dover murmured in wonder. "He actually made it look easy."

Koski's face tightened. "Their credentials had better be first-rate—and their authority better come from Coast Guard Headquarters in Washington."

Dover smiled. "Maybe they're congressmen on an inspection tour."

"Not likely," Koski said curtly.

"Shall I escort them to your cabin?"

Koski shook his head. "No. Offer them my compliments and bring them to the officers' mess." Then he grinned slyly. "Right about now, the only thing that truly interests me is a hot cup of coffee."

In precisely two minutes, Commander Koski was sitting at a table in the officers' messroom, his cold hands gratefully encircling a steaming mug of black coffee. It was nearly half drained when the door opened and Dover entered the room, followed by a chubby character with large rimless spectacles mounted on a bald head that was edged by long unkempt white hair. Although the initial effect reminded Koski of a stereotyped mad scientist, the face was round and good-natured, and the brown eyes had a crinkled grin. The stranger caught sight of the commander and marched up to the table and extended his hand.

"Commander Koski, I take it. Hunnewell—Dr. Bill Hunnewell. Sorry to inconvenience you like this."

Koski rose and shook Hunnewell's hand. "Welcome aboard, Doctor. Please sit down and have a cup of coffee."

"Coffee? Can't stand the stuff," Hunnewell said mournfully. "I'd sell my soul for a nip of hot cocoa though."

"Cocoa we've got," Koski said agreeably. He leaned back in his chair and raised his voice. "Brady!"

A steward wearing a white jacket ambled from the galley. He was long and lean and walked with a gait that could only spell Texas. "Yessir, Captain. What'll it be?"

"A cup of cocoa for our guest and two more coffees for Lieutenant Dover and—" Koski stopped and peered questioningly behind Dover. "I believe we're missing Dr. Hunnewell's pilot?"

"He'll be along in a minute." Dover bore an unhappy look on his face. It was as if he tried to signal a warning to Koski. "He wanted to be sure the helicopter was tied down securely."

Koski stared back speculatively at Dover, but then he let it go. "There you have it, Brady. And bring the pot; I could use a refill."

Brady simply nodded in acknowledgment and returned to the galley.

Hunnewell said, "It's true luxury to have four solid walls around me again. Sitting in that vibrating kite with nothing between me and the elements but a plastic bubble was enough to turn a man's hair gray." He ran his hand through the few remaining white strands surrounding his dome and grinned.

Koski set down his mug, and he wasn't smiling. "I don't think you realize, Dr. Hunnewell, just how close you came to losing the rest of your hair and yourself as well. It was pure recklessness on the part of your pilot to even consider making a flight in this weather."

"I can assure you, sir, that this trip was necessary." Hunnewell spoke in a benevolent tone, the same tone he might have used lecturing a schoolboy. "You, your crew, your ship has a vital function to perform, and time is the critical dimension. We cannot afford to lose a single minute." He pulled a slip of paper from his breast pocket and passed it across the table to Koski. "While I explain our presence, I must ask you to set an immediate course for this position."

Koski took the paper without reading its contents. "Forgive me, Dr. Hunnewell, I am not in a position to grant your request. The only order I have from the Commandant's Headquarters is to take aboard two passengers. Nothing was mentioned about giving you carte blanche to run my ship."

"You don't understand."

Koski stared piercingly over his coffee mug at Hunnewell. "That, Doctor, is the understatement of the day. Just what is your capacity? Why are you here?"

"Put your mind at ease, Commander. I'm not an enemy agent out to sabotage your precious ship. My

Ph.D. is in oceanography, and I'm currently employed by the National Underwater and Marine Agency."

"No offense," Koski said equably. "But that still leaves one question unanswered."

"Perhaps I can help clear the air." The new voice came soft but firm with an authoritative resonance.

Koski stiffened in his chair and turned to a figure who leaned negligently against the doorway—a tall, well-proportioned figure. The oak-tanned face, the hard, almost cruel features, the penetrating green eyes suggested that this wasn't a man to step on. Clad in a blue Air Force flight jacket and uniform, watchful yet detached, he offered Koski a condescending grin.

"Ah, there you are," Hunnewell said loudly. "Commander Koski, may I present Major Dirk Pitt, Special Projects Director for NUMA."

"Pitt?" Koski echoed flatly. He glanced at Dover and lifted an eyebrow. Dover only shrugged and looked uncomfortable. "By any chance the same Pitt who broke up that underwater smuggling business in Greece last year?"

"There were at least ten other people who deserve the lion's share of the credit," Pitt said.

"An Air Force officer working in oceanographic programs," said Dover, "a little out of your element, aren't you, Major?"

The lines around Pitt's eyes etched into a smile. "No more than all the Navy men who have gone to the moon."

"You have a valid point," Koski conceded.

Brady appeared and served the coffee and cocoa. He left and returned again, setting down a tray of sandwiches before retreating for the last time.

Koski began to feel uneasy in earnest now. A scientist from a prominent government agency—not good. An officer in another branch of the service with a reputation for dangerous escapades—bad news. But the combination of the two, sitting there on the other side of the table telling him what to do and where to go—absolute plague.

"As I was saying, Commander," Hunnewell said

impatiently. "We must get to that position I gave you as quickly as possible."

"No," Koski said bluntly. "I'm sorry if my attitude seems hard-nosed, but you must agree, I'm perfectly within my rights in refusing your demands. As captain of this ship, the only orders I'm obliged to obey come from either Coast Guard District Headquarters in New York or the Commandant's office in Washington." He paused to pour himself another cup of coffee. "And my orders were to take on two passengers, nothing more. I have obeyed, and now I'm resuming my original patrol course."

Pitt's eyes weighed Koski's granite features as a metallurgist might test a shaft of high-grade steel, probing for a flaw.

Suddenly he straightened up and cautiously walked over to the galley door and glanced in. Brady was busy pouring a bulky sack of potatoes into a huge steaming pot. Then Pitt, still cautiously, turned and scrutinized the alleyway outside the messroom. He could see his little game was working; Koski and Dover were exchanging confused looks between taking in his movements. Finally, seeming satisfied there were no eavesdroppers, Pitt moved to the table and sat down, leaning close to the two Coast Guard officers, lowering his voice to a murmur.

"Okay, gentlemen, here's the story. The position Dr. Hunnewell gave you is the approximate location of an extremely important iceberg."

Koski colored slightly, but managed to keep a straight face. "And what, if I may ask without sounding stupid, Major, do you class as an important iceberg?"

Pitt paused for effect. "One that has the remains of a ship imbedded under its mantle. A Russian trawler, to be exact, crammed with the latest and most sophisticated electronic detection gear Soviet science has yet devised. Not to mention the codes and data for their entire Western Hemisphere surveillance program."

Koski didn't even blink. Without taking his eyes off Pitt, he took a pouch from under his jacket and calmly began loading his corncob.

"Six months ago," Pitt continued, "a Russian trawler, bearing the name *Novgorod*, rode just a few miles off the Greenland coast and kept watching other activities at the U.S. Air Force missile base on Disko Island. Aerial photographs showed that the *Novgorod* carried every electronic reception antenna in the book, and then some. The Russians played it cool, the trawler and crew, thirty-five highly trained men, and yes, women too, never strayed within Greenland's territorial limits. She even got to be a welcome sight to our pilots, who used her as a checkpoint during poor weather. Most Russian spy ships are relieved of duty every thirty days, but this one maintained its position for a solid three months. The Department of Naval Intelligence began to wonder at the long delay. Then one stormy morning, the *Novgorod* was gone. It was nearly three weeks before her relief ship appeared. This time lag compounded the mystery—the Russians, up to then, had never broken their habit of relieving a spy ship until another one appeared on station."

Pitt paused to tap his cigarette in an ashtray. "There are only two routes the *Novgorod* would have taken home to mother Russia. One was to Leningrad via the Baltic Sea, and the other was through the Barnets Sea to Murmansk. The British and Norwegians have assured us the *Novgorod* took neither. In short, somewhere between Greenland and the European coast, the *Novgorod* disappeared with all hands."

Koski put down his mug and stared thoughtfully at its stained bottom. "It strikes me a bit strange that the Coast Guard was never notified. I know for a fact that we've received no report of a missing Russian trawler."

"It struck Washington a bit strange too. Why would the Russians keep the *Novgorod*'s loss a secret? The only logical answer is they didn't want any trace of their most advanced spy ship found by a Western nation."

Koski's lips twisted in a sarcastic grin. "You're asking me to buy a Soviet spy ship locked in an iceberg? Come now, Major, I gave up on fairy tales when I discovered there was no Oz over the rainbow or a pot of gold under it."

Pitt matched Koski's grin. "Be that as it may, it was one of your own patrol planes that spotted a ship matching the outline of a trawler in an iceberg at 47°36'N—43°17'W."

"It's true," Koski said coldly, "the *Catawaba* is the closest rescue ship to that position, but why haven't my orders to check it out come direct from District Command in New York?"

"Cloak and dagger stuff," Pitt answered. "The last thing the boys in Washington wanted was a public announcement going out over the radio. Fortunately, the pilot of the aircraft who spotted the berg waited until he landed before making a detailed location report. The idea, of course, is to go over the trawler before the Russians have a chance to catch on. I think you can appreciate, Commander, how invaluable any secret information concerning the Soviet spy fleet is to our government."

"It would seem more practical to place investigators on the iceberg who are skilled in electronics and intelligence interpretation." The subtle change in Koski's tone could hardly be called a softening, but it was there. "If you don't mind my saying so, a pilot and an oceanographer don't make sense."

Pitt looked penetratingly at Koski, across to Dover, and back to Koski again. "A false front," he said quietly, "but one with a purpose. The Russians aren't exactly primitive when it comes to espionage operations. They couldn't help but become suspicious of military aircraft milling about an area of open sea where few, if any, ships ever travel. On the other hand, National Underwater and Marine Agency aircraft are commonly known to conduct scientific projects in desolate waters."

"And your qualifications?"

"I'm experienced at flying a helicopter in Arctic weather," Pitt answered. "Dr. Hunnewell is, with little doubt, the world's leading authority on ice formations."

"I see," Koski said slowly. "Dr. Hunnewell will

study the berg before the intelligence boys crash the party."

"You have it," Hunnewell acknowledged. "If that really is the *Novgorod* under the ice, it's up to me to determine the most expedient method for entering the ship's hull. I'm sure you're aware, Commander, icebergs are a tricky lot to play with. It's like cutting a diamond; a miscalculation by the cutter, and the prize is lost. Too much thermite in the wrong place, and the ice can crack and split apart. Or, sudden and excessive melting might cause a change in the center of gravity, forcing the berg to topple upside-down. So you see, it is imperative the ice mass be analyzed before the *Novgorod* can be entered with any degree of safety."

Koski leaned back and noticeably relaxed. His eyes locked on Pitt's for a moment, and then he smiled. "Lieutenant Dover!"

"Sir?"

"Kindly oblige these gentlemen and lay a course for 47°36′N—43°17′W, full ahead. And signal District Command in New York of our intent to depart station." He watched for a change of expression on Pitt's face. There was none.

"No offense," Pitt said equably. "I suggest you drop that signal to your District Command."

"I'm not suspicious or anything, Major," Koski offered apologetically. "It's just that I'm not in the habit of cruising all over the North Atlantic without letting the Coast Guard know where their property is."

"Okay, but I'd appreciate it if you didn't mention our destination." Pitt snuffed out his cigarette. "Also, please notify the NUMA office in Washington that Dr. Hunnewell and I have arrived safely on board the *Catawaba* and will continue our flight to Reykjavik when the weather clears."

Koski raised an eyebrow. "Reykjavik, Iceland?"

"Our final destination," Pitt explained.

Koski started to say something, thought better of it, then shrugged. "I'd better show you to your quarters, gentlemen." He turned to Dover. "Dr. Hunnewell can bunk with our engineering officer. Major Pitt can move in with you, Lieutenant."

Pitt grinned at Dover, then stared back at Koski. "The better to keep an eye on me?"

"You said it, not me," Koski replied, surprised at the pained expression that crossed Pitt's face.

Four hours later Pitt was dozing on a cot that had been squeezed into the iron womb Dover called his cabin. He was tired, almost to the aching point, but too many thoughts were running through his mind to allow him entry into the paradise of deep sleep. One week ago at this time he had been sitting with a gorgeous, sex-mad redhead on the terrace of the Newporter Inn, over-looking the picturesque waterfront of Newport Beach, California. He fondly remembered caressing the girl with one hand while holding a scotch-rocks in the other, contentedly watching the ghost-like pleasure yachts glide across the moonlit harbor. Now he was alone and regrettably suffering on a plank-hard folding cot aboard a tossing Coast Guard cutter somewhere in the refrigerated North Atlantic Ocean. I must be a card-carrying masochist, he thought, to volunteer for every madcap project that Admiral Sandecker keeps dreaming up. Admiral James Sandecker, Chief Director of the National Underwater and Marine Agency, would have shied at the term madcap project—damned bung twister would have been more his style.

"Damned sorry to drag you from sunny California, but this damned bung twister has been dumped in our lap." Sandecker, a small, fire-haired, griffon-faced man, waved a seven-inch cigar in the air like a baton. "We're supposed to be engaged in scientific underwater re-search. Why us? Why not the Navy? You'd think the Coast Guard could handle its own problems." He shook his head in irritation, puffed on the cigar. "Anyway, we're stuck with it."

Pitt finished reading and then laid a yellow folder marked *confidential* on the admiral's desk. "I didn't think it was possible for a ship to freeze up in the mid-dle of an iceberg."

"It's extremely unlikely, but Dr. Hunnewell assures me it could happen."

"Finding the right berg might prove difficult; it's already been four days since the Coast Guard's sighting. That overgrown ice cube could have drifted halfway to the Azores by now."

"Dr. Hunnewell has charted the current and drift rate to within a thirty-square-mile area. If your vision is good, you shouldn't have any trouble spotting the berg, particularly since the Coast Guard dropped a red dye marker on it."

"Spotting it is one thing," Pitt said thoughtfully, "landing a helicopter on it is another. Wouldn't it be more convenient and less dangerous to arrive by—"

"No!" Sandecker interrupted. "No ships. If that thing under the ice is as important as I think it is, I don't want anyone except you and Hunnewell within fifty miles of it."

"This may come as a surprise, Admiral, but I've never set a copter down on an iceberg before."

"It's very possible no one else has either. That's why I requested you as my Special Projects Director." Sandecker smiled mischievously. "You have the annoying knack of successfully—shall we say—delivering the goods."

"This time," Pitt asked slyly, "do I have the opportunity of volunteering?"

"I wouldn't have it any other way."

Pitt shrugged helplessly. "I don't know why I always give in so easily to you, Admiral. I'm beginning to think you have me pegged as a first-class pigeon."

A broad grin rode across Sandecker's face. "You said it, not me."

The latch clicked and the cabin door swung open. Pitt lazily opened one eye in time to see Dr. Hunnewell come in. The overweight doctor did a tightrope act trying to maneuver between Pitt's cot and Dover's clothes locker before he finally reached a small chair by a writing desk. Audibly, he sighed in chorus with the chair's creaking protest as he eased his bulk past the armrests.

"How in God's name does a titan like Dover get into this thing?" he incredulously asked no one in particular.

"You're late," Pitt yawned. "I expected you hours ago."

"I couldn't go sneaking around corners or slithering through ventilators as if I was on my way to a spy convention. I had to wait for an excuse to talk to you."

"An excuse?"

"Yes. Commander Koski's compliments. Dinner is served."

"Why all the subterfuge?" Pitt asked with a cagey grin. "We have nothing to hide."

"Nothing to hide! Nothing to hide! You lie there like an innocent virgin waiting for her first communion and calmly say we have nothing to hide?" Hunnewell shook his head hopelessly. "We'll both be in front of a firing squad when the Coast Guard learns we flim-flammed them out of the use of one of their new cutters."

"Helicopters have a nasty habit, they won't fly with air in their fuel tanks," Pitt said sarcastically. "We had to have a base of operations and a place to refuel. The *Catawaba* was the only ship in the area with the necessary facilities. Besides, *you* sent that phony message from the Coast Guard Commandant—you're on the hook for that one."

"That incredible yarn about the missing Russian trawler. You can't deny that's yours from beginning to end."

Pitt placed his hands behind his head and stared at the ceiling. "I rather thought everyone enjoyed it."

"I have to hand it to you. That was the slickest con job it's been my misfortune ever to witness."

"I know. There are times when I hate myself."

"Have you considered what may happen when Commander Koski sees through our devious little plan?"

Pitt stood up and stretched. "We simply do what

any other two red-blooded American con men would
do."

"And that is?" Hunnewell prompted dubiously.

Pitt smiled. "We simply worry about it when the
time comes."

Chapter
2

Of all the oceans, only the Atlantic is totally unpredictable. The Pacific, the Indian, even the Arctic each have their personal idiosyncrasies, but all have one trait in common: they seldom fail to provide a hint of their coming moods. Not so the Atlantic, especially north of the 15th parallel of latitude. In a matter of a few hours a glassy calm sea might be transformed into a foam-whipped cauldron instigated by a Force 12 hurricane, or there are times when the Atlantic's fickle nature works in reverse. Heavy winds, heavy seas during the night may give every indication of an impending storm, yet when the dawn comes, there is nothing to see but an azure mirror beneath an empty sky. And so it was for the men on the *Catawaba* as the new sun found them cruising comfortably over a peaceful seascape.

Pitt woke slowly, his eyes coming into focus on the rear of a pair of extra-large white shorts, amply filled by Dover, who was bending over a small basin brushing his teeth.

"You've never looked lovelier," Pitt said.

Dover turned around, the toothbrush poised over his bottom left molars. "Huh?"

"I said, good morning!"

Dover merely nodded, mumbled something incoherent through the toothpaste, and turned back to the basin.

Pitt sat up and listened. The hum of engines was still there, and the only other mechanical sound came from the rush of warm air through the ventilator. The motion of the ship seemed so smooth, it was almost imperceptible.

"I don't wish to appear a rude host, Major," Dover said, smiling, "but I suggest you blossom from the sack. We should be within range of your search area in another hour and a half."

Pitt threw off the blankets and stood up. "First things first. How is your establishment classed when it comes to breakfast?"

"A two-star Michelin rating," Dover said cheerfully. "I'll even treat."

Pitt had a fast wash, decided against a shave, and quickly slipped into his flight clothes. He followed Dover into the passageway, wondering how a man as large as the lieutenant could wander around the ship without running his head into low bulkheads at least ten times a day.

They had just finished a breakfast that Pitt figured would have cost at least five dollars in any of the better hotels when a seaman came up and said that Commander Koski wanted to see them in the bridge control room. Dover followed him, with Pitt lagging a few steps behind carrying a cup of coffee. The commander and Hunnewell were crouched over a chart table as they entered the room.

Koski looked up. The outthrust jaw no longer set like the bow of an icebreaker, and the intense blue eyes seemed almost tranquil.

"Good morning, Major. Are you enjoying your stay?"

"The accommodations are a bit cramped, but the food is superb."

The hard but genuine smile came on. "What do you think of our little electronic wonderland?"

Pitt made a three-hundred-and-sixty-degree scan of the control room. It was like something out of a science fiction space movie. From floor to ceiling the four steel bulkheads stood buried behind a mechanical avalanche of computers, television monitors, and instrumented consoles. Endless rows of technically labeled switches and knobs crisscrossed the equipment, garnished by enough colored indicator lights to fill a casino marquee in Las Vegas.

"Very impressive," Pitt said casually, sipping his coffee. "Air-search radar and surface-search radar scanners, the latest Loran-type navigational equipment of medium, high and ultra-high frequencies, not to mention computerized navigational plotting." Pitt spoke with the nonchalant air of a public relations director employed by the boatyard that laid the *Catawaba*'s keel. "The *Catawaba* comes equipped from the factory with more extensive oceanographic, communications, navigational, aerological and plotting equipment than any ship its size in the world. Basically, Commander, your vessel is designed to remain in midocean under any atmospheric conditions as a weather station, to conduct search and rescue operations, and to assist in oceanographic research work. I might add that she is manned by seventeen officers and one hundred sixty enlisted men, and cost between twelve and thirteen million dollars to build at the Northgate Shipyards in Wilmington, Delaware."

Koski, Dover and all the other men in the bridge control room, with the exception of Hunnewell, who remained intent on the chart, froze. If Pitt had been the first Martian to visit earth, he couldn't have possibly been the object of more incredulous apprehensiveness.

"Don't be surprised, gentlemen," Pitt said, feeling the warmth of self-satisfaction. "I make it a habit to do my homework."

"I see," Koski said grimly. It was obvious that he didn't see. "Perhaps you might give us a clue as to why you've studied your lessons so diligently."

Pitt shrugged. "As I've said, it's a habit."

"An irritating one at that." Koski looked at Pitt with a hint of uneasiness. "I wonder if you're really what you say you are."

"Dr. Hunnewell and I are bona fide," Pitt said reassuringly.

"We'll know for certain in precisely two minutes, Major." Koski's tone suddenly turned cynical. "I like to do my homework too."

"You don't trust me," Pitt said dryly. "A pity. Your mental anxiety is all for nothing. Dr. Hunnewell and I have no intent, or the means, for that matter, of endangering the safety of your ship or crew."

"You've given me no opportunity for trust." Koski's eyes were bleak, his voice icy. "You carry no written orders, I've received no radio signals regarding your authority, nothing . . . nothing but a vague message from Coast Guard Headquarters announcing your arrival. I might point out that anyone with a knowledge of our call signal could have sent that communication."

"Nothing's impossible," Pitt said. He couldn't help but admire Koski's perception. The commander had struck the nail precisely on the head.

"If you're playing a shady game, Major, I want no part of it—"

Koski broke off to accept a signal form from a seaman, and studied it carefully, taking his time about it. A strange considering look crossed his face. Then he frowned as he passed the sheet across to Pitt. "It seems that you're a never-ending source of surprise."

If Pitt didn't look uncomfortable, he certainly felt it. The obvious exposure had been a long time coming, and he'd had plenty of time to prepare. Unfortunately, he hadn't come up with a plausible back-up story. Pitt quickly decided there was little he could do but take the form from the commander's hand and appear unconcerned. It said:

"Regarding your inquiry of Dr. William Hunnewell and Major Dirk Pitt, Dr. Hunnewell's credentials are of the highest caliber. He is Director of the California Institute of Oceanography. Major Pitt is indeed Special Projects Director for NUMA. He also is the son of Senator George Pitt. These men are engaged in oceanographic research vital to the interests of the government and are to be extended every assistance and courtesy, repeat, extended every assistance and courtesy. Also, please inform Major Pitt that Admiral Sandecker requests that the major beware of frigid women." It was signed by the Commandant of the Coast Guard.

"The defense rests," Pitt said, savoring each syllable to the hilt. Sandecker, the old fox, had used his influence to finagle the Coast Guard Commandant into playing the game. Pitt let out a deep breath and handed the message form back to Koski.

"It must be nice to have friends in high places," Koski said, a touch of anger in his voice.

"It helps on occasion."

"I have no choice but to be satisfied," Koski said heavily. "That last part, if I'm not infringing upon some sacred trust, was code?"

"No great secret," Pitt answered. "It's only Admiral Sandecker's sly way of telling Dr. Hunnewell and me to continue on to Iceland after our investigation of the iceberg."

Koski stood there for a moment not saying anything. He shook his head slowly in puzzlement and was still shaking it when Hunnewell thumped his fist on the chart table.

"There it is, gentlemen. The precise location of our ghost ship—give or take a few square miles." Hunnewell was magnificent. If he had been aware of the tension a few moments before, he showed absolutely no evidence of it. He folded the chart and shoved it into the pocket of his windbreaker. "Major Pitt, I think it best if we take off as soon as possible."

"Whatever you say, Doc," Pitt said agreeably. "I can have the chopper warmed up and ready to go in ten minutes."

"Good." Hunnewell nodded. "We're now in the area where the berg was sighted by the patrol plane. According to my calculations, at the present rate of drift, the iceberg should reach the edge of the Gulf Stream sometime tomorrow. If the ice patrol's estimate of the size is correct, the berg is already melting to the tune of a thousand tons an hour. When it hits the warmer water of the Gulf Stream, it won't last ten days.

The only unanswered question is when will the derelict be released from the ice? Conceivably it could already be lost; hopefully it's still there and will be for a few more days."

"What do you figure for the flight distance?" Pitt asked.

"Approximately ninety miles to the general vicinity," Hunnewell answered.

Koski looked up at Pitt. "As soon as you take off, I'll reduce speed to one third and maintain a heading of one-zero-six degrees. How long do you make it before we rendezvous?"

"Three and a half hours should do the job," Pitt replied.

Koski looked thoughtful. "Four hours—after four hours I'm coming into the icepack after you."

"Thank you, Commander," Pitt said. "Believe me when I say I'm grateful for your concern."

Koski believed him. "Are you certain I can't bring the *Catawaba* in closer to your search area? If you should have an accident on the berg or have to ditch in the sea, I doubt if I could reach you in time. In forty-degree water a man in full clothing only has a life expectancy of twenty-five minutes."

"We'll have to risk it." Pitt took a final sip of his coffee and stared idly at the empty cup. "The Russians might already smell a rat if one of their trawlers has sighted your Coast Guard vessel Sunday cruising in an area outside its regular patrol station. That's why the end run with the helicopter. We can stay low enough to avoid any radar scanner and still be tough to sight visually. Time is important also. A copter can get in and out of the *Novgorod*'s location in one tenth the time it would take the *Catawaba*."

"Okay." Koski sighed. "It's your show. Just see that you're back on the landing platform by . . ." he hesitated, looking at his watch . . . "no later than 1030." Then he grinned. "If you're a good boy and arrive on time, I'll have a fifth of Johnnie Walker waiting."

Pitt laughed. "Now that's what I call one hell of an incentive."

"I don't like it," Hunnewell shouted above the racket of the helicopter's engine exhaust. "We should have sighted something by now."

Pitt looked at his watch. "Timewise, we're in good shape. Still over two hours to go."

"Can't you go higher? If we double our range of vision, we'd double our chances of detecting the iceberg."

Pitt shook his head. "No can do. We'd also double the possibility of our own detection. It's safer if we stay at a hundred and fifty feet."

"We must find it today," Hunnewell said, an anxious expression on his cherub face. "Tomorrow may be too late for a second try." He studied the chart draped across his knees for a moment then picked up a pair of binoculars and focused off to the north at several icebergs floating together in a cluster.

"Have you noticed any bergs that come close to matching the description we're looking for?" Pitt asked.

"We crossed one about an hour ago that passed the size and configuration requirements, but there was no red dye on its walls." Hunnewell swung the binoculars, scanning a flat restless ocean studded with hundreds of massive icebergs, some broken and jagged, others rounded and smooth, like paper-white geometric solids thrown haphazardly over the blue sea.

"My ego is shattered," Hunnewell said mournfully. "Never since my high school trigonometry class have my calculations been so far off."

"Perhaps a change in wind direction blew the berg on a different course."

"Hardly," Hunnewell grunted. "An iceberg's underwater mass is seven times the size of what shows on the surface. Nothing but an ocean current has the slightest effect on its movement. It can easily move with the current against a twenty-knot wind."

"An irresistible force and an immovable object rolled up into one lump."

"That and much more—damned near indestructible." Hunnewell talked as he peered through the glasses. "Of course, they break up and melt soon after drifting south into warmer waters. But during their passage to the Gulf Stream, they bow neither to storm nor man. Glacier icebergs have been blasted by torpedoes, eight-inch naval guns, massive doses of thermite bombs, and tons of coal dust to soak up the sun and speed up the melting process. The results were comparable to the damage a herd of elephants might suffer after a slingshot bombardment by a tribe of anemic pygmies."

Pitt went into a steep bank, dodging around the sheer sides of a high-pinnacled berg—a maneuver that had Hunnewell clutching his stomach.

He checked the chart again. Two hundred square miles covered and nothing achieved. He said: "Let's try due north for fifteen minutes. Then head back east to the edge of the ice pack. Then south for ten minutes before we cut west again."

"One graduated box pattern to the north coming up," Pitt said. He tilted the controls slightly, holding the helicopter in a side-swinging movement until the compass read zero degrees.

The minutes wore on and multiplied and the fatigue began to show in the deepening lines around Hunnewell's eyes. "How's the gas situation?"

"That's the least of our worries," Pitt replied. "The elements we're short on at the moment are time and optimism."

"Might as well admit it," Hunnewell said wearily. "I ran out of the latter a quarter of an hour ago."

Pitt gripped Hunnewell's arm. "Hang in there, Doc," he said encouragingly. "Our elusive iceberg may be just around the next corner."

"If it is, it's defied every drift pattern in the book."

"The red dye marker. Could be it washed away in the storm yesterday?"

"Fortunately no. The dye contains calcium chloride, a necessary ingredient for deep penetration—takes weeks, sometimes months for the stain to melt away."

"That leaves us with one other possibility."

"I know what you're thinking," Hunnewell said flatly. "And you can perish the thought. I've worked closely off and on with the Coast Guard for over thirty years, and I've never known them to mistake an ice position sighting."

"That's it then. A million-ton chunk of ice evaporated into—"

Pitt left the sentence unfinished, partly because the helicopter was beginning to drift off course, partly because he glimpsed something. Hunnewell suddenly stiffened in his seat and leaned forward, the binoculars jammed against his eye sockets.

"I have it," Hunnewell cried.

Pitt didn't wait for a command; he dipped the helicopter and headed toward the direction indicated by Hunnewell's binoculars.

Hunnewell passed the glasses to Pitt. "Here, take a peek and tell me these old eyes aren't picking up a mirage."

Pitt did a juggling act with the binoculars and the helicopter's controls while fighting to keep the engine vibration from jiggling the iceberg out of focus.

"Can you make out the red dye?" Hunnewell asked anxiously.

"Like a stripe of strawberry in the middle of a scoop of vanilla ice cream."

"I can't understand it." Hunnewell shook his head. "That berg shouldn't be there. By every known law of current and drift, it should be floating at least ninety miles to the southeast."

But it was there, resting on the sharp horizon line, a massive towering hunk of ice, beautifully carved by nature, grotesquely marred by manmade chemicals. Before Pitt could lower the binoculars, the ice crystals on the berg caught the sun and reflected the brilliance into his eyes, the intensity blasting through the lenses. Temporarily blinded, he gained altitude and altered course a few degrees to remove the glare. It was nearly a full minute before the skyrockets behind his eyeballs finally faded away.

Then suddenly Pitt became aware of a dim, almost

imperceptible shadow in the water. He barely had time
to distinguish the dark shape as the helicopter skimmed
over the blue swells, not three hundred feet beneath the
landing skids. The iceberg was still a good seven miles
away when he swung around in a great half circle toward the east and the *Catawaba.*

"What in hell's the matter with you?" Hunnewell
demanded.

Pitt ignored the question. "I'm afraid we have uninvited guests."

"Nonsense! There isn't a ship or another aircraft
in sight."

"They're coming to the party through the basement."

Hunnewell's eyebrows raised questioningly. Then
he slowly slumped back in the seat. "A submarine?"

"A submarine."

"It's quite possible it may be one of ours."

"Sorry, Doc, that's wishful thinking."

"Then the Russians beat us to it." Hunnewell's
mouth twisted. "Dear God, we're too late."

"Not yet." Pitt turned the helicopter into another
circling arc, this time back toward the iceberg. "We can
be standing on the ice in four minutes. It will take the
sub at least a half hour to reach the berg. With any luck
we can find what we came for and get the hell out before their crew lands."

"That's cutting it a bit fine." Hunnewell didn't
sound very confident. "When the Russians see us running about on the berg, they won't come unarmed, you
know?"

"I'd be surprised if they didn't. Actually, the captain of that Russian sub has enough weapons at his
command to blast us to pieces anytime he has the inclination. But I'm betting he won't take the chance."

"What has he got to lose?"

"Nothing. But he gains the repercussions of a nice
fat international incident. Any commander worth a ru-
ble in his position will be certain we're in constant radio
contact with our home base, notifying them of his sub's
position and ready to scream bloody murder at the first

shot. This side of the Atlantic is our stomping grounds, and he knows it. He's too far from Moscow to play the role of a block bully."

"All right, all right," Hunnewell said. "Go ahead and set us down. I suppose even getting shot at is better than sitting another minute in this tooth-jarring mixmaster."

Pitt said no more. He made the approach and set the helicopter down without any difficulty on a small flat area of ice no more than twenty feet long by fifteen feet wide. Then, before the rotor blades had come to a final stop, he and Hunnewell jumped from the cockpit and stood on the silent iceberg wondering when the Russian submarine would surface, wondering what they would find beneath the shroud of ice that separated them from the cold unfriendly waters. They could see no life, feel no life. Their cheeks were touched lightly by a frigid breeze, but apart from that there was nothing, nothing at all.

Chapter 3

The tense minutes passed in total silence, minutes before Pitt could bring himself to say anything that was important. When at last he did, his voice sounded to him like a vague whisper. Why whisper? he thought. Hunnewell was probing the ice thirty feet away, the Russian submarine, now riding motionless on the surface, lay a quarter of a mile from the northern edge of the iceberg. Finally, Pitt managed to attract Hunnewell's attention with a voice that was still hushed by the cathedral-like silence.

"Time's running out, Doc." It still seemed he might be overheard, though the Russians couldn't have picked up his words had he shouted at the top of his voice.

"I'm not blind," Hunnewell snapped. "How long before they get here?"

"By the time they set a dinghy in the water, row in from the sub and step ashore—four hundred yards if it's an inch—it'll take them between fifteen and twenty minutes."

"We've no damned time to lose," Hunnewell said impatiently.

"Any luck yet?"

"Nothing!" Hunnewell boomed back. "The derelict must be deeper than I thought." He rammed the probe feverishly into the ice. "It's here; it's got to be here. A hundred-and-twenty-five-foot vessel couldn't have disappeared."

"Maybe the Coast Guard saw a phantom ship."

Hunnewell paused to adjust his sunglasses. "The ice patrol crew might have been fooled by their eyes, but not by their radar equipment."

Pitt moved closer to the open door of the helicopter. His gaze swung to Hunnewell, then back to the sub, and a second later he was peering through the binoculars. He studied the tiny figures that were erupting from the hatches of the low-silhouetted submarine and scrambling hurriedly across the sea-splashed deck. In less than three minutes, a large six-man dinghy was inflated, dropped beside the hull and boarded by a group of men carrying an assortment of automatic weapons. Then an indistinct popping sound came over the rolling blue water. The sound was enough—enough for Pitt to drastically cut his original time estimate.

"They're coming. Five, maybe six of them; can't tell for sure."

"Are they armed?" Hunnewell's query sounded urgent.

"To the teeth."

"My God, man!" Hunnewell shouted irritably. "Don't just stand there and gawk. Help me search for the derelict."

"Forget it." Pitt's tone was unhurried. "They'll be here in another five minutes."

"Five minutes? You said—"

"I didn't count on their dinghy having an outboard motor."

Hunnewell stared stricken at the submarine. "How did the Russians find out about the derelict? How could they have possibly known the location?"

"No great feat," Pitt answered. "One of their KGB agents in Washington undoubtedly got hold of the Coast Guard's sighting report—it's hardly a classified secret—and then dispatched every fishing trawler and submarine they had in this part of the Atlantic to search the ice field. It's an unfortunate coincidence for us, but a lucky one for them that we both discovered the iceberg at the same moment."

"It looks as if we've thrown the ball game," Hunnewell said bleakly. "They've won, and we've lost. Dammit, if we could only locate the derelict's hull, we could at least destroy it with thermite bombs and keep it out of the Russians' hands."

"To the victor goes the spoils," Pitt murmured. "All one million tons of the finest, purest, genuine Greenland ice in the Atlantic Ocean."

Hunnewell was puzzled, but said nothing. Pitt's apparent indifference made no sense.

"Tell me, Doc," Pitt continued. "What's today's date?"

"The date?" Hunnewell said dazedly. "It's Wednesday, March twenty-eighth."

"We're early," Pitt said. "Three days early for April Fools' Day."

Hunnewell's voice was flat and hard. "This is hardly the time or place for levity."

"Why not? Somebody's played a tremendous joke on us and on those clowns out there." Pitt gestured toward the rapidly approaching landing party. "You, I, the Russians, we're all starring in the greatest laugh riot ever to hit the North Atlantic. The climax of the final act comes when we all learn that there is no derelict in this iceberg." He paused to exhale a cloud of smoke. "As a matter of fact, there never was one."

Total incomprehension and the meager beginnings of hope touched Hunnewell. "Go on," he prompted.

"Besides radar contact, the crew of the patrol plane reported that they sighed the outline of a ship in the ice, yet we saw nothing before we touched down. That alone doesn't figure. They were in an aircraft flying at a probable patrol speed of two hundred miles an hour. If anything, our chances of spotting something from a hovering helicopter were far higher."

Hunnewell looked thoughtful. He seemed to be weighing what Pitt had said. "I'm not sure what you're hinting at." Then he smiled, suddenly his old cheerful self again. "But I'm getting wise to your sly mind. You must have something up your sleeve."

"No magic. You said it yourself; by every known law of current and drift, this berg should be floating ninety miles to the southwest."

"True." Hunnewell looked at Pitt with a new respect. "And the conclusion, exactly what do you have in mind?"

"Not what, but who, Doc. Someone who is leading all of us on the proverbial wild-goose chase. Someone who removed the red dye from the iceberg containing the lost ship and spread more of the same over a decoy ninety miles off the track."

"Of course, the iceberg we flew over hours ago. The same size, configuration and weight, but no red stain."

"That's where we'll find our mystery ship," said Pitt. "Right where you calculated it was supposed to be."

"But who's playing games?" Hunnewell asked, his face set in a contemplative twist. "Obviously it isn't the Russians; they're as confused as we were."

"At the moment it doesn't matter," Pitt said. "The important thing is to bid fond farewell to this floating ice palace and fly off into the blue. Our uninvited guests have arrived." He nodded down the slope of the berg. "Or perhaps you hadn't noticed?"

And Hunnewell hadn't. But he noticed it now. The first of the landing party from the submarine was leaping onto the edge of the ice. Within a few seconds, five of them came piling on the berg, walking cautiously in Pitt and Hunnewell's direction. They were dressed in black—Russian marines—and heavily armed. Even at a hundred yards, Pitt could discern the unmistakable look of men who knew exactly what they were out to do.

Pitt casually climbed aboard the helicopter, turned the ignition switch and pushed the starter. Even before the rotor blades swung into their first revolution, Hunnewell was ensconced in the passenger's seat with his safety belt tightly secured.

Before he closed the door to the cockpit, Pitt

leaned out, cupped both hands to his mouth and shouted to the advancing Russians, "Enjoy you stay, but don't forget to pick up your litter."

The officer leading the men from the submarine cocked an ear, then shrugged uncomprehendingly. He was certain that Pitt was hardly likely to shout in Russian for his benefit. As if to signal the occupants of the helicopter of his peaceful intentions, the officer lowered his automatic weapon and waved a salute as Pitt and Hunnewell relinquished possession of the iceberg and rose into the radiant blue sky.

Pitt took his time, keeping the helicopter at a minimum cruising speed and holding on a northward course for fifteen minutes. Then, after they were out of sight and radar range of the submarine, he swung around in a long circle to the southwest and by eleven fifteen they had found the derelict.

As they bore down on the great ice giant, Pitt and Hunnewell shared a strange sense of emptiness. It wasn't just the end of the long hours of uncertainty—they were already past the time limit set by Commander Koski—it was the eerie appearance of the mystery ship itself. Neither man had ever seen anything quite like it. The atmosphere around the berg had a terrifying desolation that belonged not to earth but to some dead and distant planet. Only the rays of the sun broke the inertness, penetrating the ice and distorting the lines of the ship's hull and superstructure into a constantly changing series of abstract shadows. The sight seemed so unreal that it was difficult for Pitt to accept the visible fact of its existence. As he adjusted the controls and lowered the helicopter to the ice, he half expected the entombed vessel to vanish.

Pitt tried to land on a smooth spot near the berg's edge, but the sloping angle of the ice proved too great; he finally put down directly on top of the derelict. Hunnewell leaped from the helicopter just before the skids kissed the ice, and had already paced the derelict from bow to stern when Pitt joined him.

"Odd," Hunnewell murmured, "most odd. Nothing protrudes above the surface, not even the masts and radar antenna. Every square inch is sealed solidly under the ice."

Pitt pulled a handkerchief from his flight jacket and blew his nose. Then he sniffed the air, as if testing it. "Smell anything out of the ordinary, Doc?"

Hunnewell tilted his head back and inhaled slowly. "There is something of an odor. Too faint though. I can't make it out."

"You don't travel in the right circles," Pitt said, grinning. "If you'd get out of your laboratory more often and learn a bit about life, you'd recognize the distinct aroma of burnt rubbish."

"Where's it coming from?"

Pitt nodded at the derelict under his feet. "Where else but down there."

Hunnewell shook his head. "No way. It's a scientific fact, you can't smell an inorganic substance inside a block of ice from the outside."

"The old proboscis never lies." The midday warmth was beginning to overcome the cold, so Pitt unzipped his flight jacket. "There must be a leak in the ice."

"You and your educated nose," Hunnewell said acidly. "I suggest you stop playing bloodhound and start placing the thermite charges. The only way we're going to get inside the wreck is by melting the ice mantle."

"We'll be taking a risk."

"Trust me," Hunnewell said mildly. "I'm not about to split the berg and lose the derelict, the helicopter, and ourselves as well. I intend to begin with small loads and work our way down by degrees."

"I wasn't thinking of the iceberg. I was thinking of the wrecked ship. There's a damn good chance the fuel tanks have ruptured and allowed diesel oil to slosh the entire length of the keel. If we miscalculate and ignite as much as a drop, the whole derelict goes up in one fiery puff."

Hunnewell stamped his foot on the hard-packed ice. "How do you expect to get through that—with an ice pick?"

"Dr. Hunnewell," Pitt said quietly, "I won't argue the fact that your name is known far and wide for your hyper-scientific intellect. However, like most super-brains, your mental depth for practical, everyday run-of-the-mill matters is sadly lacking. Thermite charges, ice picks, you say. Why bother with complex and muscle-exerting schemes when we can simply perform an open sesame routine?"

"You're standing on glacial ice," Hunnewell said. "It's hard and it's solid. You can't walk through it."

"Sorry, my friend, you're dead wrong," Pitt said.

Hunnewell eyed him suspiciously. "Prove it!"

"What I'm getting at is, the labor has already been done. Our Machiavelli and his merry band of busy helpers have obviously been here before us." He pointed dramatically upward. "Please observe."

Hunnewell lifted a quizzical eyebrow and looked upward and intently studied the broad face of the steep ice slope. Along the outer edges and near the lower base, only a few yards from where Pitt and Hunnewell stood, the ice was smooth and even. But beginning at the summit and working downward into the middle of the slope, the ice was as pockmarked as the backside of the moon.

"Well now," Hunnewell murmured, "it does appear that someone went to a lot of trouble to remove the Ice Patrol's red dye stain." He gave a long expressionless look at the towering ice pinnacle, then turned back to Pitt. "Why would someone chip the stain out by hand when they could have easily erased all trace with explosives?"

"I can't answer that," Pitt said. "Maybe they were afraid of cracking the berg, or maybe they didn't have explosives, who can say? However, I'll lay a month's wage that our clever little pals did more than merely chip ice. They most certainly found a way to enter the derelict."

"So all we do now is look for a flashing sign that says *enter here*." Hunnewell's tone was sarcastic. He wasn't used to being outguessed, and his expression showed that he didn't like it.

"A soft spot in the ice would be more appropriate."

"I suppose," Hunnewell said, "you're suggesting a camouflaged cover over some sort of ice tunnel."

"The thought had crossed my mind."

The doctor peered over the top of his glasses at Pitt. "Let's get on with it then. If we stand around here theorizing much longer, my testicles will probably get an acute case of frostbite."

It shouldn't have been all that difficult, not by a long shot, yet it didn't go as easily as Pitt had figured. The unpredictable occurred when Hunnewell lost his footing on the slope and slid helplessly toward a steep ledge that dropped into the icy sea. He fell forward, desperately clawing at the ice, his nails scratching and bending painfully backward through the hard surface. He slowed momentarily, but not enough. His fall happened so abruptly that his ankles were already scraping the edge of the thirty-foot drop before he thought of shouting for help.

Pitt had been busily prying up a chunk of loose ice when he heard the cry. He swung around, took in Hunnewell's deteriorating plight, had a lightning impression of how impossible rescue would be once the doctor had fallen into the freezing water, and in one swift movement tore off his flight jacket and flung himself across the slop in a flying leap, feet first, legs lifted crazily in the air.

To Hunnewell's panic-flooded brain, Pitt's move looked like an act of pure madness. "Oh, God, no, no," he shouted. But there was nothing he could do but watch Pitt hurtle toward him like a bobsled. There might have been a chance, he thought, if Pitt had stayed on the berg. Now it seemed certain that both men would die in the freezing salt water together. Twenty-five minutes, Commander Koski's words flashed through his head, twenty-five minutes was all a man had to remain alive in forty-degree water—and with all the time in the world they never could have pulled themselves back onto the sheer sides of the iceberg.

If he'd had precious moments to think about it, Pitt would have undoubtedly agreed with Hunnewell: he surely looked like a madman, skiding over the ice with his feet high above his head. Suddenly, with only a leg's length remaining before he collided with Hunnewell, Pitt brought his feet flashing down with a power and swiftness that, even in these desperate circumstances, made him grunt in pain as his heels crashed through the ice, dug in tenaciously and brought him to a muscle-jarring stop. Then, as if triggered by instinct, in the same motion he threw a sleeve of his jacket to Hunnewell.

The thoroughly frightened scientist needed no coaxing. He grasped the nylon fabric with a grip that no vise could have equaled and hung on, trembling for almost a minute, waiting for his middle-aged heart to slow down to a few beats above normal. Fearfully, he stole a glance sideways and saw what his numbed senses could not feel—the edge of the ice ledge cut across his waist at the navel.

"When you're up to it," Pitt said, his voice calm but pierced with a noticeable trace of tenseness, "try pulling yourself toward me."

Hunnewell shook his head. "I can't," he murmured hoarsely. "It's all I can do to hold on."

"Can you find a foothold?"

Hunnewell didn't answer. He only shook his head again.

Pitt bent over between his outstretched legs and tightened his grip on the jacket. "We're sitting here though the courtesy of two hard rubber heels, not steel cleats. It won't take much for the ice to crack around them." He flashed an encouraging grin at Hunnewell. "Make no sudden movement. I'm going to pull you clear of the ledge."

This time Hunnewell nodded. He felt a sick ache in his stomach, the tips of his torn fingers throbbed, his sweatsoaked face reflected the terror and pain. One thing, and one thing only, reached through his blanket of fear: the determined look in Pitt's eyes. Hunnewell stared at the lean, tan face, and in that moment he knew that Pitt's inner strength and confidence were gaining a toehold in his own frightened mind.

"Stop your blasted grinning," he said faintly, "and start pulling."

Cautiously, an inch at a time, Pitt hauled Hunnewell slowly upward. It took him an agonizing sixty seconds before he had Hunnewell's head on a plane between his knees. Then Pitt, one hand at a time, let go of the jacket and grabbed Hunnewell under the armpits.

"That was the easy part," Pitt said. "The next exercise is up to you."

His hands free, Hunnewell wiped a sleeve across his sweaty brow. "I can't make any guarantees."

"Your dividers, are they on you?"

Hunnewell's expression went blank for a moment. Then he nodded. "Inside breast pocket."

"Good," Pitt murmured. "Now climb over me and stretch out full length. When your feet are solidly on my shoulders, take out the dividers and jam them into the ice."

"A piton!" Hunnewell exclaimed, suddenly aware. "Damned clever of you, Major."

Hunnewell began hauling himself over Pitt's prostrate form, straining like a locomotive climbing the Rockies, but he made it. Then, with Pitt's hands firmly clamped on his ankles, Hunnewell pulled out the steel-pointed dividers that he normally used for plotting distances on charts and rammed them deeply into the ice.

"Okay," Hunnewell grunted.

"Now we'll repeat the process," Pitt said. "Can you hold on?"

"Make it quick," Hunnewell answered. "My hands are nearly numb."

Tentatively, one heel still imbedded in the ice as a safety measure, Pitt tested his weight on Hunnewell's legs. The dividers gripped firm. Working as swiftly and as smoothly as a cat, Pitt crept past Hunnewell, felt his hands grope over the edge of the slope where it leveled out, and wiggled up onto safe ground. He didn't waste an instant. Almost immediately, it seemed to Hunnewell, Pitt was throwing down a nylon line from the helicopter. Half a minute later, the pale and exhausted oceanographer sat on the ice at Pitt's feet.

Hunnewell gave a great sigh and gazed into Pitt's relieved face. "Do you know what I'm going to do first thing when we set foot in civilization?"

"Yes," Pitt said, smiling. "You're going to buy me the finest gourmet dinner in all Reykjavik, round up all the booze I can drink, and introduce me to a sensuous, buxom, Icelandic nymphomaniac."

"The dinner and the booze are yours—I owe you that much. The nymphomaniac, I can't promise. So many years have passed by since I've negotiated for a woman's charms, I'm afraid I've lost the touch."

Pitt laughed, clapped Hunnewell on the shoulder and helped him to his feet. "Don't sweat it, old friend. Girls are my department." He stopped abruptly and said sharply: "Your hands look like you held them against a grindstone."

Hunnewell lifted his hands and stared indifferently at the bleeding fingers. "Not really as bad as they look. A bit of antiseptic and a manicure and they'll be as good as new."

"Come on," Pitt said. "There's a first-aid kit in the copter. I'll fix them up for you."

A few minutes later, as Pitt tied the last small bandage, Hunnewell asked, "Did you find any sign of a tunnel before I took my spill?"

"It's a slick piece of work," Pitt replied. "The entire circumference of the entrance cover is beveled, a perfect match with the surrounding ice. If someone hadn't got careless and cut a small handgrip, I'd have walked right over it."

Hunnewell's face suddenly grew dark. "This accursed iceberg," he said grimly. "I swear that it bears a personal enmity against us."

He flexed his fingers and solemnly studied the eight little bandages masking the tips. His eyes seemed strained and his face looked weary.

Pitt walked over and raised a round slab of ice three feet in diameter by three inches thick, revealing a crudely carved tunnel barely large enough for one man to crawl through. Instinctively he turned his head away—a powerful, acrid stench of burnt paint, fabric and fuel, mingled with torched metal, rose from the opening.

"That should prove I can detect smells through an ice cube," Pitt said.

"Yes, you've passed the nose test," Hunnewell said smugly. "But you've failed miserably on your thermite charge theory. That's nothing but a burned-out hulk down there." He paused to give Pitt a scholarly gaze over the tops of his spectacles. "We could have blasted until next summer without doing any damage to the derelict."

Pitt shrugged. "Win a few, lose a few." He passed a spare flashlight to Hunnewell. "I'll go first. Give me five minutes before you follow."

Hunnewell crouched at the edge of the ice tunnel as Pitt knelt to enter.

"Two. I'll give you two minutes, no more. Then I'll be right behind you."

The tube, illuminated by the shattered rays of the sun through the ice crystals above, ran downward at a thirty-degree angle for twenty feet, stopping at the blackened steel plates, charred and bent, of the hull. The smell by this time was so strong that Pitt found it an effort just to breathe. He shook off the irritating odor and dragged himself to within a foot of the fire-scarred metal, discovering that the tunnel curved and paralleled the hull for another ten feet, ending finally at an open hatch, savagely twisted and distorted. He could only wonder at the white-hot temperatures responsible.

Crawling over the jagged edge of the hatchway, he stood up and swung the beam of his flashlight, surveying the heat-defaced walls. It was impossible to tell what purpose the compartment served. Every square inch was gutted by the terrible intensity of the fire. Pitt suddenly felt a dread of the unknown. He stood dead-still for several moments, forcing his mind to regain control of his emotions before he stepped across the debris toward the door leading to the alleyway and shone the light into the darkness beyond.

The beam touched the whole black length as far as the stairway to a lower deck. The corridor was barren except for the charred ashes of a carpet. It was the silence that was eerie. No creaking of the plates, no throb of the engines, no lapping of water against a weed-encrusted hull, nothing, only the complete soundlessness of a void. He hesitated in the doorway for a long minute, his first thought, conviction rather, was that something had gone terribly, terribly wrong with Admiral Sandecker's plans. This wasn't what they had been led to expect at all.

Hunnewell came through the hatchway and joined him. He stood next to Pitt, staring at the blackened walls, the distorted and crystallized metal, and the melted hinges that once held a wooden door. Wearily he leaned against the doorway, his eyes half closed, shaking his head as if coming out of a trance.

"We'll find precious little that's of any use to us."

"We'll find nothing," Pitt said firmly. "What the fire left, our unknown friends have undoubtedly picked clean." As if to emphasize his words, he played the beam on the deck, revealing several overlapping footprints in the soot traveling to and from the open hatchway. "Let's see what they've been up to."

They went out into the alleyway, stepping through the ashes and debris on the deck, moved to the next compartment, and entered. It had been the radio room. Most of the ruins were scarcely recognizable. The bunk and furniture were skeletons of charred wood, the remains of the radio equipment one congealed mess of melted metal and hardened drippings of stained solder. Their senses by now had become accustomed to the overpowering stench and the grotesque carbonized surroundings, but they weren't the least bit prepared for the hideously misshapen form on the deck.

"Oh, good God!" Hunnewell gasped. He dropped his flashlight and it rolled across the deck and came to rest against the shockingly disfigured remains of a head, illuminating the skull and teeth where they burst from the incinerated flesh.

"I don't envy him his death," Pitt murmured.

The ghastly sight was too much for Hunnewell. He staggered off into one corner and retched for several minutes. When he finally returned to Pitt's side, he looked as if he'd recently returned from the grave.

"I'm sorry," he said sheepishly. "I've never seen a cremated corpse before. I didn't have the vaguest idea what one looked like—never gave it much thought really. It's not a pretty sight, is it?"

"There's no such thing as a pretty corpse," Pitt said. He was beginning to feel a touch of sickness himself. "If that lump of ashes on the deck is any indication of things to come, we should find at least fourteen more just like it."

Hunnewell grimaced as he stooped and picked up his flashlight. Then he slipped a notebook from a pocket, held the light under his arm and flipped through several pages. "Yes, you're right. The ship sailed with six crewmen and nine passengers: fifteen in all." He fumbled a little before finding another page. "This poor devil must be the radio operator—Svendborg—Gustav Svendborg."

"Maybe, maybe not. The only one who can tell for certain is his dentist." Pitt stared at what had once been a breathing, flesh-and-blood man, and he tried to imagine how the end had come. A furnacelike wall of red and orange flame, a brief unearthly scream, the searing shock of pain that drove the mind into instant insanity, and the limbs flailing in the contorted dance of death. To die by fire, he reflected, the last seconds of life spent in indescribable agony, was an extinction abhorred by every living man and beast.

Pitt kneeled down and studied the body more closely. His eyes squinted and his mouth tightened. It must have been almost as he had visualized, but not quite. The scorched form was curled in the fetus position, the knees drawn up almost to the chin and the arms pulled tightly against the sides, contracted by the intense heat upon the flesh. But there was something else that caught Pitt's attention. He focused the flashlight on the deck beside the body, illuminating dimly the twisted steel legs of the radio operator's chair where they protruded from beneath his disfigured remains.

Hunnewell, his face void of all color, asked: "What do you find so interesting in that grisly thing?"

"Have a look," Pitt said. "It would seem that poor Gustav was sitting down when he died. His chair literally burned out from under him."

Hunnewell said nothing, only eyed Pitt questioningly.

"Doesn't it strike you strange," Pitt continued, "that a man would calmly burn to death without bothering to stand up or make an effort to escape?"

"Nothing strange about it," Hunnewell said stonily. "The fire probably engulfed him while he was hunched over the transmitter sending out a Mayday." He began to choke with sickness again. "God, we're not doing him any good with our conjectures. Let's get out of here and search the rest of the ship while I'm still able to walk."

Pitt nodded and turned and passed through the doorway. Together they made their way into the bowels of the derelict. The engine room, the galley, the salon, everywhere they went their eyes were laid on the same horrifying spectacle of death as in the radio room. By the time they discovered the thirteenth and fourteenth bodies in the wheelhouse, Hunnewell's stomach was slowly becoming immune. He consulted his notebook several more times, marking certain pages with a pencil until only one name between the padded covers remained that didn't have a neat line drawn through it.

"That's about it," he said, snapping the book shut. "We've found them all except the man we came for."

Pitt lit a cigarette and blew a long cloud of blue smoke and seemed to consider for a moment. "They were all charred so far beyond recognition, he could have been any one of them."

"But he wasn't," Hunnewell said positively. "The

right body won't be too difficult to identify, at least not for me." He paused. "I knew our quarry rather well, you know."

Pitt's eyebrows raised. "No, I didn't know."

"No secret really." Hunnewell puffed on the lenses of his glasses and polished them with a handkerchief. "The man we've lied, schemed and risked our lives to find—unfortunately, as it probably turns out, dead—attended one of my classes at the Oceanographic Institute six years ago. A brilliant fellow." He motioned toward the two cremated forms on the deck. "A pity if he ended like this."

"How can you be certain you'll be able to tell him from the others?" Pitt asked.

"By his rings. He had a thing about rings. Wore them on every finger except his thumbs."

"Rings don't make a positive identification."

Hunnewell smiled a little. "There is also a toe missing from the left foot. Will that do?"

"It would," Pitt said thoughtfully. "But we haven't found a corpse that qualifies. We've already searched the entire ship."

"Not quite." Hunnewell pulled a slip of paper from the notebook and unfolded it under the beam of his flashlight. "This is a rough diagram of the vessel. I traced a copy from the original in the maritime archives." He pointed at the creased paper. "See here, just beyond the chartroom. A narrow ladder drops to a compartment directly beneath a false funnel. It's the only entrance."

Pitt studied the crude tracing. Then he turned and stepped outside the chartroom. "The opening is here all right. The ladder is burned all to hell, but enough of the rung bracing is left to support our weight."

The isolated compartment—situated in the exact center of the hull without benefit of portholes—was ravaged even worse than the others; the steel plating on the walls curved outward, buckled like crinkled sheets of wallpaper. It appeared empty. No trace of anything that remotely resembled furnishings was left after the conflagration. Pitt was just kneeling down, poking the ashes, searching for a sign of a body, when Hunnewell shouted.

"Here!" He fell to his knees. "Over here in the corner." Hunnewell focused the light on the sprawled outline of what had once been a man, now a barely discernible pile of charred bones. Only bits of the jawbone and pelvis were recognizable. Then he bent very low and carefully brushed away an area of the remains. When Hunnewell stood up, he held several small pieces of distorted metal in his hand.

"Not proof positive perhaps. But about as certain as we'll ever get."

Pitt took the fused bits of metal and held them under the beam of his light.

"I remember the rings quite well," Hunnewell said. "The settings were beautifully handcrafted and inlaid with eight different semiprecious stones native to Iceland. Each was carved in the likeness of an ancient Nordic god."

"Sounds impressive but garish," Pitt said.

"To you, a stranger maybe," Hunnewell returned quietly. "Yet if you had known him—" His voice trailed off.

Pitt eyed Hunnewell speculatively. "Do you always form sentimental attachments to your students?"

"Genius, adventurer, scientist, legend, the tenth richest man in the world before he was twenty-five. A kind and gentle person totally untouched by his fame and wealth. Yes, I think you could safely say a friendship with Kristjan Fyrie could result in a sentimental attachment."

How strange, Pitt thought. It was the first time the scientist had mentioned Fyrie's name since they had left Washington. And it had been uttered in a hushed, almost reverent tone. The same inflection, Pitt recalled, that Admiral Sandecker had also used when he spoke of the Icelander.

Pitt was conscious of no awe as he stood over the pitiful remains of the man who had been one of the most powerful figures in international finance. As he stood there staring down, his mind simply could not associate the ashes at his feet with the flesh-and-blood person the world's newspapers referred to as the apotheosis of the swinging intellectual jetsetter. Perhaps if he had met the celebrated Kristjan Fyrie, an emotion of some sort might be present now. But then, Pitt truly doubted it. He wasn't one to impress easily. Take away the clothes of the greatest living man, his father once told him, and you behold a very embarrassed, naked and defenseless animal.

Pitt looked at the twisted metal rings for a moment and then passed them back to Hunnewell, and as he did he heard the faint sound of movement somewhere on the deck above. He froze, listening intently. But the sound had died in the blackness beyond the upper hatchway. There was something sinister in the quality of the silence that hung over the devastated cabin—a feeling that someone was observing their every motion, listening to their every word. Pitt nerved himself for an act of defense, but it was too late. A powerful light beam played into the room from the top of the ladder, blinding his eyes in its blazing glare.

"Robbing the dead, gentlemen? By God, I do believe you two are capable of most anything." The face was hidden behind the light, but the voice unmistakably belonged to Commander Koski.

Chapter 4

Without moving, without replying, Pitt stood in the middle of the charred deck. He stood there, it seemed to him, for a decade while his brain worked to explain Koski's presence. He had expected the Commander to arrive on the scene eventually, but not for at least another three hours. It was now obvious that instead of waiting until the prescribed rendezvous time, Koski had altered his heading and pushed the *Catawaba* at full speed along Hunnewell's plotted course into the ice pack as soon as the helicopter was out of sight.

Koski swung the flash beam to the ladder, exposing Dover's face beside him. "We have much to talk about. Major Pitt, Dr. Hunnewell, if you please."

Pitt thought of a cleverly worded comeback but dismissed it. Instead, he said, "Up your ass, Koski! You come down! And bring that hulking goon of an exec officer if it will make you feel any safer."

There was almost a full minute of angry silence before Koski replied, "You're hardly in a position to make rash demands."

"Why not? There's too much at stake for Dr. Hunnewell and me to sit here and suck our thumbs while you play amateur detective." Pitt knew his words were arrogant, but he had to get the upper hand over Koski.

53

"No need to get nasty, Major. An honest explanation will go a long way. You've lied since the moment you set foot on my ship. The *Novgorod* indeed. The greenest cadet at the Coast Guard Academy wouldn't think of identifying this hulk as a Russian spy trawler. The radar antennas, the highly sophisticated electronic gear you described with such authority—did the equipment evaporate? I didn't buy you and Hunnewell from the beginning, but your stories were convincing, and my own headquarters, however mysteriously, backed you up. You've used me, Major. My crew, my ship, as you would a streetcar or a service station. An explanation? Yes, I don't think it's asking too much. Merely the answer to one simple question: what in hell is coming off?"

Koski was in the fold now, Pitt thought. The cocky little commander wasn't demanding, he was asking. "You still have to come down to our level. Part of the answer lies here in the ashes."

There was a moment's hesitation, but they came. Koski, followed by the mammoth form of Dover, climbed down the ladder and faced Pitt and Hunnewell. "Okay, gentlemen, let's have it."

"You've seen most of the ship?" Pitt asked.

Koski nodded. "Enough. Eighteen years of rescue at sea, and I've never seen a vessel gutted as bad as this one."

"Do you recognize it?"

"Impossible. What's left to recognize. It was a pleasure craft, a yacht. That much is certain. Beyond that you can flip a coin." Koski looked at Pitt, a faint puzzlement in his eyes. "I'm the one who expects answers. What are you leading up to?"

"The *Lax*. Ever hear of it?"

Koski nodded. "The *Lax* disappeared over a year ago with all hands, including its owner, the Icelandic mining magnate—" he hesitated, recalling, "Fyrie, Kristjan Fryie. Christ, half the Coast Guard searched for months. Didn't find a sign. So what about the *Lax*?"

"You're standing on it," Pitt said slowly, letting his words sink in. He aimed his flashlight at the deck.

"And this cremated mess is all that's left of Kristjan Fryie."

Koski's eyes widened and the color drained from his face. He took a step forward and stared down at the thing in the yellow circle of light. "Good God, are you sure?"

"Burned beyond recognition is a gross understatement, but Dr. Hunnewell is ninety percent certain of Fyrie's personal effects."

"Yes, the rings. I overheard."

"Not much, perhaps, but considerably more than we could find on the other bodies."

"I've never seen anything like this," Koski said in wonder. "It can't be. A ship this size couldn't vanish without a trace for nearly a year and then pop up burned to a cinder in the middle of an iceberg."

"It would seem that it did just that," Hunnewell said.

"Sorry, Doc," Koski said, staring into Hunnewell's eyes. "Though I'm the first to admit that I'm not in your league when it comes to the science of ice formations, I've kicked around the North Atlantic long enough to know that an iceberg might get sidetracked by currents, drifting in circles, or scrape along the New-foundland Coast for up to three years—ample time for the *Lax,* by some remote chance, to become trapped and entombed. But, if you'll forgive the word play, the theory doesn't hold water."

"You're quite correct, Commander," Hunnewell said. "The chances are extremely remote for such an occurrence, but nonetheless conceivable. As you know, a fire-gutted ship takes days to cool. If a current or wind pushed and held the hull against the iceberg, it would only take forty-eight hours or less before this entire ship imbedded itself under the berg's mantle. You can achieve the same situation by holding a red-hot poker against an ice block. The poker will melt its way into the block until it cools. Then the ice, if refrozen around the metal, locks it tight."

"Okay, Doc, you score on that one. However, there's one important factor no one has considered."

"Which is?" Pitt prompted.

"The final course of the *Lax*," Koski said firmly.

"Nothing strange about that," Pitt offered. "It was in all the newspapers. Fyrie with his crew and passengers left Reykjavik on the morning of April tenth of last year and laid a direct heading for New York. He was last sighted by a Standard Oil tanker six hundred miles off Cape Farewell, Greenland. After that, nothing more was seen or heard of the *Lax* again."

"That's fine as far as it goes." Koski pulled his coat collar around his ears and fought to keep his teeth from chattering. "Except the sighting took place near the fiftieth parallel—too far south of the iceberg limit."

"I would like to remind you, Commander," Hunnewell said, raising an intimidating eyebrow, "that your own Coast Guard has logged as many as fifteen hundred bergs in one year below the forty-eighth parallel."

"And I'd like to remind you, Doc," Koski persisted, "that during the year in question the number of iceberg sightings below the forty-eighth parallel came to zero."

Hunnewell merely shrugged.

"It would be most helpful, Dr. Hunnewell, if you'd explain how an iceberg appeared where none existed, then with the *Lax* frozen in its clutches ignored the prevailing currents for eleven and a half months and cruised four degrees north while every other berg in the Atlantic was drifting south at the rate of three knots an hour."

"I can't," Hunnewell said simply.

"You can't?" Koski's face went blank with disbelief. He looked at Hunnewell, then at Pitt, then back to Hunnewell again. "You rotten bastards!" he said savagely. "Don't lie to me!"

"That's pretty salty terminology, Commander," Pitt said harshly.

"What in hell do you expect? You're both highly intelligent people, yet you act like a pair of mongoloids. Take Dr. Hunnewell here. An internationally renowned scientist, and he can't even explain how an iceberg can drift north against the Labrador Current. Either you're a fraud, Doc, or you're the dumbest professor on record. The plain simple truth is that it's as impossible for this berg to reverse drift as it is for a glacier to flow uphill."

"Nobody's perfect," Hunnewell said shrugging helplessly.

"No courtesy, no honest answer, is that it?"

"It's not a question of honesty," Pitt said. "We've our orders just as you have yours. Up to an hour ago Hunnewell and I were following a precise plan. That plan is now out the window."

"Uh-huh. And the next move in our game of charades?"

"The problem is, we can't explain everything," Pitt said. "Damned little in reality. I'll tell you what Dr. Hunnewell and I know. After that you'll have to draw your own conclusions."

"You could have leveled with me sooner."

"Hardly," Pitt said. "As captain of your ship you have full authority. You even have the power to disregard or challenge orders from your Commandant if you feel they endanger your crew and ship. I couldn't take a chance. We had to give you a snow job so you'd cooperate fully. Besides, we were not to confide in anyone. I'm going against those orders right now."

"Could be another snow job?"

"Could be," Pitt said, grinning, "but what's the percentage? Hunnewell and I have nothing more to gain. We're washing our hands of this mess and heading for Iceland."

"You're dropping all this in my lap?"

"Why not? Abandoned and drifting derelicts are your bag. Remember your motto, *Semper paratus,* always prepared, Coast Guard to the rescue and all that."

The twisted look on Koski's face was priceless. "I would appreciate it if you just stuck to the facts without benefit of tawdry remarks."

"Very well," Pitt said calmly. "The story I concocted on the *Catawaba* was true up to a point—the point where I substituted the *Novgorod* for the *Lax.* Fyrie's yacht, of course, wasn't carrying classified electronic equipment, or any other clandestine mechanical devices for that matter. The cargo actually consisted of eight major-league engineers and scientists from Fyrie Mining Limited, who were on their way to New York to open secret negotiations with two of our government's largest defense contractors. Somewhere on board—probably in this room—was a file of documents containing a geological survey of the ocean floor. What Fyrie's research team had discovered under the sea or where remains a mystery. This information was vitally important to a great number of people; our own defense department desperately yearned to get their hands on it. And so did the Russians; they pulled out all stops to grab it."

"The last statement explains a great deal," said Koski.

"Meaning?"

Koski exchanged knowing looks with Dover. "We were one of the ships that searched for the *Lax*—it was the *Catawaba*'s first patrol. Every time we blinked our eyes, we found ourselves crossing the wake of a Russian vessel. We were just egotistical enough to think they were observing our search patterns. Now it turns out that they were nosing after the *Lax* too."

"It also neatly ties in with the reason we butted in on your show," said Dover. "Ten minutes after you and Dr. Hunnewell left the flight pad, we received a message from Coast Guard Headquarters warning of a Russian sub patrolling around the ice pack. We tried but couldn't raise you—"

"Small wonder," Pitt interrupted. "It was essential that we maintain strict radio silence once we headed for the derelict. I took the precaution of switching the radio off. We couldn't transmit, much less receive."

"After Commander Koski notified headquarters of our failure to contact your helicopter," Dover continued, "a signal came through hot and heavy ordering us to hightail it after you and act as escort in case the sub got pushy."

"How did you find us?" Pitt asked.

"We hadn't passed two icebergs before we spotted that yellow copter of yours. It stood out like a canary on a bedsheet."

Pitt and Hunnewell looked at each other and began laughing.

"What's the joke?" Koski asked curiously.

"Luck, plain, simple, paradoxical luck," said Pitt, his face twisted in mirth. "We flew all over hell for three hours before we found this floating ice palace, and you found it five minutes after you began searching." Pitt then briefly told Koski and Dover about the iceberg decoy and meeting with the Russian submarine.

"Good Lord," Dover muttered. "Are you suggesting that we're not the first to set foot on the iceberg?"

"The evidence is plain," Pitt said. "The Ice Patrol's dyed stain has been chipped away, and Hunnewell and I found footprints in nearly every cabin of the ship. And there's more, something that takes the whole situation out of the mysterious and puts it in the category of the macabre."

"The fire?"

"The fire."

"Undoubtedly accidental. Fires have been happening on ships since the first reed boats floated down the Nile thousand of years ago."

"Murder has been going on for much longer than that."

"Murder!" Koski repeated flatly. "You did say murder?"

"With a capital M."

"Except for the excessive degree, I've observed nothing I haven't already seen on at least eight other burned-out ships during my service on the Coast Guard—bodies, stench, devastation, the works. In your honored opinion as an Air Force officer, what makes you think this one is any different?"

Pitt ignored Koski's testy remark. "It's all too perfect. The radio operator in the radio room, two engineers in the engine room, the captain and a mate on the bridge, the passengers in either their staterooms or salon, even a cook in the galley, everybody exactly where he should be. You tell me, Commander; you're the expert. What in hell kind of a fire would sweep through the entire ship, roasting everyone to a crisp without their making the slightest attempt at self-preservation?"

Koski tugged at an ear thoughtfully. "No hoses are scattered in the passageways. It's apparent no one tried to save the ship."

"The nearest body to the fire extinguisher lies twenty feet away. The crew went against all laws of human nature if they decided at the last minute to run and die at their routine duty stations. I can't imagine a cook who perferred dying in his galley to saving his life."

"That still proves nothing. Panic could have—"

"What does it take to convince you, Commander—a belt in the bicuspids with a baseball bat? Explain the radio operator. He died at his set, yet it's a known fact that a Mayday signal was never received from the *Lax* or any other ship in the North Atlantic at the time. Seems a bit odd that he couldn't have gotten off at least three or four words of a distress call."

"Keep going," Koski said quietly. His piercing eyes had an interested glint.

Pitt lit a cigarette and blew a long cloud of blue smoke into the refrigerated air, and he seemed to deliberate for a moment. "Let's talk about the condition of the derelict. You said it, Commander, you've never seen a ship gutted as badly as this one. Why? It was carrying no explosives or flammable cargo, and we can rule out the fuel tanks—they caused the blaze to spread, yes, but not to this degree on the opposite end of the ship. Why would every square inch burn with such a high intensity? The hull and superstructure are steel. And besides hoses and extinguishers, the *Lax* had a sprinkler system." He paused and pointed at two misshapen metal fixtures hanging from the ceiling. "A fire at sea usually starts at one location, the engine room, or a cargo hold, or a storage area, and then spreads from compartment to compartment, taking hours and sometimes days to fully consume a ship. I'll bet you any amount you care to cover that a fire investigator would scratch his head and cross this one off as a flash fire, one that totaled out the entire ship within a matter of minutes, setting a new record, ignited by causes or persons unknown."

"What do you have in mind for the cause?"

Pitt said, "A flamethrower."

There was a minute of appalled silence.

"Do you realize what you're suggesting?"

"You're damned right I do," Pitt said. "Right down to the violent blast of searing flame, the hideous swish of the jets, the terrible smoke from melted flesh. Like it or not, a flamethrower is the logical answer."

They were all listening now with horrified interest. Hunnewell made a choking noise in his throat as if he were going to be sick again.

"It's outlandish, unthinkable," Koski murmured.

"This entire setup is outlandish," Pitt said evenly.

Hunnewell stared at Pitt blankly. "I can't believe that everyone stood like sheep and let themselves be turned into human torches."

"Don't you see?" Pitt said. "Our fiendish friend somehow either drugged or poisoned the passengers and crew. Probably slipped a massive dose of chloral hydrate into their food or drinks."

"They all could have been shot," Dover ventured.

"I studied several of the remains." Pitt shook his head. "There were no signs of bullets or shattered bones."

"And if he waited until they were all knocked out by the poison—I prefer to think they died outright—scattered them around the ship, and then went from compartment to compartment with a flamethrower . . ." Koski left the surmise unfinished. "But what then? Where did the killer go from there?"

"Before attempting to answer that one," Hunnewell said wearily, "I wish someone would kindly explain where the murderer materialized from in the first place. He obviously wasn't one of the passengers or crew. The *Lax* sailed with fifteen men, and it burned with fifteen men. Logic dictates that this was the work of a team who boarded from another ship."

"Won't work," said Koski. "Any boarding of one

ship by another requires some sort of radio contact. Even if the *Lax* had picked up survivors from a phony shipwreck, the captain would have immediately reported it." Koski suddenly smiled. "As I recall, Fyrie's last message asked for the reservation of a penthouse suite at the Statler-Hilton in New York."

"Poor bastard," Dover said slowly. "If money and success ends like this, who needs it?" He looked at the thing on the deck again and quickly turned away. "God, what kind of maniac could murder fifteen humans at a sitting? Methodically poison fifteen men and then calmly cremate them with a flamethrower?"

"The same maniac who blows up airliners for insurance money," said Pitt. "One who can kill another human with the same lack of shattering guilt you'd experience after swatting a fly. The motive here was obviously gain. Fyrie and his people made a discovery that was extremely valuable. The United States wanted it, Russia wanted it, but a dark horse got away with it."

"Was it worth all this?" Hunnewell said with sickness in his eyes.

"It was to the sixteenth man." Pitt stared down at the grisly remains on the deck. "The unrecorded intruder who became the death of the party."

Chapter 5

Iceland, the land of frost and fire, rugged glaciers and smoldering volcanoes, an island prism of lava-bed reds, rolling tundra greens, and placid lake blues stretched under the rich gold glow of the midnight sun. Surrounded by the Atlantic Ocean, bounded by the warm waters of the Gulf Stream in the south and by the frigid polar sea to the north, Iceland rests midway as the crow flies between New York and Moscow. A strange island of kaleidoscopic scenes far less cold than its name suggests; the average temperature in the cold month of January rarely rises above that of the New England coast of the United States. To someone seeing it for the first time, Iceland seems indeed an unequaled phenomenon of beauty.

Pitt watched the jagged snow-packed peaks of the island grow on the horizon and the flashing water below the Ulysses turn from the deep blue of the great ocean depths to the rich green of the inshore surf. Then he altered the controls, and the helicopter dipped neatly on a ninety-degree angle and a parallel course along the steep lava cliffs that burst from the sea below. They passed over a tiny fishing village, nestled on a half circle bay, its roofs painted in a checkered myriad of tile reds and pastel greens; a lonely outpost at the gateway of the Arctic Circle.

"What time is it?" Hunnewell asked, awakening from a light sleep.

"Ten minutes past four in the morning," Pitt replied.

"God, to look at the sun, you'd think it was four in the afternoon." Hunnewell yawned loudly and made a vain attempt to stretch in the cramped confines of the cockpit. "About now I'd give my right arm if I could go back to sleep between the crisp white sheets of a soft bed."

"Keep your eyes propped open, it won't be long now."

"How far to Reykjavik?"

"Another half hour." Pitt paused to make a visual check of the instruments. "I could have cut north sooner, but I wanted to sightsee the coastline."

"Six hours, forty-five minutes since we left the *Catawaba*. Not bad time."

"Probably could have shaved that considerably if we weren't handicapped with an extra fuel tank."

"Without it we'd be back there somewhere trying to swim four hundred miles to shore."

Pitt grinned. "We could have always sent a Mayday to the Coast Guard."

"Judging from the mood Commander Koski was in when we took off, I doubt if he'd put himself out for us if we were drowning in a bathtub and he had his hand on the plug."

"In spite of what Koski thinks of me, I'd vote for him as admiral any time he decided to run. In my book he's a damn good man."

"You have a funny way of expressing your admiration," Hunnewell said dryly. "Except for your perceptive deduction concerning the flamethrower—my hat's off to you for that one, by the way—you really didn't tell him a damned thing."

"We gave him the truth as far as it went. Anything else would have been fifty percent guesswork. The only real fact that we omitted was the name of Fyrie's discovery."

"Zirconium." Hunnewell's gaze was lost in the distance. "Atomic number: forty."

"I barely squeaked through my geology class," Pitt said, smiling. "Why zirconium? What makes it worth mass murder?"

"Purified zirconium is vital in the construction of nuclear reactors because it absorbs little or no radiation. Every nation in the world with facilities for atomic research would give their eyeteeth to have it obtainable by the carload. Admiral Sandecker is certain that if Fyrie and his scientists did indeed discover a vast zirconium bonanza, it was under the sea close enough to the surface to be raised economically."

Pitt turned and stared out of the cockpit bubble at the dark ultramarine blue that stretched almost unrippled to the south. A fishing boat with a chain of dories sailed out to sea, the tiny hulls moving as calmly as if they were gliding across a tinted mirror. He watched them through eyes that barely saw, his mind dwelling on the exotic element that lay covered by the cold waters below.

"A hell of an undertaking," he muttered, just loud enough to be heard over the drone from the engine's exhaust. "The problems of raising raw ore from the sea bottom are immense."

"Yes, but not insurmountable. Fyrie Limited employs the world's leading experts at underwater mining. That's how Kristjan Fyrie built his empire, you know, dredging diamonds off the coast of Africa." Hunnewell spoke with what sounded like simple admiration. "He was only eighteen, a seaman on an old Greek freighter, when he jumped ship at Beira, a small port on the coast of Mozambique. It didn't take him long to catch the diamond fever. There was a boom on in those days, but the big syndicates had all the productive claims tied up. That's where Fyrie stood out from the rest—he had a shrewd and creative mind.

"If diamond deposits could be found on land not

two miles from shore, he reasoned, why couldn't they lie underwater on the continental shelf? So every day for five months he dove in the warm waters of the Indian Ocean until he found a section of the seabed that looked promising. Now the trick was scrounging the financing to buy the needed dredging equipment. Fyrie had arrived in Africa with nothing but the shirt on his back. To beg from the white moneyed interests in the territory would have been a waste of time. They would have taken everything and left him with nothing."

"One percent of something is often better than ninety-nine percent of nothing," Pitt injected.

"Not to Kristjan Fyrie," Hunnewell replied defensively. "He had a true Icelander's sense of principle—share the profits but never give them away. He went before the black people of Mozambique and sold them on forming their own syndicate, with Kristjan Fyrie, of course, as president and general manager. After the black people raised the financing for the barge and dredging equipment, Fyrie worked twenty hours a day until the entire operation was running like a computer at IBM. The five months of diving paid off—the dredge began to bring up high-grade diamonds almost immediately. Within two years Fyrie was worth forty million dollars."

Pitt noticed a dark speck in the sky, several thousand feet higher and in front of the Ulysses. "You certainly seem to have studied the Fyrie history."

"I know it sounds strange," Hunnewell went on, "but Fyrie seldom stayed with a project more than a few years. Most men would have bled the operation dry. Not Kristjan. After he made a fortune beyond his wildest dreams, he turned the whole business over to the people who financed the venture."

"Just gave it away?"

"Lock, stock and the popular barrel. He distributed every share of his stock to the native stockholders, set up a black administration that could run efficiently without him, and took the next boat back to Iceland. Of the few white men held in high esteem by the Africans, the name of Kristjan Fyrie stands right at the top."

Pitt was watching the solitary dark speck in the northern sky turn into a sleek jet aircraft. He leaned forward, screwing up his eyes against the bright blue glare. The stranger was one of the new executive jets built by the British—fast, reliable and capable of whisking twelve passengers halfway around the world in a matter of hours without a fuel stop. Pitt barely had time to realize that the stranger was painted an ebony black from nose to tail when it swept past his range of vision traveling in the opposite direction.

"What did Fyrie do for an encore?" he asked.

"Mined manganese off Vancouver Island in British Columbia and brought in an offshore oil field in Peru to name a few. There were no mergers, no subsidiaries. Kristjan built Fyrie Limited into a great industry specializing in underwater geological exploitation, nothing else."

"Did he have a family?"

"No, his parents died in a fire when he was very young. All he had was an identical twin sister. Don't really know much about her. Fyrie put her through a finishing school in Switzerland, and, so rumor has it, she later became a missionary somewhere in New Guinea. Apparently her brother's fortune meant nothing to—"

Hunnewell never finished the sentence. He jerked sideways facing Pitt, his eyes staring blankly, his mouth open in surprise but no words coming out. Pitt barely had time to see the old man slump forward, limp and dead to all appearances, as the plexiglass bubble encircling the cockpit shattered into a thousand jagged slivers and fell away. Twisting to one side and throwing up an arm to protect his face from the blasting wall of cold air, Pitt momentarily lost control of the helicopter. Its aerodynamics drastically altered, the Ulysses nosed sharply upward, almost on its end, throwing Pitt and the unconscious Hunnewell violently against their backrests. It was then Pitt became aware of the machine gun shells striking the fuselage aft of the seats. The sudden uncontrolled maneuver temporarily saved their lives; the gunner aboard the black jet had been caught off guard, adjusting his trajectory too late and sending most of his fire into an empty sky.

Unable to match the helicopter's slow speed without stalling, the mysterious jet soared forward and swung around in a hundred-and-eighty-degree turn for another assault. The bastards must have made a sharp circle east and south and west before attacking from the rear, Pitt quickly figured as he struggled to bring the helicopter on a level course, a near impossible task with a two-hundred-mile-an hour air stream tearing at his eyes. He throttled down, trying desperately to reduce the unseen force that pinned his body against the seat.

The black jet swept by again, but this time Pitt was ready for it. He pulled the Ulysses to an abrupt horizontal stop, the rotor blates frantically beating the atmosphere, raising the light craft in a straight vertical climb. The dodge worked. The pilot of the jet roared under Pitt, unable to bring the machine gun to bear. Twice more Pitt managed to shake his attacker, but it was only a question of time before his opponent compensated for his rapidly diminishing bag of tricks.

Pitt didn't kid himself. There was no escape; the battle was too one-sided. The score was seven to nothing in favor of the visitors, with only a few seconds left to play in the fourth quarter. A grim smile wrinkled around Pitt's eyes as he lowered the copter to a bare twenty feet above the water. Victory was hopeless, but there was a slight chance, an infinitesimal fingertip chance, he thought, for a tie score. He studied the ink-black aircraft as it jockied for the last pass. There was nothing left now but the mad clangor of steeljacketed bullets smashing through the thin aluminum skin of the Ulysses. Pitt steadied the small defenseless craft and hovered as the jet dove like a concrete bird, directly toward him.

The gunner, laying prone and firing out an open cargo door, played it cool this time. He laid down a steady stream of shells, waiting for the narrowing gap to carry them into the path of the helicopter. The barrage of death was only thirty yards away now. Pitt braced himself for the impact and threw the Ulyssess straight up into the attacking plane, the helicopter's rotor blades shattering as they sliced through the jet's horizontal stabilizer. Instinctively Pitt flicked the ignition switch off as the turbine engine, without the drag from the rotor, raced wildly amid the howl of tortured metal. Then the racket stopped, and the sky was silent except for the wind that whistled in Pitt's ears.

He snatched a glance at the strange jet just before it crashed into the sea, nose first, it's tail section hanging like a broken arm. Pitt and the unconscious Hunnewell weren't much better off. All they could do was sit and wait for the crippled helicopter to drop like a stone nearly seventy feet into the cold Atlantic water. When the crash came, it was much worse than Pitt had anticipated. The Ulysses fell on its side into the Iceland surf in six feet of water, a scant football field length from shore. Pitt's head whipped sideways and glanced off the door frame, sending him into a vortex of darkness. Fortunately the agonizing shock of the icy water jolted him back to dizzy wakefulness. Waves of nausea swept over him, and he knew he was only a hairbreadth away from saying To hell with it and drifting off to sleep for the last time.

His face twisted with pain, Pitt undid his seat belt and shoulder harness, taking a gulp of air before a breaking wave crest passed over the helicopter, then quickly he unfastened the insensible Hunnewell and lifted his head above the swirling water. At that instant, Pitt slipped and lost his balance as a crashing breaker knocked him from the Ulysses into the surf. Still grasping Hunnewell by a death grip on the coat collar, he battled the rolling surge as it swept him toward shore, rolling him end-over-end across the uneven rocky bottom.

If Pitt ever wondered what it was like to drown, he had a pretty good idea now. The freezing water stung every square inch of his skin like a million bees. His ears failed to pop, and his head was one tormenting ache; his nostrils filled with water, stabbing like a knife at his frontal sinus, and the thin membranes of his lungs felt as if they'd been dipped in nitric acid. Finally, after bashing his knees into a bed of rocks, he struggled to his feet, his head bursting gratefully into the pure Icelandic air. He swore to himself then and there that if he should ever decide to commit suicide, it definitely wouldn't be by drowning.

He staggered from the water onto a pebble-strewn beach, half carrying, half dragging Hunnewell like a drunk leading a drunk. A few steps beyond the tideline Pitt eased his burden down and checked the doctor's pulse and breathing; both were on the fast side but regular. Then he saw Hunnewell's left arm. It had been terribly mangled at the elbow by the machine gun bullets. As quickly as his numbed hands would allow, Pitt took off his shirt, tore off the sleeves, and tightly wrapped them around the wound to stem the flow of blood. As bad as the tissue damage looked, there was no artery spurt, so he automatically discarded the idea of a tourniquet in favor of direct pressure. Then he sat Hunnewell up against a large rock, made a crude sling, and elevated the wound to aid the control of bleeding.

Pitt could do nothing more for his friend, so he lay down on the lumpy carpet of stone and let the unwelcome pain in his body and the hated currents of nausea sweep through his body. Relaxing as much as the sickness would let him, he closed his eyes, shutting out a magnificent view of the cloud-dotted Arctic sky.

Deep unconsciousness should have held Pitt for at least several hours, but a distant alarm in the depths of his brain began signaling, and instinctively, in response to the stimuli, his eyes popped open only twenty minutes after they had closed. The scene was different; the sky and clouds were still there, but something stood in front of them. It took a second for Pitt's eyes to focus on the five children standing around him. There was no fear in their faces as they stared down at Pitt and Hunnewell.

Pitt sat up on one elbow, forced a smile—it wasn't easy—and said, "Good morning, group. Up a bit early, aren't you?"

As if on cue, the younger children looked at the

oldest, a boy. He hesitated several moments, collecting his words before he spoke. "My brothers and sisters and I were herding our father's cows on the meadow above the cliffs. We saw your—" he paused, his face blank.

"Helicopter?" Pitt prompted.

"Yes, that is it." The boy's face brightened. "Hel-i-cop-ter. We saw your helicopter lying in the ocean." A slight blush reddened his flawless Scandinavian complexion. "I am ashamed that my English is not so good."

"No," Pitt said softly. "I'm the one who is ashamed. You speak English like an Oxford professor, while I can't even off you two words in Icelandic."

The boy beamed at the compliment as he helped Pitt struggle awkwardly to his feet. "You are hurt, sir. Your head bleeds."

"I'll survive. It's my friend who is injured seriously. We must get him to the nearest doctor quickly."

"I sent my younger sister to fetch my father when we discovered you. He will bring his truck soon."

Just then, Hunnewell moaned softly. Pitt leaned over him, cradling the bald head. The old man was conscious now. His eyes rolled and stared at Pitt briefly, and then stared at the children. He was breathing heavily and tried to speak, but the words caught in his throat. There was a strange kind of serenity in his eyes as he gripped Pitt's hand, and in a strained effort murmured, "God save thee—" Then he trembled and gave a little gasp.

Dr. Hunnewell was dead.

Chapter
6

The farmer and his oldest boy carried Hunnewell to the Land Rover. Pitt rode in the back holding the oceanographer's head in his lap. He closed the glazed, sightless eyes and smoothed the few long strands of white hair. Most children would have been terrified of death, but the boys and girls who surrounded Pitt in the bed of the truck sat silently and calmly, their expressions devoid of all but total acceptance of the only certainty that waits for everyone.

The farmer, a big handsome outdoor-hardened man, drove slowly up a narrow road to the top of the cliff and through the meadows, pulling a small cloud of volcanic red dust behind the tailgate. Within minutes he stopped at a small cottage on the outskirts of a village of white farmhouses dominated by the traditional Icelandic churchyard.

A somber little man with soft green eyes enlarged by thick steelrimmed glasses came out, introduced himself as Dr. Jonsson and, after examining Hunnewell, led Pitt into the cottage where he stitched and bandaged Pitt's three-inch head gash and made him change into some dry clothes. Later, as Pitt was drinking a strong brew of coffee and schnaps forced on him by the doctor, the boy and his father entered.

The boy nodded to Pitt and spoke. "My father would consider it a great honor if he could transport you and your friend to Reykjavik if that is where you wish to go."

Pitt stood and stared a moment into the father's warm gray eyes. "You tell your father that I am deeply grateful, and that the honor is mine." Pitt held out his hand and the Icelander gripped it hard.

The boy translated. His father simply nodded and then they both turned and left the room without another word.

Pitt lit a cigarette and looked quizzically at Dr. Jonsson. "You're a member of a strange people, Doctor. You all seem to be brimming with warmth and courtesy within, but your exterior seems completely dry of any emotion."

"You'll find the citizens of Reykjavik more open. This is the country; we are born into an isolated and stark but beautiful land. Icelanders who live away from the city are not noted for gossip; we can almost come to understand each other's thoughts before we speak. Life and love are commonplace; death is merely an accepted occurrence."

"I wondered why the children appeared so unconcerned when sitting next to a corpse."

"Death to us is merely a separation, and only a visual one at that. For you see," the doctor's hand pointed through a large picture window at the gravestones in the churchyard, "they who went before us are still here."

Pitt stared several moments at the grave markers, all rising on their individual crooked angles among the green mossy grass. Then his attention was caught by the farmer, who was carrying a handcrafted pine coffin to the Land Rover. He watched attentively as the big, silent man lifted Hunnewell's form into the traditional tapered box with all the strength and tenderness of a new father with a baby.

"What is the farmer's name?" Pitt asked.

"Mundsson, Thorsteinn Mundsson. His son's name is Bjarni."

Pitt stared through the window until the coffin was pushed slowly onto the truckbed. Then he turned away. "I'll always wonder if Dr. Hunnewell would still be alive if I'd done things differently."

"Who will ever know? Remember, my friend, if you had been born ten minutes sooner or ten minutes later, your path might never have crossed his."

Pitt smiled. "I get what you mean. But the fact is, his life was in my hands, and I fumbled and lost it." He hesitated, seeing the scene again in his mind. "On the beach I passed out for half an hour after I bandaged his arm. If I had stayed awake, he might not have bled to death."

"Put your conscience to rest. Your Dr. Hunnewell did not die from loss of blood. It was the shock of his injury, the shock of your crash, the shock of below freezing sea water. No, I'm certain an autopsy will show that his aging heart gave out long before his blood. He was getting on in years, and he was not, from what I could determine, a physically athletic man."

"He was a scientist, an oceanographer, the best."

"Then I envy him."

Pitt looked at the village physician speculatively. "Why do you say that?"

"He was a man of the sea, and he died by the sea he loved, and perhaps his last thoughts were as serene as the water."

"He talked of God," Pitt murmured.

"He was fortunate, yet I feel I will be fortunate when my times comes to be laid to rest over there in the churchyard only a hundred steps from where I was born and among so many of the people I have loved and cared for."

"I wish I could share your affinity for staying in one spot, Doctor, but somewhere in the distant past one of my ancestors was a gypsy. I've inherited his wandering ways. Three years is my all-time record for living in the same location."

"An interesting question; which of us is the most fortunate?"

Pitt shrugged. "Who can tell? We both hear the beat of a different drummer."

"In Iceland," Jonsson said, "we follow the lure of a different fisherman."

"You missed your true calling, Doctor. You should have been a poet."

"Ah, but I am a poet." Dr. Jonsson laughed. "Every village has at least four or five. You will have to search far and wide for a more literate country than Iceland. Over five hundred thousand books are sold annually to two hundred thousand people, our entire population—"

He broke off as the door opened and two men walked in. They stood calm, efficient and very official in their police uniforms. One nodded a greeting to the doctor, and Pitt suddenly got the entire picture.

"You needn't have been secretive about calling the police, Dr. Jonsson. I have nothing to conceal from anyone."

"No offense, but Dr. Hunnewell's arm was obviously mangled by gun shots. I've treated enough injured hunters to know the correct signs. The law is explicit, as I'm sure it is in your country. I must report all bullet wounds."

Pitt didn't like it much, but he had little option. The two muscular policemen standing before him would hardly buy a story about a phantom black jet attacking and shooting the Ulysses full of holes before being rammed in midair. A connection between the derelict in the iceberg and the jet was neither coincidental nor accidental. He was certain now that what started out as a simple search for a missing ship had turned out to be an unwanted involvement in a complex, farflung conspiracy. He was tired—tired of lying, sick of the whole goddamn mess. Only one thought gripped his mind: Hunnewell was dead, and someone had to pay.

"Were you the pilot of the helicopter that crashed, sir?" one of the policemen inquired. An unmistakable British accent and a courteous tone, but the "sir" seemed forced.

"Yes," was all Pitt answered.

The policemen seemed taken back for a moment by Pitt's terse reply. He was blond, had dirty fingernails, and was dressed in a uniform that left his wrists and ankles showing. "Your name, and the name of the deceased?"

"Pitt, Major Dirk Pitt, United States Air Force. The man in the coffin was Dr. William Hunnewell, National Underwater Marine Agency." Pitt thought it strange that neither policeman made an attempt to write the information down.

"Your destination? It was undoubtedly the airfield at Keflavik?"

"No, the heliport in Reykjavik."

A flicker of surprise crossed the blond policeman's eyes. It was barely perceptible, but Pitt caught it. The interrogator turned to his partner, a dark-skinned, burly character with glasses, and said something in Icelandic. He swung his head toward the Land Rover outside, scowled noticeably, then turned back to Pitt.

"Could you tell me your departure point, sir?"

"Greenland—couldn't give you the name of the town. It's spelled with twenty letters, and to an American it's totally unpronounceable. Dr. Hunnewell and I were on an expedition for our government, charting icebergs in the East Greenland Current. The idea was to crisscross the Denmark Strait by refueling at Reykjavik and then head back west to Greenland on a parallel course fifty miles further north. Unfortunately we didn't plan well, ran out of fuel and crashed on the coast. That's all, give or take a few details." Pitt lied without knowing exactly why. God, he thought, it's becoming a habit.

"Where exactly did you crash?"

"How the hell should I know," Pitt said unpleasantly. "Go three blocks past the cow pasture and turn left at Broadway. The helicopter is parked between the third and fourth waves. It's painted yellow; you can't miss it."

"Please be reasonable, sir." Pitt took satisfaction at the sudden flame in the policeman's face. "We must have all the details in order to make a report to our superior."

"Then why don't you stop beating around the bush and ask about Dr. Hunnewell's bullet wounds?" The official facial expression on the dark-skinned policeman cracked in a stifled yawn. Pitt stared at Dr. Jonsson. "You did say that's the reason they're here?"

"It is my duty to cooperate with the law." Jonsson seemed hesitant to speak.

"Suppose you explain your comrade's wound," said dirty nails.

"We were carrying a rifle to shoot polar bears," Pitt said slowly. "It accidentally discharged in the crash, the bullet striking Dr. Hunnewell in the elbow."

As far as Pitt could see, the two Icelandic policemen weren't reacting at all to his sarcasm. They stood quiet, looking at him with impatient speculation— speculation, Pitt thought, at how they would subdue him if he resisted any physical demands on their part. He didn't have to wait long.

"I am sorry, sir, but you force us to take you to our headquarters for further interrogation."

"The only place you'll take me is to the American consulate in Reykjavik. I have committed no crime against the people of Iceland nor broken any of your laws."

"I am quite familiar with our laws, Major Pitt. We do not relish getting out of bed at this time of morning for an investigation. The questions are necessary. You have not answered them to our satisfaction, so we must take you to our headquarters until we can determine what happened. There you will be free to call your consulate."

"In due time, Officer, but first, would you mind identifying yourselves?"

"I do not understand." The policeman stared coldly at Pitt. "Why should we identify ourselves? It is obvious what we are. Dr. Jonsson can vouch for our authenticity." He offered no papers or the usual police identification card. All he showed was his irritation.

"There is no doubt as to your official capacity,

gentlemen," Jonsson said in an almost apologetic tone. "However, Sergeant Arnarson usually patrols our village. I do not believe I have seen you come through our village before."

"Arnarson had an emergency call in Grindavik. He asked us to answer your call until he could arrive."

"Are you being transferred to this territory?"

"No, we were just passing through on our way to the north to pick up a prisoner. We stopped in to say hello and have a cup of coffee with Sergeant Arnarson. Unfortunately, before the pot became hot, he received your call and the one from Grindavik almost simultaneously."

"Then wouldn't it be wise to hold Major Pitt until the sergeant arrives?"

"No, I think not. Nothing can be accomplished here." He turned to Pitt. "My apologies, Major. Please do not be angry at our, how do you say it in your country, *running you in*." He turned to Jonsson. "I think it best if you came along too, Doctor, in case the Major has complications from his wounds. It's merely a formality."

A strange formality, Pitt thought, considering the circumstances. He had little choice but to comply with the policeman's wishes. "What about Dr. Hunnewell?"

"We will ask Sergeant Arnarson to send a lorry for him."

Jonsson smiled, almost diffidently. "Forgive me, gentlemen, I haven't quite finished with the major's head wound. I have two more stitches to insert before he is ready for travel. If you please, Major." He stood aside and motioned Pitt back into the examining room, closing the door.

"I thought you were all through butchering me," Pitt said good-naturedly.

"Those men are imposters," Jonsson whispered.

Pitt said nothing. There was no surprise on his face as he stepped softly over to the door, put an ear against it and listened. Satisfied when he could hear voices across the next room, he came back and faced Jonsson. "You're positive?"

"Yes, Sergeant Arnarson does not patrol Grinda-vik. Also, he never drinks coffee—his system is allergic to it, so he refuses even to stock it in his kitchen."

"Your sergeant, does he stand five foot nine and weigh about one hundred and seventy pounds?"

"To the inch and within five pounds—he is an old friend. I have examined him many times." Jonsson's eyes clouded with puzzlement. "How could you describe a man you have never met?"

"The character who does all the talking is wearing Arnarson's uniform. If you look closely, you can see the outlines where the sergeant stripes used to rest on the sleeve."

"I do not understand," Jonsson said in a whisper. His face was very pale. "What is happening?"

"I don't have half the answers. Sixteen, maybe as many as nineteen men have died, and the killing will probably go on. I'd guess Sergeant Arnarson was the latest victim. You and I are next."

Jonsson looked stricken, his hands clenched and unclenched in bewilderment and despair. "You mean I must die because I have seen and talked with two murderers?"

"I'm afraid, Doctor, that you're an innocent bystander that must be eliminated simply because you can recognize their faces."

"And you, Major, why have they concocted such an elaborate scheme to kill you?"

"Dr. Hunnewell and I also saw something that we shouldn't have."

Jonsson stared into Pitt's impassive face. "It would be impossible to murder us both without creating excitement in the village. Iceland is a small country. A fugitive could not run very far nor hide very long."

"These men are no doubt professionals when it comes to killing. Someone is paying them and paying them well. An hour after we're dead, they'll probably be relaxing with a drink in one hand aboard a jetliner bound for either Copenhagen, London or Montreal."

"They seem lax for professional assassins."

"They can afford to be. Where can we go? Their

car and Mundsson's truck are in front of the house—
they'd easily cut us off before we could open a door." Pitt
swung a hand toward a window. "Iceland is open country. There aren't ten trees within fifty miles. You said it
yourself, a fugitive could not run very far nor hide very
long."

Jonsson bowed his head in silent acceptance, then
he grinned faintly. "Then our only alternative is to
fight. It is going to be difficult taking a life after spend-
ing thirty years trying to save them."

"Do you have any firearms?"

Jonsson sighed heavily. "No, my hobby is fishing,
not hunting. The only equipment I possess that might
be classed as weapons are my surgical instruments."

Pitt walked over to a white steel-framed, glass-
paneled cabinet that held an assortment of neatly arranged medical instruments and drugs, and opened the
door. "We have one convenient advantage," he said
thoughtfully. "They don't know we're wise to their
nasty little plot. Therefore, we shall introduce them to a
good old American game known as Pin the Tail on the
Donkey."

Only two more minutes had elapsed when Jonsson
opened the door to the examining room, revealing Pitt
parked on a stool holding a bandage to his bleeding
head. Jonsson motioned to the blond man who spoke
English.

"Could you please assist me for a moment? I am
afraid that I need a third hand."

The man raised his eyebrow questioningly, then
shrugged to his partner, who sat with his eyes half
closed, his over-confidence giving birth to thoughts a
thousand miles away.

Jonsson, keeping any suspicion at a low level, purposely left the door slightly ajar, but not enough to allow vision of more than a fraction of the examining
room. "If you could hold the major's head on a slight
angle with both hands, then I can finish without inter-
ruption. He keeps twitching and ruining any chance for
a neat stitch job." Jonsson winked and then spoke in

Icelandic. "These Americans are like children when it comes to pain."

The fraudulent policeman laughed and nudged the doctor with his elbow. Then he walked around in front of Pitt, bent down and gripped Pitt's head with both hands on the temples. "Come, come, Major Pitt, a few stitches are nothing. What if the good doctor had to amputate your—"

It was all over in less than four seconds—silently. With seeming indifference and nonchalance, Pitt reached up his hands and grabbed the blond man around the wrists. Surprise showed for a brief instant in the stranger's face, then true shock as Jonsson clamped a heavy gauze pad over his mouth and jammed a syringe against his neck in the same movement. The shock gave way to terror, and he moaned in his throat, a moan that could not be heard because Pitt was loudly cursing Jonsson for a nonexistent sewing operation. The eyes above the white gauze began to lose focus, and the man made a desperate effort to hurl himself backward, but his wrists were held solidly in the vise of Pitt's grip. Then the eyes turned upward and he quietly collapsed into Jonsson's arms.

Pitt quickly knelt down and pulled a service revolver from the unconscious man's belt holster and stepped softly to the door. As soundless as he was swift, he lined up the gun and jerked open the door, swinging it all the way to its stop. For a second the tough-looking brute with the spectacles sat there in stunned immobility, staring at Pitt in the doorway. Then his hand shot to his holster.

"Freeze!" Pitt ordered.

The command was ignored, and a shot blasted through the small waiting room. There are many who claim the hand is quicker than the eye, but there are few who will take the stand that the hand is quicker than a speeding bullet. The gun flew from the bogus policeman's hand as Pitt's shell tore into the wooden grip, taking a thumb along with it. Never before had Pitt seen such dazed uncomprehension and shocked pain as the paid killer stared at the bloody half-inch stump where his thumb had been. Pitt made to lower his gun, but raised and aimed it again as he caught the look on his opponent's face—mouth tightened to a thin white line, black hatred glaring out from the squinting eyes behind the glasses.

"Shoot me, Major, quickly, cleanly here!" He tapped his chest with his uninjured hand.

"Well, well, so you speak English. My compliments, you never gave me the slightest hint that you understood any of the conversation."

"Shoot me!" The words seemed to echo in the little room and in Pitt's ears for an interminable time.

"Why rush things? There's every possibility you'll hang for murdering Sergeant Arnarson anyway." Pitt pulled the hammer of the revolver back for single-action firing. "I take it I'm safe in assuming you did kill him?"

"Yes, the sergeant is dead. Now please do the same for me." The eyes were cold, yet pleading.

"You're pretty anxious to get yourself planted."

Jonsson looked but said nothing. Totally off balance, he struggled to grasp a new set of circumstances, a complete reversal of all his previous values. As a doctor, he couldn't just stand there and watch an injured man bleed profusely without aid.

"Let me take care of the hand," Jonsson volunteered.

"Stay behind me and don't move," Pitt said. "Any man who wants to die is more dangerous than a cornered rat."

"But good Lord, man, you cannot stand there and gloat over his pain," Jonsson protested.

Pitt ignored Jonsson. "Okay, four eyes, I'll make a deal with you. The next bullet goes through your heart if you tell me the name of the man who pays your salary."

The animal-like eyes behind the glasses never left Pitt's face. He shook his head silently and said nothing.

"This isn't wartime, friend. You're not betraying your god or country. Loyalty to an employer is hardly worth your life."

"You will kill me, Major. I shall make you kill me." He advanced toward Pitt.

"I'll give you credit," Pitt said. "You're a persistent bastard." He pulled the trigger and the revolver roared again, the .38 bullet smashing into the burly character's left leg just above the knee.

Rarely had Pitt seen such disbelief in a human face. The paid killer slowly sank to the floor, his left hand clutching his torn left leg, trying to stem the blood flow, his right hand lying motionless on the tile, surrounded by a growing pool of red.

"It seems our friend has nothing to say," Pitt said. He pulled back the hammer to fire again.

"Please do not kill him," Jonsson pleaded. "His life is not worth the burden on your soul. I beg you, Major, let me have the gun. He can cause no further harm."

Pitt hesitated several moments, torn between compassion and revenge. Then, slowly, he handed the revolver to Jonsson and nodded. Jonsson took it and put his hand on Pitt's shoulder as if in secret understanding.

"I am heartbroken that countrymen of mine should cause so much grief and pain to so many," the doctor said with weariness in his voice. "I will take care of these two and contact the authorities immediately. You go with Mundsson to Reykjavik and rest. You have a nasty-looking head wound, but it won't prove serious unless you aggravate it. Stay in bed for at least two days. That is a direct order from your doctor."

"There appears to be a slight obstacle to your prescription." Pitt smiled crookedly and pointed through the front doorway. "You were one hundred percent correct about creating excitement in the village." He nodded in the direction of the road where at least twenty villagers stood silently holding every type of weapon from telescopic rifles to small-bore shotguns, all aimed steadily at the door of Jonsson's cottage. Mundsson was resting his gun easily in the crook of one arm, one foot solidly on the second doorstep, his son Bjarni slightly off to one side with an old Mauser bolt-action rifle.

Pitt held both hands out where they could easily be seen. "I think now is an appropriate time, Doctor, to give me a recommendation. These good townspeople aren't sure who plays the good guys or the bad guys."

Jonsson stepped past Pitt and spoke for several minutes in Icelandic. When he finished, the guns began to lower one by one and several of the villagers drifted toward their homes while a few lingered on the road to await further developments. Jonsson extended his hand, and Pitt gripped it.

"I fervently hope you meet with success in finding the man responsible for the terrible number of senseless murders," Jonsson said. "If you should meet him, I fear for your life. You are not a killer. If you were, two men would lie dead in my home. Your concern for life, I fear, will be your defeat. I beg you, my friend, do not hesitate when the moment arrives. God and luck go with you."

Pitt threw a last salute at Dr. Jonsson and turned and stepped down the front steps to the road. Bjarni held the passenger door of the Land Rover open for him. The seat was firm and the backrest stiff, but Pitt could not have cared less; his entire body was numb. He sat there as Mundsson started the engine and shifted through the gears, steering the truck over a stretch of smooth, narrow pavement toward Reykjavik. Pitt could have easily drifted off into a dead sleep, but somewhere in the deep recesses of his mind a spark refused to go out. Something that he saw, something that was said, an undistinguishable something refused to let his mind slow down and rest. It was like a song he couldn't quite recall whose title was on the tip of his tongue. Finally, he gave it up and dozed off.

Chapter
7

Time after time, the exact number became lost, Pitt struggled up from the bottom of the rolling surf and staggered onto the beach dragging Hunnewell. Time after time, he bandaged the oceanographer's arm only to slide into darkness again. Desperately, every time the event ran through his brain like an image from a film projector, he tried to hang onto those fleeting moments of consciousness, only to lose out to the inevitable fact that nothing can change the past. It was a nightmare, he thought vaguely as he tried to tear himself away from the bloodstained beach. He gathered his strength and with a mighty effort forced his eyes open, expecting to see an empty bedroom. The bedroom was there all right, but it wasn't empty.

"Good morning, Dirk," said a soft voice. "I'd almost lost hope that you would ever wake up."

Pitt looked up into the smiling brown eyes of a long-bodied girl who sat on a chair at the foot of his bed. "The last birdie with a yellow bill who hopped upon my windowsill didn't resemble you in the slightest," he said.

She laughed, so did the brown eyes. She pushed the long strands of shining fawn-colored hair behind her ears. Then she stood up and walked around to the head of the bed with a movement that could best be described as mercury flowing down a meandering glass tube. She wore a red wool dress that clung to her precision-shaped hour-glass figure, the hem topping a pair of neatly sculptured knees. She wasn't exactly beautiful in the exotic sense nor was she overly sexy, but she was cute—damned cute—with a pert attractiveness that melted every man she met.

She touched the bandage on the side of his head, and the smile gave way to a feminine look of Florence Nightingale concern. "You've had a nasty time, hurt much?"

"Only when I stand on my head."

Pitt knew the reason for genuine anxiety; he knew who she was. Her name was Tidi Royal and her fun-and-games personality was misleading. She could pound out one hundred and twenty words a minute on a typewriter for eight hours without a yawn, and take shorthand a shade faster. The primary reasons why Admiral James Sandecker hired her as his private secretary—or so he steadfastly claimed.

Pitt pulled himself to a sitting position and peeked under the covers to see if he was wearing anything. He was, just barely—a pair of boxer shorts. "If you're here, it could only mean the admiral is close by."

"Fifteen minutes after he got your message over the consulate's radio, we were on a jet to Iceland. He's pretty shaken about Dr. Hunnewell's death. Admiral Sandecker blames himself."

"He's going to have to stand in line," Pitt said. "I got there first."

"He said you'd feel that way." Tidi tried to speak lightly but it didn't quite come off. "Guilt-ridden conscience, probably trying to redo the event in your mind."

"The admiral's extrasensory perception must be working overtime."

"Oh, no," she said. "I don't mean the admiral."

Pitt frowned quizzically.

"A Dr. Jonsson from a little village to the north called and gave the consulate very explicit instructions regarding your convalescence."

"Convalescence, crap!" Pitt snapped. "Which re-minds me. What in hell are you doing in my bedroom?"

She looked hurt. "I volunteered."

"Volunteered?"

"To sit with you while you slept," she said. "Dr. Jonsson insisted. There's been a consulate staff member sitting in this room every minute since you closed your eyes last evening."

"What time is it?"

"A few minutes past ten—A.M. I might add."

"God, I've wasted nearly fourteen hours. What happened to my clothes?"

"Thrown out in the trash, I should imagine. They weren't fit for rags. You'll have to borrow some from a staff member."

"In that case, how about rounding up something casual while I take a quick shower and shave." He tossed her his bite-is-worse-than-bark look and said, "OK, dearheart, face the wall."

She remained facing the bed. "I've always won-dered what it would be like to see you wake up in the morning."

He shrugged and threw back the covers. He was halfway through the motion of pushing himself to his feet when three things happened: his eyes suddenly saw three Tidis, the room swayed as though it was made of rubber, and his head began to ache with the mother of all aches.

Tidi stepped forward abruptly and clutched his right arm, her face reflecting the Florence Nightingale concern again. "Please, Dirk, your head isn't ready for your feet yet."

"Nothing, it's nothing. I stood up too fast." He made it to his feet and lurched into her arms. "You'd make a lousy nurse, Tidi. You get too involved with your patients."

He held onto her for several moments until the tri-plets became one and the bedroom stood at rigid atten-tion; only the ache in his head refused to diminish.

"You're the one patient I'd love to get involved with, Dirk." She held onto him tightly and made no attempt to remove her arms. "But you never seem to notice me. You'd stand next to me in an empty elevator and never recognize me at all. There are times when I doubt whether you know I exist."

"Oh, I know you exist all right." He pushed himself away and started slowly for the bathroom, refraining from facing her as he talked. "Your vital statistics are five foot seven, one hundred thirty-five pounds, thirty-six inches around the hips, an astonishing twenty-three inches at the waist, and the bust, a probable thirty-six, C-cup. All in all, a figure that belongs on the centerspread of *Playboy*. There is also the light-brown hair framing an eager, bright face enhanced by sparkling brown eyes, a pert little nose, a perfectly formed mouth flanked by two dimples that only show when you smile. Oh, yes, I almost forgot. Two moles behind the left ear and, at this moment, your heart is beating at approximately one hundred and five thumps per minute."

She stood there like a stunned winner on a TV quiz show momentarily at a loss for words. She reached up and touched the two moles. "Like wow! I can't believe I heard you. It's unreal. You like me—you really care for me."

"Don't get carried away." Pitt hesitated in the bathroom doorway and faced her. "I'm very attracted to you, as any man would be to a pretty girl, but I'm not in love with you."

"You . . . you never gave me any indication. You've never even asked me for a date."

"Sorry, Tidi. You're the admiral's personal secretary. I make it a rule never to play games that close to him." Pitt leaned against the doorframe for support. "I respect that old guy; he's much more than just a friend or boss. I won't cause complications behind his back."

"I understand," she said humbly. "But I certainly didn't figure you for the modest hero who sacrifices the heroine to a typewriter."

"The rejected virgin who throws herself into a convent isn't exactly your bag either."

"Must we get nasty?"

"No," Pitt said approvingly. "Why don't you be a good girl and scrounge me up a change of clothes. Let's see if you're as observant of my dimensions as I am of yours."

Tidi said nothing in reply, just stood there looking forlorn and curious. Finally she shook her head in a feminine display of irritation and left.

Exactly two hours later, clad in surprisingly well-fitting slacks and sport shirt, Pitt sat across a desk from Admiral James Sandecker. The admiral looked tired and old, far beyond his years. His red hair was tousled in a shaggy unkempt mane, and it was obvious from the stubble on his chin and cheeks that he hadn't shaved for at least two days. He held one of his massive cigars casually in the fingers of his right hand, stared at the long cylindrical shape for a moment, and then set it in an ashtray without lighting the end. He grunted something about being glad to see Pitt alive and still connected in all the right places. Then the weary, bloodshot eyes studied Pitt intently.

"So much for preliminaries. Your story, Dirk. Let's have it."

Pitt didn't give it to him. Instead, he said: "I just spent an hour writing a detailed report of what occurred from the time Hunnewell and I lifted off from the NUMA pad at Dulles International until the farmer and his boy brought us to the consulate. I also included my personal opinions and observations. Knowing you, Admiral, I venture to guess you've read it at least twice. I have nothing to add. All I can do now is answer your questions."

What little of Sandecker's face was open for expression seemed to indicate a certain interest, if not downright curiosity at Pitt's flagrant, insubordinate behavior. He stood up, all five foot six inches of him, revealing a blue suit that cried out for a pressing, and peered down at Pitt, a favorite tactic when he was ready to orate.

"Once was all I needed, Major." No "Dirk" this time. "When I want sarcastic remarks, I'll book Don

Rickles or Mort Sahl and be assured of a professional job. I appreciate the fact that you've been harassed by the Coast Guard and the Russians, had your butt frozen off on an iceberg looking at incinerated cadavers, not to mention getting shot at, crashing in the Atlantic Ocean, and having a man die in your arms since I pulled you off that nice warm beach in California just seventy-two hours ago. But that does not give you the unmitigated right to hard-ass your superior."

"I apologize for the disrespect, sir." The words were there, but the tone was sadly lacking. "If I seem a bit testy, it's simply because I smell a put-on. I have the distinct impression that you dropped me into an intricate maze without benefit of a road map."

"So?" An eighth of an inch lift of the heavy red eyebrows.

"To begin with, Hunnewell and I were on damn thin ice when we swindled the Coast Guard into using its finest cutter for a refueling base, or at least *I* thought we were. Not Hunnewell. He knew the whole setup was fixed from beginning to end. I thought we'd bought a jail cell when Commander Koski signaled Coast Guard Command in Washington for confirmation of our presence. I studied Hunnewell; he pored over his charts as if nothing was happening. No quiver of the hand, no indication of sweat on the brow. He was completely at ease with the situation, knowing that you had taken care of everything before we left Dulles."

"Not quite." Sandecker picked up the cigar and lit it and gave Pitt a shrewd look. "The commandant was inspecting a damn hurricane warning facility in Florida. You were already crossing Nova Scotia before I could get to him." He blew a huge cloud of smoke toward the ceiling. "Please continue."

Pitt slouched back in his chair. "A dim, nearly undistinguishable outline of a ship turns up in an iceberg. The Coast Guard doesn't have the slightest idea what registry it is. Yet four days go by and there is no investigation. The *Catawaba* is only hours away but is never notified of the sighting. Why? Somebody in the capitol with the authority, high authority, ordered hands off, that's why."

Sandecker toyed with the cigar. "I suppose you know what you're talking about, Major?"

"Hell, no . . . sir," Pitt answered. "Without the facts, I'm guessing. But you and Hunnewell didn't guess. There wasn't the slightest doubt in your minds that the derelict was the *Lax*, a ship that had been listed as missing for over a year. You had absolute proof. How or where it came from I can't say, but you had it." Pitt's green eyes blazed into Sandecker's. "At this point my crystal ball gets foggy. I was surprised, but Hunnewell was genuinely stunned when we found that the *Lax* was burned to junk. This factor wasn't in the script, was it, Admiral? In fact, everything, including your well-planned scheme, began to go down the drain. Someone you didn't count on was working against you. Someone with resources you or whatever agency in our government that is cooperating with you never considered.

"You lost control. Even the Russians were thrown off the track. You're up against a shrewd mind, Admiral. And the message is written in neon lights, this guy doesn't play for ice cream and cake at birthday parties. He kills people like an exterminator kills termites. The name of the game as advertised is zirconium. I don't buy it. People might kill one or two persons for a fortune, but not in wholesale lots. Hunnewell was your friend for many years, Admiral, mine for only a few days, and I lost him. He was my responsibility and I failed. His contributions to society outstrip anything I'm capable of. Better I'd have died on that beach instead of him."

Sandecker showed no reaction to any of this. His unblinking eyes never left Pitt's face as he sat behind the desk thoughtfully tapping the fingers of his right hand on the glass top. Then he stood up, came around the desk and put his hands on Pitt's shoulders.

"Bullshit!" he said quietly but firmly. "It was a miracle you both made it to shore. There isn't a book-maker in the world who would give odds on an un-armed helicopter knocking a machine-gun-toting jet out of the sky. I'm the one to blame. I had a hint of what was going to happen and I wasn't smart enough to read the cards. I didn't deal you in on the action because it wasn't necessary. You were the best man I could lay my hands on for a tricky chauffeur job. As soon as you got Hunnewell here to Reykjavik, I was going to put you on the next flight back to California." He paused to check his watch. "There's an Air Force reconnaissance jet leaving for Tyler Field, New Jersey, in one hour and six minutes. You can make connections for the West Coast when you get there."

"No, thanks, Admiral." Pitt rose from the chair and walked to the window, staring over the city's peaked and sun-splashed roofs. "I've heard that Icelandic women are coolly beautiful. I'd like to see for myself."

"I can make that an order."

"No good, sir. I understand what you're trying to do, and I'm grateful. The first attempt on my life and Hunnewell's was only half successful. The second was much more elaborate and cunning and was reserved for me alone. The third should be a masterpiece. I'd like to stick around and see how it's going to be staged."

"Sorry, Dirk." Sandecker was back on friendly terms again. "I'm not going to throw your life away with the wave of a hand. Before I stand at your graveside, I'll have you locked up and standing in front of a court-martial for willful destruction of government property."

Pitt smiled. "I've been meaning to talk to you about service regulations, Admiral." He came across the room and casually sat on the edge of the desk. "For the past year and a half, I have faithfully carried out all directives issued from your office. I've questioned none of them. However, the time has come, the walrus said, to get a few facts straight. Number one: if it was possible—and it isn't—for you to court-martial me, I doubt if the Air Force would take it lightly if one of their officers was tried by a naval court. Second, and most important: NUMA is not the bridge of the flagship of the fleet. Therefore, you are not my commanding office.

You are simply my boss—no more, no less. If my insubordination infuriates your senses and naval traditions, then you have no other choice but to fire me. That's the way it is, Admiral, and we both know it."

For several seconds Sandecker made no comment, but his eyes glinted with a strange sort of amusement. Then he threw back his head and began to laugh, a rolling, deep laugh that filled the room from carpet to ceiling. "God! If there is anything worse than a cocky Dirk Pitt, I hope it becomes infected with syphilis and rots in hell." He returned to the chair behind the desk and sat down, hands clasped behind his head. "OK, Dirk, I'll put you in at first string, but you'll be required to play straight ball, no fancy independent plays. Agreed?"

"You're the boss."

Sandecker winced noticeably. "Okay, out of respect for your ah . . . superior, suppose you give me the whole story from the beginning. I've read the written words, now I want to hear it orally, direct from the horse's mouth." He peered at Pitt with an expression that dared argument. "Shall we commence?"

Sandecker heard Pitt out, then said: " 'God save thee,' that's what he said?"

"That's all he said. Then he was gone. I'd hoped Dr. Hunnewell might have offered me a clue to the whereabouts of the *Lax* between the time it vanished and the time it became inbedded in the iceberg, but he volunteered nothing except a historical sketch of Kristjan Fyrie and a lecture on zirconium."

"He did as he was told. I didn't want you involved."

"That was two days ago. Now I'm involved up to my neck." Pitt leaned over the desk toward the older man. "Let's have it, you sly old fox. What in hell is going on?"

Sandecker grinned. "For your sake, I'm going to take that as a compliment." He pulled out a bottom drawer and propped his feet on it. "I hope you know what you're letting yourself in for."

"I don't have the vaguest idea, but tell me anyway."

"All right then." Sandecker leaned back in his swivel chair and puffed several times on his cigar. "This is what took place as far as it goes—too many pieces are missing for even a fifty percent glimpse at the overall picture. About a year and a half ago, Fyrie's scientists successfully designed and constructed a nuclear undersea probe that could identify fifteen to twenty different mineral elements on the ocean floor. The probe operated by briefly exposing the metallic elements to neutrons given off by a laboratory-produced element called celtinium-279. When activated by the neutrons, the elements on the ocean's bottom gave off gamma rays, which were then analyzed and counted by a tiny detector on the probe. During tests off Iceland, the probe detected and measured mineral samples of manganese, gold, nickel, titanium, and zirconium— the zirconium in huge and unheard-of amounts."

"I think I see. Without the probe, the zirconium could never be found again," Pitt said thoughtfully. "The prize then is not the rare elements, but rather the probe itself."

"Yes, the probe opens a vast and untapped frontier for undersea mining. Whoever owns it won't control the world, of course, but possession could lead to a direct reshuffling of private financial empires and a healthy shot in the arm for the treasury of any country with a continental shelf containing a rich storehouse of minerals."

Pitt was silent for a few moments. "God, is it worth all the killing?"

Sandecker hesitated. "It depends upon how bad somebody wants it. There are men who wouldn't kill for every cent in the world, and there are others who wouldn't hesitate to slit a throat for the price of a meal."

"In Washington, you informed me that Fyrie and his scientific team were on their way to the U.S. to open negotiations with our defense contractors. I take it that was a little white lie?"

Sandecker smiled. "Yes, that was actually an understatement. Fyrie was scheduled to meet with the

President and present him with the probe." He looked at Pitt, and then said more positively: "I was the first one Fyrie notified when the tests on the probe proved successful. I don't know what Hunnewell told you about Fyrie, but he was a visionary, a gentle man who wouldn't step on an ant or a flower. He knew the far-reaching good the probe would bring to mankind; he also knew what unscrupulous interests would do to exploit it once the probe fell into their hands, so he decided to turn it over to the nation that he was certain would make beneficial and charitable use of its potential—so much noble crap in my book. But you have to give the do-gooders of the earth credit; they make an honest stab at helping the rest of us ungrateful rabble." His face looked pained. "A goddamned shame. Kristjan Fyrie would be alive this minute if he'd been rotten and selfish."

Pitt grinned knowingly. It was a well-advertised fact that Admiral Sandecker, in spite of his boiler-plate exterior, was at heart a humanitarian, and he rarely disguised his disgust and hatred for greed-driven industrialists—an outspoken trait that didn't exactly make him in great demand as a guest at society dinner parties.

"Isn't it possible," Pitt asked, "for American engineers to develop our own probe?"

"Yes, in fact we already have one, but compared with Fyrie's probe, it operates with all the efficiency of a bicycle next to a sportscar. His people made a breakthrough that is ten years ahead of anything we or the Russians are currently developing."

"Any ideas on who stole the probe?"

Sandecker shook his head. "None. It's obviously a well-financed organization. Beyond that we're playing blindman's buff in a swamp."

"A foreign country would have the necessary resources to——"

"You can forget that divination," Sandecker interrupted. "The National Intelligence Agency is positive no foreign government is in the act. Even the Chinese would think twice before killing two dozen people over an innocent, nondestructive scientific instrument. No, it's got to be a private motive. For what purpose besides financial gain," he shrugged helplessly, "we can't even guess."

"All right, so the mysterious organization has the probe, so they strike a bonanza on the sea floor. How do they raise it?"

"They can't," Sandecker replied. "Not without highly technical equipment."

"It doesn't make sense. If they've had the probe over a year, what good has it done them?"

"They've put the probe to good use all right," Sandecker said seriously, "testing every square foot of the continental shelf on the Atlantic shore of North and South America. And they used the *Lax* to do it."

Pitt stared at him curiously. "The *Lax?* I don't follow."

Sandecker flicked an ash into the wastebasket. "Do you remember Dr. Len Matajic and his assistant, Jack O'Riley?"

Pitt frowned, recalling. "I air-dropped supplies to them three months ago when they set up camp on an ice floe in Baffin Bay. Dr. Matajic was studying currents below a depth of ten thousand feet, trying to prove a pet theory of his that a deep layer of warm water had the capacity to melt the Pole if only one percent of it could be diverted upward."

"What was the last you heard of them?"

Pitt shrugged. "I left for the Oceanlab Project in California as soon as they began routine housekeeping. Why ask me? You planned and coordinated their expedition."

"Yes, I planned the expedition," Sandecker repeated slowly. He screwed the knuckles of his index fingers into his eyes, then pushed the hands together and folded them. "Matajic and O'Riley are dead. The plane bringing them back from the ice floe crashed in the sea. No trace was found."

"Strange, I hadn't heard. It must have just happened."

Sandecker put another match to his cigar. "A month ago yesterday, to be exact."

Pitt stared at him. "Why the secrecy? Nothing was in print or in broadcast about their accident. As your special projects director, I should have been one of the first to be informed."

"Only one other man besides myself was aware of their deaths—the radio operator who took their last message. I've made no announcement because I intend to bring them back from their watery grave."

"Sorry, Admiral," Pitt said. "You've lost me completely."

"All right then," Sandecker said heavily. "Five weeks ago I received a signal from Matajic. Seems O'Riley, while on a scouting trek, spotted a fishing trawler that had moored to the north end of their ice floe. Not being socially aggressive, he returned to base and informed Matajic. Then together, they trudged back and paid a friendly call on the fishermen to determine if they needed assistance. An odd bunch, Matajic said. The ship flew the flag of Iceland, yet most of the crew were Arabs, while the rest represented at least six different countries including the United States. It seems a bearing had burned out in their diesel engine. Rather than drift around while repairs were made, they decided to tie up on the ice floe to let the crew stretch their legs."

"Nothing suspicious in that," Pitt commented.

"The captain and crew invited Matajic and O'Riley on board for dinner," Sandecker continued. "This courteous act seemed harmless enough at the time. Later, it was seen as an obvious attempt to avoid suspicion. By sheer coincidence, it backfired."

"So our two scientists were also on the list to see something they shouldn't have."

"You guessed it. Some years previously, Kristjan Fyrie had entertained Dr. Hunnewell and Dr. Matajic aboard his yacht. The exterior of the trawler had been altered, of course, but the instant Matajic stepped into the main salon, he recognized the ship as the *Lax*. If he had said nothing, he and O'Riley might have been alive today. Unfortunately, he innocently asked why the proud and plush *Lax* that he remembered had been converted into a common fishing trawler. It was an honest question, but one that had cruel consequences."

"They could have been murdered then and there and their bodies weighted and dropped into the sea—no one would have ever known."

"It's one thing for a ship to go down at sea with all hands. The newspapers forgot the *Lax* one week after it disappeared. But two men and a government research station, not likely. The press would have exaggerated and harped on the enigma of the abandoned ice station for years. No, if Matajic and O'Riley had to be eliminated, there were less conspicuous methods."

"Shooting an unarmed plane out of the air without telltale witnesses, for example?"

"That appears to be the pattern," Sandecker said softly. "It wasn't until our two scientists had returned to their base camp that Matajic began to have doubts. The captain of the trawler had simply passed his command off as a sister ship to Fyrie's *Lax*. It was a possibility, Matajic told himself. But if the ship earned its keep as a fishing trawler, where were the fish? Even the distinct aroma had been missing. He got on the radio and contacted me at NUMA headquarters, told me the story along with his suspicions, and suggested that the Coast Guard make a routine investigation of the trawler. I ordered them to stand by while I sent a supply plane north to return them to Washington as quickly as possible to make a detailed report." Sandecker tapped the cigar ashes into the wastebasket again, a grim expression on his face. "I was too late. The captain of the trawler must have monitored Matajic's message. The pilot made it to the ice floe and picked them up. After that, the three of them vanished."

Sandecker reached inside his breast pocket and pulled out a worn and folded piece of paper. "This is Matajic's last message."

Pitt took the paper from the admiral's hand and unfolded it across the desk. It read: MAYDAY! MAYDAY! THE BASTARD'S ATTACKING. BLACK. NUMBER ONE ENGINE IS . . . The words abruptly ended.

"Enter the black jet."

"Exactly. With his only witnesses out of the way, the captain's problem was now the Coast Guard, whom he was sure would show up at any moment."

Pitt looked at Sandecker speculatively. "But the Coast Guard didn't come. They were never invited. You've yet to fully explain why you maintained silence even after you were certain three of NUMA's men were killed, murdered like cattle by a group of traveling butchers."

"At the time I didn't really know." The vagueness wasn't like Sandecker. Normally he was as decisive and direct as a bolt of lightning. "I suppose I didn't want the sons-of-bitches responsible to have the satisfaction of knowing how successful they were—I thought it best to let them wonder. It's snatching at leaves in a hurricane, I admit, but it's just barely possible they might make an unplanned move, a mistake that will give us a slim lead to their identity when and if I resurrect the ghosts of Matajic and O'Riley."

"How did you handle the search party?"

"I notified all search and rescue units in the Northern Command that a valuable piece of equipment had fallen off of a NUMA research ship and was floating around lost. I gave out the course the plane would have taken and waited for a sighting report. There was none." Sandecker waved his cigar to indicate helplessness. "I also waited in vain for the sighting of a trawler matching the hull design of the *Lax*. It too had evaporated."

"That's why you were dead sure it was the *Lax* under the iceberg."

"Let's just say I was eighty percent certain," Sandecker said. "I also did a bit of checking with every port authority between Buenos Aires and Goose Bay, Labrador. Twelve ports recorded the entry and departure of an Icelandic fishing trawler matching the *Lax*'s altered superstructure. For what it's worth, it went under the name of *Surtsey*. *Surtsey*, by the way, is Icelandic for 'submarine.' "

"I see." Pitt groped for a cigarette and then remembered that he was wearing a stranger's clothes. "A northern fisherman would hardly troll southern waters. Working the undersea probe is the only credible explanation."

"It's as if we were presented with a pregnant rabbit," Sandecker grunted. "One solution leaves us with a new brood of unfathomable puzzles."

"Are you in contact with Commander Koski?"

"Yes. The *Catawaba* is standing by the derelict while a team of investigators combs it thoroughly. In fact, I received a signal from them just before you struggled from bed. Three of the bodies were positively established as Fyrie's crew. The rest were too badly burned to identify."

"Like an Edgar Allan Poe ghost story. Fyrie and his people and the *Lax* disappear into the sea. Nearly a year later the *Lax* turns up at one of our research stations with a different crew. Then soon after that, the same ship becomes a burned-out derelict in an iceberg with the remains of Fyrie and the original crew on board. The more I dwell on it, the more I kick myself for not catching that Air Force jet to Tyler Field."

"You were warned."

Pitt managed a sour grin as he lightly touched the bandage on his head. "One of these times I'm going to volunteer once too often."

"You're probably the world's luckiest bastard," Sandecker said. "Living through two attempts on your life in the same morning."

"Which reminds me, how are my two friendly policemen?"

"Under interrogation. But short of Gestapo torture methods, I seriously doubt if we even get so much as a name, rank and serial number out of them. They keep insisting that they're going to be killed anyway, so why should they offer us information."

"Who is doing the interrogating?"

"National Intelligence agents on our airbase at Keflavik. The Iceland government is cooperating with us every step of the way—after all, Fyrie was practically their national hero. They're just as interested in finding out what happened to the probe and the *Lax* as we are."

Sandecker paused to remove a small bit of tobacco from his tongue. "If you're wondering why NUMA is mixed up in this instead of sitting on the sidelines and cheering on the National Intelligence Agency and their army of super spies, the answer is, or I should say was, Hunnewell. He corresponded with Fyrie's scientists for months, offering his knowledge toward the ultimate success of the probe. It was Hunnewell who was instrumental in the development of celtinium-279. Only he had a rough idea of what the probe looked like, and only he could have safely disassembled it."

"That, of course, explains why Hunnewell had to be the first aboard the derelict."

"Yes, celtinium in its refined state is very unstable. Under the right conditions, it can explode with a force equal to a fifty-ton phosphate bomb, but with a pronounced characteristic difference. Celtinium fulminates at a very slow rate, burning everything in its path to ashes. Yet, unlike more common explosives, its expansion pressure is quite low, about the same as a sixty-mile-an-hour wind. It could go off and melt but not shatter a pane of glass."

"Then my flamethrower theory was a bust. It was the probe that went off and turned the *Lax* into an instant pyre."

Sandecker smiled. "You came close."

But that means the probe is destroyed."

Sandecker nodded, his smile rapidly fading. "All of it, the murders, the probe, the killers' search for undersea treasure, it went all for nothing—a terrible, terrible waste."

"It's possible that the organization behind this affair has the design and plans for the probe in its possession."

"It's more than possible." He paused, then went on almost absently. "A lot of good it will do them. Hunnewell was the only person on earth with the process for celtinium-279. As he often said, it was basically so simple that he kept it in his head."

"The fools," Pitt murmured. "They murdered their only key to constructing a new probe. But why? Hunnewell couldn't have been a serious threat unless he found something on the derelict that led to the organization and its mastermind."

"I haven't the vaguest idea." Sandecker shrugged helplessly. "Anymore than I can guess who the unseen men were who chipped the red dye marker off the iceberg."

"I wish I knew where in the hell to take the next step," Pitt said.

"I've taken care of that little matter for you."

Pitt looked up skeptically. "I hope this isn't another one of your famous favors."

"You said it yourself, you wanted to see if Iceland's women were coolly beautiful."

"You're changing the subject." Pitt looked steadily at the admiral. "Here it comes, let me guess. You're going to introduce me to a burly, steely-eyed Icelandic female government official who is going to make me sit up half the night going over the same old tired questions and answers that I've already covered. Sorry, Admiral, I'm not up to it."

Sandecker's eyes narrowed as he sighed. "Suit yourself. The girl I have in mind isn't burly or steely-eyed or a government official, for that matter. She happens to be the loveliest woman north of the sixty-fourth parallel and, I might add, the wealthiest."

"Oh, really?" Pitt suddenly came alive. "What's her name?"

"Kirsti," Sandecker said with a sly smile. "Kirsti Fyrie, Kristjan Fyrie's twin sister."

Chapter
8

If Snorri's Restaurant in Reykjavik could be picked up and placed down in any of the epicurean distinguished cities of the world, it would be instantly greeted with respectful acclaim. Its one great hall, with open kitchen and earthen ovens only a few feet from the dining area, was designed in the Viking tradition. Richly paneled walls and intricately carved doors and beams provided the perfect atmosphere for a leisurely yet elegant dinner. The menu selection was created to reward even the most finicky gourmet, and along one entire wall stood a buffet table with over two hundred different native dishes.

Pitt surveyed the crowded dining hall. The tables were filled with laughing, talkative Icelanders and their svelt, lovely women. He was standing there, his eyes taking in the scene, his nostrils basking in the rich food smells when the maitre d' came up and spoke in Icelandic. Pitt shook his head and pointed at Admiral Sandecker and Tidi Royal comfortably ensconced at a table near the bar. He made his way over to them.

Sandecker waved Pitt to a chair opposite Tidi and hailed a passing waiter in the same motion. "You're ten minutes late."

"Sorry," Pitt said. "I took a walk in the Tjarnargardar gardens and did a little sightseeing."

"Looks like you found yourself a swinging men's shop," Tidi remarked admiringly. Her wise brown eyes roved over his wool turtleneck sweater, belted corduroy jacket and plaid slacks.

"I grew tired of wearing hand-me-downs," he said, smiling.

Sandecker looked up at the waiter. "Two more of the same," he said. "What will you have, Dirk?"

"What are you and Tidi drinking?"

"Holland gin—schnapps if you prefer. It seems to be big with the natives."

Pitt twisted his mouth. "No, thanks. I'll stick with my old standby, Cutty rocks."

The waiter nodded and left.

"Where is this exciting creature I've heard so much about?" Pitt asked.

"Miss Fyrie should be along any minute," Sandecker replied.

"Just before we were attacked, Hunnewell said that Fyrie's sister was a missionary in New Guinea."

"Yes, little else is known about her. In fact, few people knew she even existed until Fyrie's will named her sole beneficiary. Then she appeared at Fyrie Limited one day and took the reins as smoothly as if she had built the empire herself. Don't get any ideas in that bedroom mind of yours. She's shrewd—just as shrewd as her brother was."

"Then why bother with the introductions. You say hands off, yet I get the distinct impression that I'm supposed to play Prince Charming. Get cozy, but not too cozy. You've chosen the wrong man, Admiral. I'm the first to admit my looks hardly put me in the Rock Hudson—Paul Newman class, but I have a nasty habit when it comes to pursuing skirts—I'm picky. I'm not geared to assault every girl that comes into sight, especially one who is the spitting image of her brother, spent half her life as a missionary, and runs a giant corporation with a mace and chain. Sorry, Admiral, Miss Fyrie hardly sounds like my type."

"I think it's disgusting," Tidi said disapprovingly, the eyebrows arched above the huge brown eyes. "NUMA is supposed to be dedicated to scientific research of the oceans. None of this talk sounds very scientific to me."

Sandecker threw her an admonishing stare, a facial display that he was unquestionably a master at projecting. "Secretaries should be seen and not heard."

Tidi was saved from further reprimand by the timely arrival of the waiter with the drinks. He set them on the table with an accomplished motion and then left.

Sandecker watched until the waiter was several tables away before he turned back to Pitt. "Nearly forty percent of NUMA's projects are designed and planned around mining the sea floor. Russia leads us by a wide margin in surface programs, the science of her fishing fleet far surpasses anything we've got. But she lags badly in deep submersibles—a damned vital piece of equipment for undersea mining. This is our strong point. We want to maintain this advantage. Our country has the resources, but Fyrie Limited has the technical knowledge. With Kristjan Fyrie we had a good, close working association. Now that he's only a memory, I don't care to see the results of our efforts lost just when our programs are on the verge of hitting paydirt. I've talked to Miss Fyrie. All of a sudden she's very noncommittal—says she has decided to reevaluate her firm's programs with our country."

"You said she's shrewd," Pitt said. "Maybe she's holding out to the highest bidder. There's nothing in the book that says she has to be as magnanimous as her brother."

"Dammit," Sandecker said irritably. "Anything is possible. Maybe she hates Americans."

"She's not alone."

"If so, there must be a reason, and we've got to find it."

"Enter Dirk Pitt, stage left."

"Precisely, but no hanky-panky. I'm taking you off the Pacific Oceanlab project definitely and putting you on this one. Forget playing secret agent while you're at it. Leave the intrigue and the dead bodies to the National Intelligence Agency. You're to act in your official capacity as special projects director for NUMA. No more, no less. If you stumble onto any information that might lead to the people who killed Fyrie, Hunnewell and Matajic, you're to pass it on."

"Pass it on to whom?"

Sandecker shrugged. "I don't know. The NIA didn't see fit to tell me before I left Washington."

"Great, I'll take out a full-page ad in the local newspaper," Pitt said sourly.

"I don't recommend it," Sandecker said. He took a long swallow from his glass and made a wry face. "God, what do they see in this stuff?" He took another swallow from a glass of water. "I have to be in Washington the day after tomorrow. That gives me enough time to smooth the way for you."

"With—ah—Miss Fyrie?"

"With Fyrie Limited. I've arranged an exchange program. I'm taking one of their top engineers with me to the States to observe and study our techniques while you're to stay here and report on theirs. Your primary job will be to restore the close relationship we once enjoyed with the Fyrie's management."

"If this Fyrie broad has been so cool toward you and NUMA, why did she consent to meet us tonight?"

"Out of courtesy. Dr. Hunnewell and her brother were good friends. His death and the fact that you made a gallant but losing attempt to save his life played on her feminine emotions. In short, she insisted on meeting you."

"She's beginning to sound like a cross between Catherine the Great and Aimee Semple McPherson," Tidi said sarcastically.

"I can't wait to meet my new boss face to face," Pitt said. Sandecker nodded. "You can in precisely five seconds—she just walked in."

Pitt turned, and so did every other male head in the restaurant. She stood in the foyer very tall and very blond, like a fantasy of womanly perfection, incredibly beautiful, as if caught in the perfect pose by the lens of a fashion photographer's camera. Her statuesque figure was encased in a long violet-colored dress of velvet with peasant embroidery on the sleeves and hem. Now she caught Sandecker's wave, and she walked over to the table, moving with a graceful flowing motion that possessed all the suppleness of a ballerina and more than the suggestion of a natural athlete. By this time all the women in the restaurant were eyeing her with instinctive envy.

Pitt pushed back his chair and rose and studied her face as she approached. It was her tan that intrigued him. The delicately clear tanned complexion somehow seemed foreign to an Icelandic woman, even one who spent a good portion of her life in the back country of New Guinea. The total effect was striking. The blond hair, a carefree casual look with a controlled tousled effect, the deep violet eyes that matched the color of her dress, she was hardly what Pitt had imagined, to say the least.

"My dear Miss Fyrie, I'm honored that you could dine with us." Admiral Sandecker took her hand and kissed it. Then he turned to Tidi, who wore a mask of friendliness. "May I introduce my secretary, Miss Tidi Royal."

The two women exchanged polite but typically cool feminine greetings.

Then Sandecker turned to Pitt. "And this is Major Dirk Pitt, the real driving force behind my agency's projects."

"So this is the brave gentleman you've told me so much about, Admiral." Her voice came across husky and terribly sexy. "I am deeply sorry for the tragic loss of Dr. Hunnewell. My brother thought very highly of him."

"We're sorry too," Pitt said.

There was a pause while they looked at each other, Kirsti Fyrie with a touch of speculation in her eyes, and with what might have been more than friendly interest. Pitt with analytical male appraisal.

He was the first to break the silence. "If I sit here staring, Miss Fyrie, it's because Admiral Sandecker failed to warn me that the head of Fyrie Limited had such mystic eyes."

"I have been paid compliments by men before, Major Pitt, but you are the first to describe my eyes as mystic."

"Purely academic," Pitt said. "The eyes are doors to the secrets a person hides from within."

"And what deep, dark shadows do you see lurking within my soul?"

Pitt laughed. "A gentleman never reveals a lady's private thoughts." He offered her a cigarette, but she shook her head. "Seriously, our eyes have something in common."

"Miss Fyrie's eyes are deep blue," Tidi said, "yours are green. What could they possibly have in common?"

"Miss Fyrie's eyes, like mine, have rays that spread from the pupil into the iris," Pitt said. "They're sometimes called flashes." He paused to light a cigarette. "I have it from the best authority, flashes are a sign of psychic powers."

"Are you clairvoyant?" Kirsti asked.

"I admit to being a failure," Pitt replied. "I always lose at poker because I have yet to read my opponent's cards or mind. How about you, Miss Fyrie, can you see into the future?"

He saw a fleeting shadow across her eyes.

"I know my destiny, therefore I can control it."

Pitt's dark, grinning features gave nothing away as he began to enter into the spirit of the eternal chase. He leaned across the table until only a few inches separated their eyes—green stared into violet.

"I take it you usually expect to get what you want?"

"Yes!" Her answer came without an instant's hesitation.

"Then suppose I told you that under no circumstances would I ever attempt to make love to you?"

"I know the sort of thing you expect me to say, Major." An expression of defiant determination animated her face. "But If I really desired you and demanded your attention, I would be playing into your hands, literally. No, I seldom bother with something I do not want. I shall totally ignore your empty rejection."

Pitt acted as if he were unconscious of any static in the atmosphere. "Why, Miss Fyrie, I hardly figured you for a cop-out artist."

She looked blank. "A cop-out artist?"

"That's American for chicken," Tidi said with a razor-sharp tongue coated with several layers of sugar.

Admiral Sandecker cleared his throat. He was thinking of what might happen if this trend in the conversation were to continue.

"I see no reason for an old man to sit here and listen to all this lighthearted talk while he's starving. Particularly when several square yards of delicious-looking food sits begging for attention only ten feet away."

"Please allow me to introduce you to our native buffet dishes," Kirsti said. "I trust Major Pitt's appetite for food is more regulated than his appetite for sex."

"Touché!" Pitt laughed. He rose and pulled back Kirsti's chair. "From this moment forward, my every move will be with moderation."

The varieties of fish seemed endless. Pitt counted over twenty different dishes of salmon and nearly fifteen of cod alone. They each returned with their plates heaped with near over-the-rim helpings.

"I see you've taken a fancy to our cured shark meat, Major." Kirsti's eyes were smiling.

"I've heard a great deal about the processing," Pitt said. "And now at last I have a chance to try it."

The smile in her lovely eyes turned to a flicker of surprise as he ate several slices. "Are you sure you're aware of how we prepare it?"

"Of course," he answered. "The species of shark found in colder waters can't be eaten fresh, so you slice it in strips and bury it in beach sand for twenty-six days and then cure it in the wind."

"You're eating it raw, you know?" Kirsti persisted.

"Is there any other way?" Pitt said as he forked another slice into his mouth.

"Don't waste your time trying to shock him, Miss Fyrie." Sandecker cast a distasteful eye at the shark meat. "Dirk's hobby is gourmet cooking. His specialty is fish, and he is an expert on international seafood preparation."

"Actually, it's quite good," Pitt managed between mouthfuls. "However, I do think the Malaysian version has a better flavor. They cure the shark meat wrapped in a seaweed called echidna. This gives it a slightly sweeter taste than the Icelandic delicacy."

"Americans usually order steak or chicken," Kirsti said. "You are the first I have known who prefers fish."

"Not entirely," Pitt said. "Like most of my countrymen, my favorite standby is still a good double hamburger with French fries and a chocolate malt."

Kirsti looked at Pitt and smiled. "I am beginning to think that you are blessed with an iron stomach."

Pitt shrugged. "I have an uncle who is San Francisco's leading bon vivant. In my own small way I'm trying to follow in his footsteps."

The rest of the meal was eaten with a minimum of small talk, everyone relaxed and comfortable in the atmosphere of friendliness and good food. Two hours later, during a strawberry and ice cream flambé, especially concocted by Pitt and an agreeable chef, Kirsti began to make apologies for an early departure.

"I hope you will not think me rude, Admiral Sandecker, but I am afraid I must leave you, Miss Royal and Major Pitt very shortly. My fiancé has insisted on taking me to a poetry reading tonight, and since I am only a woman, it is difficult to refuse his wishes." She gave Tidi a soft female look of understanding. "I'm sure Miss Royal can appreciate my situation."

Tidi instantly grasped the romantic inference. "I envy you, Miss Fyrie. A fiancé who loves poetry is a rare catch."

Admiral Sandecker beamed a felicitating smile. "My sincerest wishes for your happiness, Miss Fyrie. I had no idea you were engaged. Who is the lucky man?"

The admiral held his composure exceedingly well, Pitt thought. He knew the old man was stunned right down to his shoe soles. This new development would call for a different set of ground rules—already Pitt found himself wondering what the competition was like.

"Rondheim—Oskar Rondheim," Kristi announced. "My brother introduced us in a letter. Oskar and I exchanged pictures and corresponded for two years before we finally met."

Sandecker stared at her. "Wait a minute," he said slowly. "I think I know of him. Isn't he the one who owns an international chain of canneries? Rondheim Industries? A fishing fleet the size of Spain's navy? Or am I thinking of some other Rondheim?"

"No, that's right," Kristi said. "His executive offices are right here in Reykjavik."

"The fishing boats, painted blue, flying a red flag with an albatross?" Pitt inquired.

Kristi nodded. "The albatross is Oskar's good luck symbol. Do you know his boats?"

"I've had occasion to fly over them," Pitt said.

Of course Pitt knew the boats and their symbol. So did every fisherman of every country north of the fortieth parallel. Rondheim's fishing fleets were notorious for wiping out fishing grounds, almost to the verge of extinction, robbing the nets of the other fishermen, and dropping their own distinctive red-dyed nets inside the territorial boundaries of other countries. The Rondheim albatross carried as much respect as the Nazi swastika.

"A merger between Fyrie Limited and Rondheim Industries would result in a most powerful empire," Sandecker said slowly, almost as if he were weighing the consequences.

Pitt's mind was running along the same channels. Suddenly, his train of thought was broken when Kristi waved her hand.

"There he is. There!"

They turned and followed Kristi's gaze to a tall, snow-haired, distinguished-looking figure vigorously stepping toward them. He was fairly young, late thirties, his face strong and lined by years of ocean gales and salt air. The eyes were cool blue-gray above a strong narrow nose and a mouth that looked good-naturedly warm, though Pitt mused—rightly—that it could quickly straighten and harden to an aggressive line during business hours. Pitt mentally wrote him down as a sharp and cunning opponent. He made a note never to turn his back to him.

Rondheim stopped before the table, his even white teeth flashing in a seemingly cordial smile. "Kristi darling. How delightful you look tonight." Then he affectionately embraced her.

Pitt waited to see where the blue-gray eyes would move to next—to himself or the admiral.

He guessed wrong. Rondheim turned to Tidi.

"Ah—and who is this lovely young lady?"

"Admiral Sandecker's secretary, Miss Tidi Royal," Kirsti said. "May I present Oskar Rondheim."

"Miss Royal." He made a slight bow. "I am charmed by such interesting eyes."

Pitt had to hold his napkin to his mouth to muffle the laughter. "I think this is where I came in."

Tidi began to giggle, and Sandecker joined in with a hearty laugh that turned heads at the nearby tables. Pitt kept his eyes on Kirsti. He was intrigued by a frightened, almost panicky expression that flickered across her face before she forced a thin smile and went along with the surrounding mirth.

Rondheim didn't go along with it at all. He stood there, his eyes staring blankly in confusion and his mouth pressed tightly together in anger—one didn't need to be a mind reader to see that he wasn't in the habit of being laughed at.

"I said something humorous?" he asked.

"This seems to be the night for complimenting women on their eyes," Pitt said.

Kristi explained to Rondheim and then hurriedly introduced Sandecker.

"It is indeed a pleasure to meet you, Admiral." The cool look was back in Rondheim's eyes. "Your reputation as a mariner and oceanographer is widely known throughout seafaring circles."

"Your reputation is also widely known throughout seafaring circles, Mr. Rondheim." The admiral shook Rondheim's hand and turned to Pitt. "Major Dirk Pitt, my special projects director."

Rondheim paused a moment, making a coldly professional assessment of the man standing before him before he extended his hand, "Major Pitt."

"How do you do." Pitt gritted his teeth as Rondheim's hand closed like a vise. Pitt fought a desire to squeeze back; instead he let his hand go limp in a deadfish grip. "Good heavens, Mr. Rondheim, you're a very strong man."

"I'm sorry, Major." Rondheim winced with surprised disgust and jerked his hand back as though he had been shocked by an electrical circuit. "The men who work for me are a rugged breed and have to be treated as such. When I am off the deck of a fishing boat, I sometimes forget to act like a gentleman of the land."

"Goodness, Mr. Rondheim, you needn't apologize. I admire virile men." Pitt held up his hand and wiggled his fingers. "No harm done as long as I can still wield a brush."

"Do you paint, Major?" Kirsti asked.

"Yes, landscapes mostly. I also enjoy doing floral still lifes. There is something about flowers that inspires the soul, don't you think?"

Kirsti looked at Pitt curiously. "I would love to see your work sometime."

"Unfortunately all of my canvases are in Washington. However, I'd be delighted to present you with my impressions of Iceland while I'm here." Pitt held a finger against his lips in a feminine gesture. "Watercolors, yes, that's it. I'll do a series of watercolors. Perhaps you can hang them in your office."

"You are very kind, but I could not accept—"

"Nonsense," Pitt interrupted. "Your coastline is magnificent. I'm simply dying to see if I can capture its contrasting forces of sea and rock meeting one another in a natural eruption of light and color."

Kirsti smiled politely. "If you insist, but you must permit me to do something for you in return."

"I ask one favor—a boat. To do your shoreline justice, I must sketch it from the sea. Nothing fancy. Any small cruiser will do."

"See my dockmaster, Major. He will have a cruiser ready for you." She hesitated a moment as Rondheim loomed up and placed his hand on her neck and shoulder. "Our boats are moored at Pier Twelve."

"Come, darling," Rondheim said, white-teethed and softly. "Max is reading his new anthology tonight. We must not be late." His hand tightened, and she closed her eyes. "I hope you good people will excuse us."

"Yes, of course," Sandecker said. "It's been a very enjoyable two hours, Miss Fyrie. Thank you for joining us."

Before anyone could say anything further, Rondheim hooked his hand through Kirsti's arm and led her from the dining room. As soon as they passed beyond the door, Sandecker threw his napkin down on the table.

"Okay, Dirk, suppose you explain your little act."

"What little act?" Pitt asked innocently.

"I admire virile men," Sandecker mimicked. "That goddamned homo act—that's what I mean. All that was missing was the lisp."

Pitt leaned forward, elbows on the table, his face dead serious. "There are situations that offer a definite advantage in being underestimated. This is one of them."

"Rondheim?"

"Exactly. He's your reason behind Fyrie's sudden reluctance to cooperate with the United States and NUMA. The man is no dummy. Once he marries Kirsti Fyrie, control of two of the largest privately owned corporations in the world will come under one roof. The possibilities are immense. Iceland and its government are too small, too dependent on the future Fyrie-Rondheim cartel for its economy to offer even a token resistance against a highly financed takeover. Then, with the right strategy, the Faeroe Islands and Green-land, giving Rondheim virtual control over the North Atlantic. After that, one can only guess in which direction his ambitions lie."

Sandecker shook his head. "You're assuming too much. Kirsti Fyrie would never go along with an international power play."

"She will have no choice in the matter," Pitt said. "In marriage the spoils go to the dominant personality."

"A woman in love is blind. Is that it?"

"No," Pitt answered. "I don't think this is a match based on love."

"Now you're an expert on affairs of the heart," Sandecker said sarcastically.

"No contest," Pitt said, grinning, "but we are fortunate in having an expert in our midst who has a built-in natural intuition for such things." He turned to Tidi. "Care to give us a feminine opinion, dearheart?"

Tidi nodded. "She was terrified of him."

Sandecker looked at her speculatively. "What do you mean by that?"

"Just what I said," Tidi said firmly. "Miss Fyrie was scared to death of Mr. Rondheim. Didn't you see how he clutched her neck? I guarantee that she'll be wearing high collars for the next week until the bruises disappear.

"Are you sure you're not imagining or exaggerating?"

Tidi shook her head. "It was all she could do to keep from screaming."

Sandecker's eyes were suddenly full of hostility. "That rotten son-of-a-bitch." He gazed at Pitt steadily. "Did you catch it?"

"Yes."

This increased Sandecker's anger. "Then why in hell didn't you stop it?"

"I couldn't," Pitt said. "I would have had to step out of character. Rondheim has every reason to think I'm a faggot. I want him to go right on thinking that."

"I'd like to think you have a hazy idea of what you're doing," Sandecker said grimly. "However, I'm

afraid you backed yourself into a corner with that crap
about being an artist. I know for a fact that you can't
draw a straight line. Natural eruption of light—my
God."

"I don't have to. Tidi will handle that little chore
for me. I've seen samples of her work. It's quite good."

"I do abstracts," Tidi said, a pained look on her
pretty face. "I've never tried a true-life seascape."

"Fake it," Pitt said briskly. "Do an abstract seascape. We're not out to impress the head curator at the
Louvre."

"But I have no supplies," Tidi whined. "Besides,
the Admiral and I are leaving for Washington the day
after tomorrow."

"Your flight has just been canceled." Pitt turned to
Sandecker. "Right, Admiral?"

Sandecker folded his hands and mulled for a few
moments. "In view of what we've learned in the last
five minutes, I think it best if I hang around for a few
days."

"The change of climate will do you good," Pitt
said. "You might even get in a fishing trip."

Sandecker studied Pitt's face. "Fairy queen imita-
tions, painting classes, fishing expeditions. Would you
humor an old man and tell me what's running through
that agile mind of yours?"

Pitt picked up a glass of water and swilled the lu-
cid contents. "A black airplane," he said quietly. "A
black airplane resting beneath a watery death shroud."

Chapter
9

They found Pier Twelve at about ten in the morning and were passed through the entrance barrier by a tall, swarthy Fyrie guard. Sandecker dressed in old rumpled clothes, a floppy, soiled hat, carrying a tackle box and fishing rod. Tidi in slacks and knotted blouse warmly covered by a man's windbreaker. She held a sketching pad under one arm and a satchel-sized handbag under the other, both hands jammed deeply in the windbreaker's pockets. The guard did a classic double-take at Pitt, who brought up the rear moving along the pier in a short sissyish gait. If Sandecker and Tidi looked and dressed like a pair of fishermen, Pitt came on like the queen of the May. He wore red suede pull-on boots, multicolored striped duck pants, so tight the seams were strained beyond endurance, supported by a two-inch-wide tapestry belt and a skin-stretched purple sweater trimmed at the collar by a yellow neckerchief. His eyes blinked rapidly behind a pair of Ben Franklin glasses and his head was covered by a tasseled knit cap. The guard's mouth slowly drifted agape.

"Hi, sweetie," Pitt said, smiling slyly. "Is our boat ready?"

The guard's mouth remained agape, his eyes blank

and unable to communicate to the brain the apparition
they were focusing on.

"Come, come," Pitt said. "Miss Fyrie has generously loaned us the use of one of her boats. Which one
is it?" Pitt stared fixedly at the guard's crotch.

The guard jerked alive as if he had been kicked,
the stunned look on his face quickly turning to one of
abject disgust. Without a word he led them down the
pier, stopping in a hundred feet and pointing down at a
gleaming thirty-two-foot Chris Craft cruiser.

Pitt leaped aboard and disappeared below. In a
minute he was back on the pier. "No, no, this won't do
at all. Too mundane, too ostentatious. To create pro-
perly I must have a creative atmosphere." He looked
across the pier. "There, how about that one?"

Before the guard could reply, Pitt trotted the width
of the pier and dropped to the deck of a forty-foot fishing boat. He explored it briefly, then popped his head
through a hatchway.

"This is perfect. It has character, a crude unique-
ness. We'll take this one."

The guard hesitated for a moment. Finally, with
that twitch of the shoulders that indicated a shrug, he
nodded and left them, walking along the pier back to
the entrance, throwing a backward look at Pitt every so
often and shaking his head.

When he was out of earshot, Tidi said, "Why this
old dirty tub? Why not that nice yacht?"

"Dirk knows what he's doing." Sandecker set the
rod and tackle box down on the worn deck planking
and looked at Pitt. "Does it have a fathometer?"

"A Fleming six-ten, the top of the line. Extrasensi-
tive frequencies for detecting fish at different depths."
Pitt motioned down a narrow companionway. "This
boat was a lucky choice. Let me show you the engine
room, Admiral."

"You mean we ignored that beautiful Chris Craft
simply because it doesn't have a fathometer?" Tidi
asked disappointedly.

"That's right," Pitt answered. "A fathometer is our
only hope of finding the black plane."

Pitt turned and led Sandecker through the companionway down into the engine room. The stale air and the dank smell of oil and bilge immediately filled their nostrils, making them gasp at the drastic change from the diamond-pure atmosphere above. There was another odor. Sandecker looked at Pitt questioningly.

"Gas fumes?"

Pitt nodded. "Take a look at the engines."

A diesel engine is the most efficient means of propelling a small boat, particularly a fishing boat. Heavy, low revolutions-per-minute, slow, but cheap to run and reliable, the diesel is used in nearly every workboat on the sea that doesn't rely on sails for power, that is, except this boat. Sitting side by side, their propeller shafts vanishing into the bilge, a pair of Sterling 420 h.p. gas-fed engines gleamed in the dim light of the engine room like sleeping giants awaiting the starting switch to goad them into thunderous action.

"What in hell would a scow like this be doing with all this power?" Sandecker queried quietly.

"Unless I miss my guess," Pitt murmured, "the guard goofed."

"Meaning?"

"On a shelf in the main cabin I found a pennant with an albatross on it."

Pitt ran a hand over one of the Sterling's intake manifolds; it was clean enough to pass a naval inspection. "This boat belongs to Rondheim, not Fyrie."

Sandecker thought for a moment. "Miss Fyrie instructed us to see her dockmaster. For some unknown reason he was absent, and the pier was left in charge of that grizzled character with the tobacco-stained moustache. It makes one wonder if we weren't set up."

"I don't think so," Pitt said. "Rondheim will undoubtedly keep a tight eye on us, but we've given him no cause to be suspicious of our actions—not yet, at any rate. The guard made an honest mistake. Without special instructions he probably figured we were given permission to select any boat on the pier, so he quite naturally showed us the best of the lot first. There was nothing in the script that said we would pick this little gem."

"What is it doing here? Rondheim surely can't be hard up for dock space."

"Who cares," Pitt said, a wide grin stretching his features. "As long as the keys are in the ignition, I suggest we take it and run before the guard changes his mind."

The admiral needed no persuasion. When it came to indulging in devious games to achieve—in his mind—an honest purpose, he was sneaky to a fault. Squaring his battered hat, he lost no time in issuing the first order of his new command.

"Cast off the lines, Major. I'm anxious to see what these Sterlings can do."

Precisely one minute later, the guard came running down the pier waving his arms like a crazy man. It was too late. Pitt stood on the deck and waved back good-naturedly as Sandecker, happy as a child with a new toy, gunned the engines and steered the deceptive-looking boat out into Reykjavik harbor.

The boat was named *The Grimsi,* and her tiny squared wheelhouse, perched just five feet from the stern, made her look as though she rode in the opposite direction than her builder had intended when he laid her keel. She was a very old boat—as old as the antique compass mounted beside the helm. Her mahogany deck planks were worn smooth, but still lay strong and true, and smelled strongly of the sea. At the pier she had looked an old ungainly bathtub from her broad-beamed, stubby shape, but when the mighty Sterlings mumbled through their exhaust, her bow lifted from the water like a sea gull soaring into the wind. She seemed to delight in being carried along without effort or trouble in a buoyant sort of way.

Sandecker eased the throttles back a notch above idle and took *The Grimsi* on a slow, leisurely tour of Reykjavik harbor. The admiral might have been standing on the bridge of a battle cruiser from the regulation smile on his face. He was back on his element, and he was enjoying every minute of it. To an interested observer his passengers looked like ordinary tourists on a chartered cruise—Tidi sunning herself and aiming a camera at everything in sight, and Pitt drawing furiously on a sketch pad. Before leaving the harbor they tied up at a bait boat and purchased two buckets of herring. Then, after an animated conversation with the bait fishermen, they cast off and headed toward the sea.

As soon as they rounded a rocky point and lost sight of the harbor, Sandecker eased open the throttles and slowly pushed *The Grimsi* to 30 knots. It was a strange sight indeed to see the ungainly hull skipping over the waves like a Gold Cup hydroplane. The waves began to melt together as *The Grimsi* increased speed and lost them behind her swirling wake. Pitt found a chart of the coast and laid it on a small shelf beside Sandecker.

"It's right about here." Pitt tapped a spot on the map with a pencil. "Twenty miles southeast of Keflavik."

Sandecker nodded. "An hour and a half, no more. Not the way she moves. Take a look. The throttles are still a good two inches from their stops."

"The weather looks perfect. I hope it holds."

"No clouds in any direction. It's usually calm around the southern end of Iceland this time of year. The worst we can look forward to is meeting a bit of fog. It usually rolls in during the late afternoon."

Pitt sat down, propped his feet on the doorway and gazed out at the rocky coastline. "At least we don't have to worry about fuel."

"What do the gauges read?"

"About two-thirds full."

Sandecker's mind clicked like a Burroughs adding machine. "Ample for our purpose. No reason to conserve, particularly since Rondheim is footing the bill." With a smug, satisfied expression on his face, he jammed the throttles against their stops.

The Grimsi sat down on her stern and took off across the blue wrinkled sea, her bow splitting two giant sheets of spray. Sandecker's timing left something to be desired. Tidi was cautiously climbing the ladder from the galley, balancing a tray laden with three cups of coffee when the admiral opened up the Sterlings. The sudden acceleration caught her totally off guard and the tray flew into the air and she vanished into the galley as though jerked backward by an invisible hand. Neither Pitt nor Sandecker caught the vaudevillian fall.

Thirty seconds later she reappeared in the wheelhouse, her head thrown back in anger, her hair stringy with dampness, her blouse stained brown by coffee. "Admiral James Sandecker," she shouted, the high-pitched voice drowning out the roar of the Sterlings. "When we get back to our hotel, you can just add the cost of a new blouse and a trip to the hairdresser on your expense account."

Sandecker and Pitt stared at Tidi and then at each other in utter uncomprehension. "I could have scalded myself into a hospital," Tidi continued. "If you want me to act as your stewardess on this voyage, I suggest you show a little more consideration." With that, she whirled and disappeared into the galley.

Sandecker's eyebrows came together. "What in hell was that all about?"

Pitt shrugged. "Women rarely offer an explanation."

"She's too young for menopause," Sandecker mumbled. "Must be on her period."

"Either way, it's going to cost you a blouse and a hairdo," Pitt said mentally applauding Tidi's economic aggressiveness.

It took Tidi ten minutes to make another small pot of coffee. Considering the dip of *The Grimsi*'s keel as it soared over and smacked the crests of the swells, it was a professional feat of dexterity that she managed to climb into the wheelhouse without spilling a drop from the three cups she clutched with dogged determination. Pitt couldn't help smiling as he sipped the coffee and watched the indigo blue water pass under the old boat. Then he thought of Hunnewell, of Fyrie, of Matajic, of O'Riley, and he wasn't smiling any longer.

He still wasn't smiling as he watched the stylus on the fathometer's graph zigzag across the paper, measuring the sea floor. The bottom showed at one hundred and thirty feet. He wasn't smiling now because somewhere down there in the depths was an airplane with a dead crew, and he had to find it. If luck played into his hands, the fathometer would register an irregular hump on its chart.

He took his cross bearings on the cliffs and hoped for the best.

"Are you sure of your search pattern?" Sandecker asked.

"Twenty percent certain, eighty percent guesswork," Pitt answered. "I could have lowered the odds if I had the Ulysses as a checkpoint."

"Sorry, I didn't know yesterday what you had in mind. My formal request for salvage was acted upon only a few hours after you crashed. The Air Force airsea rescue squadron on Keflavik picked your craft out of the surf with one of their giant helicopters. You have to give them credit. They're an efficient lot."

"Their eagerness is going to cost us," Pitt said.

Sandecker paused to make a course change. "Have you checked the diving gear?"

"Yes, it's all accounted for. Remind me to buy those State Department people at the consulate a drink when we get back. Dressing up and playing bait fishermen took a bit of doing on such short notice. To anyone gawking through a pair of navy binoculars it could have only looked an innocent encounter. The diving gear was slipped on board so smoothly and inconspicuously while you were going through the routine of bait buying that I almost missed detecting the transfer from ten feet away."

"I don't like the action. Diving alone invites danger, and danger invites death. I'll have you know I'm not in the habit of going against my own orders and allowing one of my men to dive in unknown waters without the proper precautions." Sandecker shifted from one foot to the other. He was going against his better judgment, and the discomfort showed clearly in his expression. "What do you hope to find down there besides a broken airplane and bloated bodies? How do you know someone hasn't already beaten us to it?"

"There is an outside chance that the bodies may carry identification that might point to the man behind this screwed-up engima. This factor alone makes it worth an attempt to find the remains. What's more important is the aircraft itself. All identifying numbers and insignia were hidden under black paint, leaving nothing recognizable at a distance except a silhouette. That plane, Admiral, is the only positive lead we have to Hunnewell's and Matajic's murderer. The one thing black paint can't cover is the serial number of an engine, at least not on the turbine casing under the cowling. If we find the plane, and if I can retrieve the digits, it then becomes a simple matter to contact the manufacturer, trace the engine to the plane, and from there to the owner."

Pitt hesitated a moment to make an adjustment on the fathometer. "The answer to your second question," he went on, "is 'no way.' "

"You seem damned sure of yourself," Sandecker said mechanically. "As much as I hate the murderous son-of-a-bitch, I still give him credit for brains. He'd have already searched for his missing plane, knowing that the wreckage could give him away."

"True, he would have made a surface search, but this time—for the first time—we have the advantage. Nobody witnessed the fight. The children who found Hunnewell and me on the beach said they investigated only after they noticed the Ulysses laying in the surf— not before. And the fact that our friendly assassins didn't kill us when they had an ideal opportunity instead of arriving at the doctor's house much later, proves they weren't ground observers. To sum up, I'm the only survivor who knows where to look—"

Pitt broke off suddenly, his eyes concentrating on the graph and stylus. The black lines began widening from a thin waver back and forth across the paper to a small mountainlike sweep that indicated a sudden rise of eight to ten feet above the flat, sandy sea floor.

"I think we've got it," Pitt said calmly. "Circle to port and cross our wake on course one-eight-five, Admiral."

Sandecker spun the helm and made a two-hundred-and-seventy-degree swing to the south, causing *The Grimsi* to rock gently as it passed over the waves of its own wake. This time the stylus took longer to sweep to a height of ten feet before tapering back to zero.

"What depth?" Sandecker asked.

"One hundred and forty-five feet," Pitt replied. "Judging from the indication, we just passed over her from wing tip to wing tip."

Minutes later, *The Grimsi* was moored over the reading on the fathometer. The shore was nearly a mile away, the great cliffs showing off their gray vertical rock more distinctly than ever under the northern sun. At the same time, a slight breeze sprang up and began to ruffle the surface of the rolling water. It was a mild warning, a signal foretelling the beginning of rougher weather to come. With the breeze a state of chilling apprehension raised the hairs on Pitt's neck. For the first time he began to wonder what he would find beneath the cold Atlantic waters.

Chapter 10

The brilliant blue sky, free of clouds, allowed the sun to beat down and turn Pitt's black neoprene wet suit into a skintight sauna bath as he checked the old single-hose U.S. Diver's Deepstar regulator. He would have preferred a newer model, but beggars couldn't be choosy. He considered himself lucky that one of the young consulate members made a sport of diving and had the equipment on hand. He attached the regulator to the valve of an air bottle. Two single tanks were all he could scrounge. Enough for fifteen minutes' diving, and even that was stretching precious time for dives to one hundred and forty feet. His only consolation was that he wouldn't be down long enough to worry about decompression.

His last look of *The Grimsi*'s deck before the blue-green water closed over his face mask was of Admiral Sandecker sitting sleepily with fishing pole gripped in both hands and Tidi, dressed in Pitt's outlandish clothes, brown hair encased in the knit cap, studiously sketching the Icelandic shoreline. Shielded from anyone watching from the cliffs, Pitt slipped over the side behind the wheelhouse and became a part of the sea's vastness. His body was tense. Without a diving companion there was no margin for error.

The shock of the icy water against his sweating body nearly made him pass out. Using the anchor line as a guide, he followed along its vanishing outline, leaving his air bubbles to swirl and rise lazily to the surface. As he sank deeper and deeper, the light diminished and the visibility shortened. He checked his two vital references. The depth gauge read ninety feet and the orange dial on the Doxa diving watch notified him that he had been down two minutes.

The bottom gradually came into view. He automatically popped his ears for the third time and was struck by the color of the sand—a pure black. Unlike most areas of the world where the bottom sand was white, the volcanic activity of Iceland had left a carpet of soft ebony grains. He slowed his movement, spellbound by the strangeness of the dark color beneath the vast shroud of blue-green water. Visibility was about forty feet—quite good considering the depth.

Instinctively he swung around in a three-hundred-and-sixty-degree circle. Nothing was in sight. He looked up and vaguely saw a shadow pass over him. It was a small school of cod foraging near the bottom for their favorite diet of shrimp and crab. He watched a moment as they slowly slipped overhead, their slightly flattened bodies tinted a dark olive and spotted with hundreds of small brown dots. Too bad the admiral can't hook one, he thought. The smallest weighed no less than fifteen pounds.

Pitt began swimming in ever-widening circles around the anchor line, dragging a fin in the sand to mark his trail. Underwater he often saw fantasy, at deep depths his perception was distorted, danger magnified beyond clear thinking. After five circuits he saw a dim form through the blue haze. Quickly kicking his fins, he swam toward it. Thirty seconds later his hopes were broken and discarded. The form proved to be a large jagged rock poking up from the bottom like some forgotten and crumbling outpost in the middle of a desert. Effortlessly he slipped around the current-worn sides, his mind blurred, struggling for control. This couldn't be the reading on the fathometer, he thought. The peak was too conical to match that of an aircraft fuselage.

Then he saw something lying in the sand just five feet away. The black paint on the broken and bent door blended against the black sand almost to the point of invisibility. He swam forward and turned it over, recoiling in surprise for an instant as a large lobster scurried from its new home. There were no markings anywhere on the inside paneling. Pitt had to move quickly now. The plane had to be very close, but he was due to pull the valve for his reserve air, and that only left a few minutes of extra breathing—barely enough to get him to the surface.

It didn't take him long to find it. The aircraft was resting on its belly, broke in two, evidence of the impact from the crash. His breathing became harder now, signaling him that it was time to go on reserve. He pulled the valve and headed for the top. The watery ceiling over his head slowly became brighter as he rose along with his air bubbles. At thirty feet he stopped and searched for *The Grimsi*'s keel; it was important that he break water out of sight from shore. She sat like a fat duck with her props tucked into her bottom, rolling drunkenly with the swells. He stared upward at the sun to get a direction. *The Grimsi* had drifted around her anchor line on a hundred-and-eighty-degree arc so that her starboard side now faced the coast.

He pulled himself over the port freeboard and, dropping his air tank, crawled across the deck into the wheelhouse. Sandecker, without looking up, slowly placed his rod against the railing and just as slowly walked over and leaned in the doorway.

"I hope you've had better luck than I have."

"She's lying a hundred and fifty feet off the starboard beam," Pitt said. "I didn't have time to search the interior; my air was scraping bottom."

"Better get out of that suit and have a cup of coffee. Your face is as blue as a windmill on a Delftware saucer."

"Keep the coffee hot. I'll relax as soon as we've got what we came for." Pitt started for the door.

Sandecker's eyes were set. "You're not going anywhere for the next hour and a half. We still have plenty of time. The day is young. It's senseless to overdo your physical resources. You know the repetitive dive charts as well as any diver alive. Two dives to one hundred and forty feet within thirty minutes invites a case of the bends." He paused, then drove the point home. "You've seen men scream their lungs out from the agony of pain. You know the ones who lived and the ones who were paralyzed for life. Even if I pushed this old scow to the hilt, I couldn't get you to Reykjavik before two hours. Then, add another five hours on a jet to London and the nearest decompression chamber. No way, my friend. You go below and rest up. I'll tell you when you can go down again."

"No contest, Admiral; you win." Pitt unzipped the front of his wet suit. "However, I think it would be wiser to sack out above deck so that all three of us are in view."

"Who's to see? The coast is deserted, and we haven't another boat since we left the harbor."

"The coast isn't deserted. We have an observer."

Sandecker turned and gazed across the water toward the cliffs. "I may be getting old, but I don't need glasses yet. Damned if I can detect any obvious signs."

"Off to the right just beyond that rock that projects from the water."

"Can't see crap from this distance." He stared sideways at the point Pitt described. "It'd be like looking through a keyhole and seeing another eye if I picked up the binoculars and stared back. How can you be sure?"

"There was a reflection. The sun flashed on something for a moment. Probably a pair of lenses."

"Let them gawk. If anybody should ask why only two of us were on deck, Tidi was seasick and in misery on a bunk below."

"That's as good an excuse as any," Pitt said, smiling. "So long as they can't tell the difference between Tidi and me in that wild set of duds."

Sandecker laughed. "Through binoculars from a

mile away, your own mother couldn't tell the difference."

"I'm not sure how I should take that."

Sandecker turned and stared into Pitt's eyes, his lips twisting from the laugh to a wry smile. "Don't try. Just get your ass below. It's nappy time. I'll send Tidi down with a cup of coffee. And, no hanky-panky. I know how horny you get after a hard day's dive."

An eerie, yellow-gray light showed through the hatch when Sandecker shook Pitt awake. He woke slowly, mind blurred, more groggy from a catnap than from an eight-hour sleep. Pitt could feel the drop in the wave action; *The Grimsi* was barely rocking, even in the low even swells. There was no hint of a breeze. The air was damp and heavy.

"A change in the weather, Admiral?"

"A fog bank—rolling in from the south."

"How long?"

"Fifteen, maybe twenty minutes."

"Not much time."

"Enough . . . enough for a quick dive."

Minutes later Pitt had slipped into his gear and dropped over the side. Down again into a world where there is no sound, no wind; down where air is not known. He cleared his ears and kicked his fins hard and descended, his muscles cold and aching, his brain still sluggish from sleep.

He swam silently, effortlessly, as though suspended by a wire through the great fluid backdrop. He swam through the darkening colors, the blue-green now changing slowly to a soft gray. He swam with no sense of direction, save for what his instinct and the landmarks on the bottom told him. Then he found it.

His heart began pounding like a bass drum as he approached the plane cautiously, knowing from experience that once he entered the tangled wreckage, every movement would be a menace.

He flippered around to the shattered opening of the fuselage eight feet aft of the wings and was greeted by a small rosefish, no more than six inches long. Its orange-red scales contrasted vividly with the dark background and fluoresced in the dim light like a tiny Christmas tree ornament. It stared at Pitt for a moment from one beady eye set solidly under a spiny head, then began darting back and forth in front of his face mask as he entered the plane.

As soon as his eyes adjusted to the darkness, they met with a jumbled mess of seats, broken from their moorings on the floor, and wooden boxes floating in confusion against the ceiling. Tugging two of the boxes toward the opening, he pushed them out and watched until they lifted free on their way toward the surface. Then he spied a glove with its finger sockets still encasing a man's hand. The body attached by a greenish arm to the hand was jammed between the seats in the lower corner of the main cabin. Pitt pulled the corpse out and searched its clothing. He must have been the one who fired the machine gun from the doorway, Pitt reasoned. The head wasn't a pretty sight; it had been smashed to semiliquid paste, the gray matter and skull fragments straggling in reddish tentacles away from the center mass and swaying in unison with the current. The pockets of the torn black overalls covering the remains held nothing but a screwdriver.

Pitt shoved the screwdriver under his weightbelt then, half swimming, half gliding, he entered the cockpit. Except for a broken windshield on the copilot's side, the heart of the aircraft appeared empty and undamaged. But then he happened to look up at his air bubbles rising to the overhead panel and traveling like a silver snake in search of an escape exit. They eventually ran together and clustered in one corner, encircling another corpse, pushed up there by internal gases expanding under the decomposing flesh.

The dead pilot wore the same type of black overalls. A quick search revealed nothing; the pockets were empty. The little rosefish wiggled past Pitt and began nibbling on the bulging right eye of the pilot. Panting heavily, Pitt pushed the body upward out of the way. He fought an urge to vomit into his mouthpiece and waited until he regained control of his breathing again.

He glanced at the Doxa watch. He had only been down for nine minutes, not the ninety his imagination suggested. There was little time left. Quickly he groped around the small enclosure, looking for a log book, a maintenance or check-out list, anything with printing on it. The cockpit kept its secret well. There was no record of any kind. Not even a sticker with the aircraft's call letters adhering to the face of the radio transmitter.

It was like leaving the womb, being born again, when he emerged from the plane. The open water was darker now than when he had entered. After checking the tail section, he kicked over to the starboard engine. No hope here; it was almost totally buried in the bottom silt. He got lucky on the port engine. Not only was it easily accessible, but the cowling had broken off, leaving the turbine casing bare for inspection. But fate wasn't playing the game. He discovered the area where the identification plate should have been. It was gone. Only the four little brass screws that once held it remained, neatly set in their threads.

Pitt slammed his fist against the casing in frustration. It was useless to look further. He knew all identifying marks on instruments, electrical components, and other mechanical units on the plane would be erased. Silently he cursed the brain behind the thoroughness. It seemed uncanny that one man could have considered and planned for every conceivable contingency. In spite of the near freezing water, trickles of sweat rolled down his face under the mask. His mind was turning aimlessly, posing problems and questions, but impotent to come up with solutions. Without thinking, without controlled effort, his eyes began following the antics of the rosefish. It had trailed him from the cockpit and was cavorting around a silver object a few feet beyond the bow of the plane. Pitt kept his eyes on the little fish for nearly thirty seconds, aware of nothing except the sound of his exhaust bubbles, before he finally reacted and recognized the long silver tube as the hydraulic shock absorber of the nose wheel.

Swiftly he was over it, studying the cylinder carefully. The crash had torn it from the support strut and, together with the tire and wheel, had thrown the assembly out from under the nose section. It was the same story. The manufacturer's serial number had been filed from the aluminum housing. Then, as he was about to head toward the surface, he threw a last quick look down. On the end section of the housing where the hydraulic tubing had pulled from its connection, Pitt spotted a small marking: two roughly gouged letters in the metal—SC. Taking the screwdriver from his weightbelt, he etched his initials next to the other marking. The depth of his DP matched that of the SC.

Okay. No sense in hanging around, he reasoned. His air was becoming difficult to inhale—the signal that his tank was getting low. He pulled his reserve valve and moved upward. The rosefish followed him until he turned and waved his hand in its path, sending the little marine creature scurrying behind a friendly rock. Pitt smiled and nodded. His playful companion would have to find a new friend.

Pitt arched on his back at fifty feet, looking directly up at where the surface should have been, trying to get his bearings in relation to *The Grimsi*. The light was equal in all directions, only his ascending bubbles indicated the direction of his native element. It slowly began to get lighter, but it was still much darker than when he dropped off *The Grimsi*'s side. Pitt's anxious head broke water, to be engulfed by a thick cloak of fog. God, he thought, this soup makes it impossible to find the boat. To strike out for shore would have been at best a four-to-one gamble.

Pitt unshouldered his airtank harness, tied it to his already unhooked weightbelt, and let them fall together to the bottom. Now he could float comfortably, thanks to the buoyancy of his rubber wet suit. He lay quietly, barely breathing, listening for a sound through the dense gray blanket. At first he could hear only the water lapping around his body. Then his ears picked up a faint gravelly voice . . . a voice singing a flat version of "My Bonnie Lies over the Ocean." Pitt cupped his ears, amplifying the sound, determining the direction. He struck out with an easy energy-saving breast stroke for fifty feet and then stopped. The offkey singing had increased in volume. Five minutes later he touched the seaworn hull of *The Grimsi* and pulled himself on board.

"Have a nice swim?" Sandecker asked conversationally.

"Hardly enjoyable and barely profitable." Pitt unzipped the wet suit top, revealing a dense mat of black chest hair. He grinned at the admiral. "Funny thing. I could swear I heard a foghorn."

"That was no foghorn. That was a former baritone of the Annapolis Glee Club, class of '39."

"You were never in better voice, Admiral." Pitt looked Sandecker in the eye. "Thanks."

Sandecker smiled. "Don't thank me, thank Tidi. She had to sit through ten choruses."

She materialized out of the mist and hugged him. "Thank God you're safe." She clung to him, the dampness trickling down her face, her hair falling in matted tendrils.

"It's nice to know I've been missed."

She stood back. "Missed? That's putting it mildly. Admiral Sandecker and I were beginning to come unglued."

"Speak for yourself, Miss Royal," Sandecker said sternly.

"You didn't fool me for a second, Admiral. You were worried."

"Concerned is the word," Sandecker corrected. "I take it as a personal insult when any of my men get themselves killed." He turned his gaze to Pitt. "Did you find anything of value?"

"Two bodies and little else. Somebody went to a hell of a lot of work to remove the plane's identification. Every serial number on every piece of equipment had been removed before the crash. The only markings were two letters scratched on the nose gear's hydraulic cylinder." He gratefully accepted a towel from Tidi. "The boxes I sent up. Did you retrieve them?"

"It wasn't easy," Sandecker said. "They broke surface about forty feet away. Twenty tries later—I haven't cast with a pole in years—I managed to hook and reel them in."

"You opened them?" Pitt probed.

"Yes. They're miniature models of buildings . . . like dollhouses."

Pitt straightened. "Dollhouses? You mean three-dimensional architectural exhibits?"

"Call them what you want." Sandecker paused to flip a cigar stub overboard. "Damned fine craftsmanship. The detail on each structure is amazing. They even break away by floors so you can study the interior."

"Let's take a look."

"We carried them to the galley," Sandecker said. "It's as good a place as any to get you into some dry clothes and a cup of hot coffee into your stomach."

Tidi had already changed back into her own blouse and slacks. She demurely turned her back as Pitt finished stripping off the wet suit before he donned his colorful mod outfit.

He smiled while she busied herself over the galley stove. "Did you keep them warm for me?" he asked.

"Your gay threads?" She turned and stared at him, her face showing the beginning signs of a blush. "Are you kidding? You're at least eight inches taller, and you outweigh me by nearly sixty pounds. I literally swam in the damn things. It was as if I was wearing a tent. The cold air swept up my legs and out me neck and arms like a hurricane."

"I sincerely hope it didn't cause any critical damage to your vital parts."

"If you're referring to my future sex life, I fear the worst."

"My sympathies, Miss Royal." Sandecker didn't sound very convincing. He lifted the boxes onto the table and pulled off the lids. "OK, here they are, including furniture and draperies."

Pitt looked into the first box. "No indications of water damage."

"They were watertight," Sandecker offered. "Each packed so carefully the crash left them entirely intact."

To say the models were simply masterpieces of diminutive art would have been a gross understatement. The admiral was right. The detail was amazing. Every brick, every windowpane, was precise in scale and placement. Pitt lifted off the roof. He had seen model exhibits before in museums, but never workmanship like this. Nothing had been overlooked. Paintings on the walls were exacting in color and design. The furniture had tiny designs printed on the fabric. Telephones on desks had receivers that could be picked up, connected to wires that led into the walls. As a crowning touch, the bathrooms even possessed toilet paper rolls that unraveled to the touch. The first model building consisted of four floors and a basement. Pitt carefully lifted them off one at a time, studied the contents and just as carefully replaced them. Then he inspected the second model.

"I know this one," Pitt said quietly.

Sandecker looked up. "Are you sure?"

"Positive. It's pink. You don't often forget a structure built of pink marble. It was about six years ago when I entered those walls. My father was on an economic survey mission for the President, conferring with the heads of finance of Latin American governments. I took a thirty-day leave from the Air Force and acted as his aide and pilot during the trip. Yes, I remember it well, especially this exotic black-eyed little secretary—"

"Spare us your erotic escapades," Sandecker said impatiently. "Where is it located?"

"In El Salvador. This model is a perfect scaled-down replica of the Dominican Republic capitol building." He gestured toward the first model. "Judging from the design, the other model also represents the legislative offices of another South or Central American country."

"Great," Sandecker said unenthusiastically. "We've come up with a character who collects miniature capitols."

"It doesn't tell us a hell of a lot." Tidi handed Pitt a cup of coffee and he sipped it thoughtfully. "Except that the black jet was doing double duty."

Sandecker met his gaze. "You mean it was delivering these models when it changed course to shoot down you and Hunnewell?"

"Exactly. One of Rondheim's fishing trawlers probably spotted our helicopter approaching Iceland and diverted the jet by radio so it would be waiting for us when we reached the coast."

"Why Rondheim? I see nothing tangible that ties him in with any of this?"

"Any port in a storm." Pitt shrugged. "I admit I'm groping. And, at that, I'm not completely sold on implicating Rondheim myself. He's like the butler in an old movie mystery. Every piece of circumstantial evidence, every finger of doubt, points to him, making him the most obvious suspect. But in the end, our friendly butler turns out to be an undercover policeman and the least obvious character turns out to be the guilty party."

"Somehow I can't picture Rondheim as an undercover cop." Sandecker crossed the cabin and poured himself another cup of coffee. "But he's just enough of a prick for me to fervently wish that in some form or manner he's behind Fyrie's and Hunnewell's death, so we could zero in on the bastard and nail him to the floor."

"It wouldn't be easy. He's in a pretty solid position."

"If you ask me," Tidi interjected, "you two schemers are jealous of Rondheim because of his hold over Miss Fyrie."

Pitt laughed. "You have to be in love to be jealous."

Sandecker grinned at her. "Your forked tongue is showing, lady."

"I'm not being catty out of spite. I like Kirsti Fyrie."

"I suppose you like Oskar Rondheim too," Pitt said.

"I wouldn't like that snake if he was General of the Salvation Army," she said. "But you have to give the devil his due. He's got Kirsti and Fyrie Limited tucked neatly in his pocket."

"Why? Answer that!" Pitt said speculatively. "How can Kirsti love him if she's terrified of him?"

Tidi shook her head. "I don't know. I still see the pain in her eyes when he squeezed her neck."

"Maybe she's a masochist and Rondheim's a sadist," Sandecker said.

"If Rondheim is masterminding these terrible murders, you must turn everything you know over to the proper authorities," Tidi pleaded. "If you persist in pushing this thing too far, both of you might be killed."

Pitt made a sad face. "It's shameful, Admiral. Your own secretary is vastly underestimating her two favorite people." He turned and looked dolefully at Tidi. "How could you?"

Sandecker sighed. "It's almost impossible to find loyalty in an employee these days."

"Loyalty!" Tidi looked at them as if they had gone mad. "What other girl would let herself be dragged over half the world in uncomfortable military cargo planes, frozen on smelly old boats in the middle of the North Atlantic, and be subjected to constant male harassment for the meager salary I'm paid. If that isn't loyalty, I'd like to know what you typical inconsiderate men call it?"

"Crap! That's what I call it," Sandecker said. He put his hands on her shoulders and looked warmly into her eyes. "Believe me, Tidi, I value your friendship and your concern for my welfare very highly, and I'm certain Dirk prizes you just as highly. But you must understand, a close friend and three of my people have been murdered and an attempt made on Dirk here. I'm not the kind of guy who hides under a mattress and calls a cop. By God, this whole bung-twisting mess was pushed on us by persons unknown. When we find out who they are—then and only then—will I stand back and let the law and its enforcers take over. Are you with me?"

The surprise of Sandecker's sudden display of affection held, then slowly passed from Tidi's face and big tears began to well in her eyes. She pressed her head against the admiral's chest. "I feel such a monkey," she murmured. "I'm always shooting off my mouth. Next time it runs away from me, please stuff a gag in it."

"You can count on it," he said more softly than Pitt had ever heard him. Sandecker held Tidi another minute before he released her. "Okay, let's up anchor and get the hell back to Reykjavik." The old familiar gravel tone was back. "I could use a nice hot toddy."

Pitt suddenly stiffened, held up a hand for silence, and stepped to the wheelhouse doorway and listened intently. It was very faint, but it was there. Through the blanket of mist it came as a steady drone: the sound of an engine running at very high rpm's.

Chapter
11

"Do you hear it, Admiral?"

"I hear it." Sandecker was at his shoulder. "About three miles, coming fast." He concentrated for a few seconds. "I make it dead ahead."

Pitt nodded. "Coming straight toward us." He stared unseeing into the fog. "Sounds strange, almost like the whine of an aircraft engine. They must have radar. No helmsman with half a brain would run at full speed in this weather."

"They know we're here then," Tidi whispered, as though someone beyond the railing would hear.

"Yes, they know we're here," Pitt acquiesced. "Unless I'm much mistaken, they're coming to investigate us. An innocent passing stranger would give us a wide berth the minute our blip showed on his scope. This one is hunting for trouble. I suggest we provide them with a little sport."

"Like three rabbits waiting to play games with a pack of wolves," Sandecker said. "They'll outman us ten to one, and . . ." he added softly, "they're undoubtedly armed to the teeth. Our best bet is the Sterlings. Once we're under way, our visitors stand as much chance of catching us as a cocker spaniel after a greyhound in heat."

140

"Don't bet on it, Admiral. If they know we're here, they also know what boat we've got and how fast it will go. To even consider boarding us, they'd have to have a craft that could outrace *The Grimsi*. I'm banking on the hunch they've got it."

"A hydrofoil. Is that it?" Sandecker asked slowly.

"Exactly," Pitt answered. "Which means their top speed could be anywhere between forty-five and sixty knots."

"Not good," Sandecker said quietly.

"Not bad either," Pitt returned. "We've got at least two advantages in our favor." Quickly he outlined his plan. Tidi, sitting on a bench in the wheelhouse, felt her body go numb, knew that her face beneath the makeup was paper-white. She couldn't believe what she was hearing. She began to tremble until even her voice became unsteady.

"You . . . you can't mean what . . . you say."

"If I don't," Pitt said, "we're going to have bigger trouble than River City." He paused, looking at the pale, uncomprehending face, the hands twisting nervously at the knotted blouse.

"But you're planning a cold-blooded murder." For a moment her mouth mumbled soundless words, then she forced herself on. "You just can't kill people without warning. Innocent people you don't even know!"

"That will do," Sandecker snapped sharply. "We haven't got time to explain the facts of life to a frightened female." He stared at her, his eyes understanding, but his voice commanding. "Please get below and take cover behind something that'll stop bullets." He turned to Pitt. "Use the fire ax and chop the anchor line. Give me a signal when you want full power."

Pitt herded Tidi down the galley steps. "Never argue with the captain of a ship." He swatted her on the bottom. "And don't fret. If the natives are friendly, you have nothing to worry about."

He was just lifting the ax into the air when the Sterlings rumbled to life. "Good thing we didn't lay out a damage deposit," he murmured vaguely to himself as the ax sliced cleanly through the rope into the wooden railing, blasting a six-inch splinter into the sea and sending the anchor forever to the black sandy bottom.

The unseen boat was almost upon them now, the roar of its engine dying to a muted throb as the helmsman eased back the throttles in preparation for coming alongside *The Grimsi.* From where he lay on the bow, clenching and unclenching his hands around the ax handle, Pitt could hear the hull splash into the waves as the diminishing speed pushed the hydrofoil deeper in the water. He raised himself carefully, narrowing his eyes and trying vainly to pierce the heavy fog for a sign of movement. The area round the bow was in near darkness. Visibility was no more than twenty feet.

Then a shadowy bulk slowly eased into view, showing its port bow. Pitt could barely make out several dim forms standing on the forward deck, a glow behind them that Pitt knew would be the wheelhouse. It was like a specter ship whose crew appeared as dim ghosts. The large gray form arose menacingly and towered above *The Grimsi;* the stranger had a length of a hundred feet or better, Pitt guessed. He could see the other men clearly now, leaning over the bulwarks, saying nothing, crouched as if ready to jump. The automatic rifles in their hands told Pitt all he needed to know.

Coolly and precisely, no more than eight feet from the gun barrels on the specter ship, Pitt made three movements so rapidly they almost seemed simultaneous. Swinging the ax head sideways, he brought the flat face down loudly on an iron capstan—the signal to Sandecker. Then in the same swinging motion he hurled the ax through the air and saw the pick part of the head bury itself in the chest of a man who was in the act of jumping down on *The Grimsi*'s deck. They met in midair, a ghastly scream reaching from the man's throat as he and the ax fell against the railing. He hung there for an instant, the bloodless nails of one hand clenched over the wooden molding and then dropped into the gray water. Even before the sea closed over the man's head, Pitt had hurled himself on the worn planks of the deck, and *The Grimsi* leaped ahead like a frightened impala, chased by a storm of shells that swept across the deck and into the wheelhouse before the old boat had vanished into the mist.

Staying below the gunwale, Pitt crawled aft and across the threshold of the wheelhouse doorway. The floor was littered with glass and wood splinters.

"Any hits?" Sandecker asked conversationally, his voice hardly audible above the exhaust of the Sterling engines.

"No holes in me. How about you?"

"The bastards' aim was above my head. Add to that the fact that I was able to make myself three feet high, and you have a fortunate combination." He turned and looked thoughtful. "I thought I heard a scream just before all hell broke loose."

Pitt grinned. "I cannot tell a lie. I did it with my little ax."

Sandecker shook his head. "Thirty years in the Navy, and that's the first time any crew of mine every had to repel boarders."

"The problem now is to prevent a repeat performance."

"It won't be easy. We're running blind. Their goddamned radar knows our every move. Our biggest fear is ramming. With a ten-to-twenty-knot edge they're an odds-on favorite to win at blindman's buff. I can't avoid the inevitable. If their helmsman is halfway on the dime, he'll use his superior speed to pass and then cut a ninety-degree angle and catch us amidships."

Pitt considered a moment. "Let's hope their helmsman is right-handed."

Sandecker frowned uncomprehendingly. "You're not getting through."

"Lefties are a minority. The percentages favor a right-hander. When the hydrofoil begins to close in again—its bow is probably no more than four hundred yards behind our ass end this second—the helmsman will have an instinctive tendency to swing out to his starboard before he cuts in to ram us. This will give us an opportunity to use one of our two advantages."

Sandecker looked at him. "I can't think of one, much less two."

"A hydrofoil boat depends on its high speed to sustain its weight. The foils travel through the water the same as the wings of an aircraft travel through air. Its greatest asset is speed, but its greatest limitation is maneuverability. In simple English, a hydrofoil can't turn worth a damn."

"And we can. Is that it?" Sandecker probed.

"*The Grimsi* can cut two circles inside their one."

Sandecker lifted his hands from the spokes of the wheel and flexed his fingers. "Sounds great as far as it goes, except we won't know when they start their arc."

Pitt sighed. "We listen."

Sandecker looked at him. "Shut down our engines?"

Pitt nodded.

When Sandecker's hands went back on the wheel, they were white-knuckled, his mouth tight and drawn. "What you're suggesting is one hell of a gamble. All one of those Sterlings had to do is balk at the starter button and we're a sitting duck." He nodded toward the galley. "Are you thinking of her?"

"I'm thinking of all of us. Stand or run, the chances are we get deep-sixed anyway. The last dollar bet of the gambler—call it what you will, but however remote, it's a chance."

Sandecker cast a searching stare at the tall man standing in the doorway. He could see that the eyes were determined and the chin set.

"You mentioned two advantages."

"The unexpected," Pitt said quietly. "We know what they're out to do. They may have radar, but they can't read our minds. That is our second and most important advantage—the unexpected move."

Pitt looked at his Doxa watch. One-thirty, still early in the afternoon. Sandecker had cut the engines, and Pitt had to fight to stay alert—the sudden silence and the calm of the fog began a creeping course to dull his mind. Above, the sun was a faded white disc that brightened and dimmed as the uneven layers of mist rolled overhead. Pitt inhaled slowly and evenly to keep a sensation of wet and chill from penetrating his lungs. He shivered in his clothes, turned damp from the fine sparkling drops bunched in clusters on the material. He sat there on the forward hatch cover waiting until his ears lost the roar of the Sterlings, waiting until his hearing picked up the engines of the hydroplane. He didn't have to wait long. He soon tuned in the steady beat of the hydroplane as the explosions through its exhaust manifolds increased in volume.

Everything had to go perfect the first time. There could be no second chance. The radar operator on the hydroplane was probably at this instant reacting to the fact that the blip on his scope had lost headway and had stopped dead in the water. By the time he notified his commander and a decision was reached, it would be too late for a course change. The hydroplane's superior speed would have put its bow almost on top of *The Grimsi*.

Pitt rechecked the containers lying in a neat row beside him for perhaps the tenth time. It had to be the poorest excuse for an arsenal ever concocted, he mused. One of the containers was a gallon glass jar Tidi had scrounged from the galley. The other three were battered and rusty gas cans in various sizes that Pitt had found in a locker aft of the engine room. Except for their contents, the cloth wicks protruding from the cap openings and the holes punched through the top of the cans, the four vessels had little in common.

The hydroplane was close now—very close. Pitt turned to the wheelhouse and shouted, "Now!" Then he lit the wick of the glass jar with his lighter and braced himself for the sudden surge of acceleration he prayed would come.

Sandecker pushed the starter button. The 420-hp Sterlings coughed once, twice, then burst into rpm's with a roar. He swung the wheel over to starboard hard and jammed the throttles forward. *The Grimsi* took off over the water like a racehorse with an arrow imbedded in its rectum. The admiral held on grimly, clutching the

wheel and half expecting to collide with the hydroplane
bow on. Then suddenly as a spoke flew off the wheel
and clattered against the compass, he became aware
that bullets were striking the wheelhouse. He could still
see nothing, but he knew the crew of the hydroplane
were firing blindly through the fog, guided only by the
commands of the radar operator.

To Pitt the tension was unbearable. His gaze alter-
nated from the wall of fog in front of the bow to the jar
in his hand. The flame on the wick was getting danger-
ously close to the tapered neck and the gasoline sloshing
behind the glass. Five seconds, no more, then he would
have to heave the jar over the side. He began counting.
Five came and went. Six, seven. He cocked his arm.
Eight. Then the hydroplane leaped from the mist on an
opposite course, passing no more than ten feet from
The Grimsi's railing. Pitt hurled the jar.

The next instant stayed etched in Pitt's memory
the rest of his days. The frightful image of a tall,
yellow-haired man in a leather windbreaker gripping
the bridge railing, watching in shocked fascination that
deathly thing sailing through the damp air toward him.
Then the jar burst on the bulkhead beside him and he
vanished in a blast of searing bright flame. Pitt saw no
more. The two boats had raced past each other and the
hydroplane was gone.

Pitt had no time to reflect. Quickly he lit the wick
on one of the gas cans as Sandecker swept *The Grimsi*
on a hard-a-port, hundred-and-eighty-degree swing into
the hydroplane's wake. The worm had turned. The hydroplane had slowed, and a pulsating yellowish-red
glow could be easily seen through the gray mist. The
admiral headed straight for it. He was standing straight
as a ramrod now. It was certain that anybody who
might have been shooting at *The Grimsi* thirty seconds
ago would not be standing on a flaming deck in the
hope of drilling an old scow full of holes. Nor was there
now any possibility of the hydroplane ramming anything until the fire was out.

"Hit 'em again," he yelled to Pitt through the shattered forward window of the wheelhouse. "Give the bastards a taste of their own medicine."

Pitt didn't answer. He barely had time to throw the flaming can before Sandecker spun the wheel and turned across the hydroplane's bow for a third running attack. Twice more they raced from the fog, and twice more Pitt lobbed his dented cans of searing destruction until his makeshift arsenal was used up.

And then it hit *The Grimsi*, a thunderous shock wave that knocked Pitt to the deck and blew out what glass was left in the windows around Sandecker. The hydroplane had erupted in a volcanic roar of fire and flaming debris, instantly becoming a blazing inferno from end to end.

The echoes had returned from the cliffs on shore and left again when Pitt pushed himself shakily to his feet and stared incredulously at the hydroplane. What had once been a superbly designed boat was now a shambles and burning furiously down to the water's edge. He staggered to the wheelhouse—his sense of balance temporarily crippled by the ringing in his ears from the concussion—as Sandecker slowed *The Grimsi* and drifted past the fiery wreck.

"See any survivors?" Sandecker asked. He had a thin slice on one cheek that trickled blood.

Pitt shook his head. "They've had it," he said callously. "Even if any of the crew made it to the water alive, they'd die of exposure before we could find them in this soup."

Tidi entered the wheelhouse, one hand nursing a purplish bruise on her forehead, her expression one of total bewilderment. "What . . . what happened?" was all she could stammer.

"It wasn't the fuel tanks," Sandecker said. "Of that much I'm certain."

"I agree," Pitt said grimly. "They must have had explosives lying abovedecks that got in the way of my last homemade firebomb."

"Rather careless of them." Sandecker's voice was almost cheerful. "The unexpected move, that's what you said, and you were right. It never occurred to the dumb bastards that cornered mice would fight like tigers."

"At least we evened up the score a bit." Pitt should have felt sick, but his conscience didn't trouble him. Revenge—he and Sandecker had acted out of desire for self-preservation and revenge. They had made a down payment to avenge Hunnewell and the others, but the final accounting was a long way off. Strange, he thought, how easy it was to kill men you didn't know, whose lives you knew nothing about. "Your concern for life, I fear, will be your defeat," Dr. Jonsson had said. "I beg you, my friend, do not hesitate when the moment arrives." Pitt felt a grim satisfaction. The moment had arrived and he hadn't hesitated. He'd had no time even to think about the pain and death he was inflicting. He wondered to himself if this subconscious toleration of killing a total stranger was the factor that made wars acceptable to the human race.

Tidi's hushed voice broke his thoughts. "They're dead; they're all dead." She began to sob, her hands pressed tightly to her face, her body shaking from side to side. "You murdered them, burned them to death in cold blood."

"I beg your pardon, lady," Pitt said coldly. "Open your eyes! Take a good look around you. These holes in the woodwork weren't caused by woodpeckers. To quote from appropriate clichés from every western movie ever made—they drew first, or we had no choice, marshal, it was them or us. You've got the script all wrong, dearheart. We're the good guys. It was their intention to cold-bloodedly murder us."

She looked up into the lean, determined face, saw the green eyes full of understanding, and suddenly she felt ashamed. "You two were warned. I told you to gag me the next time I went hysterical and shot off my mouth."

Pitt met her gaze. "The admiral and I have tolerated you this far. As long as you keep us in coffee, we won't complain to the management."

She reached up and kissed Pitt gently, her face wet with tears and mist. "Two coffees coming up." She brushed her eyes with her fingers.

"And go rinse your face," he said, grinning. "Your eye makeup goo is halfway to your chin."

Obediently she turned and climbed down into the galley. Pitt looked at Sandecker and winked. The admiral nodded back in masculine understanding and turned back to the blazing boat.

The hydroplane was going down by the stern, sinking rapidly. The sea crowded over the gunwales and swamped the flames, hissing in a cloud of steam, and the hydroplane was gone. In seconds, only a swirling welter of oily bubbles, unidentifiable bits of flotsam, and dirty, creaming foam remained to mark the grave. It was as though the boat had been nothing but a nebulous nightmare that vanished with the passing of night.

With an extra effort of willpower, Pitt pulled his mind back to practical reality. "No sense in hanging around. I suggest we head back to Reykjavik as fast as we dare through this fog. The quicker and the farther we high tail it out of this area before the weather clears, the better for all concerned."

Sandecker glanced at his watch. It was now one forty-five. The entire action had barely lasted fifteen minutes. "A hot toddy is looking better all the time," he said. "Stand by the fathometer. When the bottom rises above a hundred feet, we'll at least know we're running too close to shore."

Three hours later and twenty miles southwest of Reykjavik they rounded the tip of the Keflavik peninsula and broke out of the fog. Iceland's seemingly eternal sun greeted them in a dazzling brilliance. A Pan American jet, arising from the runway of the Keflavik International Airport, soared over them, its polished aluminum skin reflecting the solar glare, before making a great circle toward the east and London. Pitt watched it wistfully and idly wished he were at the controls chasing the clouds instead of standing on the deck of a rolling old scow. His thoughts were interrupted by Sandecker.

"I can't begin to tell you how sad I feel about re-

turning Rondheim's boat in such shabby condition." A
sly, devilish smile cut a swath across Sandecker's face.

"Your solicitude is touching," Pitt returned sarcastically.

"What the hell, Rondheim can afford it." Sandecker took a hand off the wheel and waved it around
the shattered wheelhouse. "A little wood putty, a little
paint, new glass and it'll be good as new."

"Rondheim might well laugh away the damage to
The Grimsi, but he won't exactly roll in the aisle laughing when he learns the fate of his hydroplane and
crew."

Sandecker faced Pitt. "How can you possibly con-
nect Rondheim with the hydroplane?"

"The connection is the boat we're standing on."

"You'll have to do better than that," Sandecker
said impatiently.

Pitt sat down on a bench over a life preserver
locker and lit a cigarette. "The best plans of mice and
men. Rondheim planned well, but he overlooked the
thousand-to-one chance that we would swipe his boat.
We wondered why *The Grimsi* was tied to the Fyrie
dock . . . It was there to follow us. Shortly after we
were to cast off and begin cruising the harbor in the
luxury of the cabin cruiser, his crew would have appeared on the dock and eased this nondescript fishing
boat into our wake to keep an eye on us. If we had
acted suspiciously once we were at sea, there'd have
been no way to shake them. The cabin cruiser's top
speed probably stands near twenty knots. We know *The
Grimsi*'s to be closer to forty."

"The expressions on a few faces must have been
priceless," Sandecker said, smiling.

"Panic undoubtedly reigned for a while," Pitt
agreed, "until Rondheim could figure out an alternate
plan. I give him credit, he's a smart bastard. He's been
more suspicious of our actions than we thought. Still, he
wasn't completely sure of what we were up to. The
clincher came when we borrowed the wrong boat quite
by accident. After the shock wore off, he guessed, mis-
takenly, that we were wise to him and took it on pur-

pose to screw him up. But he now knew where we were headed."

"The black jet," Sandecker said positively. "Feed us to the fish after we pinpointed its exact position. That was the idea?"

Pitt shook his head. "I don't think it was his original intention to eliminate us. We had him fooled on the diving equipment. He assumed we would try to find the wreck from the surface and then come back later for the underwater recovery."

"What changed his mind?"

"The lookout on the beach."

"But where did he pop from?"

"Reykjavik by car." Pitt inhaled and held the smoke before letting it out and continuing. "Having us tailed by air was no problem except that eventually losing us in an Icelandic fog bank was a foregone conclusion. He simply ordered one of his men to drive across the Keflavik peninsula and wait for us to show. When we obliged, the lookout followed us along the coast road and stopped when we anchored. Everything looked innocent enough through his binoculars, but like Rondheim, we took too much for granted and overlooked one minor point."

"We couldn't have," Sandecker protested. "Every precaution was considered. Whoever was watching would have needed the Mount Palomar telescope to tell Tidi was masquerading in your clothes."

"True. But if the sun caught them where they broke surface, any Japanese seven by fifty glasses could have picked up my air bubbles."

"Damn!" Sandecker snapped. "They're hardly noticeable close up, but at a distance in a calm sea with the sun just right——" He hesitated.

"The lookout then contacted Rondheim—radiophone in his car, most likely—and told him we were diving on the wreck. Rondheim's back was to the wall now. We had to be stopped before we discovered something vital to his game. He had to lay his hands on a boat capable of matching *The Grimsi*'s speed and then some. Enter the hydroplane."

"And the something vital to his game?" Sandecker probed.

"We know now it wasn't the aircraft or its crew. All trace of identity was erased. That leaves the cargo."

"The models?"

"The models," Pitt repeated. "They represent more than just a hobby. They have a definite purpose."

"And how do you intend to find out what in hell they're good for?"

"Simple." Pitt grinned cunningly. "Rondheim will tell us. We drop them off with the consulate boys on the bait boat and then we sail right up to the Fyrie dock as if nothing happened. Rondheim will be so hungry to know if we've discovered anything. I'm counting on him to make a careless move. Then we'll shove it to him where it hurts most."

Chapter 12

It was four o'clock when they tied up to the Fyrie dock. The ramp was deserted, the dockmaster and the guard obvious by their absence. Pitt and Sandecker weren't fooled. They knew their every move had been studied the second *The Grimsi* rounded the harbor breakwater.

Before he followed Tidi and Sandecker away from the forlorn and battered little boat, Pitt left a note on the helm.

SORRY ABOUT THE MESS. WE WERE ATTACKED BY A SWARM OF RED-NECKED FUZZWORTS. PUT THE REPAIRS ON OUR TAB.

He signed it *Admiral James Sandecker.*

Twenty minutes later they reached the consulate. The young staff members who played such professional roles as bait fishermen beat them by five minutes and had already locked the two models away in the consul's vault. Sandecker thanked them warmly and promised to replace the diving gear Pitt had been forced to jettison with the best that U.S. Divers manufactured.

Pitt then quickly showered and changed clothes and took a taxi to the airport at Keflavik.

His black Volvo cab soon left the smokeless, picturesque city behind its rear bumper and headed onto the narrow asphalt belt that was the coastal road to the Keflavik airport. To his right stretched the Atlantic, at this moment as blue as the Aegean waters of the Grecian Isles. The wind was rising off the sea, and he could see a small fleet of fishing boats running for the harbor, pushed by the relentless swells. His left side took in the green countryside, rolling in an uneven furrowed pattern, dotted by grazing cattle and Iceland's famous long-maned ponies.

As the beauty of the scenery flashed by, Pitt began to think about the Vikings, those dirty, hard-drinking, love-a-fight men who ravaged every civilized shore they set foot on, and who had been romanticized beyond all exaggeration and embellishment in legends handed down through the centuries. They had landed in Iceland, flourished and then disappeared. But the tradition of the Norsemen was not forgotten in Iceland, where the hard, sea-toughened men went out every day in storm or fog to harvest the fish that fed the nation and its economy.

Pitt's thoughts were soon jolted back to reality by the voice of the cab driver as they passed through the gates of the airport.

"Do you wish to go to the main terminal, sir?"

"No, the maintenance hangars."

The driver thought a moment. "Sorry, sir. They are on the edge of the field beyond the passenger terminal. Only authorized cars are permitted on the flight line."

There was something about the cab driver's accent that intrigued Pitt. Then it came to him. There was an unmistakable American midwestern quality about it.

"Let's give it a try, shall we?"

The driver shrugged and pulled the cab up to the flight line gate and stopped where a tall, thin, gray-haired man in a blue uniform stepped from the same austere, white-painted guard shack that seemed to sit by gates everywhere. He touched his fingers to his cap brim in a friendly salute. Pitt rolled down the window, leaned out, and showed his Air Force I.D.

"Major Dirk Pitt," he snapped in an official tone, introducing himself. "I'm on urgent business for the United States government and must get to the commercial maintenance hangar for nonscheduled aircraft."

The guard looked at him blankly until he finished and then, smiling dumbly, shrugged.

The cab driver stepped from behind the steering wheel. "He doesn't understand English, Major. Allow me to translate for you."

Without waiting for an acknowledgment, the driver put an arm around the guard and gently walked him away from the car toward the gate, talking rapidly but gesturing gracefully as he rattled off a flow of words in Icelandic. It was the first chance that Pitt had a good look at his helpmate.

The driver was medium height, just under six foot, not more than twenty-six or twenty-seven years old, with straw-colored hair and the light skin that usually goes with it. If Pitt had passed him on the street, he would have pegged him as a junior assistant executive, three years out of university, eager to make his mark in his father-in-law's bank.

Finally the two men broke out laughing and shook hands. Then the driver climbed back behind the wheel and winked at Pitt as the still smiling guard opened the gate and waved them through.

Pitt said, "You seem to have a way with security guards."

"A necessity of the trade. A cab driver wouldn't be worth his salt if he couldn't talk his way past a gate guard or a policeman on a barricaded street."

"It's apparent you've mastered the knack."

"I work at it . . . Any particular hangar, sir? There are several, one for every major airline."

"General maintenance—the one that handles transient nonscheduled aircraft."

The glare of the sun bounced off the white cement taxiway and made Pitt squint. He slipped a pair of sunglasses from a breast pocket and put them on. Several huge jetliners were parked in even rows, displaying the emblems and color schemes of TWA, Pan American,

SAS, Icelandic, and BOAC, while crews of white-coveralled mechanics buried themselves under engine cowlings and crawled over the wings with fuel hoses. On the other side of the field, a good two miles away, Pitt could make out aircraft of the U.S. Air Force, undoubtedly going through the same rituals.

"Here we are," the driver announced. "Permit me to offer you my services as a translator."

"That won't be necessary. Keep the meter running. I'll only be a few minutes."

Pitt got out and walked through the side door of the hangar, a sterile giant of a building that covered nearly two acres. Five small private planes were scattered around the floor like a handful of spectators in an otherwise empty auditorium. But it was the sixth that caught Pitt's eye. It was an old Ford Tri-motor known as the Tin Goose. The corrugated aluminum skin that covered the framework and the three motors, one perched on the nose directly in front of the cockpit, the other two suspended in space by an ungainly network of wires and struts, combined to make it look to the unknowing eye a thing too awkward to fly with any degree of control or, for that matter, lift its wheels from the ground. But the old pioneering pilots swore by it. To them it was a flying son of a bitch. Pitt patted the ancient washboard sides, idly wished he could test-fly it someday, and then walked on toward the offices in the rear of the hangar.

He opened a door and moved into what appeared to be a combination locker room and rest area, wrinkling his nose from the pungent, heavy smell of sweat, cigarette smoke and coffee. Except for the coffee, the aroma bore a marked resemblance to a high school gym. He stood there a moment looking at a group of five men clustered around a large European-style ceramic coffee urn, laughing good-naturedly at a recently told joke. They were all dressed in white coveralls, some spotlessly clean, others decorated with heavy splotches of black oil. Pitt sauntered easily toward them, smiling.

"Pardon me, gentlemen, any of you speak English?"

A shaggy, long-haired mechanic sitting nearest the urn looked up and drawled, "Yeah, I speak American if that'll do."

"That will do fine," Pitt laughed. "I'm looking for a man with the initials S.C. He's probably a hydraulic specialist."

The mechanic eyed him uneasily. "Who wants to know?"

Pitt forced a friendly smile and pulled out his I.D. again.

"Pitt, Major Dirk Pitt."

For a full five seconds the mechanic sat immobile, expressionless except for the stunned widening of his eyes. Then he threw his hands in the air helplessly and then let them fall limply to his sides.

"Ya, got your man, Major. Ah knew it were too good to last." The voice reached from somewhere deep in Oklahoma.

It was Pitt's turn to become expressionless. "Like what's too good to last?"

"Mah moonlightin' activites," he drawled morosely. "Workin' as a hydraulic specialist for civilian airlines during mah off-duty hours." He stared forlornly into his coffee cup. "Ah knew it was against U.S. Air Force regulations, but the money was too good to pass up. Ah guess ah can kiss mah stripes good-by."

Pitt looked at him. "I know of no Air Force regulations that prevent an enlisted man or an officer, for that matter, from picking up a few dollars when he isn't on duty."

"Nuthin' wrong with Air Force rules, Major. It's Keflavik Base policy set by Colonel Nagel, the C.O. on our side of the field. He feels we should work on squadron aircraft durin' our time off instead of helpin' out the feather merchants. Tryin' to make a name for himself with the Pentagon brass, ah guess. But ya wouldn't be here if you didn't know all that."

"That'll do," Pitt said sharply. His gaze swung and

held on the other four men, measuring them until it drifted back to the Air Force mechanic. Then his eyes grew suddenly cold. "When you talk to a superior officer, Airman, you stand up."

"Ah don't have to kiss your ass, Major. You ain't got no uniform on—"

Two seconds was all it took. With a nonchalant ease Pitt bent over, clasped the front two legs of the mechanic's chair and flipped him over on his back and put his foot over the man's throat in one deceptive movement. The other maintenance men stood there in stunned immobility for a few seconds. Then their senses returned and they began to circle Pitt menacingly.

"Call off your flunkies or I break your neck," Pitt said, grinning pleasantly into the fear-widened eyes.

The mechanic, unable to talk with the heel of Pitt's shoe pushing against his windpipe, gestured wildly with both hands. The men stopped and moved back a step, retreating not so much from their friend's muted pleas as from the ice-cold grin on Pitt's face.

"That's a good group," Pitt said. He turned and looked down at the helpless mechanic and lifted his foot just enough to allow his prisoner to speak. "Now, then, name, rank, and serial number. Let's have it!"

"Sam . . . Sam Cashman," he choked. "Sergeant. Air Force 19385628."

"That wasn't so bad, now was it, Sam?" Pitt bent and helped Cashman to his feet.

"Ah'm sorry, sir. Ah figured that as long as ya were gonna court-martial me anyway—"

"You're lousy at figuring," Pitt interruped. "Next time keep your mouth shut. You admitted guilt when you didn't have to."

"Are ya still gonna bust me?"

"To begin with, I don't give a rat's ass whether you moonlight or not. Since I'm not stationed at Keflavik Air Force Base, I could care less about the policies—chicken shit as they are—of your Colonel Nagel. Therefore, I won't be the one to bust you. All I want is the answers to a few simple questions." Pitt stared Cashman in the eye and smiled warmly. "Now how about it? Will you help me?"

The expression on Cashman's face displayed genuine awe. "Christ Almighty, what ah wouldn't give to serve under an office like you." He extended his hand. "Ask away, Major."

Pitt returned Cashman's grip. "First question: do you usually scratch your initials in the equipment you repair?"

"Yeah, it's kind of a trademark, ya might say. Ah do good work an ah'm proud of it. Serves a purpose too. If ah work on the hydraulic system of an aircraft and it comes back with a malfunction, ah know the trouble lays where ah didn't work. It saves a lot of time."

"Have you ever repaired the nose gear of a twelve-passenger British jet?"

Cashman thought for a moment. "Yeah, about a month ago. One of those new executive twin turbine Loreleis—a hell of a machine."

"Was it painted black?"

"Ah couldn't see paint markin's. It was dark, about one-thirty in the mornin' when ah got the call." He shook his head. "Wasn't black, though. Ah'm positive."

"Any distinguishing features or anything unusual about the repair that you can recall?"

Cashman laughed. "The only distinguishin' features were the two weirdos who were flyin' it." He held up a cup, offering Pitt some coffee. Pitt shook his head. "Waal, these guys were in a terrible hurry. Kept standin' around tryin' to push me. Pissed me off plenty. Seems they made a rough landin' somewhere and busted a seal in the shock cylinder. They were damned lucky that ah found a spare over at the BOAC hangars."

"Did you get a look inside?"

"Hell no, you'd have thought they had the President on board the way they guarded the loadin' door."

"Any idea where they came from or where they were headed?"

"No way, they were tight-lipped bastards. Talked about nothin' but the repair. Must have been on a local flight though. They didn't refuel. You ain't flyin' far in a Lorelei—not from Iceland anyhow—without full tanks."

"The pilot must have signed a maintenance order."

"Nope. He refused. Said he was behind schedule and would catch me next time. Paid me though. Twice what the job was worth." Cashman was silent for a moment. He tried to read something in the man standing before him, but Pitt's face was as impenetrable as a granite statue. "What's behind these questions, Major? Mind lettin' me in on your secret?"

"No secret," Pitt said slowly. "A Lorelei crashed a couple of days ago and nothing except a portion of the nose gear was left to identify. I'm trying to trace it, that's all."

"Wasn't it reported as missin'?"

"I wouldn't be here if it was."

"Ah knew there was something fishy about them guys. That's why ah went ahead and filled out a maintenance report."

Pitt leaned over, his eyes boring into Cashman's. "What good was a report if you couldn't identify the aircraft?"

A shrewd smile split Cashman's lips. "Ah may be a country boy, but mah momma didn't drop me outta her bottom this mornin'." He stood up and tilted his head toward a side door. "Major, ah'm gonna make your day."

He led Pitt into a small dingy office furnished with only a battered desk that was decorated with at least fifty cigarette burn marks, two equally battered chairs and a huge metal filing cabinet. Cashman walked straight to the cabinet and pulled out a drawer, rummaged for a moment, found what he was looking for and handed Pitt a folder soiled with greasy fingerprints.

"Ah wasn't kiddin' ya, Major, when ah said it was too dark to make out any paint markin's. Near as ah could tell, the plane had never been touch by a brush or spray gun. The aluminum skin was as shiny as the day it left the factory."

Pitt opened the folder and scanned the maintenance report. Cashman's handwriting left much to be desired, but there was no mistaking the notation under AIRCRAFT IDENTIFICATION: Lorelei Mark VIII-B1608.

"How did you get it?" Pitt asked.

"Compliments of a limey inspector at the Lorelei factory," Cashman answered, sitting on a corner of the desk. "After replacin' the seal on the nose gear, ah took a flashlight and checked out the main landin' gear for damage or leakage, and there it was, stuck away under the right strut as pretty as you please. A green tag sayin' that this here aircraft's landin' gear had been examined and okayed by master inspector Clarence Devonshire of Lorelei Aircraft Limited. The plane's serial number was typed on the tag."

Pitt threw the folder on the desk. "Sergeant Cashman!" he snapped.

Stunned at the brusque tone, Cashman jumped erect. "Sir?"

"Your squadron!"

"Eighty-seventh Air Transport Squadron, sir."

"Good enough." Pitt's cold expression slowly worked into a huge grin and he slapped Cashman on the shoulder. "You're absolutely right, Sam. You truly made my day."

"Wish ah could say the same," Cashman sighed, visibly relieved, "but that's twice in the last ten minutes ya scared the crap outta me. Why'd ya want mah squadron?"

"So I'd know where to send a case of Jack Daniel's. I take it you enjoy good whiskey?"

A look of wonder suddenly came over Cashman's face. "By gawd, Major, you're sumthin' else. Ya know that?"

"I try." Already Pitt was plotting how to explain a case of expensive whiskey on his expense account. What the hell, screw Sandecker, he thought; the tab was worth the consequences. Screw, the word bounded out of his mind and caused him to remember something. He reached inside his pocket.

"By the way, have you ever seen this before?" He handed Cashman the screwdriver he'd found on the black Lorelei.

"Waal, waal, fancy that. Believe it or not, Major, this here screwtwister is mine. Bought it through the catalog of a tool specialty house in Chicago. It's the only one of its kind on the island. Where'd you come across it?"

"In the wreck."

"So that's where it went," he said angrily. "Those dirty bastards stole it. Ah should a known they were up to sumthin' illegal. Ya just tell me when their trial is, and ah'll be happier than a rejected hog at a packin' plant to testify against them."

"Save your leave time for a worthwhile escapade. Your friends won't be showing for a trial. They bought the farm."

"Killed in the wreck?" It was more statement than question.

Pitt nodded.

"Ah suppose ah could go on about crime not payin', but why bother. If they had it comin', they had it comin'. That's all there is to it."

"As a philosopher, you make a great hydraulic specialist, Sam." Pitt shook Cashman's hand once more. "Good-by and thank you. I'm grateful for your help."

"Glad to do it, Major. Here, keep the screwdriver for a souvenir. Already ordered a new one, so won't be needin' it."

"Thanks again." Pitt shoved the screwdriver back in his pocket, turned and left the office.

Pitt relaxed in the cab and stuck a cigarette between his lips without lighting the end. Obtaining the mysterious black jet's serial number had been a shot in the dark that paid off in spades. He really hadn't expected to find out anything. Staring through the window at the passing green pastures, he saw nothing with his eyes, idly wondering if the plane could now be tied directly to Rondheim. His mind was still wandering over the possibility when he had the vague impression that the countryside looked different than before. The fields were empty of cattle and ponies, the rolling hills flattened into a vast carpet of uneven tundra. He swung around and gazed out the other window; the sea was not where it should have been; instead, it lay to the rear of the cab, slowly disappearing over a long, low rise in the road. He leaned over the front seat.

"Do you have a date with the farmer's daughter or are you taking the scenic route to run up the meter?"

The driver applied pressure to the brake and slowed the cab, stopping at the side of the road. "Privacy is the word, Major. Merely a slight detour so we can have a little chat—"

The driver's voice froze into nothingness, and for good reason. Pitt had jammed the tip of the screwdriver half an inch into the cavity of his ear.

"Keep your hands on the wheel and get this hack back on the road to Reykjavik," Pitt said quietly, "or your right ear will get screwed into your left."

Pitt watched the driver's face closely in the rearview mirror, studying the blue eyes, knowing they would signal any sudden attempt at resistance. No shadow of an expression touched the boyish features, not even a flicker of fear. Then slowly, very slowly, the face in the mirror began to smile, the smile transforming into a genuine laugh.

"Major Pitt, you are a very suspicious man."

"If you had three attempts on your life in the last three days, you'd develop a suspicious nature too."

The laugh stopped abruptly and the bush brows bunched together. "Three attempts? I'm aware of only two—"

Pitt cut him off by pushing the screwdriver another eighth of an inch deeper into his ear. "You're a lucky man, friend. I could try and make you contribute a few choice items about your boss and his operation, but Russian KGB-style interrogation is way out of my line. Instead of Reykjavik, suppose you drive nice and easy back to Keflavik, only this time to the United States Air

Force side of the field where you can join a couple of your buddies and play charades with National Intelligence agents. You'll like them; they're experts at taking a wallflower and turning him into a babbling life of the party."

"That might prove embarrassing."

"That's your problem."

The smile was back in the rear-view mirror. "Not entirely, Major. It would, indeed, be a moment worth remembering to see your face when you discover you brought in a N.I.A. agent for questioning."

Pitt's pressure on the screwdriver didn't relax. "Very second-rate," he said. "I'd expect a better story from a high school freshman caught smoking pot in the boy's room."

"Admiral Sandecker said you wouldn't be an easy man to talk to."

The door was open now and Pitt had the opportunity to slam it. "When did you talk to the admiral?"

"In his office at NUMA headquarters, ten minutes after Commander Koski radioed that you and Dr. Hunnewell had landed safely, aboard the *Catawaba*, to be precise."

The door stayed open. The driver's answer tallied with what Pitt knew: the N.I.A. had not contacted Sandecker since he had arrived in Iceland. Pitt glanced around the car. There was no sign of life, no sign of an ambush by possible accomplices. He started to relax, caught himself, and then clenched the screwdriver until his fingers ached.

"Okay, be my guest," Pitt said casually. "But I strongly urge you to make your pitch without so much as a tic."

"No sweat, Major. Just put your mind at ease and lift my cap."

"Lift your cap?" Pitt repeated blankly. He hesitated a moment, then slowly, using his free left hand, removed the driver's cap.

"Inside, taped to the underside of the top." The driver's voice was soft, yet commanding. "There is a twenty-five caliber Colt derringer. Take it and get that damned screwdriver out of my ear."

Still using one hand, Pitt opened the breech of the derringer, rubbed his thumb over the primers of the two tiny cartridges to make sure the chambers were loaded, and then reclosed the breech and cocked the hammer. "So far, so good. Now ease out of the car and keep your hands where I can see them." He loosened his grip on the screwdriver and withdrew it from the driver's ear cavity.

The driver slid from behind the wheel, walked to the front of the car and propped himself lazily against a fender. He lifted his right hand and massaged his ear, wincing. "A clever tactic, Major. It didn't come out of any book I know."

"You should read more," Pitt said. "Ramming an icepick through the eardrum into the brain of an unsuspecting victim is an old trick used by paid killers in gang wars long before either you or I were born."

"A rather painful lesson I'm not likely to forget."

Pitt got out and pushed the front door of the car open to its stop and stood behind the interior panel, using it for a shield, the gun in his hand trained on the driver's heart. "You said you talked to Admiral Sandecker in Washington. Describe him. Size, hair, mannerisms, layout of his office—everything."

The driver needed no further coaxing. He talked for several minutes and ended up by mentioning a few of Sandecker's pet slang terms.

"Your memory is good—nearly letter-perfect."

"I have a photographic memory, Major. My description of Admiral Sandecker could have easily come from a file. Take a rundown of yourself for example: Major Dirk Eric Pitt. Born exactly thirty-two years, four months and twelve days ago at the Hoag Hospital in Newport Beach, California. Mother's name Barbara, father George Pitt, senior United States Senator from your home state." The driver droned on as if he might have been repeating a memorized spiel, as indeed he was. "No sense in going on about your three rows of combat ribbons which you never wear or your formidable reputation as a lady's man. If you like, I can give you a detailed hour-by-hour account of your actions since your left Washington."

Pitt waved the gun. "That will do. I'm impressed, of course, Mr.—ah—"

"Lillie. Jerome P. Lillie the Fourth. I'm your contact."

"Jerome P.—" Pitt made a good try but couldn't suppress an incredulous laugh. "You've got to be kidding."

Lillie gestured helplessly. "Laugh if you will, Major, but the Lillie name has been highly esteemed in St. Louis for nearly a hundred years."

Pitt thought for a moment. Then it came to him. "Lillie Beer. Of course, that's it. Lillie Beer. What's the slogan? *Brewed for the gourmet's table.*"

"Proof that it pays to advertise," Lille said. "I take it you're another one of our satisfied customers?"

"No, I prefer Budweiser."

"I can see you're going to be a hard man to get along with," Lillie moaned.

"Not really." Pitt released the derringer's hammer and threw the tiny gun to Lillie. "Be my guest. You couldn't possibly be one of the bad guys and come up with a story that wild."

Lillie fielded the gun. "Your trust is warranted, Major. I told you the truth."

"You're a long way from the brewery, or is that another story?"

"Very dull and very time-consuming. Some other time, perhaps, I'll pour out my biography over a glass of Dad's product." He calmly retaped the gun to the inside of his cap as if it was an everyday occurrence. "Now then, you mentioned a third attempt on your life."

"You offered to give me a detailed, hour-by-hour account of my actions since I left Washington. You tell me."

"Nobody's perfect, Major. I lost you for two hours today."

Pitt did some fast mental arithmetic. "Where were you around noon?"

"On the southern shore of the island."

"Doing what?"

Lillie turned away and looked across the barren fields, his face empty of all expression. "At exactly ten minutes after twelve this afternoon I was pushing a knife into another man's throat."

"Then there were two of you keeping an eye on *The Grimsi?*"

"*The Grimsi?* Ah, of course—the name of your old boat. Yes, I stumbled into the other guy quite by accident. After you and the admiral and Miss Royal took off toward the southeast, I had a hunch your anchor would drop in the area where you and Dr. Hunnewell crashed. I drove across the peninsula and arrived too late—that damned old scow was faster than I thought—you were already sketching up a storm while Admiral Sandecker was playing the role of Izaak Walton. The very picture of your contentment had me fooled completely."

"But not your competitor. His binoculars were stronger."

Lillie shook his head. "A telescope. One hundred and seventy-five power, mounted on a tripod, no less."

"Then the glint I saw from the boat was from the reflecting mirror."

"If the sun caught it right, a visible flash would be the obvious giveaway."

Pitt was silent for a moment as he lit a cigarette. The click of the lighter seemed strangely loud in the open of the barren landscape. He exhaled and looked at Lillie.

"You say you knifed him?"

"Yes, it was unfortunate, but he left me no choice." Lillie leaned over the hood of the Volvo and rubbed a palm over his forehead, seemingly ill at ease with his inner self. "He—I don't know his name, as there was no identification—was bent over the telescope talking into a portable transmitter when I crept around an outcropping of rock and literally bumped into him. His attention and mine had been focused on your boat. He didn't expect me, and I didn't expect him. To his final regret, he acted first and without fore-thought. Pulled a switchblade knife from a sleeve—rather old-fashioned, really—and leaped." Lillie made a helpless shrug. "The poor guy tried to stab instead of slash—the sure sign of an amateur. I should have taken him alive for questioning, but I got carried away during the heat of the moment and turned his knife against him."

"Too bad you didn't get to him five minutes sooner," Pitt said.

"Why is that?"

"He'd already radioed our position so his buddies could close in for the kill."

Lillie stared at Pitt questioningly.

"For what purpose? Merely to steal a few sketches or a bucket of fish?"

"Something much more important. A jet aircraft."

"I know. Your mysterious black jet. The thought had occurred that you might go looking for it when I guessed your destination, but your report failed to pin-point the exact—"

Pitt interrupted, his voice deceptively friendly. "I know for certain that Admiral Sandecker has had no contact with you or your agency since he left Washing-ton. He and I are the only ones who know what's in that report . . ." Pitt paused, suddenly remembering. "Ex-cept—"

"Except the secretary at the consulate who typed it," Lillie finished, smiling. "My compliments, your commentary was well written." Lillie didn't bother to explain how the consulate secretary passed him a copy and Pitt didn't bother to ask him. "Tell me, Major, how do you go about dredging for a sunken aircraft with nothing but a sketch pad and a fishing pole?"

"Your victim knew the answer. He detected my air bubbles through his telescope."

Lillie's eyes narrowed. "You had diving equip-ment?" he asked flatly. "How? I watched you leave the dock and saw nothing. I studied you and the admiral from the shore and neither of you left the deck for more than three minutes. After that I lost visibility when the fog rolled in."

"The N.I.A. doesn't have a monopoly on sneaky, underhanded plots," Pitt said, shooting Lillie down in flames. "Let's sit in the car and make ourselves comfortable and I'll tell you about another ordinary garden variety day in the life of Dirk Pitt."

So Pitt slouched in the rear seat with his feet propped on the backrest of the front and told Lillie what had happened from the time *The Grimsi* left the Fyrie dock until it had returned. He told what he knew for certain and what he didn't, everything, that is, except for one little indefinable thought that kept itching in his mind—a thought that concerned Kirsti Fyrie.

Chapter
13

"So you've selected Oskar Rondheim as your villain," Lillie murmured. "You haven't convinced me with any solid proof."

"I agree, it's all circumstantial," Pitt said. "Rondheim has the most to gain. Therefore, Rondheim has the motive. He murdered to get his hands on the undersea probe and he's murdered to cover his tracks."

"You'll have to do better than that."

Pitt looked at Lillie. "Okay, come up with a better one."

"As an agent in good standing with the N.I.A., I'm embarrassed to admit that I'm a bit confused."

"*You're* confused." Pitt shook his head in mock sadness. "I can't say I find it too comforting knowing our nation's security rests in your hands."

Lillie smiled faintly. "It is you who has provided the confusion, Major. It is you who has broken the chain."

"What chain?" Pitt said. "Or am I supposed to guess?"

Lillie hesitated a moment before answering. Finally he looked directly at Pitt.

"During the last eighteen months a chain of strange circumstances has been forged link by link, country by country, from the southernmost tip of Chile to the northern border of Guatemala. Secretly, through a complex series of clandestine maneuvers, the great mining companies of South America have slowly merged into one giant syndicate. Outwardly it's business as usual, but behind the locked and barred doors of their respective administrations, the policies governing their operations come directly from a single unknown voice."

Pitt shook his head. "Not possible. I can name at least five countries that have nationalized their mining cartels. There's no way they could tie in with a private company beyond their borders."

"None the less, it's a documented fact. Where the mines have been nationalized, the management is controlled by an outside organization. The Parnagus-Janios high-grade iron ore pits of Brazil, the Domingo bauxite mines of the Dominican Republic, the government silver mines of Honduras, they all take their directives from the same person or persons."

"How did you gather your information?"

"We have many sources," Lillie said. "Some within the mining companies themselves. Unfortunately, our contacts have not infiltrated top-level management."

Pitt mashed his cigarette into an ashtray recessed within the car door. "Nothing mysterious about someone attempting to gain a monopoly. If they have the guts to pull it off, more power to them."

"A monopoly is bad enough," Lillie said. "The names of the men we've been able to uncover, who are high on the totem pole, include twelve of the wealthiest men in the Western World—all possessing vast financial powers in mineral exploitation. And each with tentacles so long that they reach out and control over two hundred industrial corporations." Lillie paused, staring at Pitt. "Once they gain a monopoly they can force the prices of copper, aluminum, zinc and several other commercial ores halfway to the moon. The resulting inflation would devastate the economies of at least thirty na-

tions. The United States, of course, being one of the
first to go to its knees."

"It doesn't necessarily follow," Pitt said. "If that
happens, they and their financial empires would be
sucked down too."

Lillie smiled and nodded. "That's the catch. These
men, F. James Kelly of the U.S., Sir Eric Marks of
Great Britain, Roger Dupuy of France, Hans Von
Hummel of Germany, Iban Mahani of Iran, and others—each worth close to ten figures—are all loyal to
their respective countries. Any one of them might chisel
and cheat on taxes, but none of them would willingly
send his government over the brink of economic disaster."

"Then where's the profit motive?"

"We don't know."

"And Rondheim's connection?"

"None, except his relationship with Kirsti Fyrie
and her offshore mining interests."

There was a long silence; then Pitt said slowly,
"The burning question, then, is where do you fit in?
What does the takeover of Latin American mining syndicates have to do with Iceland? The N.I.A. didn't send
you up here to play cab driver just to learn the local
highway system. While your brother agents are lurking
behind potted plants watching Kelly, Marks, Dupuy and
the others, your assignment is to keep an eye on another
member of the money boys' group. Shall I mention the
name or would you like it written on paper and sealed
in an envelope by Price Waterhouse?"

Lillie stared at him for a moment, considering.
"You're shooting in the dark."

"Am I?" Pitt was homing in now. "Okay, let's
drag out the suspense and digress for a moment. Admiral Sandecker said he checked every port authority between Buenos Aires and Goose Bay and found twelve
that recorded the entry and departure of an Icelandic
fishing trawler matching the remodeled *Lax*. What he
should have said was that he *had* them checked. Someone else did the actual work for him and that someone
was the N.I.A."

"Nothing out of the ordinary in that," Lillie said flatly. "Records are sometimes easier for us to obtain than a government agency concerned with marine life."

"Except you already had the information before Sandecker requested it."

Lillie said nothing. He didn't have to. His grim expression was all the motivation Pitt needed to continue.

"One evening a couple of months ago, I ran into an Army communications officer in a bar. It was a slow night and neither of us felt like partying or chasing girls, so we just sat around and drank together until closing time. He had just finished a tour of duty at the Smytheford radio-communications station on Hudson Bay, Canada—a complex of two hundred radio masts forming a huge dish on a thousand-acre site. Don't ask me what his name and rank were so you can turn him in for divulging military secrets. I've forgotten them anyway."

Pitt hesitated a moment to shift his feet to a more comfortable position before he went on.

"He was proud of the installation, especially so since he was one of the engineers who helped design and construct it. The sophisticated equipment, he said, was capable of electronically monitoring every radio transmission north of New York, London and Moscow. After the installation was completed, he and his crew of Army engineers were politely ordered to leave for duty elsewhere. It's only guesswork on his part, of course, but he was certain that it's currently being operated by the National Intelligence Agency which specializes in undercover eavesdropping on behalf of the Department of Defense and the Central Intelligence Agency. A rather interesting assumption when you consider that Symtheford is advertised as a satellite tracking station."

Lillie leaned forward. "Just where is all this leading to?"

"To two gentlemen named Matajic and O'Riley. Both deceased."

"You think I knew them?" Lillie asked curiously.

"Only by name. I see little reason to explain who they were. You already know. Your people at Smytheford monitored Matajic's message to Sandecker identi-

fying the long-lost *Lax*. It must have meant little to your
intelligence analysts at the time, but their electronic ears
undoubtedly pricked up when they received the pilot's
last message seconds before the black jet blasted all
three men into the sea. At this point, the plot thickens.
Admiral Sandecker played it cagy and handed the Coast
Guard a phony story about missing equipment, request-
ing air-sea search in the area NUMA's plane disappeared. Nothing was found . . . or at least nothing
was reported. The Coast Guard struck out, but the
N.I.A. didn't—they had the *Lax* and its mysterious
crew pinpointed right from the start. Every time the
ship radioed its home base in Iceland, the Smytheford
computers plotted its exact position. Now the experts at
your headquarters in Washington began to smell a connection between the lost undersea probe and the mining
operations takeover in South America, so they back-
tracked and traced the ship's movements up and down
the Atlantic Coast. When Sandecker asked for the same
information, they discreetly waited a few days and then,
fighting to keep a straight face, handed him a previously prepared copy."

"Do you honestly expect me to admit to any of
this?"

"I don't much give a damn what you admit to,"
Pitt said wearily. "I'm merely pointing out a few facts of
life. Put them all together and they spell the name of
the man you have under surveillance here in Iceland."

"How do you know it isn't a woman?" Lillie
probed.

"Because you've reached the same conclusions I
have—Kirsti Fyrie may control Fyrie Limited, but Oskar Rondheim controls Kirsti Fyrie."

"So we're back to Rondheim."

"Did we really ever leave him?"

"Clever, clever deduction, Major Pitt," Lillie murmured.

"Care to fill in any gaps?"

"Until I receive orders to the contrary, I can't
fully brief an outsider on all the details of our operation." Lillie's voice carried an official tone that didn't

quite come off. "I can, however, acknowledge your conclusions. You are quite correct in everything you've said. Yes, the N.I.A. picked up Matajic's message. Yes, we tracked the *Lax.* Yes, we feel Rondheim is in some way connected with the mining syndicate. Beyond that there is little I can officially tell you that you don't already know."

"Since we've become such close friends," Pitt said, grinning, "why don't you call me Dirk?"

Lillie was gracious in defeat. "Have it your way. But don't you dare call me Jerome—it's Jerry." He held out his hand. "Okay, partner. Don't make me sorry I took you into the firm."

Pitt returned the grip. "Stick with the kid here and you'll go places."

"That's what I'm afraid of." Lillie sighed and gazed over the barren countryside for a moment as if weighing the turn of events. Finally he broke his thoughts and looked at his watch. "We'd better head back to Reykjavik. No thanks to you, I've got a busy night ahead of me."

"What's on your agenda?"

"First, I want to contact headquarters as soon as possible and pass on the serial number of the black jet. With a bit of luck they should be able to run a make and have the owner's name back to us by morning. For your sake, after all the trouble you went to, I hope it provides an important lead. Second, I'm going to poke around and see where that hydroplane was moored. Somebody has got to know something. You can't keep a craft like that a secret on an island this small. And third, the two scaled replicas of South American capitol buildings. I'm afraid you threw us a weird twist when you fished them from the briny deep. They must have a functional purpose. They may be vital to whoever built them, or they may not. Just to play safe, I'd better request Washington to fly in an expert on miniatures and have every square inch of those models thoroughly examined."

"Efficient, industrious, professional. Keep it up. I may slowly become impressed."

"I'll try to do my best," Lillie said sarcastically.

"Would you like an extra hand?" Pitt asked. "I'm free for the evening."

Lillie smiled a smile that made Pitt feel a twinge of uneasiness. "Your plans are already made, Dirk. I wish I could trade places with you, but duty calls."

"I'm afraid to ask what's on your nasty little mind," Pitt said dryly.

"A party, you lucky dog. You're going to a poetry reading party."

"You've got to be kidding."

"No, I'm serious. By special invitation from Oskar Rondheim himself. Though I suspect it was Miss Fyrie's idea."

Pitt's eyebrows came together over his penetrating green eyes. "How do you know this? How *could* you know this? No invitation arrived before you picked me up at the consulate."

"A trade secret. We *do* manage to pull a rabbit out of the hat occasionally."

"Okay, I'll concede a point and stick a gold star on your chart for the day." It was beginning to get chilly so Pitt rolled up his window. "A poetry reading," he said disgustedly. "God, that ought to be a winner."

Chapter
14

It is debated among Icelanders whether the great house, sprawling over the crest of the highest hill above Reykjavik, is even more elegant than the President's mansion at Bessastadir. This could be argued until both structures crumbled to dust, mostly because there is no real case for comparison. The President of Iceland's residence is a model of classic simplicity, while Oskar Rondheim's modern edifice looked as if it had been spawned by the unleashed imagination of Frank Lloyd Wright.

The entire block in front of the ornate grille doors was lined with limousines representing every expensive auto manufacturer of every country: Rolls-Royce, Lincoln, Mercedes-Benz, Cadillac. Even a Russian-built Zis stood temporarily in the circular driveway, unloading its cargo of formally dressed passengers.

Beyond the entryway, eighty to ninety guests drifted in and out of the main salon and the terrace, conversing in a spectrum of different languages. The sun, which had been hidden off and on by a stray cloud, shone brightly through the windows even though it was just past nine o'clock in the evening. At the far end of the great salon, Kirsti Fyrie and Oskar Rondheim anchored the receiving line under a massive crest bearing the red albatross and greeted each arriving guest.

Kirsti was radiantly beautiful, gowned in white silk with gold trim, her blond hair elegantly wound Grecian style. Rondheim, tall and hawklike, towered beside her, his thin lips cracking in a smile only when politeness required. He was just greeting the Russian guests and smartly steering them toward a long table set with even rows of caviar and salmon and embellished by a huge silver punch bowl, when his eyes widened a fraction and the forced smile froze. Kirsti stiffened suddenly as the murmur of the guests died to a strange stillness.

Pitt swept into the room with all the flourish of a matinee idol whose grandiose entrances were his stock-in-trade. At the head of the stairway he stopped and took the handle of a lorgnette, hanging around his neck by a small gold chain, and held the tiny single lens up to his right eye and surveyed the startled audience who unabashedly stared back at him.

No one could really blame them, even an authority on etiquette. Pitt's outfit looked like a cross between a Louis XI court costume and God knew what. The red jacket sported ruffles on the collar and sleeves while a pair of brocaded yellow breeches tapered and disappeared into the red suede boots. Around his waist he wore a brown silk sash, whose tasseled end hung to within inches of his knees. If Pitt had been searching for an eye-shattering effect, he achieved his purpose with honors. After building the scene to its peak, he daintily walked down the stairway and approached Kirsti and Rondheim.

"Good evening, Miss Fyrie . . . Mr. Rondheim. How good of you to invite me. Poetry readings are absolutely my favorite soirees. I wouldn't miss one for all the lace in China."

She gazed at Pitt, fascinated, her lips parted. She said huskily: "Oskar and I are happy you could come."

"Yes, it's good to see you again, Major——" The words stuck in Rondheim's throat as he forgot and grasped Pitt's dead-fish handshake.

Kirsti, as if sensing an embarrassing situation in the

making, quickly asked, "You're not wearing your uniform tonight?"

Pitt casually swung the lorgnette around on its chain. "Heavens no. Uniforms are so drab, don't you think? I thought it would be amusing if I came in mufti this evening so no one would recognize me." He laughed loudly at his own left-handed joke, turning every head within hearing distance.

To Pitt's extreme pleasure, Rondheim visibly forced himself to smile courteously. "We had hoped Admiral Sandecker and Miss Royal might also attend."

"Miss Royal will be along shortly," Pitt said, staring across the room through his eyeglass. "But I'm afraid the admiral isn't feeling well. He decided to retire early. Poor fellow, I can't blame him after what happened this afternoon."

"Nothing serious, I hope." Rondheim's voice betrayed a lack of concern for Sandecker's health that was as obvious as his sudden interest in the reason behind the admiral's incapacity.

"Fortunately, no. The admiral only suffered a few cuts and bruises."

"An accident?" Kirsti asked.

"Dreadful, simply dreadful," Pitt said dramatically. "After you were so kind to offer us the loan of a boat, we cruised to the south side of the island where I sketched the coastline while the admiral fished. About one o'clock we found ourselves enveloped by a nasty fog. Just as we were about to return to Reykjavik, a horrible explosion occurred somewhere in the mist. The blast blew out the windows in the wheelhouse, causing a few small cuts about the admiral's head."

"An explosion?" Rondheim's voice was low and hoarse. "Do you have any idea as to the cause?"

"Afraid I haven't," Pitt said. "Couldn't see a thing. We investigated, of course, but with visibility no more than twenty feet, we found nothing."

Rondheim's face was expressionless. "Very strange. You are sure you saw nothing, Major?"

"Absolutely," Pitt said. "You're probably thinking along the same lines as Admiral Sandecker. A ship might have hit an old World War Two mine or possibly a fire broke out and touched off its fuel tanks. We notified the local coastal patrol. They have nothing to do now but wait and see what vessel is reported as missing. All in all a terrifying experience—" Pitt broke off as Tidi approached. "Ah, Tidi, here you are."

Rondheim turned on the smile again. "Miss Royal." He bowed and kissed her hand. "Major Pitt has been telling us of your harrowing experience this afternoon."

The bastard, Pitt thought. He can't wait to pump answers out of her. Tidi looked cute and frisky in a blue full-length dress, her fawn hair falling straight and natural down her back. Pitt hung his arm loosely around her waist, letting the hand slip down out of sight, and pinched her soft bottom. He smiled as he looked down into those wide brown eyes—eyes that possessed a wise, knowing quality.

"I missed most of it, I'm afraid." She reached behind her back and, clutching Pitt's hand discreetly, twisted his little finger until he gave in and just as discreetly removed his arm from her waist. "The blast knocked me against a cupboard in the galley." She touched a small swelling on her forehead, the purplish bruise neatly covered by makeup. "I was pretty much out of it for the next hour and a half. Poor Dirk here trembled and threw up all the way back to Reykjavik."

Pitt could have kissed her. Tidi had picked up the situation without the bat of an eye and come through like a trooper.

"I think it's time we mingled,'" he said, taking her by the arm and whisking her off toward the punch bowl.

He passed her a cup of punch and they helped themselves to the hors d'oeuvres. Pitt had to fight from yawning as he and Tidi drifted from one group to another. An experienced party-goer, Pitt usually mixed with ease, but this time he couldn't seem to make a beachhead. There was an odd atmosphere about this function. He couldn't put his finger on it, yet there was something definitely out of place. The usual subdivisions were present—bores, the drunks, snobs and the backslappers. Everyone they joined who could speak English was quite polite. No anti-American sentiments—a favorite ploy during most conversations involving guests of other nations—came to the surface. To all outward appearances, it seemed like the common, middle-of-the-road get-together. Then suddenly he had it. He bent down and whispered in Tidi's ear.

"Do you get the feeling we're *persona non grata?*"

Tidi looked at him curiously. "No, everyone seems friendly enough."

"Sure, they're sociable and polite, but it's forced."

"How can you be certain?"

"I know a warm, sincere smile when I see one. We're not getting any. It's as though we're in a cage. Feed and talk to the animals, but don't touch."

"That's silly. You can't really blame them for being uneasy when they talk to someone who's dressed the way you are."

"That's the catch. The oddball is always, without fail, the center of attraction. If I wasn't dead sure, I'd say this was a wake."

She looked up at Pitt with a sly smile. "You're just nervous because you're way out of your league."

He smiled back. "Care for an explanation?"

"See those two men over there?" She nodded her head sideways to her right. "Standing by the piano?"

Pitt casually rolled a slow glance in the direction Tidi indicated. A small, rotund, lively little man with a bald head was gesturing animatedly as he spoke in rapid bursts into a wiry, thick white beard no more than ten inches from his nose. The beard belonged to a thin, distinguished-looking man with silver hair that fell well below his collar, giving him the appearance of a Harvard professor. Pitt turned back to Tidi and shrugged. "So?"

"You don't recognize them?"

"Should I?"

"You don't read the society pages of *The New York Times.*"

"*Playboy* is the only publication I bother with."

She threw him a typical feminine disgusted-with-the-male-of-the-species expression and said: "It's a pretty sad state of affairs when the son of a United States Senator can't identify two of the richest men in the world."

Pitt was only half listening to Tidi. It took a few seconds for her words to sink in. But then they slowly began to register and he turned his head and brazenly stared at the two men who were still heavily involved in conversation. Then he swung back and gripped Tidi's arm so hard she winced.

"Their names?"

Her eyes flew wide in surprise. "The bald-headed fat man is Hans Von Hummel. The distinguished-looking one is F. James Kelly."

"You could be mistaken."

"Maybe . . . no, I'm positive. I saw Kelly once at the President's Inaugural Ball."

"Look around the room! Recognize anyone else?"

Tidi quickly did as she was told, scanning the main salon for a familiar face. Her gaze stopped not once, but three times. "The old fellow with the funny-looking glasses sitting on the settee. That's Sir Eric Marks. And the attractive brunette next to him is Dorothy Howard, the British actress—"

"Never mind her. Concentrate on the men."

"The only other who looks vaguely familiar is the one who just came in, talking to Kirsti Fyrie. I'm pretty sure he's Jack Boyle, the Australian coal tycoon."

"How come you're such an authority on millionaires?"

Tidi gave a cute shrug. "A favorite pastime for a lot of unmarried girls. You never know when you might meet one, so you prepare for the occasion even if it only comes off in your imagination."

"For once your daydreams paid off."

"I don't understand."

"Neither do I except this is beginning to look like a meeting of the clan."

Pitt pulled Tidi out on the terrace and slowly walked her to a corner away from the mainstream of

the crowd. He watched the small groups of guests milling about the expansive double doors, catching them
looking his way and then turning back, not in embarrassment, but rather as if they were scientists observing
an experiment and discussing its probable outcome. He
began to get the uneasy feeling that coming into Rondheim's lair was a mistake. He was just in the process of
thinking up an excuse to leave when Kirsti Fyrie spied
them and came alongside.

"Would you care to be seated in the study? We're
almost ready to begin."

"Who is giving the reading?" Tidi asked.

Kirsti's face brightened. "Why, Oskar, of course."

"Oh, dear God," Pitt mumbled under his breath.

Like a lamb to slaughter, he let Kirsti lead him to
the study with Tidi tagging behind.

By the time they reached the study and found a
seat among the long circular rows of plush armchairs
grouped around a raised dais, the room was nearly
brimming to capacity. It was small consolation, but Pitt
considered he and Tidi fortunate to sit in the last row
near the doorway, offering a possible means of unnoticed departure when the opportunity arose. Then his
hopes went up in smoke—a servant closed and bolted
the doors.

After a few moments, the servant turned a rheostat
and dimmed the lights, throwing the study into solid
darkness. Then Kirsti climbed the dais and two soft,
pink spotlights came on, giving her the aura of a sculptured Greek goddess standing serenely on her pedestal
in the Louvre. Pitt mentally undressed her, trying to
imagine what an awesome picture she would have made
in that revealing condition. He stole a glance at Tidi.
The enraptured quality of her expression made him
wonder if it were possible that her thoughts were similar
to his. He groped for her hand, found it and squeezed
the fingers tightly. Tidi was so absorbed with the vision
on the dais, she didn't even notice or respond to Pitt's
touch.

Standing there motionless, soaking up the stares

from an audience who sat invisible beyond the glare of the spotlights, Kirsti Fyrie smiled confidently with that inner glow of self-assurance that only a woman truly secure in her loveliness can possess.

She bowed her head toward the hushed bodies in the darkness and began to speak. "Ladies and gentlemen, distinguished guests. Tonight, our host, Mr. Oskar Rondheim, will offer for your enjoyment his latest work. This he will read in our native Icelandic tongue. Then, since most of you understand English, he will read selected verses from the marvelous new contemporary Irish poet, Sean Magee."

Pitt turned and whispered to Tidi. "I should have fortified myself with at least ten more cups of that punch."

He couldn't see Tidi's face. He didn't have to—he felt her elbow jab him sharply in the ribs. When he turned back to Kirsti, she had disappeared and Rondheim had taken her place.

It might have been said that Pitt suffered the agonies of the damned for the next hour and a half. But he didn't. Five minutes after Rondheim began delivering his Icelandic saga in a rolling monotone, Pitt was sound asleep, content in the fact that no one would notice his lack of poetry appreciation in the darkened surroundings.

No sooner had the first wave of unconsciousness swept over him than Pitt found himself back on the beach for the hundredth time, cradling Dr. Hunnewell's head in his arms. Over and over he watched helplessly as Hunnewell stared vacantly into Pitt's eyes, trying to speak, fighting desperately to make himself understood. Then finally, barely uttering those three words that seemingly had no meaning, a cloud passed over his tired old features and he was dead. The strange phenomenon of the dream wasn't its actual recurrence, but rather the fact that no two sequences were exactly the same. Each time that Hunnewell died, something was different. In one dream the children would be present on the beach as they had been in reality. In the next, they would be missing, nowhere in sight. Once the black jet circled overhead, dipping its wings in an unexpected salute. Even Sandecker appeared in one scene, standing over Pitt and Hunnewell and sadly shaking his head. The weather, the layout of the beach, the color of the sea—they all differed from fantasy to fantasy. Only one small detail always remained faithfully—Hunnewell's last words.

The audience's applause woke Pitt up. He stared at nothing in particular, stupidly gathering his thoughts. The lights had come on and he spent several moments blinking and getting his eyes accustomed to the glare. Rondheim was still on the dais, smugly accepting the generous acclaim. He held up his hands for silence.

"As most of you know, my favorite diversion is memorizing verse. With all due modesty, I must honestly state that my acquired knowledge is quite formidable. I would, at this time, like to put my reputation on the block and invite any of you in the audience to begin a line of any verse that comes to your mind. If I cannot finish the stanza that follows or complete the poem to your total satisfaction, I shall personally donate fifty thousand dollars to your favorite charity." He waited until the murmur of excited voices tapered to silence once more. "Shall we begin? Who will be first to challenge my memory?"

Sir Eric Marks stood. "'Should the guardian friend or mother—' Try that one for an introduction, Oskar."

Rondheim nodded. "'Tell the woes of wilful waste, Scorn their counsel, scorn their pother; You can hang or drown at last!'" He paused for effect. "'One and Twenty' by Samuel Johnson."

Marks bowed in acknowledgment. "Absolutely correct."

F. James Kelly rose next. 'Finish this one if you can and name the author. 'Now all my days are trances, And all my nightly dreams—'"

Rondheim hardly skipped a beat. "'Are where thy grey eye glances, And where thy footstep gleams—In what ethereal dances, By what eternal streams!' The title is 'To One in Paradise' and it was written by Edgar Allan Poe."

"My compliments, Oskar." Kelly was visibly impressed. "You rate an A plus."

Rondheim looked about the room, a smile slowly spreading across his chiseled face as a familiar figure rose in the back. "Do you wish to try your luck, Major Pitt?"

Pitt looked at Rondheim somberly. "I can only offer you three words."

"I accept the challenge," Rondheim said confidently. "Please state them."

" 'God save thee,' " Pitt said very slowly, almost as if he were skeptical of any additional lines.

Rondheim laughed. "Elementary, Major. You've done me the kindness of allowing me to quote from my favorite verse." The contempt in Rondheim's voice was there; everyone in the room could feel it. " 'God save thee, ancient Mariner, From the fiends, that plague thee thus. Why look'st thou so? With my crossbow I shot the Albatross. The sun now rose upon the right. Out of the sea came he, Still hid in mist, and on the left Went down into the sea. And the good south wind still blew behind, But no sweet bird did follow, Nor any day for food or play Came to the mariners' hollo. And I had done a hellish thing, And it would work 'em woe. For all averr'd I had kill'd the bird That made the breeze to blow.' " Then suddenly Rondheim stopped, looking at Pitt curiously. "There's little need to continue. It's obvious to all present that you have asked me to quote 'The Rime of the Ancient Mariner' by Samuel Taylor Coleridge."

Pitt began to breathe a little easier. The light suddenly became brighter at the end of the tunnel. He knew something that he hadn't known before. It wasn't over yet, but things were looking up. He was glad now that he had played the proverbial long shot. The gamble had paid off in unexpected answers. The nightmare of Hunnewell's death would never trouble his sleep again.

A satisfied smile touched his lips. "Thank you, Mr.

Rondheim. Your magnificent memory serves you well."

There was something about Pitt's tone that made Rondheim uneasy. "The pleasure is mine, Major." He didn't like the smile on Pitt's lips; he didn't like it at all.

Chapter
15

Pitt suffered for another half hour as Rondheim continued to awe the audience with his vast repertoire of verse. At last the program was over. The doors were opened and the crowded room drained into the main salon, the women escorted onto the terrace to engage in small talk and sip a sweet alcoholic concoction passed about by the servants, the men directed to the trophy room for cigars and one hundred-year-old Rouche brandy.

The cigars were carried into the room within a sterling silver case and presented for everyone's selection except Pitt. He was blithely ignored. After the lighting ritual, each man holding his cigar over a candle, warming it to the desired temperature, the servants passed around the Rouche brandy, the heavy, yellow-brown fluid in exotically designed snifter glasses. Again Pitt was left empty-handed.

Apart from himself and Oskar Rondheim, Pitt counted thirty-two men gathered around the flames crackling in the immense fireplace at the end of the trophy room. The reaction to Pitt's presence, as expressed by the faces, was interesting. No one even noticed him. For a fleeting moment he pictured himself a ghost with no substance that had just walked through the wall and was waiting for a séance to begin so that he could put in a spiritual appearance. Or so he thought. He could have imagined all sorts of strange scenes, but there was no imagining the blunt, circular gun barrel that was pressing into his spine.

He didn't bother to see whose hand held the gun. It would have made little difference. Rondheim answered any doubt.

"Kirsti!" Rondheim stared behind Pitt. "You are early. I didn't expect you for another twenty minutes."

Von Hummel produced a handkerchief, mopped a brow that soaked the monogrammed linen and asked: "The girl he arrived with, has she been readied?"

"Miss Royal has been made quite comfortable," Kirsti said, staring right through Pitt. There was something in her tone that left him with a feeling of doubt.

Rondheim came over and took the gun from her hand as though he was a concerned parent. "Guns and beauty do not go together," he scolded. "You must allow a man to guard the major."

"Oh, I rather enjoyed it," she said in a throaty tone. "It's been so long since I've held one."

"I see no reason to delay any further," Jack Boyle said. "Our timing is complex. We must proceed at once."

"There is time," Rondheim said tersely.

A Russian, a short, stocky man with thinning hair, brown eyes and a limping gait, stood and faced Rondheim. "I believe you owe us an explanation, Mr. Rondheim. Why is this man," he nodded in Pitt's direction, "being treated like a criminal? You told myself and the other gentlemen here he is a newspaperman and that it would not be wise to speak too freely with him. Yet, that is the fourth or fifth time tonight you have referred to him as Major."

Rondheim studied the man before him, then set down his glass and pushed the button on a telephone. He didn't lift the receiver or talk into it, only picked up his glass and sipped at the remaining contents.

"Before your questions are answered, Comrade Tamareztov, I suggest you look behind you."

The Russian called Tamareztov swung around. Everyone swung around and looked to their rear. Not Pitt, he didn't have to. He kept his eyes straight ahead at a mirror that betrayed several hard-looking, expressionless men in black coveralls, who suddenly materialized at the opposite end of the room, AR-17 automatic rifles braced in the firing position.

A round-shouldered, heavy character in his middle seventies, with blue knifing eyes deep set in a wizened face, grasped F. James Kelly by the arm. "You invited me to join you tonight, James. I think you know what this is all about."

"Yes, I do." When Kelly spoke, the pained look in his eyes was plainly visible. Then he turned away.

Slowly, very slowly, almost unnoticed, Kelly, Rondheim, Von Hummel, Marks and eight other men had grouped themselves on one side of the fireplace, leaving Pitt and the remaining guests standing opposite the flames in utter bewilderment. Pitt noted, with a touch of uneasiness, that all the guns were aimed at his group.

"I'm waiting, James," the old blue-eyed man said, his voice commanding.

Kelly hedged, looked rather sadly at Von Hummel and Marks. He waited expectantly. They finally nodded back, assuring him of their approval.

"Have any of you heard of Hermit Limited?"

The silence in the room became intense. Nobody spoke, nobody answered. Pitt was coolly calculating the chances of escape. He gave up, unable to bring the odds of success below fifty to one.

"Hermit Limited," Kelly went on, "is international in scope, but you won't find it on any stock exchange because it is vastly different in administration from any business you're familiar with. I don't have time to go into all the details of its operation, so just let me say that Hermit's main goal is to achieve control and take possession of South and of Central America."

"That's impossible," shouted a tall, raven-haired man with a pronounced French accent. "Absolutely unthinkable."

"It's also good business to do the impossible," Kelly said.

"What you've suggested is not business, but political power madness."

Kelly shook his head. "Madness maybe, but political power with selfish and inhuman motives, no." He searched the faces on the other side of the fireplace. They were all blank with disbelief.

"I am F. James Kelly," he said softly. "In my lifetime I have amassed over two billion dollars in assets."

No one present doubted him. Whenever the *Wall Street Journal* listed the one hundred wealthiest men in the world, Kelly's name always stood at the top.

"Being wealthy carries tremendous responsibilities. As many as two hundred thousand people depend on me for their living. If I was to fail financially tomorrow, it would cause a recession that would be felt from one end of the United States to the other, not to mention the many countries around the world that depend upon my subsidiary companies for a high percentage of their local economies. Yet, as these gentlemen around me can testify, riches do not guarantee immortality. Very few of the rich are remembered in the history books."

Kelly looked almost ill as he paused. No one in the room did anything but breathe until he continued.

"Two years ago I began thinking about what I would leave after I was gone. A financial empire fought over by parasitic business associates and relatives, who had only counted the days till my funeral so they could grab the spoils. Believe me, gentlemen, it was a pretty dismal thought. So I considered methods to distribute my assets in ways that would benefit mankind. But how? Andrew Carnegie built libraries, John D. Rockefeller set up foundations for science and education. What would do the most good for the peoples of the world regardless of white, black, yellow, red, or brown skins? Regardless of nationalities? If I had listened to my human emotions, it would have been an easy decision to use my money to assist the Cancer Crusade, the Red Cross, the Salvation Army or any one of the thousand medical centers or universities around the country. But was it really enough? Somehow it sounded too easy. I decided upon a different direction—one that would have a lasting impact on millions of people for hundreds of years."

"So you plotted to use your resources to become the self-proclaimed messiah of the poverty-stricken Latin nations," Pitt said.

Kelly offered Pitt a condescending smile. "No, you're quite mistaken, Major—ah—"

"Pitt," Rondheim provided. "Major Dirk Pitt."

Kelly gazed at Pitt thoughtfully. "Are you by chance any relation to Senator George Pitt?"

"His errant son," Pitt acknowledged.

Kelly stood like a wax statue for a moment. He turned to Rondheim but only received a stone face in return. "Your father is a good friend," he said woodenly.

"Was," Pitt said coldly.

Kelly fought to keep his composure. It was apparent that the man was deeply troubled by his conscience. He downed his brandy, took a second to collect his thoughts, and went on.

"It has never been my intention to play God. Whatever path I chose had to come from a means far more calculating, far less emotional than the human mind."

"Computers!" the word fell from the lips of Kelly's elderly friend. "Hermit Limited was the project you programmed into the computers at our data processing division nearly two years ago. I remember it well, James. You closed down the entire complex for three months. Gave everyone a vacation with pay—a display of generosity that you've seldom demonstrated before or since. Loaned the use of the equipment, you said, to the government for a top secret military project."

"I was afraid even then you might have guessed my intentions, Sam." It was the first time Kelly had called the old gentleman by name. "But systems analysis provided the only efficient solution to the problem I presented myself. The concept could hardly be classed as revolutionary. Every government has its think tanks. The space systems devised for our rocketry and moon projects have been utilized for everything from diagnosing crime reports to improving surgical procedures. Programming a computer to select a country or geographic location that is ripe for a controlled and developed utopian atmosphere and the method to achieve that goal is not as farfetched as any of you might think."

"It's sheer science fiction."

"In this day and age we all deal in science fiction, do we not?" Kelly answered. "Consider this, gentlemen. Of all the nations of the world, the nations of Latin America are the most vulnerable to outside penetration, primarily because they have not had to face foreign encroachment in well over a hundred years. They were protected by a wall, a wall built by the United States and called the Monroe Doctrine."

"The American government will take a very dim view to your grandiose scheme," said a tall man with white hair, white eyebrows and solemn eyes.

"By the time their agents have penetrated Hermit Limited's organization we will have proven our intentions with solid accomplishments," Kelly said. "They will not bother us. In fact, I predict they will discreetly give us a green light and provide whatever aid they consider possible without international repercussion."

"I take it you don't intend to go it alone," Pitt probed.

"No," Kelly tersely answered. "After I satisfied myself that the program was sound and had every chance to succeed, I approached Marks, Von Hummel, Boyle and the other gentlemen you see here who possessed the financial means to make it a reality. They thought as I did. Money is to be used for the common good of all. Why die and leave nothing but a large bank account or a few corporations that soon forget who planted their seed and nourished them to financial maturity? We then met and formed Hermit Limited. Each of us owns equal shares of stock and has an equal voice on the board of directors."

"How do you know one or more of your partners

in crime won't get greedy?" Pitt smiled faintly. "They may swindle a country or two for themselves."

"The computer chose well," Kelly said, undaunted. "Look at us. No one is under the age of sixty-five. What do we have left? One, two, maybe with luck ten years. We are all childless. Therefore, no heirs. What does any one of us have to gain by excessive avarice? The answer is simple. Nothing."

The Russian shook his head incredulously. "Your scheme is absurd. Even my own government would never consider such drastic and reckless action."

"No government would," Kelly said in patient explanation. "But there lies the difference. You think only in political terms. In the history of man, no nation or civilization has ever fallen except by internal revolution or by foreign invasion. I intend to write a new chapter by accomplishing the impossible by adhering to strict business principles."

"I can't say as I recall murder being taught as a required course in business administration school," Pitt said, calmly lighting a cigarette.

"An unfortunate but necessary part of the plan," returned Kelly. "Methodical assassination is perhaps a more fitting term." He turned to the Russian. "You should have your KGB agents read the *Ismailians*, Comrade Tamareztov. It goes into great detail concerning the methods used by a Persian sect of fanatics that spread terror through the Mohammedan world in 1090 A.D. The word *Assassin* is their dark memorial to the ages."

"You're as mad as they were," the Frenchman said severely.

"If you believe that," Kelly said slowly, "you're very naive."

The Frenchman looked dazed. "I do not understand. How can you—"

"How can my associates here and I take over an entire continent?" Kelly finished. "Basically, it's elementary. Purely a problem of economics. We start with an impoverished country, gain control of its monetary resources, discreetly eliminate its key leaders and buy it out."

"You wax lyrical, James," said the old man. "You'll have to do better."

"There is genuis in simplicity, Sam. Take, for example, Bolivia. A country whose people are close to starvation . . . in many cases the income per family barely exceeding twenty dollars a year. Its whole economy is based on the Peroza copper mines. Gain control of the mines and you gain control of the country."

"I should think Bolivia's army will have something to say about a foreign-inspired takeover," Pitt said, pouring a glass to the brim with brandy.

"Quite right, Major Pitt." Kelly smiled, then said briskly: "But armies have to be paid. Each has its price, particularly its generals. If they refuse to be bought, it is then a simple matter of elimination. Again, a business principle. In order to build a more efficient organization, you discard the deadwood and replace with hardworking, dedicated individuals." He paused a moment, unconsciously smoothing his beard. "After Hermit Limited assumes the administration of the government, the army shall be gradually disbanded. And why not? It is only a drain on the economy. Again, you could compare an army to a company that is losing money. The obvious solution is to close the doors and write it off as a tax loss."

"Have you forgotten the people, James?" It was Sam who spoke. "Do you truly expect them to stand idly while you turn their country upside down?"

"Like any going concern, we have an advertising and marketing department. As with a new product about to be introduced on the market, we have a detailed promotional campaign all worked out. People only know what they see and hear in the media to which they have access. One of our first steps was to purchase, under a local citizen's name, of course, whatever newspapers, radio and television stations that were available."

Pitt said: "I assume you don't envision a free press in your Shangri-La?"

"A free press is purely a form of permissiveness," Kelly said impatiently. "Look what it has done to the United States. Print anything so long as its filthy, scandalous, sensational—anything to sell more papers in order to obtain more paid advertising. The so-called free press in America has stripped every moral fiber from a once great nation and left nothing but a stagnant pile of garbage in the closets of the people's minds."

"Granted, the American press isn't perfect," Pitt said. "But they at least make an effort to get at the truth and expose autocrats like yourself."

Pitt quickly fell silent, surprised at himself for making a speech. He had come close to falling out of character. He knew now that if there was a slight thread of hope for escape, it lay in his continued masquerade as one of the gay boys. "Goodness, I didn't mean to get carried away."

Frowning, baffled, Kelly lifted his eyes to look again at Rondheim. His silent question was answered with a disgusted shrug.

The old man called Sam broke the silence. "After you buy out one country, James, how do you intend to take over the rest? Even you and your associates, as you call them, haven't the capital to gain financial control of the entire continent in one fell swoop."

"True, Sam, even our combined resources can only go so far. But we can make Bolivia, for example, into an organized and fruitful society. Try and imagine it, with no corruption at the administrative level, the military, except for a token force, eliminated, the agriculture and the industry all geared toward providing a better life for the people, the consumers." The intensity in Kelly's voice began to rise. "Again business principle, sink every nickel and dime into growth. None goes for profit. Then, when Bolivia is established as the utopian prototype, the envy of all the peoples on the continent, then we shall annex her neighboring countries, one by one."

"The poor and the hungry waiting breathlessly to be swept into paradise," the Frenchman said contemptuously. "Is that it?"

"You think you exaggerate," Kelly said indifferently, "but you hit the truth closer than you intended. Yes, the poor and the hungry will be eager to snatch at any straw that guarantees an immensely higher standard of living."

"The domino theory impelled by noble thoughts," Pitt added.

Kelly nodded. "As you say, noble thoughts. And why not? Western civilization has a constant history of rebirths impregnated by noble thoughts. We businessmen, as perhaps the largest and most powerful influence of the last two hundred years, now have a golden opportunity to determine whether another brilliant rebirth shall occur or whether a civilization that lies in the gutter shall remain there and stop breathing forever.

"At this point I must admit to being a stick-in-the-mud. I hold a number of doctrines that have been poohpoohed by the best academic minds of higher learning. I entertain the thought that organization is better than confusion. I prefer profit to loss, strong means to gentle persuasion to accomplish a goal. And I'm dead certain that sound business rules are more valuable than political ideologies."

"Your grand design has a flaw," Pitt said, helping himself to another brandy. "A deviation that could easily screw up the works."

Kelly stared at Pitt speculatively. "Your brain against the most advanced techniques of computer science? Come now, Major. We've spent months programming every possibility, every abnormality. You're merely playing games."

"Am I?" Pitt downed the brandy as if it were water and said to Kelly: "How do you explain Rondheim and Miss Fyrie? They hardly pass the age requirements for executive material of Hermit Limited. Rondheim is short by twenty years. Miss Fyrie . . . well, ah . . . she doesn't even come close."

"Miss Fyrie's brother, Kristjan, was an idealist, like myself, a man who was searching for a way to raise people from the mud of poverty and misery. His acts of generosity in Africa and other parts of the world where his business transpired led us to make an exception. Unlike most hardheaded businessmen, he used his wealth for common good. When he tragically lost his life, we, the board of directors of Hermit Limited," he bowed to the men seated around him, "voted to elect Miss Fyrie in his place."

"And Rondheim?"

"A fortunate contingency we had hoped for, but not counted on. Though his extensive fishing facilities appeared an enticing asset toward developing the fishing industry of South America, it was his hidden talents and useful connections that swung the pendulum in his favor."

"The superintendent of your liquidation department?" Pitt said grimly. "The leader of your private sect of Ismailians?"

The men around Kelly looked at each other, then at Pitt. They looked in silence with curiosity written on their faces. Von Hummel wiped his brow for the fiftieth time and Sir Eric Marks rubbed his hand across his lips and nodded at Kelly, a movement that did not go unnoticed by Pitt. Swinging the sash around his waist semicomically, Pitt walked over to the table and poured himself another glass of the Rouche, a last drink for the road, because he knew Kelly never meant for him to leave the house through the front door.

"You guessed that?" Kelly said in an even voice.

"Hardly," Pitt said. "After you've had three attempts on your life, you kind of get to know these things."

"The hydroplane!" Rondheim snapped savagely. "You know what happened to it?"

Pitt sat down and sipped the brandy. If he had to die, at least he had the satisfaction of knowing he held the stage at the end.

"Terribly sloppy of you, my dear Oskar, or should I say the late captain of your last boat. You should have seen the look on his face just before my Molotov cocktail hit him."

"You damned queer!" Rondheim said, his voice shaking with fury. "You lying faggot!"

"Sticks and stones, my dear Oskar," Pitt said carelessly. "Think what you may. One thing is certain. Due to your negligence, you'll never see your hydroplane and crew again."

"Can't you see what he's trying to do?" Rondheim took a step toward Pitt. "He's trying to turn us against each other."

"That will do!" Kelly's tone was cold, his eyes commanding. "Please go on, Major."

"You're very kind." Pitt downed his brandy and poured another. What the hell, he thought, might as well deaden whatever pain that was coming. "Poor Oskar also bumbled the second attempt. I don't have to go into the sorry details, but I'm sure you're aware that his two feeble-brained assassins are talking like women on a party line right this minute to agents of the National Intelligence Agency."

"Damn!" Kelly spun around to Rondheim. "Is that true?"

"My men never talk." Rondheim glared at Pitt. "They know what will happen to their relatives if they do. Besides, they know nothing."

"Let us hope you're right," Kelly said heavily. He came and stood over Pitt, staring with a strangely expressionless gaze that was more disturbing than any display of animosity could ever have been. "This game has gone far enough, Major."

"Too bad. I was just getting warmed up, just getting to the good part."

"It isn't necessary."

"Neither was killing Dr. Hunnewell," Pitt said. His voice was unnaturally calm. "A terrible, terrible mistake, a sad miscalculation. Doubly so, since the good doctor was a key member of Hermit Limited."

Chapter
16

For perhaps ten shocked, incredulous seconds Pitt let his words soak in as he sat nonchalantly in an armchair, cigarette in one hand, glass in the other, the very picture of relaxed boredom. Not so Rondheim and the other members of Hermit Limited. Their faces were as uncomprehending as if each had just come home and found his wife in bed with another man. Kelly's eyes widened and his breath seemed to stop. Then slowly he began to gain control again, calm, quiet, the professional businessman, saying nothing until the right words formed in his mind.

"Your computers must have blown a fuse," Pitt continued. "Admiral Sandecker and I were on to Dr. Hunnewell right from the start." Pitt lied, knowing there was no way Kelly or Rondheim could prove otherwise. "You wouldn't be interested in how or why."

"You are mistaken, Major," Kelly said impatiently. "We would be most interested."

Pitt took a deep breath and made the plunge. "Actually our first tipoff came when Dr. Len Matajic was rescued—"

"No! That cannot be," Rondheim gasped.

Pitt gave silent thanks to Sandecker for his wild plan to resurrect the ghosts of Matajic and O'Riley. The opportunity was handed to him on a silver platter, and he could see no reason not to use it to kill time.

"Pick up the phone and ask the overseas operator for Room 409 at Walter Reed General Hospital in Washington. I suggest you request person-to-person; your call will go through faster."

"That will not be necessary," Kelly said. "I have no reason to doubt you."

"Suit yourself," Pitt said carelessly, fighting to keep a straight face, laying his bluff successfully. "As I started to say, when Dr. Matajic was rescued, he described the *Lax* and its crew in vivid detail. He wasn't fooled for a minute by the alterations to the superstructure. But, of course, you know all this. Your people monitored his message to Admiral Sandecker."

"And then?"

"Don't you see? The rest was simple deduction. Thanks to Matajic's description, it didn't take any great effort to trace the ship's whereabouts from the time it disappeared with Kristjan Fyrie to when it moored on the iceberg where Matajic had his research station." Pitt smiled. "Because of Dr. Matajic's powers of observation—the crew's suntans hardly spelled a fishing trip in North Atlantic waters—Admiral Sandecker was able to figure the *Lax*'s previous course along the South American coast. He then began to suspect Dr. Hunnewell. Rather clever of the admiral now that I look back on it."

"Go on, go on," Kelly urged.

"Well, obviously the *Lax* had been utilizing the undersea probe to find new mineral deposits. And just as obviously, with Fyrie and his engineers dead, Dr. Hunnewell, the co-inventor of the probe, was the only one around who knew how to operate it."

"You are exceedingly well informed," Kelly said wryly. "But that hardly constitutes proof."

Pitt was on tricky ground. So far he had been able to skirt around the National Intelligence Agency's involvement in Hermit Limited. And Kelly had yet to be baited into offering any further information. It's time, he amusedly told himself, to tell the truth.

"Proof is it? Okay, will you accept the words of a dying man? Straight from the horse's mouth. The man in question is Dr. Hunnewell himself."

"I don't believe it."

"His last words before he died in my arms were: 'God save thee.'"

"What are you talking about?" Rondheim shouted. "What are you trying to do?"

"I meant to thank you for that, Oskar," Pitt said coldly. "Hunnewell knew who his murderer was—the man who gave the order for his death. He tried to quote from 'The Rime of the Ancient Mariner.' It was all there, wasn't it? You quoted it yourself: 'Why look'st thou so? With my crossbow I shot the Albatross.' Your trademark, Oskar, the red albatross. That's what Hunnewell meant. 'For all averr'd I had kill'd the bird That made the breeze to blow.' You killed the man who helped you probe the sea floor." Pitt was feeling cocky now; the warmth from the brandy was spreading comfortingly through his body. "I can't match your memory for quoting the verse verbatim, but if my memory serves me correctly, the Ancient Mariner and his ship of ghosts were met by a hermit near the end—another tie-in. Yes, it was all in the verse. Hunnewell pointed the finger of guilt with his dying breath and you, Oskar, stood up and unwittingly pleaded guilty."

"You sent your arrow in the right direction, Major Pitt." Kelly idly stared at the smoke from his cigar. "But you aimed at the wrong man. I gave the order for Dr. Hunnewell's death. Oskar merely carried it through."

"For what purpose?"

"Dr. Hunnewell was beginning to have second thoughts about Hermit Limited's methods of operation—quite old-fashioned thoughts really: thou shall not kill and all that. He threatened to expose our entire organization unless we closed down our assassination department. A conditon that was impossible to accept if we were to have any chance for ultimate success. Therefore, Dr. Hunnewell had to be discharged from the firm."

"Another business principle, of course."

Kelly smiled. "It is that."

"And I had to be swept under the carpet because I was a witness," Pitt said as if answering a question.

Kelly simply nodded.

"But the undersea probe?" Pitt asked. "With Hunnewell and Fyrie—the geese who laid the golden eggs—dead, who is left with the knowledge to build a second-generation model?"

The confident look was back in Kelly's eyes. "No one," he answered softly. "But then no one is required. You see, our computers have now been programmed with the necessary information. With proper analysis of the data, we should have a working model of the probe within ninety days."

For a brief moment, Pitt stood silent, caught unprepared by the unexpected disclosure. Then he quickly shook off his surprise at Kelly's statement. The brandy was beginning to get to him now, but his mind was still running with the smoothness of a generator.

"Then Hunnewell no longer served a useful purpose. Your data-processing brains discovered the secret of producing celtinium-279."

"I compliment you, Major Pitt. You possess a penetrating discernment." Kelly glanced impatiently at his watch and nodded to Rondheim. Then he turned and said, "I'm sorry, but I'm afraid the time has come, gentlemen. The party is over."

"What do you intend on doing with us, James?" Sam's eyes burned into Kelly's until the billionaire turned and avoided the stare. "It's obvious you told us your secrets as a courtesy to our curiosity. It's also obvious you can never let us walk from this house with those secrets in our heads."

"It's true." Kelly looked at the men standing opposite the fireplace. "None of you can be permitted to tell what you heard here tonight."

"But why?" old Sam asked philosophically. "Why expose us to your clandestine operation and thereby seal our death warrants?"

Kelly tiredly rubbed his eyes and leaned back in a large overstuffed leather chair. "The moment of truth, the denouement." He sadly searched the faces across the room. They were pale with shock and disbelief.

"It is now eleven o'clock. In exactly forty-two hours and ten minutes, Hermit Limited will open its doors for business. Twenty-four hours later we will be running the affairs of our first client, or country, if you prefer. In order to make this historical event as inauspicious as possible, we need a diversion. A disaster that will attract headlines and cause anxious concern among the leaders of world governments while our plan is carried off practically unnoticed."

"And we are your diversion," said the tall white-haired man with the solemn eyes.

After a long wordless stare, Kelly simply said, "Yes."

"The innocent victims of a disaster spawned by computers to make headlines. God, it's barbaric!"

"Yes," Kelly repeated, "but necessary. In your own ways, to your own countries, you are important men. You represent the industry, government and science of five different nations. Your combined loss will be considered a worldwide tragedy."

"This must be some sort of insane joke," Tamareztov shouted. "You cannot simply shoot two dozen men and their wives down like animals."

"Your wives will be returned to your lodgings safe and unharmed, and unknowing." Kelly set his glass on the mantel. "We have no intention of shooting anyone. We intend to rely on Mother Nature to do the job, with a little help, of course. After all, shootings can be traced, accidents merely regretted."

Rondheim motioned the black coveralled men with the guns to move in closer. "If you please, gentlemen, roll up one of your sleeves."

As if on cue, Kirsti left the room and quickly returned carrying a small tray set with bottles and hypodermic syringes. She set the tray down and began filling the syringes.

"I'll be damned if you'll stick a needle in my arm," one of the men in Pitt's group exploded. "Shoot me now and get it over—" His eyes went glassy as a guard's rifle butt caught him behind the ear and he slumped to the floor.

"Let us have no further arguments," Rondheim said grimly. He turned to Pitt. "Come into the next room, Major. In your instance, I shall deal with you on a personal basis." He waved the gun he had taken from Kirsti toward a doorway.

Rondheim, followed by two of his guards, escorted Pitt along a wide hall, down a circular flight of stairs into another hall, then shoved roughly through the second of several doorways lining both sides of the second passageway. Pitt, letting himself go loose, stumbled awkwardly, fell to the floor, then scanned the room.

It was an immense room, painted stark white; a large pad lay in the middle of the floor, surrounded by an array of body-building equipment, brightly lit by long rows of fluorescent light fixtures. The room was a gymnasium, better and more expensively equipped than any Pitt had ever seen. The walls were decorated with at least fifty posters depicting the many karate movements. Pitt silently acknowledged a well-conceived and laid-out training room.

Rondheim passed the small automatic to one of the guards. "I must leave you for a moment, Major," he said dryly. "Please make yourself comfortable until I return. Perhaps you would care to loosen up your muscles. May I suggest the parallel bars." With that he laughed loudly and left the room.

Pitt stayed where he was on the floor and studied the two guards. One was a tall, ice-faced and hard-eyed giant nearly six feet four. The dark hair circling his prematurely bald head made him look like a monk, an illusion shattered by the semi-automatic rifle cradled in a pair of huge, hairy hands. He returned Pitt's stare with a look that dared Pitt to try and escape, a possibility made one hundred percent hopeless by the second guard. He stood and filled up the door to the hallway, his shoulders coming within an inch of touching both sides of the vertical framework. Except for a big, red face, heavily moustached, he could have passed inspection with an army of apes. He let his rifle hang loosely in a hand that came nearly to his knees.

Five minutes passed—five minutes during which Pitt carefully planned his next move, five minutes in which the guard's hard eyes never left him. Then suddenly, the door on the far side of the gym opened and Rondheim walked in. He had changed from his dinner jacket into the white, loose-fitting attire of a karate disciple, clothing that Pitt knew was called a gi. Rondheim stood there for a moment, an assured, confident smile taut on his thin lips. Then he walked softly across the floor on bare feet and stepped onto the heavy mat, facing Pitt.

"Tell me, Major. Are you familiar with karate or Kung-Fu?"

Pitt uneasily eyed the narrow black belt that was knotted around Rondheim's waist and fervently prayed that the warm glow of the brandy would ease the beating he felt certain was coming. He simply shook his head.

"Perhaps judo?"

"No, I abhor physical violence."

"A pity. I had hoped for a more worthy opponent. But it is no less than I suspected." He idly fingered the Japanese characters embroidered on his belt "I have my doubts about your masculinity, yet Kirsti thinks you are more manly than you act. We shall soon see."

Pitt forced back the hate and projected a quaver of fear. "Leave me alone; leave me alone!" His voice was high-pitched now, almost a screech. "Why do you want to hurt me? I've done nothing to you." His mouth was working in short jerks from a contorted face. "I lied to you about blowing up your boat. I never saw it through the fog—I swear. You must believe—"

The two guards looked at each other and exchanged sickened expressions, but Rondheim's face went far beyond mere revulsion—he looked positively nauseated.

"Enough!" he shouted commandingly. "Stop this drivel. I never believed for a moment you had the courage to attack and destroy my boat and crew."

Pitt stared wildly about him, a look of blind stupid terror in his eyes that might have been painted there. "You have no reason to kill me. I'll tell no one anything. Please! You can trust me." He started to move toward Rondheim, his hands upturned, pleading.

"Stand where you are!"

Pitt froze. His planned act was working. He could only hope now that Rondheim would quickly tire of a victim who put up no defense, no resistance at all.

"A major in the United States Air Force," Rondheim grimaced. "I'll wager you are nothing but a spineless homosexual who used your father's influence to acquire rank—the lowest form of vermin, living off your own excretion. Soon you will know what it is to feel pain from the hands and feet of another man. A shame you will not enjoy the time to look back and reflect on your most punishing lesson in the art of self-defense."

Pitt stood there like a panic-frozen elk about to be brought down by the hounds. He stood there mumbling incoherently as Rondheim moved to the middle of the mat and assumed one of the many opening stances of Karate.

"No, wait—"

Pitt choked the words off in his throat, threw back his head and spun sideways in one convulsive movement. He had caught the tiny shift in Rondheim's eyes, the beginning of the lightning thrust as the Icelander came in with a reverse punch that connected on Pitt's cheekbone, a half-solid blow that would have caused much more damage than a bruised swelling if Pitt hadn't rolled with the impact. He reeled back two steps and stood there as if stunned, swaying dazedly to and fro as Rondheim advanced slowly, the trace of a sadistic smile in the thin, chiseled features.

Pitt had made a mistake by ducking, had almost given himself away by revealing his quick reflexes. He had to fight to keep his mind turned on the rules. It wasn't easy. No normal man who knows how to take care of himself enjoys standing idle while being beaten to a pulp. He gritted his teeth and waited, holding his body loosely to absorb the blows from Rondheim's next attack. He didn't wait but a few seconds.

Rondheim scored with a roundhouse kick to the head that rammed Pitt full in the face, knocking him off the mat against a row of horizontal exercise bars set into the wall. Pitt lay on the floor in silence, tasting the blood from his crushed lips and feeling his loosened teeth.

"Come, come, Major." Rondheim spoke soothingly, tauntingly. "Up on your feet. The lesson's barely begun."

Pitt pushed himself groggily to his feet and stumbled drunkenly onto the mat. The urge to counterpunch Rondheim was stronger than ever now, but he knew his only course was to play out his role.

Rondheim lost no time in working on him again. A quick combination of sledgehammer blows to the head that never seemed to end, followed by a front kick to the exposed rib area, and Pitt felt rather than heard one of his ribs snap. As if in slow motion, Pitt sunk to his knees and slowly slumped forward onto his face, so badly injured that blood and vomit mingled freely in his mouth and flowed onto the mat in an ever-widening pool. He didn't need a mirror to know he was being worked over fearfully, his face distorted in grotesque mutilation, both eyes rapidly closing, lips ballooned in a purplish mass of torn meat, one nostril of his nose split open.

The daggerlike pain in his chest and the agony of his torn face rose in giant waves and pounded him to the verge of blackness; yet he was surprised to find his mind was still functioning normally. Instead of allowing the painless oblivion of unconsciousness to swoop in, he willed himself to fake it, setting his teeth against a groan that would have given his deception away.

Rondheim was infuriated. "I'm not through with this slimy faggot." He motioned to one of the guards. "Revive him."

The one with the bald head walked to a nearby bathroom, soaked a towel and none too gently wiped the blood from Pitt's face and then compressed the now reddened cloth behind his neck. When Pitt didn't respond, the guard left again and returned with a small vial of smelling salts.

Pitt coughed once, twice, then spit a gob of blood on the guard's boot, taking grim satisfaction that it was no accident. He rolled over onto his side and looked up at Rondheim looming over him.

Rondheim laughed softly. "You seem to have difficulty staying awake in class, Major. Perhaps you are becoming bored." His voice suddenly chilled. "Stand up! You have yet to finish your—ah—course of instruction."

"Course? Instruction?" Pitt's words came blurred, semi-intelligibly through his bloated, broken lips. "I don't get what you mean—"

Rondheim answered by lifting his heel and jamming it in Pitt's groin. Pitt's whole body shuddered and he groaned, the agony tearing him apart.

Rondheim spat on him. "I said stand up!"

"I . . . I can't."

And then Rondheim leaned down and struck Pitt with a shuto blow to the back of the neck. There was no fighting it, no faking it this time: Pitt blacked out for real.

"Bring him around again!" Rondheim yelled insanely. "I want him on his feet."

The guards stared uncomprehendingly; even they were beginning to tire of Rondheim's bloody game. But they had little choice except to work over Pitt like a couple of trainers over a punchdrunk boxer until he emitted the barest signs of consciousness. It didn't take a medical specialist to determine that Pitt could have never stood unaided. So the guards, each with one arm, held Pitt up, his body sagging between them with the dead weight of a wet bag of Portland cement.

Rondheim pounded the defenseless battered body until his gi was soaked through with sweat, the front splotched with blood.

Pitt, in those tortured moments between light and darkness, found himself losing his grip of any emotion, of all intelligence; even the pain was beginning to fade into one massive dull throb. Thank God for the brandy, he thought. He'd never have been able to survive up to this point, taking so much brutality from Rondheim's hands without reacting, if it hadn't been for the alcohol's numbing effects. Now he didn't need it. His physical resources were nearly gone, his mind was slipping from control, losing contact with reality, and the most terrible part was that he could do nothing about it.

Rondheim threw a particularly vicious and accurately aimed kick to Pitt's stomach. As the light passed from Pitt's eyes for the sixth time and the guards released their grip, letting his limp body drop to the mat, the sadistic lust on Rondheim's face slowly faded. He stared vacantly at his bloody and swollen knuckles, his chest heaving as his breath came in quick pants from the exertion. He dropped to his knees, grabbed Pitt by the hair, turning the head so that the throat was exposed, and then he lifted his right hand, palm open, in preparation to deliver the finishing stroke, the *coup de grâce*, a killing judo chop that would snap Pitt's head backward, breaking his neck.

"No!"

Rondheim kept the hand poised, and slowly turned. Kirsti Fyrie stood in the doorway, a look of fear and horror on her face. "No," she said, "please . . . no! You can't!"

Rondheim kept the hand poised. "What does he mean to you?"

"Nothing; but he is a human being and deserves better. You are cruel and ruthless, Oskar. Not altogether unbecoming qualities in a man. But they should be tempered with courage. Beating a defenseless and half-dead man is little different from torturing a helpless child. There is no courage in that. You disappoint me."

Rondheim's hand slowly dropped. He rose, swaying tiredly, and staggered to Kirsti. Tearing the clothing from the upper part of her body, he slapped her viciously across the breasts. "You warped whore," he grasped. "I warned you never to interfere. You who have no right to criticize me or anyone else. It's easy for you to sit by on your pretty ass and watch while I do the dirty work."

She lifted a hand to strike him, her beautiful features contorted in hatred and anger. He caught her wrist and held it, twisting until she uttered a cry.

"The basic difference between a man and a woman, my dove, is physical strength." He laughed at her helplessness. "You seem to have forgotten that."

Rondheim roughly pushed her out the door and turned to the guards. "Throw that queer bastard in with the others," he ordered. "If he is fortunate and opens his eyes once more, he can have the satisfaction of knowing he died among friends."

Chapter
17

Somewhere in the black pit of unconsciousness Pitt began to see light. It was vague, dim like the bulb of a flashlight whose batteries were gasping out their last breath of energy. He struggled toward it. Desperately he reached out, once, twice, making several agonizing attempts to touch the yellow glow he knew was his window to the conscious world outside his mind. But each time he thought it was within his grasp, it moved further away and he knew he was slipping backward into the void of nothingness once more. Dead, he thought vaguely, I'm dead.

Then he became aware of another force, a sensation that shouldn't have been there. It was coming through the void, becoming stronger, more intensified with each passing moment. Then he had it, and he knew he was still among the living. Pain, glorious, tormenting pain. It burst upon him in one crushing, agonizing wave, and he moaned.

"Oh, thank you, God! Thank you for bringing him back!" The voice, it sounded miles away. He pushed his mind into second gear and then it came again. "Dirk! It's Tidi!" There was a second's silence, a second in which Pitt became increasingly aware of the brightening light and the stinging smell of pure, fresh air and a soft arm tenderly cradled around his head. His vision was blurred and distorted; he could vaguely distinguish a dim form leaning over him. He tried to speak but could do no more than groan, mumble a few incoherent words and stare at the shadowy figure above.

"It seems our Major Pitt is about to be reborn."

Pitt could barely make out the words. The voice wasn't from Tidi's lips, that much he was certain; the tone was too deep, too masculine.

"They worked him over pretty thoroughly," said the unidentified voice. "Better he'd died without regaining consciousness. Judging from the looks of things, none of us will live to see—"

"He'll make it." It was Tidi again. "He's got to . . . he's just got to. Dirk is our only hope."

"Hope . . . Hope?" Pitt whispered. "Dated a girl named Hope once."

The agony in his side stabbed and twisted like white-hot iron, but strangely his face felt nothing; the tortured flesh was numb. Then he knew why, knew why he saw only shadows. His sight, or at least thirty percent of it, returned as Tidi lifted a piece of thin damp fabric, the nylon of her pantyhose, from his face. Pitt's torn and swollen features felt nothing because Tidi had been constantly soaking the cuts and bruises in ice water from a nearby mud puddle to relieve the intense swelling. The mere fact that Pitt could see anything at all through the tiny slits around his bloated eyes attested to her successful efforts.

Pitt focused his eyes with difficulty. Tidi was gazing down at him, her long fawn-colored hair framing a pale and anxious face. Then the other voice spoke and the tone was no longer strange.

"Did you get the license number of the truck, Major: Or was it a bulldozer that mashed your already ugly profile?"

Pitt turned his head and looked into the smiling, but tight-muscled face of Jerome P. Lillie. "Would you believe a giant with muscles like tree trunks?"

"I suppose," Lillie said expectantly, "your next

words will be—*if you think I look bad, you should see the other guy.*"

"You'd be disappointed. I didn't lay so much as a fingertip on him."

"You didn't fight back?"

"I didn't fight back."

Lillie showed pure astonishment. "You stood there and took . . . took this terrible beating and did nothing?"

"Oh, will you two shut up!" Tidi's voice held a mixture of irritation and distress. "If any of us are to survive, we must get Dirk on his feet. We can't just sit here and gossip."

Pitt pulled himself to a sitting position and gazed in agony through a red haze of pain as his broken rib cried in protest. The unthinking sudden movement made his side feel as if someone had squeezed his chest between a giant pair of pliers and twisted. Carefully, gently, he eased himself forward until he could see around him.

The sight that met his eyes looked like something out of a nightmare. For a long moment he stared at the unreal scene and then at Tidi and Lillie, his face a study of bewildered incomprehension. Then a shred of understanding crept into his head and with it some certainty of where he was. He reached out a hand to steady himself and muttered to no one in particular.

"My God, it's not possible."

For maybe ten seconds, maybe twenty, in one of those silences they refer to as pregnant, Pitt sat there, as stiff and unmoving as a dead man, staring at the broken helicopter a scant ten yards away. The jagged remains of the hulk lay half sunk in mud at the bottom of a deep ravine whose walls rose in sharp sloping angles to seemingly come together and meet a hundred feet toward the Iceland sky. He noted that the shattered craft was large, probably one of the Titan class, capable of carrying thirty passengers. Whatever colors or markings the copter may have been painted originally, it was impossible to recognize them now. Most of the fuselage back of the cockpit was crumpled like a bellows, the remaining framework a myriad of twisted metal.

Pitt's first frightful impression, the one that ruled his confused mind, was that no one from the crash could have lived. But there they were: Pitt, Tidi, Lillie, and scattered about the steep slopes of the ravine in unnatural pain-contorted positions, the same group of men who had stood beside Pitt in Rondheim's trophy room, the same group who had opposed F. James Kelly and Hermit Limited.

They all appeared to be alive, but most were badly injured; the grotesque angles of their arms and legs revealed a terrible array of smashed and broken bones.

"Sorry to ask the inescapable question," Pitt mumbled, his voice hoarse, though now under control, "but . . . what in hell happened?"

"Not what you think," Lillie replied.

"What then? It's obvious . . . Rondheim was abducting all of us somewhere when the aircraft crashed."

"We didn't crash," Lillie said. "The wreck has been here for days, maybe even weeks."

Pitt stared incredulously at Lillie, who seemed to be lying comfortably on the damp ground, oblivious of the wetness soaking through his clothing. "You'd better fill me in. What happened to these people? How did you come to be here? Everything."

"Not too much to my story," Lillie said quietly. "Rondheim's men caught me snooping around the Albatross docks. Before I had a chance to uncover anything, they hustled me off to Rondheim's house and threw me in with these other gentlemen."

Pitt made a move toward Lillie. "You're in pretty rough shape. Let's have a look."

Impatiently Lillie waved him back.

"Hear me out. Then get the hell away from here and get help. No one is in immediate danger of dying from their injuries—Rondheim saw to that. Our primary peril is exposure. The temperature is under forty degrees now. In another few hours it will be freezing. After that, the cold and the shock will take the first of us. By morning there will be nothing in this goddamn ravine but frozen bodies."

"Rondheim saw to that? I'm afraid—"

"You don't get it? You're slow on the trigger, Major Pitt. It's obvious, the carnage you see here was never caused by accident. Immediately after our sadistic friend Rondheim beat you to a pulp, we were each given a heavy dose of Nembutal and then, very coldly and methodically, he and his men took us one at a time and fractured whatever bones they thought were necessary to make it appear as though we were all injured in the crash of the helicopter."

Pitt stared at Lillie but said nothing. Totally off balance, his mind was in a whirlpool of disbelief, his thought desperately seeking to sort out a set of circumstances that defied comprehension. The way he felt, he would have been prepared to believe anything, but Lillie's words were too macabre, too monstrous to consider.

"My God, it's not possible." Pitt screwed his eyes shut and shook his head in slow frustration. "It has to be some kind of insane nightmare."

"Nothing insane about the reason," Lillie assured him. "There is a method to Kelly's and Rondheim's madness."

"How can you be sure?"

"I'm sure—I was the last one they put under the drug—I overheard Kelly explaining to Sir Eric Marks how this whole unreal tragedy was conceived by Hermit Limited's computers."

"But for what purpose? Why the savagery? Kelly could have simply put us on another aircraft and dropped it over the ocean without a trace, with no chance for survivors."

"Computers are a hard lot; they only deal in cold facts," Lillie murmured wearily. "To their respective governments, the men suffering around us are important figures. You were at Rondheim's little party. You heard Kelly explain why they had to die—their deaths are meant to be a diversion, to buy time and to grab headlines and the attention of world leaders while Hermit

Limited pulls off its coup without international interference."

Pitt's eyes narrowed. "That doesn't explain away the sadistic cruelty."

"No, it doesn't," Lillie admitted. "However, in Kelly's eyes the end justifies the means. A disappearance at sea was probably fed into the computer's banks but undoubtedly rejected in favor of a sounder plan."

"Like producing the bodies at an opportune time."

"In a sense, yes," Lillie said slowly. "World focus on a disappearance at sea would have faded in a week or ten days—the search would have obviously been called off since no one could live long floating in the frigid North Atlantic."

"Of course," Pitt nodded. "The vanishing act of the *Lax* was an ideal example."

"Exactly. Kelly and his rich friends need all the time they can buy to become entrenched in whatever country it is they intend to take over. The longer our State Department is diverted by the loss of high-ranking diplomats, the harder it will be when they get around to putting the screws on Hermit Limited's operations."

"This way, Kelly can have the advantage of an extended search." Pitt's voice was quiet but positive. "And when hope begins to grow dim, he can arrange for an Icelander to stumble accidentally on the crash site and the bodies. And Kelly can reap the advantage of an extra two weeks while the world mourns and government leaders are concentrating on speeches at the funeral processions."

"Every alternative was neatly considered. We were all supposedly on a flight to Rondheim's northern estate for a day of salmon fishing. His group, the Hermit Limited bunch, were going to come on the next flight. At least, that's the story that will be handed out."

"What's to stop someone from accidentally discovering us at any moment?" Tidi asked, gently dabbing a trickle of blood from Pitt's swollen mouth.

"It's fairly obvious," Pitt said, thoughtfully surveying the immediate surroundings. "We can't be seen unless that someone is standing practically on top of us.

Add to that the fact we're probably in the most uninhabited area of Iceland, and the odds of being found begin to stretch to infinity."

"Now you can clearly see the picture," Lillie said. "The helicopter had to be placed in the narrow confines of the ravine and then destroyed because it could not have been purposely crashed with any degree of accuracy—a perfect undetectable location. A search plane directly overhead could have no more than a second to spot the debris, a million-to-one chance at best. The next step was to scatter our bodies around the area. Then, after two or three weeks of decomposition, the most a competent coroner could determine is that some of us died from injuries sustained from the phony crash and the rest from exposure and shock."

"Am I the only one who can walk?" Pitt asked harshly. His broken ribs ached like a thousand sores, but the hopeful stares, the miserable bit of optimism in the eyes of the men who knew death was only a few hours away, forced him to ignore the pain.

"A few can walk," Lillie answered. "But with broken arms, they'll never make it to the top of the ravine."

"Then I guess I'm elected."

"You're elected." Lillie smiled faintly. "If it's any consolation, you have the satisfaction of knowing Rondheim is up against a tougher man that his computers projected."

The encouragement in Lillie's eyes became the extra impetus Pitt needed. He rose unsteadily to his feet and looked down at the figure lying stiffly on the ground.

"Where did Rondheim bust you?"

"Both shoulders and—I'm guessing—my pelvis." Lillie's tone was as calm as if he were describing the fractured surface of the moon.

"Kind of makes you wish you were back in St. Louis running the brewery, doesn't it?"

"Not really. Dear old Dad never had much confidence in his only son. If I . . . if I'm not alive and kicking when you come back, tell him—"

"Read him the riot act yourself. Besides, my heart wouldn't be in it." Pitt had to fight to keep his voice from faltering. "I never liked Lillie beer anyway."

He turned away and knelt over Tidi.

"Where did they hurt you, dearheart?"

"My ankles are a little off center." She smiled gamely. "Nothing serious. I'm just lucky, I guess."

"I'm sorry," Pitt said. "You wouldn't be lying here if it wasn't for my bungling."

She took his hand and squeezed it. "It's more exciting than taking dictation and typing the admiral's letters."

Pitt bent over and lifted her in his arms and carried her tenderly a few feet and laid her beside Lillie. "Here's your big chance, you little gold digger. A real live millionaire. And for the next few hours he's a captive audience. Mr. Jerome P. Lillie, may I present Miss Tidi Royal, the darling of the National Underwater Marine Agency. May you both live happily ever after."

Pitt kissed her lightly on the forehead, stumbled awkwardly once more to his feet and walked unsteadily over the water-soaked ground to the old man he knew simply as Sam. He thought of the distinguished manner, the warm, piercing eyes he had seen in the trophy room as he stared down and saw the legs, twisted outwards like the crooked branches of an oak tree, the blue eyes dulled by pain, and he forced himself to smile a confident, hopeful smile.

"Hang in there, Sam." Pitt leaned over and gently grasped the old man's shoulder. "I'll be back with the prettiest nurse in Iceland before lunchtime."

Sam's lips gave the barest hint of a grin. "To a man my age, a cigar would prove much more practical."

"A cigar it is."

Pitt leaned over and shook Sam's hand. The blue eyes suddenly came to life and the old man raised up, gripping Pitt's outstretched hand with an intensity that Pitt didn't think was possible, and the lines of the tired, drawn face lightened into determined hardness.

"He must be stopped, Major Pitt." The voice was low, almost an insistent whisper. "James must not be allowed to go through with this terrible thing. His purpose glories in goodness, but the people he has surrounded himself with, glory only in greed and power."

Pitt only nodded without speaking.

"I forgive James for what he has done." Sam was talking, almost rambling to himself. "Tell him his brother forgives—"

"My God!" Pitt's shock showed in his face. "You're brothers?"

"Yes, James is my younger brother. I remained in the background these many years, handling the financial details and problems that plague a giant multinational corporation. James, a master at wheeling and dealing, enjoyed the center of attraction. Until now, we were a pretty successful combination." Sam Kelly bowed his head in a barely perceptible sign of farewell. "God bring you luck." And then a smile slowly stretched across his face. "Don't forget my cigar."

"You can count on it," Pitt murmured. He turned away, his mind swirling with conflicting images and emotions, then slowly clearing and settling on one permanent irresistible purpose that held his mental processes in a viselike grip. The driving force, the hatred that had been smoldering within him since Rondheim lashed out with the first crippling blow, now exploded into an intense burning flame that consumed his mind to the expulsion of all else, but then his thoughts were pulled back to reality by the low voice of the Russian diplomat, Tamareztov.

"The heart of a good Communist goes with you, Major Pitt."

Pitt barely paused to reply. "I'm honored. It's not often a Communist has to rely on a capitalist to save his life."

"It is not an easy pill to swallow."

Pitt stopped and looked down at Tamareztov in slow speculation, noting the arms lying limply on the ground, the unnatural angle of the left leg. Then his face softened.

"If you promise not to hold any party indoctrination lectures while I'm gone, I'll bring you back a bottle of vodka."

Tamareztov stared back at Pitt curiously. "A display of Yankee humor, Major? But I think you really mean what you say about the vodka."

A grin touched the corners of Pitt's lips. "Don't misread my intentions. Since I'm already taking a short walk to the corner liquor store, I merely thought I'd save you the trip." Then, before the uncomprehending Russian could reply, Pitt turned and began climbing the embankment toward the top of the ravine.

Cautiously at first, a few inches at a time, trying to move at a pace that favored his cracked ribs, Pitt clawed at the soft, slippery earth and pulled himself upward without looking in any direction except straight ahead. The first twenty feet were easy. Then the slope steepened and the soil became more firm, making it difficult to dig the shallow hand and toeholds which afforded his only source of support.

The climb itself became a purgatory, punctuated by the agony of his injuries. All emotion had drained away, his movements became mechanical, dig and pull, dig and pull. He tried to keep count of each foot gained but lost track after thirty, his mind totally void of all mental function.

He was like a blind man moving through the daylight in a blind world, and the only sense he still possessed was the sense of touch. Then for the first time fear came to him—not fear of falling or fear of injury, but the honest, cold fear of failing over twenty people whose lives depended on his reaching that line between earth and sky that seemed so far above him. Minutes passed that seemed like hours. How many? He didn't know, would never know. Time as a means of measurement no longer existed. His body was simply a robot going through repeated motions without the benefit of constant commands from the mind.

He began counting again, only this time he stopped at ten. Then one minute of rest, he told himself, no more, and he began again. His breath was coming in heaving gulps now, his fingers were raw, the ends of the nails jagged and spotted with blood, his arm muscles aching from the continuous effort—a sure sign his body was about spent. Sweat trickled down his face, but the irritating tickle could not be felt through his agonized flesh. He paused and looked up, seeing little through the swollen slits that were his eyes. The edge of the ravine blended into a nebulous line of angles and shadowy profiles that defied any judgment of distance.

And then suddenly, almost with a sense of surprise, Pitt's hands found the soft, crumbling edge of the slope. With strength he didn't think was possible, he pulled himself up onto flat ground and rolled over on his back, laying inert and to all appearances, dead.

For nearly five minutes, Pitt lay rigid, only his chest moving with the pulsating rise and fall of his breath. Slowly, as the waves of total exhaustion receded to a level of sufferable tolerance, he pulled himself to his feet and peered into the bottom of the narrow chasm at the tiny figures below. He cupped his hands to yell, then decided against it. There were no words he could think of to shout that had any meaning, any encouragement. All the people below could see was his head and shoulders over the level of the steep cliff. Then with a wave of the hand, he was gone.

Chapter
18

Pitt stood like a solitary tree on a great empty plain. A dark green mosslike vegetation spread in every direction as far as he could see, edged on one horizon by a range of high hills and cloaked by a sun-whitened mist on two others. Except for a few small rises dotting the desolate landscape, most of the ground was nearly flat. At first he thought he was completely alone. But then he saw a tiny snipe that soared across the sky like a dart in search of an unseen target. It came closer, and from a height of two hundred feet it circled and looked down at Pitt, as if curiously inspecting the strange animal that stood out so vividly in red and yellow plumage against the center of the unending green carpet. After three cursory sweeps, the little bird's inquisitiveness waned and it fluttered its wings against the air and continued on its seeming flight to nowhere.

As if perceiving the bird's thoughts, Pitt stared down at his offbeat clothing and murmured vaguely to himself, "I've heard of being all dressed up with no place to go, but this is ridiculous."

The sound of his voice suddenly woke him up to the fact that his mind was working again. He felt the relief that was due from overcoming the exhausting climb from the ravine, the high elation of being alive with a hope of finding help before the people below died from the near-freezing temperatures. Jubilantly he struck out across the tundra toward the distant hills.

Fifty feet, no further, that was as far as Pitt got when it abruptly hit him. He was lost. The sun was high above the skyline. There were no stars to guide him. North, south, east and west were words that meant nothing, had no definition in terms of measurement or accuracy. Once he entered the mist that was crawling across the land toward him, he would have no guideline, no landmarks to take a sight on. He was lost, adrift without any sense of direction.

For once that cold, damp morning, he didn't feel the grip of fear. It wasn't that he knew fear would cloud his thoughts, confuse his reasoning. He was consumed with sharp anger that he should have been so beautifully tricked into complacency, so ignorantly unaware that he was stumbling to his death. Every contingency, the computers of Hermit Limited, his archenemy, had mechanically figured on every contingency. The stakes were too high in the murderous game that Kelly, Rondheim and their group of incredibly ruthless business associates were playing. But he swore to himself that he wasn't going to be forced to land on Boardwalk and pay a rent he couldn't afford without passing Go. He stopped, sat down and took stock.

It didn't take any great ingenious deduction to determine that he was sitting somewhere in the middle of the uninhabited part of Iceland. He tried to remember what little he had learned about the Eden of the North Atlantic, what few facts he had absorbed when studying the flight maps on board the *Catawaba*. The island stretched one hundred ninety miles from north to south, he recalled, and nearly three hundred miles from east to west. Since the shortest distance between two points was north and south, the other two directions were eliminated. If he traveled south, there was every possibility that he would run onto the Vatnajökull ice mass, not only Iceland's but Europe's largest glacier, a great frozen wall that would have signaled the end of everything.

North it was, he decided. The logic behind his decision bordered on the primitive, but there was another reason, a compelling urge to outsmart the computers by traveling in the direction least expected, a direction that offered the least obvious chance of success. The average man in similar circumstances would have probably headed toward Reykjavik, the largest sprawl of civilization, far to the west and south. That is undoubtedly, he hoped, what the computers had been programmed for—the average man.

Now he had an answer, but it was only half an answer. Which way was north? Even if he knew for certain, he had no means to follow it along a straight line. The accepted fact that a man who was right-handed would eventually make a great arc to his right without any landmarks to guide him, came back to haunt Pitt's thoughts.

The whine of the jet engines interrupted his reverie and he looked up, holding his hand to shield his eyes from the glare of the cobalt blue sky, sighting a commercial airliner cruising serenely ahead of its long white contrails. Pitt could only wonder at the aircraft's course. It could have been heading anywhere: west to Reykjavik, east to Norway, southeast to London. There was no way to tell for certain unless he had a compass.

A compass, the word lingered in his mind, savored like the thought of an ice-cold beer by a man dying of thirst in the middle of the Mojave Desert. A compass, a simple piece of magnetic iron mounted on a pivot and floating in a mixture of glycerin and water. Then a light suddenly clicked on deep in the recesses of his brain. A long-forgotten bit of outdoor lore he'd learned many years before during a four-day hike in the Sierras with his old Boy Scout troop began to break through the fog-shrouded barrier of time.

It took him nearly ten minutes of searching before he found a small pool of water trapped in a shallow depression beneath a dome-shaped hill. Quickly, as dexterously as his raw and bleeding fingers would allow, Pitt unclasped the brown sash and tore off the pin that held it in place. Wrapping one end of the long silk material around his knee, he knelt and pulled it taut with his left hand and with his right began stroking the pin from head to tip in a single direction against the silk, building friction and magnetizing the tiny piece of metal.

The cold was increasing now, creeping into his sweat-soaked clothes and forcing a spasm of shivers to grip his body. The pin slipped through his fingers, and he spent useless minutes probing the mossy ground cover until he discovered the little silver sliver by accidentally running it a quarter of an inch under a fingernail. He was almost thankful for the pain, as it meant there was still feeling in his hands. He kept pushing the pin back and forth across the silk, careful not to let it slip through his fingers again.

When he felt satisfied that further friction would add nothing more, he rubbed the pin over his forehead and nose, covering it with as much skin oil as it could hold. Then he took two slender bits of thread from the lining of his red jacket and doubled them loosely around the pin. The tricky part of the operation was yet to come, so Pitt relaxed for a moment flexing his fingers and massaging them much like a piano player preparing to tackle Chopin's Minute Waltz.

Feeling he was ready, he gingerly picked up the two loops and with painstaking slowness lowered the pin into the calm little pond. Holding a deep breath, Pitt watched the water bend under the weight of the metal. Then ever so gently his fingers cautiously slid the threads apart until the pin swam by itself, kept afloat by the oil and the surface tension of the water.

Only a child at Christmastime, staring wide-eyed at an array of gifts under the tree, could have experienced the same feeling of wonder that Pitt did that moment as he sat entranced and watched that crazy little pin swing leisurely in a half circle until its head pointed toward magnetic north. He sat there unmoving for a full three minutes, staring at his makeshift compass, almost afraid that if he blinked his eyes, it would sink and disappear.

"Let's see your goddamned computer come up with that one," Pitt murmured to the empty air.

A tenderfoot might have impatiently started running in the direction the pin pointed, mistaken in the assumption that a compass always faithfully aims its point toward true north. Pitt knew that the only place where a compass would unerringly indicate the North Pole was a small area in the Great Lakes between the United States and Canada where by chance the North and Magnetic Poles come into line. As an experienced navigator, he was also aware that the Magnetic Pole lay somewhere beneath Prince of Wales Island above Hudson Bay, approximately one thousand miles below the Arctic Pole and only a few hundred miles above Iceland. That meant that the pin was pointing a few degrees north of west. Pitt figured his compass declination at about eighty degrees, a rough guess at best, but at least he was certain that north now stood at a near right angle to the head of the pin.

Pitt took his bearing and picked the rudimentary compass needle out of the water and started walking into the mist. He hadn't covered a hundred yards when he could taste the blood springing from the open cuts on his inner lips, the teeth loosened in his gums, and with all he had already suffered, the pain inaugurated by Rondheim's kick to the groin, which made it impossible for him to walk without a heavy limping gait. He forced himself to keep going, to cling tenaciously to the thread of consciousness. The ground was rough and uneven and he soon lost count of the number of times he stumbled and fell, wrapping his arms around his chest in a vain attempt to deaden the torture from the cracked ribs.

Luck stayed with him and the mist disappeared after an hour and a half, offering him a chance to take advantage of the many hot springs he passed and orient his bearings with the compass pin. Now he could line up a landmark to the north and keep shifting from one landmark to the next until he was sure he was straying. Then he would stop and take another compass reading and begin the process over again.

Two hours became three. Three hours became four. Each minute was an infinite unit of misery and suffering, of aching cold, of intense burning pain, of fighting for control of his mind. Time melted into an eternity which Pitt knew might not end until he fell against the soft, damp grass for the last time. In spite of his determination, he began to have doubts that he would live through the next few hours.

One step in front of the other, an endless cycle that slowly pushed Pitt further and further into total exhaustion. His thoughts had no room now for anything but the next landmark, and when he reached it, he concentrated every ounce of his sinking energy on the next one. Logic was nearly nonexistent. Only when he heard a muted alarm going off somewhere in the dim corners of his brain, warning him that he was straying off course, did he stop at a steaming sulfur pool to regain a heading with his compass.

Even twelve hours ago to Pitt seemed like twelve years, then his reflexes had been razor-edged, honed and pointed for any necessary mental command, but now as he set the pin in the water his trembling hands failed him and the ingenious little compass slipped beneath the surface and shot to the bottom of the deep crystal-clear pool. Pitt had time to grab it before it sank out of reach, but he could only sit there and stare transfixed for wasted seconds before he reacted to the setback. Then it was too late, far too late, for his hope for finding his way out of Iceland's barren island plateau was lost.

His puffed eyes were almost totally closed, his legs cramped from exhaustion, and his breath coming in agonized gasps that broke the clear still air, but he struggled to his feet and stumbled forward, urged on by an inner strength he didn't know existed. For the next two hours he blundered along in a void all of his own. Then, in the middle of climbing a small eight-foot embankment, his body turned off the switch to consciousness and collapsed like a deflated balloon just inches from the top of the ridge.

Pitt knew he had crossed over the threshold from physical sensibility to the inertness of twilight sleep. But something didn't quite jell. His body was dead; all pain was gone, all feeling, even human emotion seemingly had died. Yet, he could still see, though his total panorama consisted only of grass-covered ground no more than a few inches in front of his eyes. And he could hear, his ears relayed a throbbing sound to a numbed brain that refused to relay any explanation as to the cause or the distance from which the strange coughing beat came.

Then suddenly there was silence. The sound had died away, leaving only the vision of green blades wavering slightly in a whisper breeze. Something in the desolation over which he had stumbled was out of context. The superhuman, courageous effort had been wasted, the responsibility to the people back in the freezing ravine now evaporated into the empty atmosphere. Pitt was past caring or knowing or sensing now, he could relinquish his hold on life and peacefully die under the cold Norse sun. It would have been so easy to let go and fall into the black pit of no return except for something that didn't belong in the picture, an illusion that shattered the whole conception of death.

A pair of boots, two worn leather boots, standing in front of Pitt's unseeing eyes where only a moment before was an empty plot of wild grass. And then phantom hands rolled him over on his back and he became aware of a face framed by the vacant sky—a stern face with sea-blue eyes. Gray hair flowed around a broad forehead like the helmet on a warrior in a Flemish painting. An old man, aged somewhere beyond seventy years, wearing a worn turtleneck sweater, bent and touched Pitt's face.

Then without saying a word, with surprising strength for a man of his years, he lifted Pitt up and carried him over the rise. Through the cobwebs of his mind, Pitt began to wonder at the sheer coincidence, the miracle, which indeed it was, that led to his discovery. No more than one easy stride over the small summit lay a road; he had fallen within spitting distance of a small dirt road that paralleled a tumbling glacial river of white froth, rushing swiftly through a narrow gorge of black lava rock. Yet the sound Pitt's ears had detected came not from the roar of the falling water, but from the exhaust of an engine belonging to a battered, dust-covered British-made jeep.

Like a child placing a doll in a highchair, the old Icelander set Pitt in the front passenger seat of the jeep. Then he climbed behind the wheel and steered the rugged little vehicle over the winding road, stopping every so often to open a closed cattle gate, an operation that became routine as they entered a section of rolling hills divided by lush green meadows bursting with plovers that clouded the sky at the approach of the jeep. They stopped in front of a small farmhouse with white side-boards and a red roof. Pitt shrugged off the supporting hands and staggered into the living room of the comfortable little house.

"A telephone, quickly. I need a telephone."

The blue eyes narrowed. "You are English?" the Icelander asked slowly in a heavy Nordic accent.

"American," Pitt answered impatiently. "There are two dozen seriously injured people out there who will die if we don't get help to them soon."

"There are others on the plateau?" There was no concealing the astonishment.

"Yes, yes!" Pitt nodded his head violently. "God, man, the phone. Where do you keep it?"

The Icelander shrugged helplessly. "The nearest telephone lines are forty kilometers away."

A great tidal wave of despair swept over Pitt only to ebb and vanish at the stranger's next words.

"However, I have a radio transmitter." He motioned to a side room. "Please, this way."

Pitt followed him into a small, well-lit, but spartan room, the three primary pieces of furniture being a chair, a cabinet and an ancient hand-carved table holding a gleaming transmitter, not more than a few months from manufacture; Pitt could only marvel at the latest equipment being used in an isolated farmhouse. The Icelander crossed hurriedly to the transmitter, sat down and began twisting the array of dials and knobs. He switched the radio to SEND, selected the frequency and picked up the microphone.

He spoke a few words rapidly in Icelandic and waited. Nothing came back over the speaker. He shifted the transmitting frequency fractionally and spoke again. This time a voice answered almost immediately. The pressure of the race against death made Pitt as tense as a guy wire in a hurricane gale, and in total indifference to his pain and fatigue he paced the floor while his benefactor conversed with the Reykjavik authorities. After ten minutes of explanation and translation, Pitt requested and received a call from the American Embassy.

"Where in the goddamned hell have you been?" Sandecker's voice exploded over the speaker so loudly that it might have come from the doorway.

"Waiting for a streetcar, walking in the park," Pitt snapped back. "It makes no difference. How soon before a team of medics can be assembled and in the air?"

There was a tense silence before the admiral answered. There was, he knew, a tone of urgent insistence in Pitt's voice, a tone Sandecker had seldom heard from Pitt's lips. "I can have a team of Air Force paramedics ready to load in thirty minutes," he said slowly. "Would you mind telling me the reason behind your request for a medical unit?"

Pitt didn't answer immediately. His thoughts were barely able to focus. He nodded thankfully as the Icelander offered him the chair.

"Every minute we waste with explanations, someone may die. For God's sake, Admiral," Pitt implored, "contact the Air Force and get their paramedics loaded on helicopters and supplied to aid victims of an air disaster. Then while there's time, I can fill you in on the details."

"Understood," Sandecker said without wasting a word. "Stand by."

Pitt nodded again, this time to himself, and slumped dejectedly in the chair. It won't be long now, he thought, if only they're in time. He felt a hand on his shoulder, half turned and managed a crooked smile up at the warm-eyed Icelander.

"I've been a rude guest," he said quietly. "I haven't

introduced myself or thanked you for saving my life."

The old man offered a long, weathered hand. "Golfur Andursson," he said. "I am chief gillie for the Rarfur River."

Pitt gripped Andursson's hand and introduced himself and then asked, "A chief gillie?"

"Yes, a gillie is also the river warden. We act as guides for fishermen and watch over the ecology of the river, much like a conservationist in your own country who protects the natural resources of your inland water grounds."

"It must be lonely work——" Pitt's mouth stopped working and he gasped as a sharp pain in his chest nearly carried him into blackness. He clutched the table, fighting to remain conscious.

"Come," Andursson said. "You must let me tend to your injuries."

"No," Pitt answered firmly. "I must stay by the radio. I'm not leaving this chair."

Andursson hesitated. Then he shook his head and said nothing. He disappeared from the room and returned in less than two minutes carrying a large first-aid case and a bottle.

"You are lucky," he said smiling. "One of your countrymen fished the river just last month and left this with me." He held up and proudly displayed a fifth of Seagram's V.O. Canadian Whiskey. Pitt noticed that the seal on the cap had not been broken.

Pitt was on his fourth healthy swig and the old river warden had just finished binding his chest when the radio crackled and Sandecker's gravel voice broke into the room again.

"Major Pitt, do you read me?"

Pitt lifted the microphone and pressed the transmitting switch. "Pitt here. I read you, Admiral."

"The paramedics are mustering at Keflavik and Iceland's civilian search and rescue units are standing by. I'll maintain radio contact and coordinate their efforts." There was a momentary silence. "You have a lot of worried people here. Keflavik has no report of a missing plane, either military or commercial."

Rondheim wasn't taking any chances, Pitt thought. The bastard was taking his own sweet time about reporting his overdue and missing guests. Pitt breathed deeply and took another shot of the V.O. Then he replied:

"Notification isn't scheduled yet."

Total uncomprehension broke in Sandecker's voice. "Come again. Please repeat."

"Trust me, Admiral. I can't even begin to answer a tenth of the questions that must be running through everyone's mind, especially over the radio—I repeat—especially over the radio."

Somehow, Pitt thought, the names of the internationally known men back in the ravine had to be kept from the news services for at least the next thirty-six hours: time enough to stop Kelly, Rondheim and Hermit Limited before they could be warned and go underground. He had to give the admiral credit. Sandecker caught Pitt's implication of the need of secrecy almost immediately.

"Your message is understood. Can you give me the location? Use your reverse coordination map."

"Sorry, I know of no such—"

"Dammit!" Sandecker shouted, turning the speaker into a thunderbolt of distorted static. "Do as you're ordered."

Pitt sat and stared dumbly at the radio's speaker for nearly thirty seconds before Sandecker's hidden meaning began to register in his weary mind. The admiral was offering him a chance to answer questions without giving away valid information, by replying in the contrary. He mentally kicked himself for letting Sandecker outdo him in the verbal gymnastics.

Pitt flicked off the mike switch and turned to Andursson. "How far is the nearest town and in what direction?"

Andursson vaguely pointed out the window. "Sodafoss . . . we are exactly fifty kilometers south of its town square."

Pitt quickly added to the Icelander's figure to allow for the distance he had stumbled across the plateau and turned back to the radio. "The aircraft came down approximately eighty kilometers north of Sodafoss. I repeat, eighty kilometers north of Sodafoss."

"Was the aircraft civilian or military?"

"Military."

"How many survivors?"

"Can't say for certain. Two, maybe four."

Pitt could only hope the admiral would grasp the total number of twenty-four. The feisty old oceanographer didn't fail him.

"Let us hope we can have them safe and sound by this time tomorrow." Sandecker's intimation of twenty-four hours quickly settled any doubt. He paused, and then his voice came through low, quiet with a strong inflection of concern. "Is Miss Royal with you?"

"Yes."

Sandecker didn't reply immediately. Pitt could almost see the sudden paling, almost hear the sudden intake of breath. Then the admiral said, "Has she . . . has she given you any trouble?"

Pitt thought a moment, trying to piece together the right words. "You know how women are, Admiral, always complaining. First it was an imaginary ache in her ankles, now she claims she's freezing to death. I'll be eternally grateful if you use all haste in taking this griping female off my hands."

"Will do all possible at this end to grant your request." The gravel-like tone was back now. "Stand by."

Pitt hummed softly to himself. This was taking too much time, each minute was precious, each second irreplaceable. He looked at his watch. Exactly one o'clock—seven hours since he crawled out of the ravine. He felt a sudden chill and took another swallow from the bottle.

The radio crackled again. "Major Pitt."

"Come in, Admiral."

"We have a problem here. Every helicopter on the island is grounded. The paramedics will have to be air-dropped from a transport."

"Do you understand? It is imperative that helicopters be used. The survivors must be airlifted out. And most important, Admiral. I must lead the search—repeat—I must lead the search. The crash site is invisible from the air. Your rescue party could search for days and never find it."

Pitt could sense the gloom at the other end. Sandecker took a long time in answering. Then he spoke wearily, defeated, as if he were delivering the last rites, which indeed he very nearly was.

"Negative to your request. There are seven copters on the island. Three belong to the Air Force, four to the Icelandic Search and Rescue Department. All are grounded due to maintenance problems." Sandecker paused, then went on slowly. "The possibility seems remote, but our people and the local government authorities smell sabotage."

"Oh, Christ!" Pitt murmured, and suddenly his blood ran cold. Every contingency. The term came back to haunt him again and again. Kelly's computers had built the wall ever higher against hope of rescue. And Rondheim's coldly efficient gang of killers had carried out the mechanical commands to the letter.

"Do you have enough flat ground for a light plane to land and pick you up?" Sandecker probed expectantly. "If affirmative, you could direct a rescue drop from the air."

"A small plane might make it," Pitt said. "I have a level meadow here the length of a football field."

Outside, unnoticed by Pitt, the sun, a perfect orange disk in the northern latitudes, was being rapidly overtaken by great rolling black clouds that soon surrounded and cut off its bright glow. A chilling breeze had sprung up and was bending the grass in the meadows and hills. Pitt became aware of Andursson's hand on his shoulder and the sudden dimming light in the room at the same time.

"A storm from the north," Andursson said solemnly. "It will snow within the hour."

Pitt threw back the chair and hurriedly crossed the room to a small double window. He stared through the glass, his eyes unbelieving, and he struck his fist against the wall in despair.

"God, no!" he whispered. "It would be suicidal for the paramedics to parachute through a blinding snowstorm."

"Nor could a light plane fly through the turbulence," Andursson said. "I have seen the coming of many northerns and have known their ferocity. This will be a bad one."

Pitt weaved drunkenly back to the radio and collapsed in the chair. He held his cut and swollen face in his hands and muttered softly, "God save them. God save all of them now. Hopeless, hopeless."

Sandecker came over the radio, but Pitt sat unhearing. "Your exact position, Major. Can you give me your exact position?"

Andursson reached over Pitt and took the microphone. "One minute, Admiral Sandecker," he said firmly. "Please stand by."

He took Pitt's right hand and gripped it hard. "Major Pitt, you must control your mind." He looked down, his eyes bright with compassion. "'The knot of death, though it be bound like stone, may be unravelled by he who knows the frail strand.'"

Pitt slowly looked up into Andursson's eyes. "So, I have another poet on my hands."

Andursson simply nodded his head shyly.

"This has certainly been my week for poets," Pitt sighed. Then he swore softly to himself. He had already spent far too much time in needless talk and useless pity, and time was running short. He needed a plan, a device, a gimmick to reach those who put their trust in him. Computers make mistakes, he told himself. Those cold electronic monsters can make an error—an error that may be infinitesimal, but none the less the possibility exists. There is no emotion built into their wiring, no sentiment, no room for nostalgia.

"Nostalgia," Pitt said out loud, rolling the word on his tongue, savoring every syllable, repeating it at least three more times.

Andursson stared at him strangely. "I do not understand."

"You'll soon see," Pitt said. "I'm not waiting to

find the frail strand in your poetic knot of death. I'm going to cut it with blades."

The old man looked more lost than ever. "Blades?"

"Yes, propeller blades. Three of them, to be exact."

Chapter
19

There are many wondrous sights to behold in this
world, but to Pitt nothing, not even a thirty-story rocket
blasting into outer space or a needle-nosed supersonic
transport streaking across the sky at twice the speed of
sound could ever look half as incredibly beautiful as
that old Ford tri-motor, the famed Tin Goose, pitching
and rolling awkwardly in the fitful wind, curtained by
the black folds of giant menacing clouds. Braced against
the increasing gale, he watched intently as the ancient
aircraft, graceful in its ugliness, circled Andursson's
farm once before the pilot eased back on the throttles,
skimmed less than ten feet over a fence and set it down
in the meadow where the wide-set landing wheels rolled
to a complete stop in less than two hundred feet from
touchdown.

Pitt turned to Andursson. "Well, good-by, Golfur.
Thank you for all you've done for me . . . for all of
us."

Golfur Andursson shook Pitt's hand. "It is I who
thank you, Major. For the honor and opportunity to
help my fellow brother. God go with you."

Pitt couldn't run, his cracked ribs wouldn't permit
that, but he covered the distance to the tri-motor in less
than thirty seconds. Just as he reached the right side of

the fuselage, the door flew open and willing arms reached down and pulled him into the cramped, narrow cabin.

"Are you Major Pitt?"

Pitt looked into the face of a great bull of a man, tan-faced, with long blond sideburns. "Yes, I'm Pitt."

"Welcome back to the roaring twenties, Major. This is a helluva idea, using this old flying fossil for a rescue mission." He held out his hand. "I'm Captain Ben Hull."

Pitt took the massive paw and said, "Best we move out if we expect to beat the snow."

"Right you are," Hull boomed briskly. "No sense in getting ticketed for overparking." If Hull was mildly shocked at Pitt's damaged face or his strange-looking clothes, he concealed it well. "We ran this trip without a copilot, a reserved seat in your name, Major. Figured you'd want front row balcony to lead us to the wreck."

"Before I signed off, I asked Admiral Sandecker for a couple of items—"

"Got news for you, Major. That old sea dog carries a big mean stick. Seems he pulled every plug to get them on board before we took off." He pulled a package from his parka and raised an inquiring eyebrow. "Beats the hell out of me why you'd want a bottle of Russian vodka and a box of cigars at a moment like this."

"It's for a couple of friends," Pitt said, smiling. He turned and made his way past ten men ranged in various relaxed positions along the floor of the cabin— large, quiet, purposeful-looking men dressed in arctic weather gear. They were men who were trained in scuba diving, parachute jumping, survival, and nearly every phase of emergency medicine except surgery. A wave of confidence surged through Pitt just from observing them.

Ducking his head to clear the low cockpit door, Pitt moved into the cramped confines and eased his sore body into the worn and cracked leather bucket seat, sitting vacant on the copilot's side. As soon as he was safely strapped in, he turned and found himself staring into the grinning face of Sergeant Sam Cashman.

"Howdy, Major." Cashman's eyes widened. "God Amighty, who stomped on your face?"

"Tell you over a drink sometime." Pitt glanced at the instrument panel, quickly familiarizing himself with the old-fashioned gauges. "I'm a bit surprised to see—"

"To see a sergeant flyin' this mission instead of a genuine flight officer," Cashman finished. "You got no choice, Major. Ah'm the only one on the whole island who's checked out on this old bus. Ain't she a winner? She'll take off and land on a dollar bill and give you change."

"Okay, Sergeant. You're in command. Now let's swing this bird into the wind and get her up. Bear due west along the river until I tell you to cut south."

Cashman merely nodded. Deftly he jockeyed the Tin Goose on a hundred-and-eighty-degree turn until it faced into the wind at the far side of the meadow. Then he shoved the three throttles forward and sent the lumbering old airliner bouncing and shuddering on its way, ever closer to the fence on the opposite end of the field, no more than three hundred feet away.

As they lurched past the front of Golfur Andursson's little house with the plane's tail wheel still glued to the ground, Pitt began to have a vague idea of what Charles Lindbergh's thoughts must have been when he urged his heavily laden Spirit of St. Louis off the muddy runway of Roosevelt Field back in 1927. It seemed impossible to Pitt that any aircraft short of a helicopter or light two-seater could leave the earth in so small a space. He shot a fast look at Cashman and saw only icy calmness and total relaxation. Cashman was indifferently whistling a tune, but Pitt couldn't quite make out the melody above the roar of the trio of two-hundred-horsepower engines.

There was no doubt, Pitt reflected. Cashman certainly displayed the image of a man who knew how to handle a plane, especially this one. With two-thirds of the meadow gone, Cashman eased the control column forward and lifted the tail wheel and then pulled back, floating the plane a few feet above the turf. Then to

Pitt's horror, Cashman suddenly dropped the tri-motor back hard on the ground no more than fifty feet in front of the fence. Pitt's horror turned to amazement as Cashman jerked the controls back against his chest and literally bounced the old Tin Goose over the fence and threw it into the air.

"Where in hell did you learn that little trick?" Pitt said, exhaling a great sigh of relief. It was then he recognized the tune Cashman was whistling as the theme from the old movie, "Those Magnificent Men in Their Flying Machines."

"Used to be a crop duster in Oklahoma," Cashman replied.

"How did you wind up as a mechanic in the Air Force?"

"One day the junker ah was flyin' developed a nasty cough. Plowed up a farmer's pasture and butchered his champion beef sire years before its time. Everybody in the county was out to sue me. Ah was flat broke so ah split the scene and enlisted."

Pitt couldn't help smiling as he peered through the windshield at the river two hundred feet below. From that height he could easily spot the sloping ridge where Andursson had found him. He saw something now he didn't expect to find. Almost imperceptibly, he became aware of a long even line against the landscape that trailed off toward the south. He pushed open the little side window and looked again. It was there all right: the dark shade of green against the lighter tinted tundra. His footprints, where they had sunk into the soft vegetation, had left a path that was easy to follow as the white line down the center of a highway.

Pitt caught Cashman's eye and motioned earthward. "To the south. Follow that dark trail to the south."

Cashman banked the plane and stared for a moment out the side window. Then he cocked his head in acknowledgment and turned the nose of the tri-motor southward. Fifteen minutes later he could only wonder at the unerring trail Pitt had made during his trek to the river. Except for a few occasional deviations around rough or uneven ground, the man-made mark on the earth was almost as straight as a plumb line. Fifteen minutes, that was all the old antique needed to cover the same distance that had taken Pitt several hours.

"I have it now," Pit shouted. "There, that crack-like depression where my path ends."

"Where do you want me to set her down, Major?"

"Parallel to the rim of the ravine. There's a flat area running about five hundred feet east and west."

The sky was darkening by the moment—darkening with the mist of falling snow. Even as Cashman made his landing approach, the first flakes began dotting the windshield, streaking to the edges of the glass before being blown into the sky by the airstream. Pitt's race had been won, but only by the barest of margines.

Cashman made a safe landing, a smooth landing considering the rugged terrain and the difficult wind conditions. He timed his run so that the cabin door of the tri-motor ended up within ten yards of the steep drop-off.

The wheels had hardly rolled to a halt when Pitt leaped from the plane and was stumbling, sliding to the bottom of the ravine. Behind him, Hull's men began methodically unloading supplies and arranging them on the dampening ground. Two of the paramedics uncoiled ropes and threw them down the slopes in preparation of bringing up the survivors. Pitt ignored all this. He had one driving desire: to be the first into that chilling pit of hell.

He came upon Lillie still stretched out on his back with Tidi huddled over him, his head cradled in her arms. She was talking to Lillie, saying words Pitt couldn't understand, her voice no more than a weak, hoarse whisper; she seemed trying her best to smile, but her lips barely curved in a pitiful grimace and there was little pleasantry in either the voice or the eyes. Pitt walked up behind her and gently touched her wet-streaked hair.

"It seems you two have become rather close friends."

Tidi twisted around and stared dazedly at the figure standing over her. "Good Lord, you've come back." She reached out and touched his hand. "I thought I heard an airplane. Oh, God, this is wonderful, you've come back."

"Yes," Pitt smiled faintly, then nodded at Lillie. "How is he?"

"I don't know," she said wearily. "I just don't know. He slipped into unconsciousness about half an hour ago."

Pitt knelt down and listened to Lillie's breathing. It was slow and steady. "He'll make it. This guy has guts ten miles long. The big question is whether he'll ever walk again."

Tidi pressed her face against Pitt's hand and began to sob, her breath coming in convulsive shudders, the shock, the pain, and the relief washing over her in rolling waves. He held her tightly saying nothing. He was still holding her shivering body and stroking her hair as he would a little girl when Captain Hull approached.

"Take the girl first," Pitt said. "Her ankles are broken."

"My men have set up an aid tent above the slopes. There's a stove warming in it now. She'll be comfortable there until the Icelandic Search and Rescue Team can transport her to Reykjavik." Hull wiped his eyes tiredly. "Their cross-country vehicles are homing in on our radio signals now."

"Can't you airlift her out?"

Hull shook his head. "Sorry, Major. That old tri-motor can only carry eight stretcher cases on one trip. I'm afraid the first load will have to be the most critically injured. This is one occasion where the ladies will have to go last." He nodded down at Lillie. "How bad is this one?"

"Fractured shoulders and pelvis."

Two of Hull's men appeared carrying an aluminum basket stretcher. "Take the man first," he ordered. "And see that you handle him gently. This one is a back injury."

The paramedics carefully eased Lillie's inert form

into the stretcher and attached the ropes for the ascent
to the top of the ravine. Pitt couldn't help but be impressed and thankful for the efficiency and smoothness
of the lifting lines. Just three minutes later Hull had returned for Tidi.

"Okay, Major. I'll take the little lady."

"Handle her with care, Captain. She happens to be
Admiral Sandecker's private secretary."

Apparently nothing startled Hull for long. The surprise only flickered in his eyes for an instant. "Well,
well," he boomed. "In that case, I'll escort the lady myself."

Hull tenderly picked Tidi up in his massive arms
and carried her to a waiting basket. Then true to his
word, he climbed along beside her all the way to the top
of the slope and saw her comfortably bedded down inside the warm tent before he returned to direct the rescue operation.

Pitt pulled the package from under his arm and
moved slowly across the broken bottom of the ravine
until he stood over the Russian diplomat. "Mr. Tamareztov, how are you getting along?"

"A Russian relishes the cold, Major Pitt." He
cupped a small handful of snow that had fallen across
his chest. "Moscow would not be Moscow without a full
season of snow. To me it is the same as desert sand to
an Arab; a curse that is part of one's very existence."

"Are you in pain?"

"An old Bolshevik never admits to pain."

"A pity," Pitt said.

"A pity?" Tamareztov repeated. He looked at Pitt
suspiciously.

"Yes, I was about to offer you a little something
that's guaranteed to relieve discomfort caused by hay
fever, headache and indigestion."

"More Yankee humor, Major?"

Pitt let a slight grin touch his face. "Yankee sarcasm," he said. "The prime reason why we're so often
misunderstood by people of other countries. The average American has a sarcastic streak down his back that

defies intelligent comprehension." He sat down next to Tamareztov and produced the bottle of vodka. "For example, you see before you the fruits of my trip to the corner liquor store."

Tamareztov could only stare incredulously.

"A promise made is a promise kept." Pitt cradled the Russian's head and tilted the bottle to the injured man's lips. "Here, drink some of this."

Tamareztov easily drained a quarter of the bottle before Pitt eased it away. He nodded his head and mumbled his thanks. Then his eyes took on a warm penetrating expression. "Domestic, true Soviet domestic. How in the world did you manage that?" he asked.

Pitt tucked the bottle in Tamareztov's armpit. "It was on sale," he said. Then he rose and turned to leave.

"Major Pitt."

"Yes?"

"Thank you," Tamareztov said simply.

He was white with snow, lying there vacantly staring at the clouds when Pitt found him. His face, calm and serene, had the expression of a man untouched by pain, a man who was happy and content and at last at peace with himself. A medic was bending over, examining him.

"Heart?" Pitt asked softly, somehow afraid he might wake him.

"Considering his age, that's as safe a bet as any, sir." The medic turned and motioned to Hull, who was standing but a few feet away. "Shall we evacuate him now, Captain?"

"Leave him lay," Hull said. "It's our job to save the living. This man is dead. As long as there is a chance to keep any one of these people from joining him, our attention must go to them."

"You're right, of course," Pitt said wearily. "This is your show, Captain."

Hull's tone softened. "You know this man, sir?"

"I wish I had known him better. His name is Sam Kelly."

The name obviously meant nothing to Hull. "Why don't you let us take you topside, Major. You're in a pretty bad way yourself."

"No, I'll stay with Sam here." Pitt reached over and gently closed Kelly's eyes for the final time and lightly brushed the snowflakes from the old wrinkled face. Then he took a cigar he recognized as Sandecker's special brand from the box and slipped it into Kelly's breast pocket.

Hull stood unmoving for nearly a minute, groping for words. He started to say something but thought better of it and instead simply nodded his head in silent understanding. Then he turned and plunged back to work.

Chapter
20

Sandecker closed the file and put it down and leaned forward as if he were about to spring. "If you're asking for my permission, the answer is an unequivocal no!"

"You place me in an awkward position, Admiral." The words came from a man who sat facing Sandecker. He was short and seemed almost as broad as the chair. He wore a nondescript black suit with a white shirt decorated by a black silk tie. Unconsciously, every so often, he ran his hand over a bald head as if searching for hair that once might have existed, and he peered through gray eyes that never blinked under Sandecker's blazing stare. "I had sincerely hoped we would have no disagreement. However, since that is not to be, I must inform you that my presence here is purely an act of courtesy. I already possess the orders for Major Pitt's reassignment."

"By whose authority?" Sandecker asked.

"They were signed by the Secretary of Defense," the other man replied matter-of-factly.

"You wouldn't mind showing me the orders." Sandecker said. He was playing his last pawn and he knew it.

"Very well." His opponent sighed. He reached into

his briefcase and pulled out a set of papers and handed them to Sandecker.

Silently the admiral read the orders. Then his lips twisted in a wry smile. "I didn't really stand a chance, did I?"

"No, you didn't."

Sandecker looked down at the papers in his hands again and shook his head. "You're asking too much . . . too much."

"I don't enjoy this sort of thing, but time is a commodity we can't afford. This whole scheme, a naive scheme, spawned by Hermit Limited is totally impractical. I admit it sounds inspiring and all that. Save the world, build a paradise. Who knows, maybe F. James Kelly has the answer for the future. But at the moment, he is the leader of a gang of maniacs who have murdered nearly thirty people. And, exactly ten hours from now, he plans to assassinate two heads of state. Our course is determined by one elementary fact—he must be stopped. And Major Pitt is the only one who is physically capable of recognizing Kelly's hired killers."

Sandecker threw the papers on the desk. "Physically capable. Nothing but goddamned words that have no feeling." He pushed himself from the chair and began pacing the room. "You're asking me to order a man who has been like a son to me, a man who has been beaten within an inch of death, to get up from a hospital bed and track down a gang of vicious killers six thousand miles from here?" Sandecker shook his head. "You don't know the half of what you're demanding from human flesh and blood. There are limits to a man's courage. Dirk has already done far more than was expected of him."

"Granted that courage is reduced by expenditure. And I agree that the major has done more than was thought humanly possible. God knows there are few if any of my men who could have pulled that rescue off."

"It could be we're arguing over nothing," Sandecker said. "Pitt may not be in any condition to leave the hospital."

"I'm afraid your fears . . . or should I say hopes?

. . . are groundless." The bald man checked through a brown folder. "I have here a few observations from my agents, who by the way have been guarding the major." He paused, reading, then went on. "Excellent physique, constitution like a bull, unique rapport with . . . ah . . . the nurses. Fourteen hours of rest, intensive care and massive vitamin injections plus the finest muscle therapy known by the top doctors in Iceland. He has been stitched, massaged and taped. Fortunately, the only major damage was to his ribs and at that the fractures were minor. All in all, he's a sorry mess, but I can't be particular. I'd take him if they were lowering him into a coffin."

Sandecker's face was cold and blank. He turned as one of the embassy secretaries poked her head around a door.

"Major Pitt is here, sir."

Sandecker glared at the fat man. Surprise edged into his voice. "You bastard, you knew all along he would do it."

The fat man shrugged and said nothing.

Sandecker stiffened. His eyes looked resentfully into the fat man's. "Okay, send him in."

Pitt came through the door and shut it behind him. He moved stiffly across the room to a vacant sofa and very slowly eased into the soft cushions. His entire face was swathed in bandages, only the slits for his eyes and nose plus the top opening for a patch of black hair gave any indication of life beneath the rolls of white gauze. Sandecker tried to look behind the bandages. The deep green eyes that were visible never seemed to flicker.

Sandecker sat down behind the desk and clasped his hand behind his head. "Do the doctors at the hospital know where you are?"

Pitt smiled. "I suspect they'll wonder in another half hour."

"I believe you've met this gentleman." Sandecker motioned to the fat man.

"We've talked over the telephone," Pitt answered. "We haven't been formally introduced . . . at least not with proper names."

The fat man moved quickly around the desk and offered Pitt his hand. "Kippmann, Dean Kippmann."

Pitt took the hand. It was a fooler. There was nothing weak and fat about the grip. "Dean Kippmann," Pitt repeated. "The chief of the National Intelligence Agency. There's nothing like playing with the big leaguers."

"We deeply appreciate your help," Kippmann said warmly. "Do you feel up to a little air travel?"

"After Iceland, a little South American sun couldn't hurt."

"You'll enjoy the sun all right." Kippmann stroked the skin on his head again. "Particularly the southern California variety."

"Southern California?"

"By four o'clock this afternoon."

"By four o'clock this afternoon?"

"At Disneyland."

"At Disneyland?"

Sandecker said patiently: "I'm well aware that your destination isn't exactly what you had in mind. But we can do without the echo."

"With respects, sir, none of this figures."

"Until an hour ago, those were our words precisely," Kippmann said.

"Just what have you got in mind?" Pitt asked.

"This." Kippmann pulled more papers from his seemingly bottomless briefcase and studied them briefly. "Until we were able to question you and the other survivors who were physically up to it, we had only a sketchy idea at best as to the purpose behind Hermit Limited. We knew it existed, and we were fortunate to ferret out a small percentage of their business dealings, but their ultimate goal, the brains, the money behind the entire operation remained a mystery—"

Pitt broke in guardedly. "But you had a lead. You suspected Dr. Hunnewell."

"I'm glad you didn't tumble sooner, Major. Yes, the N.I.A. was trailing Dr. Hunnewell. No concrete evidence, of course. That's why we set him up—in the hope he would lead us to the men at the top of the organization."

"Oh, God, it *was* a setup!" It wasn't easy to combine a sour exclamation and an anguished moan in the same breath, but Pitt pulled it off. "The whole goddamned scene on that iceberg was a setup."

"Yes, Hunnewell came to our attention when he so thoughtfully provided all the right solutions for Fyrie Limited's undersea probe, but offered absolutely nothing toward the efforts under development in his own country."

"Then emtombing the *Lax* was a neat little piece of deception," Pitt said. "That was your drawing card. Hunnewell was bound to come forward as an investigator when the admiral here asked him out of what seemed sheer coincidence. Hunnewell probably couldn't believe his luck. He immediately volunteered, not to see what happened to his old friend Kristjan Fyrie—he'd already guessed that—or to inspect the strange phenomenon of a ship locked in ice, but rather to discover what had become of his precious undersea probe."

"Again, yes, Major." Kippmann handed Pitt several glossy photographs. "Here are pictures taken from the submarine that kept a watch on the *Lax* for almost three weeks. They show an unusual feature about the crew."

Pitt ignored him and looked up at Sandecker severely and steadily. "The truth comes out at last. The *Lax* was found by the search fleet and then tailed until it burned."

Sandecker shrugged. "Mr. Kippmann took the trouble to notify me of that interesting little fact only last night." The tight grin on his griffinlike features hardly indicated friendliness toward Kippmann.

"Reproach us if you will," Kippmann said seriously, "but it was vital that you both were kept on the sidelines as much as possible. If Kelly or Rondheim or particularly Hunnewell had smelled your connection with us, our whole operation would have bombed." He stared at Pitt, his voice low. "Major, you were simply to act as pilot and escort for Hunnewell while he inspected the *Lax*. You then were to fly him to Reykjavik where we would have again taken over our observation of his movements."

"It didn't quite work out that way, did it?"

"We underestimated the other side," Kippmann said candidly.

Pitt inhaled on a cigarette and idly watched the smoke curl toward the ceiling. "You haven't explained how the *Lax* came to be in the iceberg. Nor have you shed any light on what happened to the pirate crew, or given a hint as to how Fyrie and his crew and scientists could disappear for over a year and then suddenly have their charred bodies turn up on the ship again."

"The answer to both questions is simple," Kippmann said. "Fyrie's crew never left the ship."

Sandecker took his hands from behind his head and slowly leaned forward, placing them palms down on the desk in front of him. His eyes were rock-hard. "Matajic reported a crew of Arabs, not fair-haired Scandinavians."

"That's true," Kippmann agreed. "I think if you gentlemen will oblige me by glancing at these photographs, you'll see what I mean about the crew."

He passed the prints to Sandecker and extra copies to Pitt. He then sat down in a chair and lit a cigarette after inserting it in a long holder. Kippmann was totally relaxed. Pitt was beginning to think the man would have yawned if he'd been stabbed in the crotch.

"Please note photo number one," Kippmann said. "It was taken with a very sharp telephoto lens through a periscope. As you can see, it clearly shows ten crew members going about their duties on various parts of the ship. There isn't a dark-skinned man in the bunch."

"Coincidence," Sandecker said guardedly. "The Arabs Matajic reported seeing might have been below."

"A slim possibility, Admiral, providing we stopped at one picture. However, the other photos were taken at different times and on different days. By comparing them all together, we get a count of approximately fourteen men, not one of Arab ancestry. Surely, gentlemen, if there were even one Arab on that ship, he would have had to make an appearance during a three-week period." Kippmann broke off and tapped his cigarette holder against the rim of an ashtray. "Also, we have definitely identified the faces in the photographs as the same people who set sail on the *Lax* shortly before it vanished."

"And what of Matajic?" Sandecker asked, probing. "He was a top scientist, trained in accurate observation. Surely he was positive of what he saw—"

"Matajic saw men who were made up to look like other nationalities," Kippmann said. "The crew should have been masters at disguise by the time he stumbled onto them—remember they had visited a number of ports. They took no chances of recognition. It's only guesswork, of course, we'll never know for certain, but it's fairly safe to say the crew caught O'Riley watching them and slipped into their phony pose before Matajic came on board for supper."

"I see," Pitt said mildly. "And then what?"

"You can guess the rest, if you don't already know it." Kippmann toyed with his cigarette holder a moment and then continued. "Somehow, it's not difficult to imagine, the celtinium-279 ignited and transformed the *Lax* into a floating incinerator. Our submarine could only stand by and watch helplessly—it happened so quickly, there were no survivors. Fortunately the Navy had put a fast-thinking skipper in command of the sub. A storm was approaching and he knew it was only a question of time before the red-hot plates on the *Lax*'s hull cooled and contracted, bursting their seams and letting the sea water flood in and sink her, a finale further speeded by the Force Eight storm building on the horizon."

"So he turned a twenty-million-dollar submarine into a tugboat and nudged the burning hulk against a convenient iceberg until it melted its way inside." Pitt sat there looking at Kippmann, his expression pleasant.

"Your theory is quite correct, Major," Kippmann said thinly.

"Not my theory." Pitt smiled. "Dr. Hunnewell's. It

was he who came up with the hot poker in ice pro-
posal."

"I see," Kippmann said, but he didn't.

"The next question that interests me directly"—
Pitt hesitated, mashing out his cigarette—"is why did
you send Hunnewell and me chasing all over the North
Atlantic hunting down a particular iceberg after you
erased all of its distinguishable markings? Why did you
set Hunnewell up to find the *Lax* and then deliberately
try to hide it?"

Impassively Kippmann stared at Pitt. "Thanks to
you, Major, my men were forced to work their asses off
in freezing temperatures, chipping the Coast Guard's
red dye marker from the iceberg simply because you
showed up two days ahead of schedule."

"You were going over the *Lax* with a fine-toothed
comb and hadn't finished when Hunnewell and I appeared on the scene. Is that it?"

"Precisely," Kippmann said. "Nobody expected
you to fly a helicopter through the aftermath of the season's worst storm."

"Then your men were there—" Pitt broke off,
looked at Kippmann for a long speculative moment,
then went on quietly, "Your agents were concealed on
the berg the entire time Hunnewell and I explored the
Lax."

Kippmann shrugged. "You didn't give us a chance
to pull them off."

Pitt half rose from the couch. "You mean they
stood by and did nothing when Hunnewell and I
damned near fell from the berg into the sea, no rope, no
help, no encouraging word, nothing?"

"In our business we have to be ruthless." Kippmann offered a tired smile. "We don't like it, but we have
to. It's just that it's the nature of the game."

"A game?" Pitt said. "A fantasy of intrigue? A
sport of make-believe dog eat dog? You're in a rotten
occupation?"

"A never-ending cycle, my friend," Kippmann said
acidly. "We didn't start out to be this way. America has

always been the good guy. But you can't play white knight when the other side uses every dirty rule in the book."

"Granted, we're the land of suckers, always believing that good never fails to triumph over evil. But where does that leave us? Back in Disneyland?"

"I'll come to that in due time," Kippmann said with restraint. "Now then, from what you and the others in the hospital reported, Hermit Limited intends to make their move approximately nine hours and forty-five minutes from now. Their first step will be to assassinate the leader of the Latin American country that they plan to take over. Am I correct?"

"That's what the man said," Pitt nodded. "Beginning with Bolivia."

"You shouldn't believe all you hear, Major. Kelly only used Bolivia as an example. He and his group aren't strong enough for a country that size. He's too much of a businessman to make a grab until he is ninety percent sure of a profit."

"The target could be any one of half a dozen countries," said Sandecker. "How in hell can you be sure which one it is?"

"We have computers too," Kippmann said with some satisfaction. "The processed data narrowed the choice down to four. Major Pitt helpfully narrowed it down to two."

"You've lost me," Pitt said. "How could I—"

"The models you dredged from the sea," Kippmann cut in quickly. "One is the exact replica of the capitol building of the Dominican Republic. The other is the government legislative chambers of French Guiana."

"A fifty-fifty chance at best," Sandecker said slowly.

"Not really," Kippmann said. "It's the honored opinion of the N.I.A. that Kelly and his little troop will try for a double-header."

"Both countries at once?" Sandecker looked at Kippmann inquiringly. "You can't be serious?"

"Yes, we're serious, and if you'll pardon the expression, we're deadly serious."

"What can Kelly hope to gain by splitting his efforts?" Pitt asked.

"Trying for the Dominican Republic and French Guiana at the same time isn't the gamble it seems." Kippmann pulled a map from the folder and smoothed it on Sandecker's desk. "On the northern coast of South America you have Venezuela, and British, Dutch and French Guiana. Further north, a day's passage by boat, a few hours' flight by plane, the island that contains Haiti and the Dominican Republic. Strategically it's a beautiful situation."

"In what way?"

"Suppose," Kippmann said thoughtfully, "just suppose a dictator who ruled Cuba also ruled Florida as well."

Sandecker looked at Kippmann, his face set and intense. "By God, it is a beautiful situation. It would only be a matter of time before Hermit Limited, operating on the same island, strangled Haiti's economy and took over."

"Yes, then using the island as a base, they could slowly spread into the central Latin countries and absorb them one by one."

Pitt's voice was impassive. "History recalls that Fidel Castro tried to infiltrate the mainland countries and failed on every occasion."

"Yes," Kippmann repeated. "But Kelly and Hermit Limited have the one thing Castro lacked—a foothold. Kelly will have French Guiana." He paused in reflection a moment. "A foothold as sure and as firm as the Allies had in 1944 when they invaded France at Normandy."

Pitt shook his head slowly. "And I thought Kelly was insane. The bastard just might do it. He just might pull his fantastic scheme off."

Kippmann nodded. "Let us say, considering all facts, at the present time the odd makers would probably lay their bets in favor of Kelly and Hermit Limited."

"Maybe we should let him do it," Sandecker said. "Maybe he was somehow meant to have his utopia."

"No, it is not meant to be," Kippmann said calmly. "It can never happen."

"You seem pretty certain," Pitt said.

Kippmann stared at him and grinned thinly. "Didn't I tell you? One of the birds that tried to kill you in that doctor's office decided to cooperate. He told us quite a story."

"It seems there are a number of things you forgot to tell us." Sandecker grunted acidly.

Kippmann went on. "Kelly's glorious enterprise is doomed to failure; I have it on the best authority." He paused, his grin broadening. "As soon as Hermit Limited is entrenched in the Dominican Republic and French Guiana, there will be a proxy fight among the board of directors. Major Pitt's passing acquaintance, Mr. Oskar Rondheim, intends to eliminate Kelly, Marks, Von Hummel and the rest and take over as chairman of the board. Sad to say, Mr. Rondheim's future intentions will hardly be classed as honorable and benevolent."

Tidi was sitting prettily in a wheelchair beside Lillie's bed when Pitt entered the hospital room, followed by Sandecker and Kippmann.

"The doctors tell me you'll both live," Pitt said, smiling. "Just thought I'd . . . ah . . . drop by and offer my farewells."

"You're leaving?" Tidi asked sadly.

"Afraid so. Someone has to identify Rondheim's triggermen."

"You—be careful," she stammered. "After all you went through to save us, we don't want to lose you now."

Lillie raised his head stiffly. "Why didn't you say something out there in the ravine?" he asked seriously. "God, I had no idea your ribs were kicked in."

"It made no difference. I was the only one who could walk. Besides, I never fail to get carried away when I have a good audience."

Lillie smiled. "You had the best."

Pitt asked, "How's your back?"

"I'll be in this miserable body cast longer than I care to think about, but at least I'll be able to dance again when it comes off."

Pitt stared down at Tidi. Her face was pale and tears were beginning to well in her eyes and Pitt understood.

"When the big day arrives," Pitt said, forcing a grin, "we'll celebrate with a party, even if it means I have to drink your old man's beer."

"That I'll have to see."

Sandecker cleared his throat. "Ah . . . I take it that Miss Royal is as good a nurse as she is a secretary."

Lillie grasped Tidi's hand. "I'd break a bone every day of the week if it always meant meeting someone like her."

There was a short pause. "I think we should be leaving," Kippmann said. "Our Air Force transportation is waiting even now."

Pitt leaned down and kissed Tidi and then shook Lillie's hand. "Look after yourselves. I'll be expecting an invitation to that party soon." He turned his palms upward and shrugged helplessly. "God only knows where I'll be able to find a date who'd be seen in public with a battered face like this."

Tidi laughed at that. He squeezed her shoulder and then turned and left the room.

In the car on the way to the air base, Pitt stared out the window, his eyes unseeing, his mind back in the hospital. "He'll never walk again, will he?"

Kippman shook his head sadly. "It's doubtful . . . very doubtful."

Fifteen minutes later, without a further word being spoken, they arrived at the Keflavik Air Field to find an Air Force B-92 reconnaissance bomber waiting by the terminal. Another ten minutes and the supersonic jet was speeding down the runway, soaring out over the ocean.

Sandecker, alone in the terminal, watched the plane lifting into the azure sky, his eyes following it until it disappeared into the distance of the cloudless horizon. Then, wearily, he walked back to the car.

Chapter
21

Because of the seven-hour time gain in flying from east to west and the twelve-hundred-mile-per-hour-plus speed of the jet bomber, it was still on the morning of the same day he left Iceland when a bleary-eyed Pitt yawned, stretched in the confined limitations of the tiny cabin, and looking idly out the navigator's side window, watched the tiny shadow of the aircraft dart across the green slopes of the Sierra Madre mountains.

And what now? Pitt smiled wryly back at his reflection in the glass as the bomber now swung out of the foothills and across the smog-blanketed San Gabriel Valley. Gazing down at the Pacific Ocean as it came into view, he cleared his mind of the past and directed it on the immediate future. He didn't know how nor did he have even a remote scrap for a plan, but he knew, no matter the obstacles, he knew he was going to kill Oskar Rondheim.

His mind abruptly returned to the present as the landing gear thumped down and locked into place at the same moment that Dean Kippmann nudged him on the arm.

"Have a nice nap?"

"Slept like the dead."

The B-92 touched down and the engines screamed

as the pilot threw the thrust into reverse. The day outside looked warm and comfortable and the California sun gleamed blindingly on the long rows of military jets parked along the taxiways. Pitt read the twelve-foot-high letters painted across a giant hangar: WELCOME TO EL TORO MARINE AIR STATION.

The bomber's engines slowly died and an automobile sped over the apron as Pitt, Kippmann and the Air Force crew climbed down a narrow ladder to the concrete. Two men unreeled from a blue Ford stationwagon and approached Kippmann. Greetings and handshakes were exchanged. Then they all walked back to the car. Pitt, left standing with nothing to do, followed them.

Beside an open car door the three men huddled together and conversed in undertones while Pitt stood several feet away and enjoyed a cigarette. Finally Kippmann turned and came over.

"It seems we're about to crash a family reunion."

"Meaning?"

"They're all here. Kelly, Marks, Rondheim, the whole lot."

"Here in California?" Pitt asked incredulously.

"Yes, we had them traced as soon as they left Iceland. The serial number you found on that black jet came home a winner. Hermit Limited purchased six of the same model with consecutive numbers from the factory. We have every one of the remaining five planes under surveillance at this moment."

"I'm impressed. That was fast work."

Kippmann dropped a smile. "Not all that tough. It might have been if the planes had been scattered around the globe, but as it is, they're all sitting neatly side by side exactly eight miles from here at the Orange County Airport."

"Then Kelly's headquarters must be nearby."

"In the hills behind Laguna Beach, a fifty-acre complex," Kippmann said, pointing in a southwesterly direction. "Incidentally, Hermit Limited has over three hundred employees on the payroll who think they're doing classified political analysis for their own government."

"Where do we go from here?"

Kippmann motioned Pitt into the car. "Disneyland," he said solemnly, "to stop a double murder."

They pulled onto the Santa Ana Freeway and headed north, weaving in and out of the light morning traffic. As they passed the Newport Beach turnoff, Pitt couldn't help wondering if the beautiful redhead he had met on the beach just a few days ago would still be there waiting at the Newporter Inn.

Kippmann produced two photographs and shoved them in front of Pitt. "Here are the men we're trying to save."

Pitt tapped the face in one of the photos. "This is Pablo Castile, President of the Dominican Republic."

Kippmann nodded. "A brilliant economist and one of the leading members of the Latin American right. Since his inauguration he has begun an ambitious program of reforms. For the first time the people of his country are projecting an atmosphere of confidence and optimism. Our state department would hate like hell to see Kelly screw things up just when there's hope of the Dominican Republic becoming economically stable."

Pitt held up the other photo. "I can't place him."

"Juan De Croix," Kippmann said. "A highly successful doctor of East Indian ancestry. Leader of the People's Progressive Party—won the election only six months ago. Now President of French Guiana."

"If I remember my current events, he's got problems."

"He's got problems, all right," Kippmann agreed. "French Guiana is less prosperous than the British or Dutch Guianas. A movement for independence developed five years ago, but it was only under the threat of a revolution that the French permitted a new constitution and a general election. De Croix, of course, walked off with the votes and proclaimed total independence. He's got an uphill battle. His country suffers from tropical diseases of every type and from chronic shortages of domestic food. I don't envy him; no one does."

"De Croix's government is vulnerable," said Pitt thoughtfully. "But what of Castile's cabinet, aren't his ministers strong enough to survive his death?"

"With the people, maybe. But the Dominican army isn't too faithful. A military junta would no doubt take over, except in this case Kelly has obviously bought off the generals."

"How is it both of these men are at the same place at the same time?"

"If you'd read the papers, you'd know the leaders of the Western Hemisphere have just finished a conference in San Francisco for the Alliance of Economic and Agricultural Progress. De Croix, Castile and several other Latin leaders are doing a little sightseeing on the way home. It's that simple."

"Why didn't you stop them from entering the park?"

"I tried, but by the time our internal security forces could act, it was too late. De Croix and Castile have already been in the park for two hours and both refuse to leave. We can only keep our fingers crossed that Rondheim's killers stick to their time schedule."

"Cutting it a bit fine, aren't you?" Pitt said slowly.

Kippmann shrugged indifferently. "Some things you can control, others you can only stand by and watch."

The car turned off the freeway onto Harbor Boulevard and soon pulled up to the employees' gate, and while the driver showed his credentials and asked directions from the guard, Pitt leaned out the window and watched the monorail train pass overhead. They were at the north end of the park and all he could see over the landscaped mounds that surrounded the buildings was the top half of the Matterhorn and the turrets on the Fantasyland castle. The gate was pushed open and they were passed in.

By the time Pitt walked down the underground hallway to the park security offices, he was beginning to think how good that hospital bed in Reykjavik had felt and wondered how soon he could fall into a replacement. He wasn't sure what he expected to find in the park security offices but he had hardly envisioned what he stepped into.

The main conference room was huge; it looked like a scaled-down version of the war room at the Pentagon. The main table ran for at least fifty feet and was circled by over twenty people. There was a radio in one corner and the operator was busily pointing out locations to a marker who stood on a ramp beneath a map that must have stretched ten feet high and covered half the facing wall. Pitt walked slowly around the table and stood under the beautifully contoured and painted map of Disneyland. He was studying the many colored lights and the trail of blue fluorescent tape the marker was laying through the park traffic areas when Kippmann tapped him on the shoulder.

"Ready to go to work?"

"My body is still running on Iceland time. It's past five o'clock there. I could stand a little bracer."

"I'm sorry, sir." The words came from a big man, a tall pipe-smoking man whose eyes stared out at Pitt from behind fashionable rimless glasses. "Alcohol has never been permitted in any area of the park since we opened. And we intend to keep it that way."

"Sorry about that," Pitt said good-naturedly. He looked at Kippmann expectantly.

Kippmann took the cue. "Major Dirk Pitt, allow me to introduce Mr. Dan Lazard, Chief of Park Security."

Lazard's grip was firm. "Mr. Kippmann has filled me in concerning your injuries. Do you think you're up to this?"

"I can handle it," Pitt said somberly. "But we'll have to do something about my bandaged profile—it's a bit conspicuous."

A glint of amusement came into Lazard's eyes. "I think we can fix it so no one will notice your bandages—not even the nurse who taped them."

Later Pitt stood in front of the full-length mirror and struck a menacing pose. He was torn between uttering laughter or a stream of four-lettered words from embarrassment as he stared at the life-sized figure of the Big Bad Wolf, who impolitely stared back at him.

"You've got to admit," Kippmann said, fighting back a chuckle, "your own mother wouldn't recognize you in that rig."

"I suppose it *is* in keeping with my character," Pitt said. He removed the wolf's head, sat down in a chair and sighed. "How much time have we left?"

"Another hour and forty minutes to go before Kelly's deadline."

"Don't you think I should be sent in the game now? You're not leaving me much time to spot the killers . . . if I can spot them."

"Between my men, the park security staff and agents from the F.B.I., there must be close to forty people concentrating every effort on stopping the assassination. I'm saving you for when we come down to the wire."

"Scraping the bottom of the barrel for a last-ditch attempt." Pitt leaned back and relaxed. "I can't say I agree with your tactics."

"You're not working with amateurs, Major. Every one of those people out there are pros. Some are dressed in costumes like you, some are walking hand in hand like lovers on a holiday, some are playing the part of families enjoying the rides, others have taken over as attendants. We even have men stationed on roofs and in the dummy second-story offices with telescopes and binoculars." Kippmann's voice was soft, but it carried total conviction. "The killers will be found and stopped before they do their dirty work. The odds we've stacked against Kelly meeting his goal and deadline are staggering."

"Tell that to Oskar Rondheim," Pitt said. "There's the flaw that knocks the hell out of your good intentions—you don't know your adversary."

The silence lay heavy in the small room. Kippmann rubbed his palms across his face, then shook his head slowly, as if he were about to do something he intensely disliked. He picked up the ever-present briefcase and handed Pitt a folder marked simply 078-34.

"Granted, I haven't met him face to face, but he is no stranger to me." Kippmann read from the folder. " 'Oskar Rondheim, alias Max Rolland, alias Hugo von Klausen, alias Chatford Marazan, real name Carzo Butera, born in Brooklyn, New York, July 15, 1940.' I could go on for hours about his arrests, his convictions. He was pretty big along the New York waterfront. Organized the fishermen's union. Got muscled out by the syndicate and dropped from sight. Over the past few years we kept close tabs on Mr. Rondheim and his albatross industries. We finally put two and two together and came up with Carzo Butera."

A sly grin crept across Pitt's face. "You've made your point. It would be interesting to see what your scandal sheet has to say about me."

"I have it right here," Kippmann said, matching Pitt's grin. "Care to see it?"

"No, thanks. It couldn't tell me anything that I don't already know," Pitt said flatly. "I would be interested though in seeing what you have on Kirsti Fyrie."

Kippmann's expression went blank and he looked as if he had been shot. "I was hoping you wouldn't get around to her."

"You have her file also." It was more statement than question.

"Yes," Kippmann answered briefly. He saw there was no way out, no argument that would stand. He sighed with uneasiness and handed Pitt file number 883-57.

Pitt reached out and took the folder. For ten minutes he examined the contents, leafing very slowly, almost reluctantly from documents to photos, from reports to letters. Then finally, like a man in a dream, he closed the folder and gave it back to Kippmann.

"I can't believe it. It's ridiculous. I won't believe it."

"I'm afraid what you read is true, all of it." Kippmann's voice was quiet, even.

Pitt pulled the back of his hand across his eyes. "Never, never in a thousand years would I have . . ." His voice faded away.

"It threw us out of gear too. Our first hint came when we could find no trace of her on New Guinea."

"I know. I'd already pegged her for a phony on that score."

"You knew? But how?"

"When we had dinner together in Reykjavik, I described a recipe that called for shark meat wrapped in a seaweed known as echidna. Miss Fyrie accepted it. Rather strange behavior from a missionary who spent years in the jungles of New Guinea, don't you think?"

"How the hell should I know." Kippmann shrugged. "I don't have the vaguest notion as to what an echidna is."

"An echidna," Pitt said, "is an egg-laying spiny anteater. A mammal very common to the landscape of New Guinea."

"I can't say I blame her for missing the catch."

"How would you react if I said I was going to barbecue a New York cut steak wrapped in porcupine quills?"

"I'd say something."

"You've got the idea."

Kippmann stared at Pitt with an admiring look. "What put you on to her in the first place? You wouldn't have tricked her without a nudge, without a suspicious hint."

"Her tan," Pitt answered. "It was shallow—not burned deep like one acquired after years and months spent in a tropic jungle."

"You, sir, are very observant," Kippmann murmured thoughtfully. "But why . . . why bother to trip up someone you barely knew?"

"Partly for the same reason I'm standing here in this ridiculous wolf suit," Pitt said grimly. "I volunteered for your little manhunt for two reasons. One, I've got a score to even with Rondheim and Kelly, no more, no less. Second, I'm still Special Projects Director for NUMA, and as such, my primary duty is to obtain the plans for Fyrie's undersea mineral probe. That's why I conned Kirsti—she knows where the blueprints are hidden. By knowing something I shouldn't have, it gave me a wedge, a lever to get to her."

Kippmann nodded. "Now I understand." He sat on the edge of a desk and toyed with a letter opener. "Okay, after I have Kelly and his group in custody, I'll turn her over to you and Admiral Sandecker for questioning."

"Not good enough," Pitt snapped. "If you want my continued cooperation as an identifying witness, then you must promise me a few minutes alone with Rondheim. And full and complete custody of Kirsti Fyrie."

"Impossible!"

"Not really. Rondheim's future physical condition can matter little to you."

"Even if I turned my back so you could kick him in the teeth, I couldn't let you have Kirsti Fyrie."

"You could," Pitt said positively. "Mostly because she isn't yours to give. If you're lucky, you might pin an accomplice charge on her. But that might strain our relations with Iceland, an event that wouldn't make our State Department exactly jump for joy."

"You're wasting your breath," Kippmann said impatiently. "She will be convicted of murder along with all the rest."

"Yours is not to convict, yours is to apprehend and arrest."

Kippmann shook his head. "You don't understand—"

He broke off as the door opened wide. Lazard stood framed in the doorway, his face ashen.

Kippmann stared at him curiously. "Dan, what is it?"

Lazard wiped his brow and slumped into an empty chair. "De Croix and Castile have suddenly changed their planned excursion. They've shaken their escort and disappeared somewhere in the park. God only knows what can happen before we find them."

Frowning, baffled, Kippmann's face expressed a moment of utter uncomprehension. "Christ!" he exploded. "How could it happen? How could you lose them with half the federal agents in the state guarding their party?"

"There are twenty thousand people out there in the park right this minute," Lazard said in a patient tone. "It doesn't take any great feat of cleverness to misplace two of them." He shrugged helplessly. "De Croix and Castile bitched about our heavy security precautions from the second they stepped through the main gate. They went to the john together and gave us the slip by ducking out a side window, just like a pair of kids."

Pitt stood up. "Quickly, do you have their tour and scheduled stops?"

Lazard stared at him for a moment. "Yes, here, each amusement and exhibit and their time schedules." He handed Pitt a Xeroxed sheet of paper.

Pitt rapidly glanced at the schedule. Then a slow grin cut his face as he turned to Kippmann. "You'd better send me into the game, coach."

"Major," Kippmann said unhappily. "I have the feeling I'm about to be blackmailed."

"As they say during campus riots, will you meet our demands?"

The slumping of Kippmann's shoulders displayed as sure a sign of defeat as if he'd waved a white flag. He stared at Pitt. The eyes that stared back were disconcertingly steady.

Kippmann nodded. "Rondheim and Miss Fyrie are yours. They're staying in the Disneyland Hotel across the street. Adjoining rooms, 605 and 607."

"And Kelly, Marks, Von Hummel and the rest?"

"They're all there. Hermit Limited reserved the entire sixth floor." Kippmann rubbed his face uncomfortably. "Just what do you have in mind?"

"Rest easy. Five minutes with Rondheim. Then you can have him. Kirsti Fyrie I keep. Call her a little bonus from the N.I.A. to NUMA."

Kippmann gave up completely. "You win. Now where are De Croix and Castile?"

"The obvious." Pitt smiled at Kippmann and La-

zard. "The most obvious place where any two men who
passed their childhood near the Spanish Main would
head."

"God, you've hit it," Lazard said almost bitterly.
"The last stop on the schedule—*The Pirates of the Caribbean.*"

Next to the cleverly engineered apparitions in the
Disneyland Haunted House, The Pirates of the Caribbean is the most popular attraction in the world-famous
park. Constructed on two underground levels that oc-
cupy nearly two acres, the quarter-of-a-mile boat ride
carries awed passengers through a maze of tunnels and
vast rooms decorated as roving pirate ships and pillaged
seaside towns, manned by almost a hundred lifelike figures that not only match the best of Madame Tussaud's,
but who also sing, dance and loot.

Pitt was the last one up the entrance ramp to the
landing where the attendants assist the paying customers
into the boats at the start of the fifteen-minute excursion. The fifty or sixty people waiting in line waved to
Pitt and made smiling remarks about his costume as he
made his way behind Kippmann and Lazard. He waved
back, wondering what the expressions on their faces
would be if he were to suddenly whip off his wolf's
mask and display his bandaged face. He could see at
least ten small children who would never again want the
Three Little Pigs read at bedtime.

Lazard grasped the managing attendant by the
arm. "Quickly, you must stop the boats."

The attendant, a blond, lanky boy no more than
twenty years of age, simply stood there in mute uncomprehension.

Lazard, obviously a man who disliked wasted
conversation, moved hurriedly across the landing to
the controls, disengaged the underwater traction chain
that pulled the excursion boats, set the handbrake and
turned to face the stunned boy again.

"Two men, two men together, have they taken the
ride?"

The dazed boy could only stammer. "I . . . I

don't know for sure, sir. There . . . there's been so many. I can't recall them all——"

Kippmann stepped in front of Lazard and showed the boy the photographs of Castile and De Croix. "Do you recognize these men?"

The boy's eyes widened. "Yes, sir, now I remember." Then a frown spread across his youthful face. "But they weren't alone. There were two other men with them."

"Four!" Kippmann shouted, turning about thirty heads. "Are you sure?"

"Yes, sir." The boy nodded his head violently. "I'm positive. The boat holds eight people. The first four seats held a man and woman with two kids. The men in the photographs took the rear seats with two other men."

Pitt arrived just then, his breath coming in short pants, his hand clutching the handrail as he fought off the pain and exhaustion. "Was one of them a big guy with a bald head, hairy hands? And the other, red-faced with a huge moustache and shoulders like an ape?"

The boy stared dumbly for a moment at Pitt's disguise. Then his expression took on a half smile "You hit them exactly. A real pair. Like tough-looking Mutt and Jeff characters."

Pitt turned to Kippmann and Lazard. "Gentlemen," he said, his voice slightly muffled under the rubber wolf's head, "I think we've just missed our boat."

"For God's sake!" Kippmann murmured in exasperation. "We can't just stand here."

"No." Lazard shook his head. "We can't do that." He nodded at the boy. "Call extension 309. Tell whoever answers that Lazard has relocated the missing party in The Pirates of the Caribbean. Tell them it's a red situation—the hunters are in there too." He turned back to Kippmann and Pitt. "The three of us can work along the catwalks and the backdrops until we reach them, and only hope we're not too late."

"How many boats ago did they board?" Pitt asked the boy.

"Ten, maybe twelve. They should be sitting about

halfway, probably somewhere between the burning village and the cannon battle."

"This way!" Lazard almost snapped the words. He disappeared through a doorway at the end of the landing marked EMPLOYEES ONLY.

As they moved into the blackness that cloaked the mechanical workings of the pirates, the sound of voices from the passengers of the stalled boats could be heard murmuring throughout the cavernous amusement ride. Castle and De Croix, as well as their assassins, Pitt reflected, could have little suspicion as to the delay, but even so, it didn't seem to matter: there was every possibility that Kelly's and Rondheim's scheme had already been carried out. He fought off the ache in his chest and followed the squat, dim form of Kippmann past a storyland setting of five pirates burying a treasure chest. The figures seemed so lifelike it was difficult for Pitt to believe they were only electronically controlled mannequins. He was so engrossed in the simulated reality of the scene that he rammed into Kippmann, who had stopped abruptly.

"Easy, easy," Kippmann protested.

Lazard motioned to them to stay where they were as he moved catlike along a narrow corridor and leaned over the railing of a workman's gallery running over the canal that supported the boats. Then he waved Pitt and Kippmann forward.

"We got lucky for a change," he said. "Take a look."

Pitt, his eyes not yet accustomed to the dark, stared below at a sight that never was—a wild fantasy night scene containing a band of at least thirty pirates burning and looting what seemed to be a replica of a miniature Port Royal or Panama City. Flames were shooting out of several buildings. while silhouettes of laughing buccaneers chased screaming make-believe girls around and around the back-lighted windows. Boisterous singing was reverberating out of hidden speakers, giving the illusion that rape and pillage were merely good clean fun.

The canal the boats circuited through cut between the town buildings, shifting the viewers' eyes from a pair of pirates trying vainly to get a mule to pull a wagonload of their loot on the left to a trio of their shipmates drinking on a pile of wildly swaying wine barrels on the right. But it was the center of the canal that drew Pitt's attention. There in a boat almost directly under a bridge that ran over the water were Castile and De Croix, happily pointing out details of the wondrous scene like two schoolboys playing hookey at a Friday matinee. And, sitting ominously like disinterested statues on the seat directly in back of the South American Presidents, Pitt could make out the two men who had held his arms while Rondheim had battered him to a pulp only two days before in Reykjavik.

Pitt glanced at the luminous dial of the orange-faced Doxa watch on his wrist. Still an hour and twenty minutes before Kelly's countdown. Too early, far too early, yet there were two of Rondheim's killers sitting not three feet from their intended victims. A very large piece was missing from the puzzle. He had no doubt that Kelly told the truth about his timetable and that Rondheim would stick to it. But would he? If Rondheim meant to take over Hermit Limited, it stood to reason that he just might make a change in plans.

"This is your show, Dan." Kippmann spoke softly to the security director. "How do we take them?"

"No guns," Lazard said. "The last thing we want is a stray shot killing a child."

"Maybe we'd better wait for reinforcements," Kippmann said.

"No time," Lazard said. "We've kept the boats stopped too long already. Everyone is starting to get edgy, including those two characters in back of Castile and De Croix."

"Then we'll have to take a risk." Kippmann wiped a handkerchief across his damp brow. "Get the boats moving again. Then as soon as the one with our friends begins to cross under the bridge, we'll take them."

"Okay," Lazard agreed. "The bridge will give us

enough cover to close within five feet. I'll work around and come out of that doorway under the grogshop sign. Kippmann, you hide behind the mule and wagon."

"Need an extra hand?" Pitt asked.

"Sorry, Major." Lazard gave Pitt a cool stare. "You're hardly in shape for hand-to-hand combat." He paused and gripped Pitt's shoulder. "You could pull off a vital role though."

"Say the word."

"By standing on the bridge in your wolf costume and mingling with the pirates, you could distract those two in the boat long enough to give Kippmann and myself a few more seconds of insurance."

"I guess it beats hell out of matching wits with the three little pigs," Pitt said.

As soon as Lazard found a call phone and ordered the attendant to start the canal boats moving in two minutes, he and Kippmann dropped into the burning village behind the realistic-looking building fronts and took their positions.

After he stumbled over the stuffed body of a pirate who supposedly had passed out from too much wine, Pitt reached down and relieved the mannequin of its cutlass and was surprised to find that it was a steel replica of the real thing. Even at close range he could only marvel at the true-to-life appearance of the mechanical pirates. The glass eyes set in brown wax faces stared unerringly in whatever direction the head was set, and the eyebrows raised up and down in unison with the lips as the strains of "Sixteen Men on a Dead Man's Chest" boomed from speakers concealed within their aluminum-frame bodies.

Pitt moved to the center of the arched bridge over the canal and joined in the singing amid three merry buccaneers who sat with their legs dangling over the fake stone parapet, swirling their cutlasses around in circles in tune with the songfest. Pitt in his Big Bad Wolf suit and the frolicking pirates presented a strange sight to the people in the boat as they waved and sang the famous old seafaring ditty. The children, a girl about ten and a boy, Pitt guessed, no more than seven, soon recognized him as the three-dimensional cartoon character and began waving back.

Castile and De Croix also laughed and then saluted him in Spanish, pointing and joking to themselves while the tall, bald assassin and his accomplice, the broad-shouldered brute, sat stony-faced, unmoved by the performance. It occurred to Pitt that he was on thin ice, on which not merely a false move, but the tiniest miscalculation of any detail could spell death to the men, woman and children who sat innocently enjoying his antics.

Then he saw the boat move.

The bow was just passing under his feet when the shadowy figures of Kippmann and Lazard leaped from their cover, sprinted through the mass of animated figures and dropped into the rear of the boat. The surprise was complete. But Pitt hadn't noticed. No fuss, no elaborate flourish, no token words of warning, he coldly and efficiently shoved the blade of his cutlass under the armpit and into the chest cavity of the pirate sitting nearest him.

A curious thing happened. The pirate dropped his cutlass, his lips contorted into a soundless oval, eyes registering astonishment and shock, a shock almost immediately replaced by a final awareness. Then the eyes turned up in the head and he fell forward splashing into the now empty canal beneath the bridge.

The second pirate failed to react in the split second when he might have parried Pitt's swing. He started to say something. Then, with cutlass still dripping red, Pitt put all his strength into a backhand slash that bit into the base of the pirate's neck at the left shoulder blade. The man grunted and flung up the opposite arm, made as if to roll clear, but his feet slipped on the uneven flooring of the bridge and he came down on both knees, falling over sideways in a rubbery heap, blood pulsing from his half-opened mouth.

Pitt had one fleeting glimpse of a flashing metallic glint in the fiery light, and the instinctive slight inclination of his head saved his life as the third pirate's cutlass sliced through the crooked top hat that was perched on the wolf mask. Too far; Pitt had pushed his luck too far. He had caught two of Rondheim's men before they knew what was happening, but the third had gained sufficient time to counter Pitt's attack and catch him off balance.

Blindly fending off the lunging thrusts, staggering backward under the fury of the other man's assault, Pitt hurled himself convulsively sideways and over the parapet, and plunged into the cool water of the canal. Even as he dived, Pitt had heard the swish of the pirate's blade as it hissed through the empty air where his body had stood only an instant before. And then there was the sudden shock as his shoulder collided with vicious force against the shallow bottom of the canal. The pain exploded in him and everything seemed to dissolve and stop.

"Yo ho ho, sixteen men on a dead man's chest." God, Pitt thought through the haze, why don't those mechanical bastards sing something else? Like a diagnostic specialist, he carefully explored his bruised body—the areas of pain, the position of his arms and legs in the flame-sparkled water. His ribs felt as if they were burning inside his chest, the fire spreading into his back and shoulders. Pulling himself onto the landing, Pitt stood up unsteadily, swayed and only kept erect by using the cutlass as a cane, somewhat bewildered to find the hilt still imbedded tightly in his right hand.

He crouched on one knee, fighting to catch his breath, waiting for his heart to slow down to a reasonably normal rate and scanned the make-believe set, his eyes trying desperately to pierce the darkness beyond the flaming half light. The bridge was empty, the third pirate was gone, and the boat was just disappearing around a curve into the next gallery. He turned in the opposite direction just in time to see another sightseeing boat approaching up the canal.

All these things he noted mechanically, without consciously classifying their significance. All he could think of was that a killer was somewhere close by, disguised as one of the pirates. He felt helpless, the mannequins all began to look alike, and the action on the bridge had happened with such speed that he hadn't been able to perceive any details of the man's costume.

Almost frantically, he tried to plan the next step. There was no more chance in the world for surprise on his part—the human pirate knew what Pitt looked like, while he was helpless to detect the real from the fake and had now lost the opportunity to move first. Even as these thoughts flashed through Pitt's mind, he knew he must act.

A second later, he was half running, half stumbling along the quay, gasping at every step as waves of pain shot through every tendon of his body. He burst through a black curtain and into the next stage set. It had a huge domed chamber dimly lit for a nighttime scene.

Built into the far wall, a scaled-down version of a pirate's corsair ship, complete with dummy crew and Jolly Roger rippling in a breeze urged on by a hidden electric fan, fired stimulated broadsides from replica cannon across fifty feet of water and over the heads of the people in the excursion boat at a miniature fortress sitting high atop a jagged cliff on the opposite side of the cavernous chamber.

It was too dark to make out any details on the excursion boat. Pitt could detect no movement at the stern and he felt certain that Kippmann and Lazard had everything under their command—everything, that is, that was within their reach. As his eyes began to penetrate the heavy darkness, of the simulated nighttime harbor between the ship and the fortress, he saw that the bodies in the boat were all huddled below the sides of the hull. He was about halfway up the maintenance ramp to the deck of the corsair ship when he knew why, when he heard a strange sound, the almost silent thump of a gun with a silencer.

And then suddenly he was standing in back of a form in a pirate costume who was holding something in his hand and pointing it at the little boat in the water. Pitt looked at him curiously, with only a detached sort of interest. He raised the cutlass and brought the flat side of the blade down on the pirate's wrist.

The gun vanished over the railing and into the water below. The pirate swung around, the white hair falling from under a scarlet bandanna that was knotted around his head, the cold blue-gray eyes flashing with anger and frustration, the lines about the mouth deeply etched. He searched the comical figure that had so coolly killed two of his comrades. His voice was hard and metallic.

"It seems I am your prisoner."

Pitt wasn't fooled for an instant. The words were only a stall, a curtain to shield the lightning move that would surely come. The man behind the voice was dangerous and he was playing for high stakes. But Pitt had more than an edged weapon—he had a newly found strength that was suddenly coursing through his body like a gathering tidal wave. He began to smile.

"Ah—so it is you, Oskar."

Pitt paused significantly, watching Rondheim like a cat. Holding Hermit Limited's chief executioner on the end of the cutlass. Pitt pulled off the rubber wolf's head. Rondheim's face was still set and hard, but the eyes betrayed total incomprehension. Pitt dropped the mask, bracing himself for the moment he had planned for but never really believed would happen. Slowly, he unwrapped the bandages with one hand, letting the gauze fall to the deck in little unraveled piles, building the suspense. When he finished, he gazed steadily at Rondheim and stood back. Rondheim's lips began to work in a half-formed question and dazed expression spread across his features.

"Sorry you can't recall the face, Oskar," Pitt said quietly. "But you didn't leave a great deal to recognize."

Rondheim stared at the swollen eyes, the bruised and puffed lips, the sutures that laced the cheekbones and eyebrows, and then his mouth fell open and in a whisper he breathed, "Pitt!"

Pitt nodded.

"It's not possible," Rondheim gasped.

Pitt laughed. "I apologize for ruining your day, but

it just goes to prove that you can't always trust a computer."

Rondheim looked at Pitt long and searchingly. "And the others?"

"With one exception, they're all alive and mending the broken bones you so generously dispensed." Pitt focused his gaze beyond Rondheim's shoulder and saw that the excursion boat was safely entering the next gallery.

"Then it's back to you and me again, Major. Under conditions more favorable to you than those I enjoyed in the gym. But don't get your hopes up." A sort of smile twisted the tight lips. "Fairies are no match for men."

"I agree," Pitt returned. He hurled the cutlass over Rondheim's head into the water and stood back. He looked down and examined his hands. They would have to do the job. He took several slow deep breaths, ran his hands through his wet hair, rubbed them roughly on the sides of his costume and then gave a final flex to his fingers. He was ready.

"I misled you, Oskar. Round one was an unequal contest. You had the numbers, the planning and the initiative from the beginning. How are you alone, Oskar, without your paid help to prop your victims? How are you when you're on strange ground? You still have time to escape. Nothing stands between you and a chance for freedom except me. But there's the rub, Oskar. You have to get by me."

Rondheim's teeth showed. "I don't need anyone to break you, Pitt. My only regret is that I don't have the time to stretch out your next lesson in pain."

"Okay, Oskar, so much for the psychological bullshit," Pitt said calmly. He knew exactly what he was going to do. True, he was still weak and dead tired, but that was more than canceled out by the self-determination, the invisible figures of Lillie, Tidi, Sam Kelly, Hunnewell and the rest who stood at his side giving him strength he could have never possessed alone.

An uncertain smile came to Rondheim's mouth as

he crouched in a karate stance. The smile didn't last. Pitt hit him. He hit Rondheim with a right cross, a perfectly timed punch that jerked Rondheim's head sideways and staggered him into the ship's main mast.

Deep down Pitt had known that he had little chance of taking Rondheim in a prolonged fight, that he couldn't hold the other man off for more than a few minutes, but he had schemed and timed for the element of surprise, the one advantage that played on his side before the karate blows could lash his face again. As it turned out, the advantage was a small one.

Rondheim was incredibly tough; he had taken a hard blow, yet he was already recovering. He sprang from the mast and threw a kick to Pitt's head, missing by a scant inch as Pitt ducked easily away. The ill timing cost him. Pitt caught Rondheim with a series of left jabs and another short, hard right that sent him to his knees on the deck, holding a hand to a broken, bleeding nose.

"You've improved," Rondheim whispered through the streaming blood.

"I said I misled you." Pitt was hanging back tensed in a half boxing, half judo position, waiting for Rondheim's next move. "In reality, I'm about as queer as Carzo Butera."

With the sound of his true name, Rondheim could see death's fingers reaching out to touch him, but he kept his voice under iron control, his bleeding face an expressionless mask. "It seems I underestimated you, Major."

"You were an easy man to lead astray, Oskar, or should I call you by the name on your birth certificate? No matter, your run has played out."

Mouthing a string of curses through blood-specked lips, his face now frozen in insane hate, Rondheim flung himself at Pitt. He hadn't taken a second step when Pitt brought an uppercut from the deck and rammed it as solidly as a sledgehammer into Rondheim's teeth. Pitt had given it everything he had, thrown his shoulder and body into it with such force that his ribs screamed in agony and he knew even as he did it that he could never marshal the strength to do it again.

There came a dull squish sound, mingled with a muffled cracking noise. Rondheim's teeth were jerked from their sockets and imbedded in torn lips as Pitt's wrist snapped. For two or three seconds Rondheim seemed to straighten and stand there poised like a frame frozen in a movie projector, then, with the unbelievably slow, irrevocable finality of a falling tree, he crumbled to the deck and lay still.

Pitt stood and panted through clenched teeth, his right wrist hanging limply at his side. He stared up at the little lights flashing from the make-believe cannon on the fortress and then he noticed that the next excursion boat was passing through the chamber. He blinked his eyes to focus more clearly and the sweat ran into them and stung. There was something he had to do. At first the thought repulsed him, but he shook it aside, determined that there could be no other way.

He stepped over the sprawling legs of the unconscious man and bent down, propping one of Rondheim's arms against the deck and the bottom base of the railing. Then, raising one of his feet, he stomped on it, shuddering inwardly as the bone broke a few inches below the elbow. Rondheim stirred sluggishly and moaned.

"That's for Jerome Lillie," Pitt said, his voice bitter.

He repeated the process with Rondheim's other arm, noting with grim satisfaction that his victim's eyes had opened and were staring vacantly, pupils enlarged, in a glassy state of physical shock.

"Score that one for Tidi Royal."

Pitt moved automatically as he turned Rondheim's body so that the legs were pointing in the opposite direction, propped as the arms had been on the deck and railing. The thinking, emotional part of Pitt's mind was no longer part of his brain. It floated outside its cranial vault, keeping enough contact to pull the strings that made the hands and feet work. Inside the bruised, cut, and in some places, disjointed shelter, the machine was quietly, smoothly ticking over. The deathly exhaustion and pain were pushed into the background, forgotten for the moment until his mind regained full control. Then he jumped on Rondheim's left leg.

"Mark that up for Sam Kelly."

Rondheim screamed a scream that died in his throat. The glazed blue-gray eyes stared upward into Pitt's. "Kill me," he whispered. "Why don't you kill me?"

"If you lived for a thousand years," Pitt said grimly, "you could never make up for all the pain and misery you've caused. I want you to know what it's like, feel the agony as your bones part, the helplessness of lying there and watching it happen. I should break your spine like you did Lillie's; watch you rot your life away in a wheelchair. But that would be wishful thinking, Oskar. Your trial might last a few weeks, even months, but there isn't a jury in the world that won't hand you a death sentence without leaving the box. No, I'd be doing you a favor by killing you, and that would never do. This one is for Willi Hunnewell."

There was no grin on Pitt's face, no gleam of anticipation in the deep green eyes. He leaped for the fourth and final time and the hoarse, horrible scream of pain rolled over the ship's decks, echoed through the chamber, then slowly faded and died.

With a feeling of emptiness, almost sadness, Pitt sat there on a hatch cover and stared down at the broken figure of Rondheim. It wasn't a pretty sight. The fury within him had found its outlet and now he felt totally drained as he waited for his lungs and heart to slow back to normal.

He was sitting there like that when Kippmann and Lazard came charging across the deck, followed by a small army of security men. They said nothing. There was nothing they could say, at least not for a full sixty seconds, not until the full significance of what Pitt had done became clear to them.

Finally Kippmann broke the silence. "A little rough on him, weren't you?"

"It's Rondheim," Pitt said vaguely.

"Rondheim? Are you sure?"

"I seldom forget a face," Pitt said. "Especially when it belongs to a man who kicked the hell out of me."

Lazard turned to look at him. His lips twisted in a wry smile. "What was it I said about you hardly being in shape for hand-to-hand combat?"

"Sorry I couldn't get to Rondheim before he started popping away with his silencer," Pitt said. "Did he hit anyone?"

"Castile was nicked in the arm," Lazard said. "After we cold-cocked those two clowns in the stern seat, I turned and saw you playing Errol Flynn on the bridge. I knew then we weren't out of the woods yet, so I threw myself over the family up front and forced them to the bottom of the boat."

"Likewise with our visitors from Latin America." Kippmann smiled and rubbed a bruise on his forehead. "They thought I was crazy and gave me a rough go for a minute."

"What happens to Kelly and Hermit Limited?" Pitt asked.

"We'll arrest Mr. Kelly along with his internationally wealthy partners, of course, but the chances of convicting men of their stature are almost impossible. I should imagine the governments involved will hurt them where it hurts them most—in the pocketbook. The fines they'll probably have to pay should build the Navy a new aircraft carrier."

"That's a small price to pay for the suffering they've caused," Pitt said wearily.

"None the less, it is a price," Kippmann murmured.

"Yes . . . yes, it is that. Thank God they were stopped."

Kippmann nodded to Pitt. "We have you to thank, Major Pitt, for blowing the whistle on Hermit Limited."

Lazard smiled suddenly. "And I'd like to be the first to express my gratitude for your Horatius-at-the-bridge act. Kippmann and I couldn't be standing here now if you hadn't taken the cue when you did." He put his hand on Pitt's shoulder. "Tell me something. I'm curious."

"About what?"

"How did you know those pirates on the bridge were real flesh and blood?"

"As the man once said," Pitt said casually, "there we were just sitting on the bridge, eyeball to eyeball . . . and I could swear I saw the other guys blink."

Epilogue

It was a pleasant Southern California evening. The day's smog had cleared away and a cool breeze from the west carried the strong, clean smell of the Pacific Ocean through the center garden of the Disneyland Hotel, soothing the soreness of Pitt's injuries and tranquilizing his mind for the task ahead. He stood silent, waiting for the glass-enclosed elevator to descend along the exterior of the building.

The elevator hummed and stopped and the doors slid open. He scratched an imaginary itch in his eye and lowered his head, shielding his face as a young man and woman, arm in arm, laughing gaily to themselves, stepped past him without noticing his worse-for-wear features or the arm enclosed in a plastic cast and supported by a black cloth sling.

He entered and pushed the button marked six. The elevator rose swiftly, and he turned and looked through the windows at the skyline of Orange County. He took a deep breath and slowly exhaled, watching the sparkling carpet of lights spread and widen toward the dark horizon as the first three floors slid by. The lights blinked in the crystal air, reminding him of a jewel box.

It hardly seemed like two hours since the park doctor had set his wrist and Pitt had showered and shaved and eaten his first solid meal since leaving

Reykjavik. The doctor was quite definite that he go to a hospital, but Pitt wouldn't hear of it.

The doctor had said sternly, "You're a fool, you're damn near dead on your feet. You should have given up and collapsed hours ago. If you don't get your butt between the sheets of a hospital bed, you're going to experience a first-class breakdown."

"Thanks," Pitt had said shortly. "I'm grateful for your professional concern, but there's one more act to play out. Two hours—no more—then I'll dedicate what's left of my body to medical science."

The elevator slowed and stopped, the door opened and Pitt stepped onto the soft red carpet of the sixth-floor foyer. He abruptly halted in midstep to keep from colliding with three men who were waiting to go down. Two of the men he took to be Kippmann's agents. Of the third man, the one slumped head downward in the middle, there was no doubt, it was F. James Kelly.

Pitt stood there blocking their way. Kelly slowly lifted his head and stared at Pitt vacantly, unrecognizing. Finally Pitt broke the uneasy silence.

"I'm almost sorry your grand scheme failed, Kelly. In theory, it was glorious. In execution, it was impossible."

Kelly's eyes widened by slow degrees and the color drained from his face. "My God . . . is that you, Major Pitt? But no . . . you're . . ."

"Supposed to be dead?" Pitt finished, as if it no longer mattered too much except to himself.

"Oskar swore he killed you."

"I managed to leave the party early," Pitt said coldly.

Kelly shook his head back and forth. "Now I understand why my plan failed. It seems, Major, that fate cast you in the role of my avenging nemesis."

"Purely a matter of my being at the wrong place at the wrong time."

Kelly smiled thinly and nodded to the two agents. The three of them entered the waiting elevator.

Pitt stood aside, then suddenly said, "Sam left you a message."

Kelly took seconds to recover. "Is Sam—"

"Sam died out on the tundra," Pitt finished. "Near the end he wanted you to know he forgave you."

"Oh, God . . . oh, God," Kelly moaned, his fingers covering his eyes.

For many years afterward, Pitt carried the mental picture of Kelly's face just before the elevator door closed. The stricken lines, the dull, lifeless eyes, the ashen skin. It was the face of a man who looked as if he was strangling.

Pitt tried the door with the numerals 605. It was locked. He walked down the hall and turned the doorknob to Room 607. It opened. He quietly stepped over the threshold and eased the door closed. The room was cool and dark. The smell of stale cigar butts invaded his nostrils before he passed through the entry hall. The odor was all he needed to know it was Rondheim's room.

Moonlight filtered through the drapes, casting long shapeless shadows as he searched through the bedroom, noting that Rondheim's clothes and luggage was undisturbed. Kippmann had kept his word. His men had been careful not to alert Kirsti Fyrie or give her the slightest warning of Rondheim's fate or the sudden demise of Hermit Limited.

He moved toward a shaft of yellow light that split the half-open door to the adjoining room. He entered, treading softly, noiselessly like a night animal ready to spring. It could hardly be called a room, a plush suite would have been a fairer description. It consisted of a hall, a living room with an amply stocked bar, a bathroom and a bedroom, edged on one side by a large sliding glass door that led to a small balcony.

All the rooms were empty except the bathroom; the sound of running water told him that Kirsti was in the shower. Pitt walked over to the bar, casually poured himself a Scotch on the rocks and just as casually eased into a long comfortable sofa. Twenty minutes and two drinks later, Kirsti emerged from the bathroom. She was wearing a green silk kimona, loosely sashed at the waist. Her golden hair danced around her head like a sun-colored halo. She looked incredibly fresh and lovely.

She walked through the bedroom into the living room and was in the midst of mixing herself a drink when she saw Pitt's reflection in the mirror behind the bar. She stood there as if suddenly struck by paralysis, very pale, with an expression of uncertainty on her face.

"I suppose," Pitt said quietly, "the appropriate thing for a gentleman to say when a beautiful woman leaves her bath is, Behold, Venus arises from the waves."

She turned and the look of uncertainty slowly turned to one of curiosity. "Do I know you?"

"We've met."

She clutched the edge of the bar, silent, her eyes searching him. "Dirk!" she whispered softly. "It's you. It's really you. Thank God, you're still alive."

"Your concern for my welfare comes a little late."

They stared at each other, green eyes locked on violet.

"Elsa Koch, Bonny Parker and Lucretia Borgia," he said, "all could have taken lessons from you on how to kill friends and influence enemies."

"I had to do what I've done," she said faintly. "But I swear to you I have killed no one. I was unwillingly pulled into the vortex by Oskar. I never dreamed that his association with Kelly would lead to death for so many."

"You say you've killed no one."

"Yes."

"You're lying."

She gazed at him oddly. "What are you talking about?"

"You killed Kristjan Fyrie!"

She looked at him now as if he'd gone mad. Her lips were trembling, and her eyes—those lovely violet eyes—were dark with fear.

"You can't mean what you're saying," she gasped. "Kristjan died on the *Lax;* he was burned . . . burned to death."

The time had come, Pitt told himself, to settle the

account, balance the entries, tally the final score. He leaned forward.

"Kristjan Fyrie didn't die a fiery death on a ship in the North Atlantic—he died under a surgeon's scalpel on an operating table in Veracruz, Mexico."

Pitt let it sink in. He took a couple of sips of his drink and lit a cigarette. The words were not easy for him. He watched her without speaking.

Kirsti's mouth had fallen open. She closed it quickly and numbly searched for something to say. She was on the verge of tears that would never come. Then she lowered her head and covered her face with her hands.

"I have it on good authority," Pitt continued. "The operation took place at the Sau de Sol Hospital and the surgeon was a Dr. Jesus Ybarra."

She looked up with an expression of agony. "Then you know everything."

"Almost. There are still a couple of loose ends."

"Why do you torture me by beating around the bush? Why don't you come out and say it."

Pitt spoke calmly. "Say what? That you're really Kristjan Fyrie? That there never was a sister. That Kristjan died at the exact moment you were born?" He shook his head. "What difference would it make? As Kristjan you weren't willing to accept the sex your body had given you so you undertook sex conversion surgery and became Kirsti. You came into this world a transsexual. Your genes crossed you up. You weren't satisfied with the hand nature dealt you so you made a change. What more is there?"

She came from behind the bar and leaned against the leather-padded surface. "You can never know, Dirk. You can never know what it is to lead a frustrating and complicated existence, playing the strong, virile male adventurer on the outside while inside you are a woman longing to be free."

"So you escaped the shell," Pitt said. "Slipped away to Mexico to a surgeon who specializes in conversions. You took hormone injections and silicone implants for your . . . ah . . . chest. Then you soaked up the sun on a Veracruz beach, getting a tan while your incision healed. Later, at the appropriate time, you showed up in Iceland claiming to be your long-lost sister from New Guinea.

"What astonishing confidence you must have had to think you could get away with it," Pitt continued. "I've met a few slick operators in my short life span, but by God, Kirsti, or Kristjan, or whoever, you've got to be the shrewdest bastard . . . or rather, bitch that ever came down the pike. You took everyone. You conned Admiral Sandecker into thinking you were going to turn the undersea probe over to our government. You faked a thousand men and their ships and aircraft into a wild-goose chase, searching for a ship that was never missing. You beguiled Dr. Hunnewell, an old friend, into identifying a charred body as your own. You used Fyrie Limited's personnel—and they died carrying out your orders. You used Rondheim. You used Kelly. And you even tried to use me in the hope I might erase Oskar. Too bad the bubble had to burst. The first step to all frauds is to cheat oneself. At that you were a raving success."

Kirsti had moved slowly around to a small traveling case on an end table, lifted out a tiny Colt twenty-five automatic and leveled it on Pitt's chest. "Your accusations are not nearly as neat and organized as you think. You're groping, Dirk; you're groping in the dark like a blind man."

Pitt glanced at the gun and then nonchalantly turned away and ignored it. "Suppose you show me the light."

She looked uncertainly at Pitt, but she still held the gun as steady as a statue. "I had every intention of turning the undersea probe over to your country. My original plan was to put my scientists and engineers on board the *Lax* and send them to Washington for the presentation ceremonies. Then on the voyage across the North Atlantic, Kristjan Fyrie was to have been lost overboard."

"In the meantime, you had flown to Mexico for the operation."

"Yes," Kirsti answered softly. "But the totally unexpected, and unforeseen coincidence, spelled disaster to the new life I had so carefully planned. Dr. Jesus Ybarra was a member of Hermit Limited."

"So he blew the whistle and informed Rondheim."

Kirsti nodded. "From that moment on I was Oskar's slave. He threatened to expose my transition to the world if I didn't turn my business resources over to him and Kelly. I had no choice. If my secret had become known, the resulting scandal would have wrecked Fyrie Limited and shattered the economy of my country."

"Why the masquerade with the *Lax?*"

"Now that Oskar and Kelly controlled me, they were not about to let the sea probe out of their hands. So they created a fraudulent story about the *Lax*'s disappearance. You must admit, it was an efficient situation. To the world the sea probe was lost on the bottom of the sea."

"And so was Kristjan Fyrie."

"Yes, it also served my purpose."

"That doesn't explain the alteration to the *Lax*'s superstructure," Pitt persisted. "Why wasn't the sea probe simply removed and installed on another ship?"

For the first time she smiled. "The sea probe is a complicated piece of equipment. A ship must literally be designed around it. To have taken it from the *Lax* and reinstalled it in a nondescript fishing trawler would have taken months. While everyone was searching for her, the *Lax* was secretly being facelifted in a cove on the eastern coast of Greenland."

"And Dr. Hunnewell, how did he figure in the picture?"

"He worked with me in developing the probe."

"I know, but why you? Why not with someone in his own country?"

She looked at him and studied his face for a long moment. "I paid for the research and development with no strings attached. The technological corporations in the United States wanted to tie up his services and all his experimental results. Dr. Hunnewell despised doing anything that reeked of commercial profit."

"Yet he became associated with Kelly and Hermit Limited."

"When the *Lax* was prospecting the sea floor off Greenland, the probe malfunctioned. Dr. Hunnewell was the only one with the technical knowledge to suggest a quick repair. Kelly flew him there from California. A very persuasive talker, that F. James Kelly. He sold Dr. Hunnewell on joining Hermit Limited to save the world. The doctor couldn't resist. He was always what you Americans call a do-gooder." A pained expression crossed Kirsti's face. "He came to regret his decision, and he died for it."

"That explains the fire on the ship," Pitt said thoughtfully. "You underestimated Dr. Hunnewell. He didn't fall under the spell of Kelly. He saw through the whole dirty scheme. He didn't like what he saw on the *Lax*—Rondheim's crew holding your scientists prisoners. It's even likely your people on the ship slipped him the facts on Dr. Matajic's and his assistant's deaths. Hunnewell knew then he had to do something to stop Kelly so he wired the probe, timing it to self-destruct after he was in the air and on his way back to the States. Only he made a mistake. Something even he didn't understand about the reactive elements of celtinium caused it to ignite and not only destroy the probe but the entire ship and the crew as well. I was there when he set foot on the *Lax* again. I saw the stunned expression on his face when he realized what he'd done."

"It was my fault," Kirsti said shakily. "I am to blame. I should have never divulged Dr. Hunnewell's name to Oskar and Kelly."

"Kelly guessed what had happened and ordered Rondheim to silence Hunnewell."

"He was my oldest friend," Kirsti moaned softly. "And I signed his death warrant."

"Did he know about you?"

"No, Oskar simply told him I was in the hospital recuperating from an illness."

"He was a better friend than you knew," Pitt said. "He falsely identified a body on the *Lax* as yours. Dr

Hunnewell did it so the Kristjan Fyrie he knew wouldn't be implicated when he went to the authorities and spilled the damaging facts about Hermit Limited. Unfortunately, evil triumphed over good. Rondheim got to him first." Pitt shook his head sadly and sighed. "Then enter Dirk Pitt, stage left."

Kirsti shivered visibly. "That's why I insisted on meeting you. I had to express my gratitude for your attempt to save his life. I am still in your debt."

Pitt rolled the cool glass over his forehead. "Too late; it makes little difference now," he said wearily.

"It does to me. That's why I saved you from being beaten to pieces by Oskar." Her voice began to tremble. "But I . . . I can't save you a second time. I must protect myself, Dirk. I am sorry. Please do not move and make me pull the trigger. You must wait until Oskar arrives."

Pitt shook his head again. "Don't look for Oskar to come bounding in here to rescue you. At this moment, your ex-slavemaster is lying unconscious, encased in half a ton of plaster in a hospital bed. Surrounded, I might add, by a bevy of National Intelligence agents. They may have to push him to the gallows in a wheelchair, but walk or ride, he will surely swing."

The gun wavered a hair. "What do you mean?"

"It's done, over with. You're free. Hermit Limited and its management just went belly up."

Strangely, Kirsti didn't accuse Pitt of insanity. "I want to believe you, but how can I?"

"Pick up the phone and call Kelly, Marks, Von Hummel, or your friend Rondheim. Or better yet, search every room on the sixth floor."

"And what do you expect me to find?"

"Nothing, nothing at all. They've all been arrested." Pitt finished the drink and set it down. "You and I are the only ones left. Courtesy of the N.I.A. You're my bonus—a little side gift—for services rendered. Love it or hate it, your soul has passed from Rondheim to me."

The room swayed around Kirsti as the truth of Pitt's words took hold. She had wondered why Rondheim had not contacted her, why Kelly had not visited her as he had promised, why there had been no ring of the phone, no knock at the door for nearly two hours. She steadied herself, quickly accepting the realization of what had taken place.

"But . . . what of me? Am I to be arrested also?"

"No, the N.I.A. knows of your new status. They put two and two together and figured that Rondheim was blackmailing you. They considered taking you in as an accomplice, but I talked them out of it."

The gun was gently laid on the end table. An awkward silence descended. Finally Kirsti stared at Pitt and said, "There is a price; there always has to be a price."

"It's cheap enough considering your past mistakes . . . mistakes you can never buy back even with your fortune. But you can clean the slate and make a new life without outside intrusion. All I want is your guarantee for close and continued cooperation between Fyrie Limited and NUMA."

"And?"

"The memory banks in Kelly's computers contain enough data to build a new undersea probe. I speak for Admiral Sandecker when I say he would like you to head up the project."

"That's all, nothing more?" she asked incredulously.

"I said the price was cheap."

She gazed levelly at him. "Tomorrow, next week, the coming year, how can I be sure you will not decide to raise the interest rate?"

Pitt's eyes turned cold and his voice was like ice. "Don't put me in the same league with your other playmates. Mass murder and extortion have never turned me on. Your secret is safe with me, and it's even safer with the N.I.A.—they'll see to it that Rondheim, Kelly and Ybarra will never get within fifty feet of a press reporter."

She hesitated. "I'm sorry, truly sorry. What else can I say."

He didn't answer, just looked at her.

She turned and gazed out the window at the park.

The turrets of the Magic Castle were lit up like a birthday cake. The families were gone now. The young couples had taken over and were strolling along the park walkways and streets, hand in hand, breathing in the make-believe romantic atmosphere.

"And where do you go from here?" she asked.

"After a short vacation, I'll go back to NUMA headquarters in Washington and begin work on a new project."

She turned to look at him. "And if I asked you to come to Iceland with me and become a member of my board of directors?"

"I'm not the board-of-director type."

"There must be some other way for me to show my gratefulness."

She came toward Pitt and stood in front of him. A knowing smile curled her lips, the doelike eyes grew soft and there seemed to be faint signs of dampness on her forehead.

"All will be as you ask," she said slowly. She raised her hand and her fingers lightly touched his battered face. "Tomorrow I will see Admiral Sandecker and affirm out mutual efforts." She hesitated and stood back from him. "I must, however, extract a small cost in return."

"And that is?"

She loosened the sash and shrugged the kimono from her shoulders to the floor, standing there in the relaxed classical pose of the nude. Under the light from the lamp, she was like a sun-bronzed figure crafted to exacting satin smoothness by the patient hands of a master sculptor. The full rounded lips were slightly open with excitement and impatience. The soft violet eyes gave forth a silent invitation. Her features and body could only be described as magnificent: a perfectly constructed monument to the miracle of medical science.

"If it's any compliment," she said in a throaty voice, "I never for a minute believed your gay act."

"It takes one to know one."

She turned pale. "What I became is not the same."

"What you became is a cold, shrewd, calculating witch."

"No!"

"Kristjan Fyrie was a warm, honest lover of humanity. Your change was emotional as well as physical. People to you are only to be used, to be thrown away when their usefulness ends. You're cold and you're sick."

She shook her head. "No . . . no! I've changed. Yes. But I'm not cold . . . not cold." She held out her arms. "Let me prove it."

They stood in the center of the room, facing each other silently. And then she saw the expression forming on Pitt's face, and her arms slowly dropped to her sides. She looked dazed, those exotic eyes were stricken. She stared at his face with a strange, paralyzed intentness. Pitt's features were coldly menacing. The purplish bruises, the swollen flesh, the jagged cuts all worked together in one terrible mask of disgust. His eyes no longer saw her loveliness. He could only see the unidentifiable ashes of what had once been men. He saw Hunnewell dying on a lonely beach. He remembered the face of the captain of the hydroplane before he disappeared in flames. He knew the pain of Lillie, Tidi, and Sam Kelly. And he knew Kirsti Fyrie was partly responsible for their suffering and for some—their deaths.

Kirsti paled and backed away a step. "Dirk, what's the matter?"

"God save thee," he said.

He turned and opened the door. The first few steps toward the elevator were the hardest. Then it got easier. By the time he reached the main floor, walked to the curb and hailed a cab, the old confident, relaxed composure was back.

The driver opened the door and dropped the flag. "Where to, sir?"

Pitt sat there a moment in silence. Then suddenly he knew where he had to go. He had no choice. He was what he was.

"The Newporter Inn. And a compassionate red head . . . I hope."

ABOUT THE AUTHOR

CLIVE CUSSLER spent several years in advertising. He now writes full time in Arvada, Colorado, where he lives with his wife and children. He hails from California, where his hobby of deep-sea diving provided him with the background for Dirk Pitt's career. Clive Cussler is also the author of *The Mediterranean Caper* and *Raise the Titanic!*

A Special Preview of
the exciting opening pages of the
sensational new novel by

Clive Cussler

VIXEN 03

Another shattering suspense tale featuring
Dirk Pitt—this time in a search for a missing
plane that leads to a deadly confrontation.

Oblivion

Buckley Field, Colorado—January 1954

The Boeing C-97 Stratocruiser bore the look of a crypt. Perhaps the image was bred by the cold winter night, or perhaps it came from the gusting snow that was piling an icy shroud on the wings and fuselage. The flickering lights from the cockpit windshield and the fleeting shadows of the maintenance crew served only to exaggerate the chilling scene.

Major Raymond Vylander, United States Air Force, did not care for what he saw. He watched silently as the fuel truck drove away and vanished into the stormy darkness. The loading ramp was dropped from the rear of the great whalelike belly, and then the cargo doors slowly swung closed, cutting off a rectangle of light that spilled onto a heavy-duty forklift. He shifted his gaze slightly and stared at the twin rows of white lights bordering the eleven-thousand-foot Buckley Naval Air Station runway that stretched across the plains of Colorado. Their ghostly luminescence marched into the night and gradually faded behind the curtain of falling snow ...

Admiral Walter Bass, who sat on the edge of a desk, neatly folded a meteorological chart, then patted his sweating forehead with a handkerchief and nodded at Vylander.

"The weather front is moving off the eastern slope of the Rockies. You should break out of the overcast somewhere over the Continental Divide."

"Providing I can get that big-assed bird off the ground."

"You'll do it."

"Lifting a heavy plane with a full fuel load and a cargo weighing seventy thousand pounds in the middle of a blizzard with a thirty-knot crosswind from a ground altitude of five thousand feet isn't exactly a garden-variety takeoff."

"Every factor has been carefully considered," Bass said coldly. "Your wheels should leave the earth with a margin of three thousand feet of runway to spare."

Vylander dropped into a chair like a deflated balloon. "Is it worth risking the necks of my crew, Admiral? Just what is so damned vital to the U. S. Navy that it has to drag an Air Force plane out in the middle of nowhere in the dead of night to haul some junk to an island in the Pacific Ocean?"

For a moment Bass's face flushed, and then it softened. When he spoke, it was gently, almost apologetically. "It's painfully simple, Major. That junk, as you call it, is a top-priority cargo destined for a highly classified test program. Since your Stratocruiser was the only heavy transport within a thousand miles that can do the job, the Air Force consented to put her on temporary loan to the Navy. They threw you and your crew into the bargain, and that's all there is to it."

Vylander shot Bass a penetrating stare. "I don't mean to sound insubordinate, Admiral, but that's not all, not by a long shot."

Bass walked around the desk and sat down. "You're to consider it a routine flight, nothing more."

"I'd appreciate it, sir, if you'd throw me a bone and enlighten me as to what's inside those canisters in my cargo cabin."

Bass avoided his eyes. "Sorry, it's highly classified material."

Vylander knew when he was licked. He swayed wearily to his feet, picked up the vinyl folder containing his flight plan and charts, and walked toward the door. Then he hesitated and turned. "In the event we have to ditch—"

"Don't! If an in-flight emergency develops," Bass said solemnly, "you ride her down into a nonpopulated area."

"That's asking too much."

"I'm not making a formal request; I'm giving an order! You and your crew are not to abandon the aircraft between here and your destination, regardless of how dire the circumstances."

Vylander's face clouded. "Then I guess that's it."

"There is one more thing."

"Which is?"

"Good luck," Bass said, his lips edging into a tight grin. . . .

Admiral Bass stood in the Buckley control tower and watched the Stratocruiser crawl like a pregnant bug across the snow-swept field. A phone was clutched in his hand and he spoke quietly into the receiver.

"You may inform the President that Vixen 03 is preparing for takeoff."

"When do you figure its estimated time of arrival?" asked the stern voice of Charles Wilson, Secretary of Defense, through the earpiece.

"Allowing for a fuel stop at Hickam Field, in Hawaii, Vixen 03 should touch down in the test area approximately 1400 hours Washington time."

"Ike has scheduled us for 0800 hours tomorrow. He insists on a detailed briefing of the upcoming experiments and a running report on Vixen 03's flight progress."

"I'll take off for Washington immediately."

"I don't have to paint you a picture, Admiral, of what would happen if that plane crashed in or near a major city."

Bass hesitated in what seemed a long and terrible silence. "Yes, Mr. Secretary, it would indeed be a nightmare none of us could live with."

"The manifold pressure and the torque read a shade low across the board," announced Sergeant Burns. He watched over the engineer's panel with the intensity of a ferret.

"Enough to abort?" Gold asked hopefully.

"Sorry, Lieutenant. Internal-combustion engines won't perform in the thin mountain air of Denver like they will at sea level. Considering the altitude, the gauge readings are par for the course."

Vylander gazed at the strip of asphalt ahead. The snowfall had lightened, and he could almost see the halfway marker. His heart began to throb a little faster, keeping time with the rapid beat of the windshield wipers. God, he thought to himself, it looks no bigger than a shuffleboard court. As if in a trance, he reached over and picked up his hand mike.

"Buckley Control, this is Vixen 03. Ready to roll. Over."

"She's all yours, Vixen 03," the familiar voice of Admiral Bass scratched through the headphones. "Save a big-chested native girl for me." . . .

As soon as he broke through the clouds and leveled the Stratocruiser out at sixteen thousand feet on a westerly heading over the Rockies, Vylander motioned to Gold.

"Take her. I'm going to make a check aft."

Gold looked at him. The major did not normally relinquish the controls so early in the flight.

"Got her," Gold acknowledged, placing his hands on the yoke.

Vylander released his seat belt and shoulder harness and stepped into the cargo section, making sure the door to the cockpit was closed behind him.

He counted thirty-six of the gleaming stainless-steel canisters, firmly strapped to wooden blocks on the deck. He began carefully checking the surface area of each canister. He searched for the usual stenciled military markings denoting weight, date of manufacture, inspector's initials, handling instructions. There were none.

After nearly fifteen minutes he was about to give up and return to the cockpit when he spotted a small aluminum plate that had fallen down between the blocks. It had an adhesive backing, and Vylander felt a tinge of smugness as he matched it to a sticky spot of stainless steel where it had once been bonded. He held the plate up to the dim cabin light and squinted at its smooth side. The tiny engraved marking confirmed his worst fear.

He stood for a time, staring at the little aluminum plate. Suddenly he was jolted out of his reverie by a lurch of the aircraft. He rushed across the cargo cabin and threw open the door to the cockpit.

It was filled with smoke.

"Oxygen masks!" Vylander shouted. He could barely make out the outlines of Hoffman and Burns. Gold was completely enveloped in the bluish haze. He groped his way to the pilot's seat and fumbled for his oxygen mask, wincing at the acrid smell of an electrical short circuit.

"Buckley Tower, this is Vixen 03," Gold was yelling into a microphone. "We have smoke in the cockpit. Request emergency-landing instructions. Over."

"Taking over the controls," said Vylander.

"She's yours." Gold's acceptance came without hesitation.

"Burns?"

"Sir?"

"What in hell's gone wrong?"

"Can't tell for sure with all this smoke, Major." Burns's voice sounded hollow under the oxygen mask. "It looks like a short in the area of the radio transmitter."

"Buckley Tower, this is Vixen 03," Gold persisted. "Please come in."

"It's no use, Lieutenant," Burns gasped. "They can't hear you. Nobody can hear you. The circuit breaker for the radio equipment won't stay set."

Vylander's eyes were watering so badly he could hardly see. "I'm bringing her around on a course back to Buckley," he announced calmly.

But before he could complete the hundred-and-eighty-degree turn, the C-97 started to vibrate abruptly in unison with a metallic ripping sound. The smoke disappeared as if by magic and a frigid blast of air tore into the small eneclosure, assailing the men's exposed skin like a thousand wasps. The plane was shaking herself to pieces.

"Number-three engine threw a propeller blade!" Burns cried.

"Jesus Christ, it never rains . . . Shut down three!" snapped Vylander, "and feather what's left of the prop."

Gold's hands flew over the control panel, and soon the vibration ceased. His heart sinking, Vylander gingerly tested the controls. His breath quickened and a growing dread mushroomed inside him.

"The prop blade ripped through the fuselage," Hoffman reported. "There's a six-foot gash in the cargo-cabin wall. Cables and hydraulic lines are dangling all over."

"That explains where the smoke went," Gold said wryly. "It was sucked outside when we lost cabin pressure."

"It also explains why the ailerons and rudder won't respond," Vylander added. "We can go up and we can go down, but we can't turn and bank."

"Maybe we can slue her around by opening and closing the cowl flaps on engines one and four," Gold suggested. "At least enough to put us in the landing pattern at Buckley."

"We can't make Buckley," Vylander said. "Without number-three engine, we're losing altitude at the rate of nearly a hundred feet a minute. We're going to have to set her down in the Rockies."

His announcement was greeted with stunned silence. He could see the fear grow in his crew members' eyes, could almost smell it.

"My God," groaned Hoffman. "It can't be done. We'll ram the side of a mountain for sure."

"We've still got power and some measure of control," Vylander said. "And we're out of the overcast, so we can at least see where we're going."

"Thank heaven for small favors," grunted Burns.

"What's our heading?" asked Vylander.

"Two-two-seven southwest," answered Hoffman. "We've been thrown almost eighty degrees off our plotted course."

Vylander merely nodded. There was nothing more to say. He turned all his concentration to keeping the Stratocruiser on a lateral level. But there was no stopping the rapid descent. Even with full-power settings on the remaining three engines, there was no way the heavily laden plane could maintain altitude. He and Gold could only sit by impotently as they began a long glide earthward through the valleys surrounded by the fourteen-thousand-foot peaks of the Colorado Rockies.

Soon they could make out the trees poking through the snow coating the mountains. At 11,500 feet the jagged summits began rising above their wing tips. Gold flicked on the landing lights and strained his eyes through the windshield, searching for an open piece of ground. Hoffman and Burns sat frozen, tensed for the inevitable crash.

The altimeter needle dipped below the ten-thousand-foot mark. Ten thousand feet. It was a miracle they had made it so low; a miracle a wall of rock had not risen suddenly and blocked their glide path. Then, almost directly ahead, the trees parted and the landing lights revealed a flat, snow-covered field.

"A meadow!" Gold shouted. "A gorgeous, beautiful alpine meadow five degrees to starboard."

"I see it," acknowledged Vylander. He coaxed the slight course adjustment out of the Stratocruiser by jockeying the engine-cowl flaps and throttle settings.

There was no time for the formality of a checklist run-through. It was to be a do-or-die approach, textbook wheels-up landing. The sea of trees disappeared beneath the nose of the cockpit, and Gold cut off the ignition and electrical circuits as Vylander stalled the Stratocruiser a scant ten feet above the ground. The three remaining engines died and the great dark shadow below quickly rose and converged upon the falling fuselage.

The impact was far less brutal than any of them had a right to expect. The belly kissed the snow and bumped lightly, once, twice, and then settled down like a giant ski. How long the harrowing, uncontrolled ride continued Vylander could not tell. The short seconds passed like minutes. And then the fallen aircraft slid clumsily to a stop and there was a deep silence, deathly still and ominous.

Burns was the first to react.

"By God . . . we did it!" he murmured through trembling lips.

Gold stared ashen-faced into the windshield. His eyes saw only white. An impenetrable blanket of snow had been piled high against the glass. Slowly he turned to Vylander and opened his mouth to say something, but the words never came. They died in his throat.

A rumbling vibration suddenly shook the Strato-cruiser, followed by a sharp crackling noise and the tortured screech of metal being bent and twisted.

The white outside the windows dissolved into a dense wall of cold blackness and then there was nothing—nothing at all.

At his Naval Headquarters office in Washington, Admiral Bass vacantly studied a map indicating Vixen 03's scheduled flight path. It was all there in his tired eyes, the deeply etched lines on his pale sunken cheeks, the weary slump of his shoulders. In the past four months Bass had aged far beyond his years. The desk phone rang and he picked it up.

"Admiral Bass?" came a familiar voice.

"Yes, Mr. President."

"Secretary Wilson tells me you wish to call off the search for Vixen 03."

"That's true," Bass said quietly. "I see no sense in prolonging the agony. Navy surface craft, Air Force search planes, and Army ground units have combed every inch of land and sea for fifty miles along either side of Vixen 03's plotted course."

"What's your opinion?"

"My guess is her remains are resting on the seabed of the Pacific Ocean," answered Bass.

"You feel she made it past the West Coast?"

"I do."

"Let us pray you're right, Admiral. God help us if she crashed on land."

"If she had, we'd have known by now," Bass said.

"Yes"—the President hesitated—"I guess we would at that." Another pause. "Close the file on Vixen 03. Bury it, and bury it deep."

"I'll see to it, Mr. President."

Bass set the receiver in its cradle and sank back in his chair, a defeated man at the end of a long and otherwise distinguished Navy career.

He stared at the map again. "Where?" he said aloud

to himself. "Where are you? Where in hell did you go?"

The answer never came. No clue to the disappearance of the ill-fated Stratocruiser ever turned up. It was as though Major Vylander and his crew had flown into oblivion.

Colorado—September 1988

Dirk Pitt released his hold on sleep, yawned a deep, satisfying yawn, and absorbed his surroundings. It had been dark when he arrived at the mountain cabin and the flames in the great moss-rock fireplace along with the light from the pungent-smelling kerosene lamps had not illuminated the knotty-pine interior to its best advantage.

His vision sharpened on an old Seth Thomas clock clinging to one wall. He had set and wound the clock the previous night; it had seemed the thing to do. Next he focused on the massive cobwebbed head of an elk that stared down at him through dusty glass eyes. Slightly beyond the elk was a picture window that offered a breathtaking vista of the craggy Sawatch mountain range, deep in the Colorado Rockies.

As the last strands of sleep receded, Pitt found himself faced with his first decision of the day: whether to allow his eyes to bask in the majesty of the scenery or to feast them on the smoothly contoured body of Colorado congresswoman Loren Smith, who sat naked on a quilted rug, engrossed in yoga exercises.

Pitt discerningly opted for Congresswoman Smith.

She was sitting cross-legged, in the lotus position, leaning back and resting her elbows and head on the rug. The exposed nest between her thighs and the small tautened mounds on her chest, Pitt decided, put the granite summits of the Sawatch to shame.

"What do you call that unladylike contortion?" he asked.

"The Fish," she replied, without moving. "It's for firming up the bosom."

"Speaking as a man," Pitt said with mock pompousness, "I do not approve of rock-hard boobs."

"Would you prefer them limp and saggy?" Her violet eyes angled in his direction.

"Well . . . not exactly. But perhaps a little silicone here and a little silicone there . . ."

"That's the trouble with the masculine mind," she snapped, sitting up and brushing back her long cinnamon hair. "You think all women should have balloon-sized mammaries like those insipid drones on the centerfolds of chauvinist magazines."

"Wishing will make it so."

She threw him a pouting look. "Too bad. You'll have to make do with my thirty-four B-cuppers. They're all I've got."

He reached out, wrapped an iron arm around her torso, and dragged her half on, half off the bed. "Colossal or petite"—he leaned down and lightly kissed each nipple—"let no woman accuse Dirk Pitt of discrimination."

She arched up and bit his ear. "Four whole days alone together. No phones, no committee meetings, no cocktail parties, no aides to hassle me. It's almost too good to be true." Her hand crept under the covers and she caressed his stomach. "How about a little sport before breakfast?"

"Ah, the magic word."

She threw him a crooked smile. " 'Sport' or 'breakfast'?"

"What you said before, your yoga position." Pitt leaped out of bed, sending Loren sprawling backward onto her sculptured bottom. "Which way is the nearest lake?" . . .

"A quarter of a mile over the hill behind the cabin. Table Lake. Dad used to catch his limit of trout there all the time."

"Thanks to you"—he peered at her sternly—"I'm getting a late start."

"Tough."

"I didn't bring any fishing gear. Your dad leave any around?"

"Under the cabin, in the garage. He used to keep all his tackle down there. Keys to the door lock are on the mantel."

The lock was stiff from nonuse. Pitt spit on it and twisted the key as hard as he dared without breaking it. At last the tumblers gave and he squeaked the old twin doors open. After waiting a minute to adjust his eyes to the darkened enclosure, he stepped inside and looked around. There was a dusty workbench with its tools all neatly hanging in place. Cans of various sizes lined several shelves, some containing paint, some containing nails and assorted hardware.

Pitt soon found a fishing-tackle box under the bench. The pole took a little longer to find. He barely made one out in a dim corner of the garage. What seemed to be a piece of bulky equipment shrouded under a canvas drop cloth stood in his way. He couldn't quite reach the fishing pole, so he tried climbing over the obstruction. It shifted under his weight and he fell backward, clutching the drop cloth in a vain effort to catch his balance before both ended up on the dirt floor of the garage.

Pitt cursed, brushed himself off, and gazed at what barred him from an afternoon of fishing. A puzzled frown gripped his features. He knelt down and ran his hand over the two large objects he had accidentally uncovered. Then he rose and walked outside and called Loren.

She appeared over the balcony. "What's your problem?"

"Come down here a minute."

Begrudgingly, she donned a soft beige trench coat and went downstairs. Pitt led her inside the garage and pointed. "Where did your father find those?"

She bent forward and squinted. "What are they?"

"The round yellow one is an aircraft oxygen tank. The other is a nose gear, complete with tires and wheels. Damned old, judging by the degree of corrosion and the grime."

"They're news to me."

"You must have noticed them before. Don't you ever use the garage?"

She shook her head. "Not since I ran for office. This is the first time I've been to Dad's cabin since he died in an accident three years ago."

"You ever hear of a plane crashing around here?" Pitt probed.

"No, but that doesn't mean it hasn't happened. I seldom see any neighbors, so I have little opportunity to catch up on local gossip. . . ."

Harvey Dolan, principal maintenance inspector for the Air Carrier District Office of the FAA, lifted his glasses to the light and, detecting no smears, clamped them on a pyramid-shaped nose . . .

"Please observe," Dolan said with a professional flourish. He produced a ball-point pen from a breast pocket and probed it about like a pointer. "We have before us the frontal landing gear of an aircraft, an aircraft that weighed in the neighborhood of seventy or eighty thousand pounds. It was a propeller-driven craft, because the tires were not constructed for the stresses of a high-speed jet landing. Also, the strut design is of a type that has not been built since the nineteen fifties. Therefore, its age is somewhere between thirty and forty-five years. The tires came from Goodyear and the wheels from Rantoul Engineering, in Chicago. As to the make of the aircraft and its owner, however, I'm afraid there isn't too much to go on."

"So it ends here," Pitt said.

"You throw in the towel too early," said Dolan. "There is a perfectly legible serial number on the strut. If we can determine the type of ship this particular nose-gear model was designed for, then it becomes a simple matter of tracing the strut's number through the manufacturer and establishing the parent aircraft."

"You make it sound easy."

"Any other fragments?"

"Only what you see."

"How did you come to bring them here?"

"I figured that if anybody could identify them, it would be the Federal Aviation Administration." . . .

"Ordinarily I'd call in research technicians from our engineering division. But I think I'll take a stab in the dark and try a shortcut. Phil Devine, maintenance chief over at United Airlines, is a walking encyclopedia on aircraft. If anyone can tell us at a glance, he can."

"He's that good?" asked Pitt.

"Take my word for it," Dolan said with a knowing smile. "He's that good."

"A photographer you ain't. Your lighting is lousy."

A nonfiltered cigarette dangled from the lips of Phil Devine as he studied the Polaroid pictures Dolan had taken of the nose gear. Devine was a W. C. Fields-type character—heavy through the middle, with a slow, whining voice.

"I didn't come here for an art review," replied Dolan. "Can you put a make on the gear or not?"

"It looks vaguely familiar, kind of like the assembly off an old B-twenty-nine."

"That's not good enough."

"What do you expect from a bunch of fuzzy pictures —an absolute, irrefutable ID?"

"I had hoped for something like that, yes," Dolan replied, unruffled.

Pitt was beginning to wonder if he was about to referee a fight. Devine read the uneasy look in his eyes.

"Relax, Mr. Pitt," he said, and smiled. "Harvey and I have a standing rule: we're never civil to each other during working hours. However, as soon as five o'clock rolls around, we cut the hard-assing and go out and have a beer together."

"Which I usually pay for," Dolan injected dryly.

"You government guys are in a better position to moonlight," Devine fired back.

"About the nose gear . . ." Pitt said, probing quietly.

"Oh yeah, I think I might dig up something." Devine rose heavily from behind his desk and opened a closet filled from floor to ceiling with thick black-vinyl-bound books. "Old maintenance manuals," he explained. "I'm probably the only nut in commercial aviation who hangs on to them." He went directly to one volume buried among the mass and began thumbing through its pages. After a minute he found what he was looking for and passed the open book across the desk. "That close enough for you?"

Pitt and Dolan leaned forward and examined an exploded-view line drawing of a nose-gear assembly.

"The wheel castings, parts, and dimensions"—Dolan tapped the page with his finger—"they're one and the same."

"What aircraft?" asked Pitt.

Boeing Stratocruiser," answered Devine. "Actually I wasn't that far off when I guessed a B-twenty-nine. The Stratocruiser was based on the bomber's design. The Air Force version was designated a C-ninety-seven."

Pitt turned to the front of the manual and found a picture of the plane in flight. A strange-looking aircraft: its two-deck fuselage had the configuration of a great double-bellied whale.

"I recall seeing these as a boy," Pitt said. "Pan American used them."

"So did United," said Devine. "We flew them on the Hawaii run. She was a damned fine airplane."

"Now what?" Pitt turned to Dolan.

"Now I send the nose gear's serial number to Boeing, in Seattle, along with a request to match it with the parent aircraft. I'll also make a call to the National Transportation Safety Board in Washington, who will tell me if they show any lost commercial Stratocruisers over the continental United States."

"And if one turns up missing?"

"The FAA will launch an official investigation into the mystery," Dolan said. "And then we'll see what turns up."